ETERNALLY BOUND

THE ALLIANCE SERIES, BOOK 1

BRENDA K DAVIES

BRENDA K. DAVIES

ALSO FROM THE AUTHOR

Books written under the pen name

Brenda K. Davies

The Vampire Awakenings Series

Awakened (Book 1)

Destined (Book 2)

Untamed (Book 3)

Enraptured (Book 4)

Undone (Book 5)

Fractured (Book 6)

Ravaged (Book 7)

Consumed (Book 8)

Unforeseen (Book 9)

Forsaken (Book 10)

Coming 2019/2020

The Alliance Series

Eternally Bound (Book 1)

Bound by Vengeance (Book 2)

Bound by Darkness (Book 3)

Bound by Passion (Book 4)

Coming August 2019

The Road to Hell Series

Good Intentions (Book 1)

Carved (Book 2)

The Road (Book 3)

Into Hell (Book 4)

Hell on Earth Series

Hell on Earth (Book 1)

Into the Abyss (Book 2)

Kiss of Death (Book 3)

Coming Fall 2019

Historical Romance

A Stolen Heart

Books written under the pen name

Erica Stevens

The Coven Series

Nightmares (Book 1)

The Maze (Book 2)

Dream Walker (Book 3)

Coming June 2019

The Captive Series

Captured (Book 1)

Renegade (Book 2)

Refugee (Book 3)

Salvation (Book 4)

Redemption (Book 5)

Broken (The Captive Series Prequel)

Vengeance (Book 6)

Unbound (Book 7)

The Kindred Series

Kindred (Book 1)

Ashes (Book 2)

Kindled (Book 3)

Inferno (Book 4)

Phoenix Rising (Book 5)

The Fire & Ice Series

Frost Burn (Book 1)

Arctic Fire (Book 2)

Scorched Ice (Book 3)

The Ravening Series

The Ravening (Book 1)

Taken Over (Book 2)

Reclamation (Book 3)

The Survivor Chronicles

The Upheaval (Book 1)

The Divide (Book 2)

The Forsaken (Book 3)

The Risen (Book 4)

CHAPTER ONE

STANDING ON THE BALCONY, Ronan's eyes scanned the bodies writhing below him. The only thing he found enticing about the vast amount of flesh on display was breaking the necks of every person in the club. He tried to shake the impulse off, but his fangs throbbed in his gums at the thought, and it dug deeper into him with every passing second.

His entire existence had revolved around one mission: protect the innocents of this world whether they be human or vampire. It was a mission he'd followed for over a thousand years, but with every passing day, the bloodlust growing within him dragged him closer to the edge he'd seen so many other vampires plummet over.

Some of those other vampires he'd believed to be far better and stronger than him, yet they'd given into their more sinister impulses. And somehow, he remained and now stood as the oldest vampire in existence, not just within his close-knit group of men, but throughout all the vampires.

Every day he woke, he questioned if that day would be the day he fell too and became the thing he despised the most, a Savage. He didn't try to tell himself that he would never give in. He'd done that for many years, but this past year he'd come to realize it may be inevitable that he succumbed to the bloodlust beckoning him. If he didn't kill himself before that happened, he would start to kill the innocents he protected.

It was the killing himself first part that would be tricky. Savage vampires thrived on the blood of innocents, but they weren't stupid or lost to the madness of the death they delivered. No, many of them remained intelligent and calculating, and they didn't want to die. A vampire who gave himself over to their inhumanity simply saw nothing wrong with what they were doing. The blood they consumed warped them into believing a vampire's true nature was to kill and they were only living the way vampires were supposed to live.

No matter how much he despised Savages, if he gave in, he would most likely come to believe that too.

Perhaps they were right, but Ronan refused to believe vampires were meant to be little more than animals who ruthlessly slaughtered the weaker masses.

However, it didn't matter what he believed or what he didn't, he was teetering toward the Savage side. When he went over, would his men, or even multiple vampires, be capable of taking him out as he had taken out so many of those who had fallen before him?

That was a question he dreaded he would find out the answer to soon. The fine line he walked became thinner with every passing day, and with every death he delivered to the Savages amongst his kind. The thrill of killing the vampires he hunted had once satisfied him, but that was centuries ago. Now, it *barely* kept the demon part of him at bay.

The emptiness within him would never be filled. There wasn't enough blood, wasn't enough death to begin to satisfy him anymore. He faced the same bleak concept that the many who had fallen before him also faced: an eternity of nothing, or the possibility that giving into their more savage nature would finally fill the emptiness inside.

For some vampires, it hadn't been a difficult choice.

How much more time do I have?

His hands tightened on the railing, twisting over the cool metal as his teeth clamped together and his fangs slid free to press against the back of his lips.

I will not be one of them!

He told himself this every day when he opened his eyes and the emptiness greeted him, but it sounded hollow then, and it did again now. Even amongst those who were born vampires, the purebreds such as himself, he was an anomaly and stronger than the rest. The turned vampires battled their darker natures too, but not as badly as the purebreds did. Because turned vamps were human before becoming vampires, they had more humanity in them than purebreds did.

If he gave himself over to the darkness, he would never know this sensation of being torn in two again, and he would slaughter hundreds, possibly thousands, before being stopped, if he could be stopped.

No matter what, he couldn't lose control like that. He didn't like humans overly much, but there were rules, and they must be obeyed if the vampire race was to continue undetected. Vampires were far stronger than humans, but they were also vastly outnumbered by mortals.

Fear would have humans turning on them, slaughtering them, and studying them like lab rats. Some, if not many of the mortals, may try to become vampires, which would create more Savages. If such a thing happened, the vampire food supply would be depleted and the world would fall into chaos.

The rules had to be strictly followed.

This had been instilled into him from the moment of his birth. His parents had made sure he knew he would one day lead and keep the vampire and human races protected. That he would become a Defender, a vampire who protected the innocents and made sure the rules were obeyed. Things may be far different now than when his parents had been alive, but that mission still drove him every day.

Beside him, Declan shifted his stance as he glanced at Ronan from the corner of his eye. Declan's eyes were so pure gray, they appeared silver as he surveyed the scene beneath them. He ran a hand through his dark auburn hair before tugging at the ends.

At six hundred years of age, Declan was the second oldest of their group, younger than only him. They'd been fighting together since Declan had reached maturity at twenty-four. Ronan had known Declan for his entire life, yet he still didn't know all of Declan's secrets.

He did know that he'd never seen his friend so apprehensive about a possible kill before, and he didn't understand it. He'd expected Declan to be eager to destroy Joseph. Ronan suspected Declan's apprehension was because his father had been the last Defender to give into his Savage nature, and it was stirring up old memories, rather than the fact they were now hunting one of their own.

Joseph had been a powerful fighter and ally for nearly fifty years. However, he and Declan had been like two dogs circling each other whenever they were in the same room. Declan's more easygoing nature had abraded with Joseph's austere personality.

In truth, Ronan had never liked Joseph either and never considered him a friend as he did the other Defenders who worked with him, but Joseph had been a strong fighter and had made it all the way through the rigorous training every purebred that worked with him had to endure.

Ronan had seen little of Joseph over the years as he'd run the training facility for turned and purebred vamps who wished to hunt Savages. Months ago, Joseph had given in to his bloodlust and become a Savage. Ronan had been trying to track him down ever since, but Joseph knew how they operated and how to fly under their radar. Not even Brian, a turned vamp who sometimes helped them to track down Savage vamps, could pinpoint Joseph's location, until now.

Brian had called a few hours ago to let him know he'd gotten a track on Joseph in this area of Providence, Rhode Island. This club was the most likely place to attract Joseph. A club full of drunk humans was a homing beacon for vampires on the prowl. It was easy to prey on the humans here, and if Ronan got the chance, he would feed here tonight.

Feeding could wait; for now, they were on the hunt for something else.

His eyes swept the dance floor once more. Unable to take the flashing lights in places such as this, he'd put on a pair of dark sunglasses before entering, but the pulse of the flashing lights still made his head pound. The thumping beat of the music vibrated the floor beneath his feet. His gaze landed on the DJ. He ran his tongue over his fangs as he contemplated tearing the man's throat out to end the annoying beat.

What had happened to real music like Beethoven and Chopin? He'd even take some Duke Ellington, Frank Sinatra, or Billy Joel over this. This crap was enough to drive the best of vampires over the edge, and he was far from the best. But the humans liked it as they ground against each other with a frenzy the equivalent of foreplay.

Movement behind him drew his attention to Killean and Saxon as they approached from the shadows. The few humans who had been standing nearby shrank away from Killean and vanished down the stairs.

"Anything?" Ronan demanded of them.

Killean shook his head as his golden-tiger eyes went past Ronan to the dance floor. A scar sliced straight down from his deep brown hairline and over his right eye before ending halfway down his cheek. Killean had come to work with Ronan when he was fifty-two, that had been four hundred years ago, and Ronan still had no idea what had caused that scar or who had given it to him. He knew it had been inflicted on Killean before he'd become a fully mature vampire only because it remained.

Next to Killean, Saxon folded his arms over his chest and his hazel eyes drifted toward the ceiling. His dark blond hair stood up in spikes around his head. "Something else might have attracted him away from here," Saxon said. "There may be another club or bar or something we missed nearby."

Or Joseph had managed to elude them again. Ronan's teeth ground together as he released the railing. He wasn't looking forward to killing the vampire he'd once considered an ally, but he wanted this over with. With Joseph's purebred status, knowledge of the way they worked, and complete disregard of human and vampire life, he was far more lethal than many of the other Savages they'd dealt with. It had been centuries since one of their own had given in to their savage nature.

As far as Ronan could tell, going by the increased amount of disappearances, people who'd had their throats cut, and animal attacks since Joseph had given in, he'd killed over a hundred people and was averaging at least one a day. That didn't include the amount of vampires he'd slaughtered too.

With every human death, Joseph grew in power, but he also became weaker. By now, Ronan knew his old ally couldn't tolerate the sun anymore. Holy water and crucifixes would affect him, and soon enough, he wouldn't be able to cross large bodies of water, if he still could now.

Movement on the dance floor drew his attention as a tall man with black hair glided through the crowd with ease. Some of the women stopped dancing to flirt with him and the three men trailing him. All the men continued through the crowd as if they didn't see the women.

Ronan grasped the rail again as he watched the four of them. Judging by the way they carried themselves and the thick coats they wore when the humans had all checked theirs, Ronan knew what they really were...

"Hunters," he murmured. "And not human hunters, but born ones."

The born vampire hunters sometimes took in humans who knew of the existence of vampires. The hunters trained these humans how to kill vampires, but often those human hunters were bait for vampires. The hunters believed vampires were the monsters, but the practice of using the humans as bait was more ruthless than anything Ronan had ever done to a human.

"Bastards," Killean hissed so low that Ronan barely heard him.

"Well, that made this night a lot less fun," Declan said and leaned his hip against the rail.

"Do you think they're tracking Joseph?" Saxon inquired.

"I don't know," Ronan replied as he watched the four men disappear beneath the balcony. "Watch the stairs. If they come this way, be prepared to fight."

Saxon and Killean slipped back toward the stairs, moving through the few humans gathered in the shadows. Most of the mortals were entangled with someone else, or multiple someone elses. A few were huddling together, seeking a fix from their drug of choice.

Ronan had come here to destroy Joseph, but now they may also have to take out an enemy they hadn't expected—an enemy that didn't have to be an enemy, if the hunters weren't so fucking stupid. But throughout the history of vampires and hunters, and despite their common ancestors, the hunters had always believed all vamps were bad. There was no reasoning with them; there was only surviving them.

He'd done what he had to do to survive before and killed a couple of hunters in his lifetime. If it became necessary, he would do it again tonight.

CHAPTER TWO

KADENCE WATCHED from the shadows as her brother, Nathan, disappeared down the stairs to the club with her fellow hunters, Asher, Logan, and Jayce, following him. Nathan would *kill* her if he knew she was here, or more likely lecture her for hours on end, but she wasn't going to sit this hunt out. She was forced to sit out most of her life; she wouldn't miss this.

She just had no idea how to get into that club. Her gaze ran over the line of people snaking around the side of the building and waiting to get inside. The man at the front of the line held a red rope. He'd let her brother in as soon as Nathan approached him. Kadence had never met the man before, and if she had to wait in line, she would never make it inside in time. She didn't know how or why, but she'd always somehow known things over the years, and her instincts were telling her this would be the night and she had to get inside now.

Just as her instincts had told her when her father was killed. She shuddered at the memory of the sweeping, empty feeling that had descended over her the second her father left this world. Hours later his death was confirmed, but it had been no surprise to her when she saw his body. Her fingers dug into her palms at the reminder of how ineffective she'd been. Yes, she'd known when he died, but she hadn't known in time to try to prevent that death.

Now she knew that tonight was the night they would find the vamp who had murdered her father. She'd been working on trying to break out of the stronghold for a while, but she'd known tonight was the night she *had* to go. She'd buried her anxiety over the prospect of being on the other side of the walls that had encompassed her for most of her life, and put her escape plan into motion.

As a hunter, she'd been trained on how to kill a vamp, but as a female hunter, she'd never been allowed to actually fight a vamp or to mingle with humans. This was the first time she'd been out of the hunter stronghold in twenty years, and the last time was only because they'd relocated from Virginia to Massachusetts when an upswing of vampire activity drew them to the area.

Most times, she understood why she was kept so sheltered, but she resented it *all* the time. There was so much of the world to see, so much to explore and learn outside of the thousands of books she'd poured through in her lifetime. She knew hunters were vital to keeping the human population safe from the monsters that came out at night, but did that mean her life had to be sacrificed?

Kadence sighed and her shoulders hunched forward. Yes, that's exactly what it meant.

As her dad had always told her, one life was nothing compared to the billions of lives relying on the hunter race to continue. Yes, they could recruit humans, and they did, but it was necessary to continue the pure hunter line as well. However, it was often difficult for a female hunter to conceive so the women were protected and the men fought.

She'd been privileged to be born into her role as a future wife and mother—or at least that's what she'd been told, repeatedly, over the years. She didn't think being locked away to the point of claustrophobia and already betrothed to Logan was all that lucky, but her opinion didn't matter.

Next month she would be living out her purpose as a wife. Kadence's skin crawled at the reminder of her impending nuptials. Logan was a good, strong, capable man, but he was more like a brother to her than a husband. There was no spark between them, at least not on her end.

She had no idea what a spark with a man felt like, but she'd read about it in some of the romance novels in the stronghold. In those books, a spark was *extremely* important. But those were books and this was reality, and in her reality there were no sparks with her soon-to-be husband.

Because her father had been the leader of the hunters and her brother now was, she'd been paired with the strongest available hunter. And as Nathan's second-in-command, Logan was one of the best.

Kadence blew out a breath as she watched the unmoving line. She had no idea what one had to do to get inside, but she hadn't managed to escape the stronghold to be deterred now. It had taken a *lot* of planning to break free. She hadn't been prepared for this, but she would figure it out.

Thrusting her shoulders back, Kadence brushed her braid over her shoulder and slipped from the shadows. The January air chilled her cheeks as she approached the mountain of a man holding the rope. At first, his chestnut eyes ran dismissively over her, but then they became more leisurely in their perusal of her. Kadence frowned at him before waving her hand after where Nathan and the others had gone down the steps.

"Nathan is my brother," she said.

"Is that so?" the man inquired with a smirk.

"Yes."

"Then why didn't you enter with him?"

Kadence grappled to come up with a response. Glancing down the line of people, she noticed most of them were focused on the phones in their hands. A few were watching her, some with interest, others with hostility.

"I forgot my phone at home and couldn't call to let him know I was running late. He probably assumed I'd changed my mind about meeting him here," she lied with ease and flashed the man her best smile.

The man's eyes ran over her one more time. Kadence stilled her fingers when they fidgeted with the edges of her sleeves. She was so far out of her element here, awkward in a way she'd never been before. If she'd been a human woman, she would be comfortable with talking to this man, she would know what to say, but all she knew was what she'd been raised to know, vampires, marriage, babies.

Fresh resentment shot through her. *Life could be worse.* She told herself this a thousand times a day, but it had yet to fully sink in.

She should be grateful for all she had, instead of resentful of everything denied her. Still, she wanted to push this guy out of her way and stroll into the club instead of standing here like a moron with a growing group of humans peering curiously at her.

"Next time, come with him," the man said and lifted the rope before he stepped aside.

"Oh, come on! This is bullshit! Nathan is my brother too!" a chorus of voices shouted from the line.

Kadence ignored all of them as she hastened down the steps toward the thumping beat coming from behind the closed door below. Before she could open the door, it swung inward to reveal a woman holding it for her. The woman smiled at her as the music increased to the point where Kadence's head pounded in rhythm with it.

"You can check your coat," the woman said and waved her arm at a window behind her. A man stood there resting his elbows on the wooden windowsill, but he straightened when he saw Kadence.

"No, thank you." Kadence pulled her coat closer against her as she turned away from the woman. She didn't know much about humans, but her books, her family, and other hunters had told her enough about the human world to know the weapons tucked into her coat would not be welcome here.

Hurrying down the hall, she walked toward the music. She worried Nathan would discover her here, but she couldn't deny the thrill of excitement running through her at being free and finally seeing something of the human world.

Granted, it was for the worst reason possible that she was out of the stronghold, and she had no idea how to interact with this world, but she was *free*.

Stepping out of the hall, she found herself standing at the edge of a dance floor. Kadence gawked at the spectacle of all the humans moving and jumping around before her. She and her friend, Simone, had spent a lot of time dancing in each other's rooms over the years, but she'd never seen anything like this.

The complete inhibition, lack of clothing, and energy of the place fascinated her as much as it unnerved her. The aromas of sweat and alcohol intermingled so completely with each other that she could barely separate the two. There was nothing like this in the stronghold. Simone would be in absolute awe when Kadence went back and told her what she'd seen here.

Went back...

Kadence shook her head to clear it of the sadness creeping through her at the thought of returning to the stronghold—a place that was a beautiful prison for her and so many other women. Granted, most of the women there didn't think of it that way, but she'd give anything to spread her wings and break free of her gilded cage.

Not the time, she told herself sternly. *You are here for a reason.* Her gaze scanned over the crowd as she searched for the vampire who had murdered her father. She also kept an eye out for her brother.

Ronan's gaze honed in on the woman who emerged from the hallway to stand at the edge of the dance floor. Her silver blonde hair, dangling in a braid over her shoulder to her left breast, reflected the colors flashing over her in an array of reds, blues, and yellows. The lights played over her delicate features and lit the awe on her face as she stared at the humans.

A smile tugged at the corners of her full mouth when a group danced close by her. Many of the people below displayed more flesh than they covered, but Ronan found his gaze riveted on her fully clothed body in its form-fitting black pants, which were tucked into ankle-high, black boots. Her calf-length, black coat pushed back as she settled her hands on her hips to watch the crowd. Beneath the coat, she wore a black turtleneck that hugged her breasts, slender waist, and rounded hips. She looked to be a good five inches shorter than him at about five-seven.

Her smile slid away and her hands fell from her hips as she surveyed the crowd with a far more serious eye. Then her head fell back, her gaze locked onto his, and he was treated to a full-on view of her striking beauty.

The image of her body, naked beneath his and moving in a sensuous dance against his sheets, caused his cock to harden. He felt like he had when he'd been twelve and first discovering the joys of the female body, before the enjoyment of sex had faded away over the many years of his death-filled life. He couldn't recall the last time he'd desired a woman, but it had never been with this intensity.

For the first time in centuries, he lusted after a woman, and he would have her.

CHAPTER THREE

THE AIR RUSHED out of Kadence's lungs when she spotted the man above. Though his eyes were shaded with sunglasses, she knew he was focused on her. Butterflies fluttered to life within her stomach as she drank in the details of the man.

Not handsome, she wouldn't define him as that, but definitely intriguing. Her fingers itched to trace the contoured planes of his high cheekbones and the stubble lining his square jaw. His sable eyebrows drew together over the bridge of his roman nose as he watched her. She had no idea why he was wearing sunglasses inside, but she would give anything to pull them off and reveal the color of his eyes.

Sparks. For the first time in her life, she understood the romance novels as she was hit with the urge to get closer to this man, to touch him like she'd never touched another. To slip that coat from his shoulders and run her hands over him before rising on her toes to kiss him. The possibility of those arms wrapping around her and drawing her close had her taking a step forward.

A woman bumped into her, knocking her back and tearing her attention away from the man. Kadence blinked as she was jarred back to reality. Her gaze ran over the humans before she retreated from the dance floor to hover on the edge. She refused to look up again for fear she would be lost to the strange pull that man had over her. She'd come here for a reason, and she would not be deterred from it.

It had seemed odd the man wore sunglasses inside, but that faded when she realized some of the other men and women also wore them. Must be some human fashion thing, she decided.

"Hello, sugar," Declan purred from beside Ronan. "I think she might make a *very* tasty treat."

Ronan didn't have to look at him to know Declan had also spotted the woman. In a crowd of nearly a hundred humans, she stood out as clearly as the full moon from the stars. Declan leaned forward to inspect the woman more closely.

"Don't," Ronan snarled, half tempted to throw his friend over the railing.

He had no idea where the impulse came from. He was not an easy man, but he was tolerant. He'd learned centuries ago that giving into anger and having a temper were pointless. However, the way Declan looked at the woman, as if he could see straight through her clothes, had Ronan ready to punch him.

Declan's head turned toward him. "Claiming her for yourself tonight?"

"We have a mission," Ronan bit out. The thick sunglasses may be shading his eyes, but he knew Declan was aware that he remained focused on the woman.

"After the mission then?"

Ronan tore his attention away from her to look at Declan. His friend's casual air vanished; he straightened away from the railing and took an abrupt step back. Ronan didn't have time to contemplate Declan's reaction to him before the rancid stench of garbage wafted through the air. His gaze returned to the dance floor as he searched for the source of the smell.

The crowd of people flowed away from the corner as Joseph glided out of the shadows from the entryway. Yet even as the humans moved away from him, some of the women and men practically tripped over themselves to get closer to him.

A vampire's innate ability to lure someone closer drew the humans to Joseph like a bee to nectar. Their instincts told them this was no nectar, but a Venus flytrap set to spring and devour them whole. Unfortunately for these humans, Joseph's lure won out over their flight-or-fight instincts.

Ronan looked to the woman only twenty feet away from Joseph. His lips skimmed back when the woman's gaze locked on Joseph strolling through the crowd. Unlike the other females, she didn't saunter toward the vampire. Instead, her hand went to something at her side.

Ronan's eyes narrowed at her unusual reaction. The black-haired, male hunter emerged again at the edge of the dance floor, drawing the woman's gaze to him.

Kadence wanted to kick herself when Nathan spotted her from the other side of the dance floor. She'd *finally* succeeded in breaking free of the stronghold, finally made it here, and she'd been busted within five minutes of walking into the club. So much for being a stealthy hunter.

She'd completely blown it, and now she would never have another opportunity to be free again. Nathan would make sure of that. If the monster didn't die tonight, she'd never be able to witness it.

Going by what she'd been told about him and the odor coming from him, she'd known the minute the vampire who killed her father came into eyesight. She'd also forgotten about everything else as her blood thrummed with the need to see the monster slaughtered.

For a second, Ronan watched as the hunter and woman locked eyes, and then the male was moving toward her so fast that the humans didn't register his passing. The born hunters may not be vampires, but they certainly weren't entirely human either.

Ten feet before the hunter reached the woman, he stopped in the middle of the dance floor. His head swiveled and his nostrils flared as his gaze locked on Joseph. The hunter's eyes darted between the woman and Joseph before he closed the distance to the woman.

Ronan couldn't hear what they said to each other over the thumping music, but when the man snatched the woman's arm, she yanked it away from him and planted her hands on her hips. A low growl rumbled up Ronan's throat. Joseph was right there, yet he found himself thinking about breaking the hunter's hand for daring to touch her when she obviously didn't welcome it.

For daring to touch her when it was all that *he* wanted to do.

The woman's hands moved through the air as she spoke; the man's followed suit as they faced off. Then, the crowd parted and Joseph moved within feet of them. Joseph's attention remained on the women at his sides as he walked by the male hunter. The man and woman stopped speaking as they focused on Joseph. Their faces filled with a hatred Ronan suspected ran deeper than a hunter's normal animosity toward vampires.

When Joseph was out of sight, the man took hold of the woman's arm and led her over to join the three other hunters standing beside the dance floor. The woman moved with the same lethal speed as the man, confirming her as what she was. Ronan shoved aside the disappointment slithering through him at the realization the woman was completely off limits.

"A female hunter," he murmured.

"I thought they were a myth," Declan stated.

"Apparently not," Ronan said as his gaze returned to Joseph. It didn't matter who or what the woman was, all that mattered was ending this tonight. He only hoped the hunters stayed out of his way.

He'd prefer not to have to kill them too.

"Let's go."

He stalked toward where Killean and Saxon stood at the top of the stairs. Lucien, one of his best fighters, was on his way to meet them, but Ronan didn't think he'd make it in time for this battle. Lucien had reluctantly agreed to take over the running of the training facility after Joseph turned Savage. Ronan had expected to destroy Joseph sooner, so he hadn't bothered to move the training facility out of New York or find someone else to run it yet, but that would change if Joseph wasn't brought down tonight.

Stepping off the last stair, Ronan paused to survey the crowd before following Joseph's stench through the club. Any vampire who killed a human took on the aroma of trash and decay. If they didn't kill again, eventually the smell faded away. The more a vampire killed, the more rotten they smelled. Roadkill mixed with feces and month-old bodies sometimes became preferable to the odor some Savages emitted. However, only a purebred vampire could detect the odor.

Joseph had been having more fun than Ronan realized, judging by the scent of him.

Winding through the crowd, Ronan caught another glimpse of the black-haired, male hunter on his left. His gaze instinctively sought the woman, who now stood with one of the other men. That man had his hand around her slender bicep while she glowered at him.

Kadence considered kicking Logan in the nuts to break free of her fiance's hold, but she was afraid if she made a move now, she would scare the vampire they hunted away, or worse, get Nathan killed. Logan's displeasure beat against her. She didn't care that he was mad at her; he would have to get used to her not doing what she was told once they were married.

Logan had to know she wasn't the proper, well-behaved hunter she was supposed to be. Everyone in the stronghold knew that. She'd gotten in more trouble over the years than all the other women combined.

At one time, Nathan and his friends had laughed over her antics.

They'd stopped laughing years ago, and they certainly weren't laughing tonight. Jayce and Asher both stared at her as if she were a ten-legged, alien cat who had dropped on their heads from a beam above. Nathan refused to look at her as he tapped his foot and ran a hand through his black hair.

She tilted her head back to look at Logan. Unlike the man on the balcony, Logan was definitely what most would consider handsome with his pine-colored eyes, light brown hair, and refined features. Unfortunately, his handsomeness did nothing for her. She tried to tug her arm free again, but his hold on her only intensified.

"Let me go," she commanded.

"No." The simple refusal set her teeth on edge.

Ronan watched the woman trying to break free of the man's hold on her. He almost detoured to yank her away from the hunter, but there was no time for that, and the last thing they needed was a fight with the hunters tonight. Slipping through the shadows, he tracked Joseph to one of the back doors.

The expression on Joseph's face was one of boredom as a human woman ground her hips against his while rubbing her breasts on his chest. Joseph's head came up and a smile curved his mouth when his eyes latched onto Ronan's over the sea of human heads separating them.

Bending low, Joseph whispered something in the woman's ear before sinking his fangs into her throat. Joseph tore a chunk out of the woman's neck and spit it out. The woman's scream was drowned out by the beat of the music as she staggered back. Her hand flew to the wound as blood poured from between her fingers.

"Shit!" Ronan shouted. "Saxon, take care of her!"

He didn't care if the woman lived or died, but if she somehow survived this, she couldn't be allowed to tell the tale of the man who had torn her throat out with his teeth. If she died, she couldn't do so with the evidence of a vampire's fangs on her. It would only attract more hunters if she did.

Joseph spun and crashed into the back door, flinging it open and vanishing into the alley beyond. The woman slumped to the side and fell into him. Ronan steadied her as the coppery scent of her blood hit him. Ignoring the lure of her blood, he pushed her over to Saxon.

From the corner of his eye, he saw another door to the alley swinging closed. He glanced back to see the female hunter standing at the edge of the dance floor. Ronan hesitated when he realized they'd left her alone, but she didn't show any sign of following her brethren out the door. Then, he spotted the man who had been holding her jogging toward the other exit. The man stopped beside the door and leaned against the wall before glancing back at the woman.

Turning away from them, Ronan didn't look back as he followed Joseph out the door. The hunter woman was no concern of his; her relatives in the alley were.

CHAPTER FOUR

RONAN STEPPED INTO THE ALLEY, his eyes and ears attuned to his environment as he searched for Joseph and the hunters. Garbage pushed up the lids of the dumpsters lining the brick wall of the buildings across from him. The refuse flowing over the sides of the dumpsters helped to mask Joseph's scent.

Declan's and Killean's booted feet thudded on the concrete behind Ronan as he turned to the left and started walking that way. A few lazy snowflakes spiraled from the sky. The club was close enough to the ocean that a shift in the wind brought the briny scent of low tide on the air with it. The alley was unnaturally silent; the predators lurking amid it had scared off the rats who resided within.

The end of his coat beat against his calves as the alley split off and he continued down another corridor. Tucked within the inner pockets of his coat were a couple of stakes and a small crossbow. However, he mostly relied on his hands and his fangs when in battle and didn't like to weigh himself down with weapons. He also didn't like to deny himself the pleasure of an up-close and personal kill. It was what kept the demon in him at bay after all.

He'd avoid killing the hunters if he could. He didn't want to bear the stench of garbage and the increased vulnerability to the sun that their deaths would bring him. The hunters may not be entirely human, but their blood staining a vampire's hands had the same effect a human's did.

Although the hunters wouldn't hesitate to slaughter any of them, he didn't consider them his enemy, not completely. They were more of a nuisance that sometimes had to be stomped. The hunters meant well, but they didn't know the difference between the vampires who killed humans for amusement and those who didn't.

They've never known the difference, Ronan thought bitterly.

The hunters had killed many Savage vampires over the years, but they'd also destroyed some of the good ones. Thankfully, they hadn't killed as many of the good ones as they had Savages. Vampires who didn't kill tended to stay off their radar. They led peaceful lives, and unlike the Savages, they didn't draw attention to themselves by leaving a trail of bodies or missing people behind them.

Ronan turned another corner, stopping instantly when he spotted Joseph at the end of the alley. Joseph stood before a ten-foot-high brick wall, studying the blockade before him. More garbage than before overflowed the dumpsters and spilled onto the asphalt. Most of the bags had been torn open and picked through by the animal scavengers and probably some humans.

Ronan clenched and unclenched his hands as he studied his old ally. Joseph could have easily cleared the wall and been out of here by now, so why did he remain?

Declan and Killean halted beside him as Joseph glanced over his shoulder at them. The grin that split his face revealed his lethal fangs as he turned to face them. The hazel of Joseph's eyes briefly flickered through the red encompassing them as he gave a come-and-get-it gesture with his hands.

"Something's not right here," Ronan murmured to the others. "He's trying to set us up for something."

"What though?" Declan inquired.

"I don't know, but stay alert."

Declan and Killean spread out to the sides of him as the three of them prowled down the alley. Ronan didn't know why Joseph had chosen to stay, but he wasn't going to rush him until he knew what the Savage vampire had up his sleeves.

They had to approach this cautiously, but in his head, he heard the seconds of a clock ticking away. When they exited the club, the hunters must have gone the other way in the alley, but they would come this way eventually. They had to take Joseph down before the hunters arrived on the scene.

At one time, Ronan's body would have been alive with the thrill of the impending kill. Now he experienced no excitement as he closed in on the fallen Defender. Joseph's elongated canines sliced his bottom lip, and the scent of garbage grew stronger as blood trickled down his chin from the gash.

Joseph crouched down before launching himself at Ronan's chest. It was a move Joseph never would have made before becoming Savage, but the increased strength he'd experienced with his kills made him far more brazen. Despite that increased strength, Ronan had no fear Joseph could take him down. It would take far more than Joseph alone to do so.

Ronan swung out at him, catching him squarely beneath the jaw and flinging him into one of the dumpsters. Metal dented with a loud bang. Garbage spewed onto the ground and rats screeched as they scattered into the gloomy recesses of the alley. Joseph came up spitting blood as he launched off the dumpster.

"So you're going to kill me now? You're going to kill one of your own?" Joseph inquired. "So much for loyalty, hey, Ronan?"

Ronan circled him as Joseph moved toward the wall and Declan and Killean closed in on him. "You're not one of us anymore, Joseph," Ronan replied.

"You have no right to judge me. You're closer to the edge than I ever was."

Ronan didn't flinch at the assessment; it was true after all.

"Obviously not," Declan replied, "considering you're the one we're hunting."

Hatred twisted Joseph's features; Declan grinned at him in return. Joseph snarled, but this time instead of coming for Ronan, he charged straight at Declan whose smile only widened as he braced himself for Joseph's attack. Joseph lowered his shoulder and crashed into Declan, sending him reeling into the wall.

Declan didn't go down beneath Joseph. Instead, he clasped his hands together and drove them into Joseph's back. Joseph grunted as he wrapped his arms around Declan's waist, lifted him up, and bashed him into the wall again. Declan swung an uppercut that broke Joseph's hold on him and staggered Joseph back a few feet.

Before he could fully recover, Ronan grabbed Joseph by the collar of his shirt and yanked him back. His hand encircled his throat, crushing Joseph's windpipe as he pinned him to the wall. Pulling his arm back, Ronan fisted his hand in preparation to drive it through Joseph's chest and end this.

"Ronan!" Killean's shout alerted him to the threat he'd missed while focused on the kill.

A whistling reached him in time for him to turn to the side, but not in time to avoid the bolt completely. A piercing pain shot through his shoulder as the weapon impaled him from behind. Stumbling slightly forward, he nearly lost his grip on Joseph as a burning sensation spread through the thick muscle of his shoulder. Turning his head, he spotted three of the hunters at the other end of the alley. The black-haired one had an empty crossbow aimed at him.

Joseph grabbed the end of the bolt and twisted it. Ronan involuntarily released his hold on him when numbness spread through his shoulder. Joseph's hands flew to his brutalized throat. Broken sounds issued from him as he clawed at his flesh and his eyes rolled in his head. Ronan had no idea what he was trying to say, and he didn't care.

"Ronan!"

Declan's shout enabled him to dodge the next arrow one of the other hunters fired at him, an arrow aimed straight at his heart. He plucked the arrow from the air and shattered it in his fingers before leveling the hunters with a murderous stare. Two of them took a step away from him, but the black-haired one held his ground as he focused on Joseph.

Without warning, the black-haired hunter barreled down the alley with his shoulder lowered. He plowed into Joseph, running him backward as he kept his shoulder buried in Joseph's sternum. Joseph and the hunter tumbled into the dumpsters. Garbage spilled over them, momentarily burying them both beneath a wave of trash.

Ronan didn't move as Joseph and the hunter thrashed on the ground. He wasn't the only one startled by the uncharacteristically reckless display from a hunter. Declan and Killean remained unmoving as the hunter punched Joseph with enough force to crack a cheekbone. The next blow he delivered shattered Joseph's nose. Blood splattered Joseph's shirt and sprayed onto the concrete within inches of Ronan's boots.

He'd never seen a hunter behave like this. Whenever he'd encountered them, they'd always been methodical and careful as they worked together. They never let their emotions rule them or broke ranks. Even the hunter's partners were thrown off as they had yet to attempt moving in for their own kills.

The hunters didn't remain stunned into immobility for long. While what Ronan assumed was their leader continued to pummel Joseph, the other two inched forward. One held a crossbow at the ready, its arrow aimed straight at Declan's heart. The other trained a 9mm on Killean. Unless the gun was loaded with wooden bullets, it wouldn't kill them. However, it would still hurt them enough to slow them down and make it easier for them to be killed.

The one holding the crossbow kept glancing between Ronan and Declan, but the hunter didn't aim the crossbow at him again. The two remaining hunters must have decided Ronan's injury didn't make him much of a threat. They couldn't be more wrong.

Ronan scanned the alley behind them, but the woman and the other hunter they'd been with were nowhere to be seen. He turned his attention back to the ugly situation they now faced. The black-haired hunter was dragging Joseph's beaten form up behind him as he climbed to his feet.

At one time, seeing a fellow Defender so broken and bruised would have enraged him, but Joseph wasn't one of them anymore. Ronan couldn't help feeling a grudging admiration for the damage the hunter had inflicted on the Savage. If it had been any other Savage, Ronan would have walked away and allowed the hunters to have them, but he had to make sure Joseph died this night. The fallen Defender knew far too many of their secrets to risk him continuing to live.

Ronan's lips skimmed back when the black-haired hunter's azure eyes fell on him. At about six four, the hunter was a good four inches taller than him, and lean in build.

"This doesn't have to happen," Ronan said. "We don't have to fight each other. Give us Joseph and walk away."

The hunter bared his teeth and his hand clamped down on Joseph's already crushed throat. Joseph's head lulled forward on his shoulders before it snapped up. The black-haired hunter's eyes were full of antipathy as they held Ronan's. He didn't have to say a word; Ronan knew the real fight was about to begin.

Signaling Declan and Killean, he moved to the side, putting himself in a better position to go after the hunter with the crossbow. Ronan charged at him just as the black-haired hunter's command to kill them rang through the air.

The hunter holding the crossbow caught his charge out of the corner of his eye. Startled, he spun toward Ronan, but he was too late. Grabbing the end of the bow, Ronan ripped it from the hunter's hands. He drove a fist into the man's nose, shattering it before he shoved the hunter into a dumpster.

A gunshot rang out. Killean's grunt could be heard over the ensuing echo of the shot as it reverberated off the brick walls surrounding them. Another shot fired, but this time it cracked off brick. Either Killean or Declan had managed to subdue the hunter with the gun.

CHAPTER FIVE

"WHAT WERE YOU THINKING COMING HERE?" Logan demanded when she crept forward to stand at his side within the club.

Kadence barely glanced at him before focusing on the doorway Nathan and the others had exited through. Her hand slid to the stake in the inner pocket of her coat. "I should be out there," she whispered.

Logan grasped her shoulders, spinning her to face him. Kadence blinked at him, startled by the harshness of his handsome face as he glared at her. "You have no business being here at all!" he barked at her.

"You have no business telling me what to do!"

"I have every right to tell you what to do. We're to be married soon, and you've put yourself, your brother, and our entire way of life at risk by coming here. I will not have it!"

The one thing her instructors had always hated most about her was her willful streak, but she wouldn't be ordered around by anyone. Not her father, not her brother, and certainly not the man who she had no choice about marrying.

"I will not have you talking to me in such a way," she grated from between her teeth. "We may be getting married, but no one will order me around, Logan. Not even my husband."

She jerked out of his grasp and gave him a scathing glance before focusing on the door again. Around them, people danced and swayed, the lights flashed over the walls and floor, but she tuned it all out to focus on hearing anything from the outside world. Her father's line of hunters had always been the strongest; it was why their line had been the leader of the hunters since the beginning. She and Nathan were faster and stronger than the others, their senses more honed.

Because she was a woman, she would not have been allowed to lead even if she were the only living descendent, but she carried the strength of that line in her blood. If Nathan were killed before he could produce an heir, her husband would lead the hunters until she produced a male heir who would one day take control. If she had only a female child, her daughter would face the same fate. Only three times in their history had someone outside of their line been a leader until an heir was born.

"I am only trying to keep you safe," Logan said.

He broke her concentration on the outside when he rested his hand on her shoulder. His finger slid up to stroke her cheek. She resisted cringing away from the tender touch. She loved Logan as a friend, she always had and always would, but she was well aware his feelings for her were more than friendly.

He clasped his hand possessively around her nape, drawing her a step closer. Kadence stiffened beneath his touch, but it was something she would have to get used to if she were going to survive her marriage to him.

Her stomach rolled at the thought of their wedding night, and the many nights that would follow, before she blocked it out. If she pondered it too much, she would never make it through the wedding ceremony, never mind the next hundred and fifty or so years they could possibly be married, if Logan didn't get killed on a hunt.

A gunshot from outside barely registered through the music, but she knew what she'd heard. Plunging forward, she slammed into the bar on the door and shoved it open. The cold air robbed her breath as the second gunshot sounded.

Logan grabbed her arm, pushing her back toward the club. "Get inside!"

Kadence staggered backward, but she didn't turn toward the closing door. Instead, she followed Logan down the alley, running as fast as her legs would carry her. One vampire versus three hunters, her brother and the others should have easily taken him down. Yet, she could hear the sounds of fists hitting flesh, the twang of a bolt firing, and the scuffle of numerous feet from deeper within the alley.

Something had gone wrong.

Not my brother, please not my brother too. She couldn't handle it if she lost her father and Nathan.

Her brother was the only family she had left. Nathan wouldn't stand in the way of her marriage; as the leader, he would follow tradition, no matter how unhappy it made her. However, he would be there for her to lean on when she needed it. She hadn't complained to him about her marriage—she couldn't when he had enough weighing on him right now—but she knew he was aware she wasn't happy about it.

Just as she knew that being the newly appointed leader wasn't something he wanted, though he'd never said it to her. As twins, they had always been close. They'd been closer when they were younger, before Nathan went into training and she was forced to learn how to be the perfect wife and mother. They followed separate courses in life, but he'd still been her best friend over the years, her rock.

Legs aching, lungs straining for air, Kadence flew around a corner of the alley and skidded to a halt. The alley reeked of the coppery scent of fresh blood and garbage. Bile rolled up her throat, and it took all she had to keep from vomiting. The last time she had smelled blood so strongly…

Memories of her father's broken body tried to drag her under before she locked them away.

She found Nathan instantly, unharmed and holding *the vampire* in his grasp. Hatred blurred her vision as she gazed at the creature who had murdered her father and torn her life apart. The vamp was beaten and bloody, and though she scented him on the air, it was not his odor filling her nostrils now. This scent was different, spicier, and held no hint of the evil pouring from the vamp.

Her eyes latched onto a heavily muscled man shoving Asher aside. Blood poured from Asher's broken nose, but it wasn't his blood she smelled either. It was the blood of the man who had shoved Asher away. A man with lethal fangs fully extended and an overwhelming aura of power emanating from him.

Disbelief screamed through her as she recognized him as the man who had been standing on the balcony watching her. The man who had finally made her understand some of what she'd read in those romance novels. A man who was *not* a man at all, but one of the twisted freaks who thrived on killing.

How could his blood smell like that? All vampires smelled like rot! Over the years, the male hunters had captured some vampires and brought them to the stronghold for training purposes. They'd allowed the women of the camp to get close enough to detect the stench vampires emitted. It was a smell she would never forget.

As this vamp turned toward her, she saw the bolt protruding from his shoulder and the blood oozing from the puncture. His coat was pushed back, his black shirt ripped open to expose a slash of bronzed flesh across his broad chest.

His sunglasses remained in place, but she knew he watched her. Molten lava spread through her veins as those covered eyes exposed her and ripped her soul bare. He stared *into* her in a way no other ever had. Kadence shuddered while her heart leapt into her throat. Despite the fangs and the fact he was a creature she'd been born to hate, she couldn't deny her pull toward him.

Shock slid through Ronan as he stared at the female hunter. He hadn't expected her to leave the club, to come out here, and he certainly hadn't expected the rapt way she watched him. He'd seen many beautiful women over the thousand years of his life, but none of them had captivated him in such a way.

The battle and his men faded away as he stared at her. The wind tugged at her silvery hair, whipping the loose strands of it around her oval-shaped face. Her azure eyes watched his every move. The look on her face said she couldn't figure him out, but then he had no idea what to make of this woman either.

Kadence felt time crawl by as they gazed at each other, but when Logan suddenly crashed into the vamp, she realized only mere seconds had passed. Asher barely dodged out of the way of the vamp and Logan as Logan propelled the vamp into the brick wall.

"Ronan!" the auburn-haired man shouted.

"I'm fine," the one wearing the sunglasses grunted, and she realized he was Ronan.

Kadence took a step forward to stop Logan from attacking him, but then her heritage, her *common sense*, kicked in and disgust at herself filled her gut. He was a vampire for crying out loud! What was the matter with her?

Her first time out of the stronghold and she was having the warm and fuzzies for her worst enemy. She was an idiot and a pitiful excuse for a hunter.

Taking a deep breath, she struggled to control the accelerated beat of her heart as Ronan hit Logan, knocking him backward. "Declan, go that way," Ronan ordered with a wave of his hand at the auburn-haired man. "Killean, that way," he commanded the one with the scar.

Kadence's hands went to two of the stakes tucked into her inner coat pocket when she realized there were two *more* vamps in the alley. Declan moved to the right as Jayce fired a shot at Killean, hitting him in the shoulder. Killean lunged forward, knocking the gun from Jayce's hand with one blow.

Killean jerked Jayce forward, but instead of sinking his fangs into Jayce's throat and tearing it out, he threw Jayce away from him. Killean could have killed Jayce, there was no denying that. Instead, he'd pushed him away. Kadence's mind spun as she tried to understand what she'd seen, but none of it made any sense.

"Kadence! Get out of here! Now!"

Nathan's bellow made her cringe, but she wouldn't follow his command. She had to witness what happened here. Kadence gasped when Logan brandished a stake and tried to plunge into Ronan's chest. Ronan grabbed Logan's hand and tore the stake away as if Logan were no more than a child. With a flick of his fingers, he tossed the stake aside.

His lethal fangs gleamed in the dim light of the alley, but instead of striking, he pushed Logan away from him like Killean had. Kadence watched as the vamps lined up on one side of the alley, with the hunters moving to position themselves on the other side. The vamp who had killed her father thrashed in her brother's grasp, his red eyes blazing like rubies in the sun. His florid face and wheezing breaths led her to believe his windpipe had been crushed at some point.

"We are at a crossroads," Ronan stated.

His deep voice sent shivers down her spine. Kadence shook herself. No matter how compelling she found him to be, he was a vampire, plain and simple.

So caught up in her own confusion and emotions, she failed to notice what had happened during the fight. Her brother and the hunters were lined up on their side, closest to the wall, with the vampires lined up before them.

Which would have been fine. Her brother had her father's killer. Kadence was more than happy to leave here with him, more than happy to go somewhere else to dispose of the monster, while they left the rest of the vamps alone, for now.

The real problem was that she'd been separated from the hunters and was stuck behind the vampires.

CHAPTER SIX

"Do you plan to fight to the death?" Ronan asked.

"If that's what it takes, considering it will be your deaths, not ours," Nathan replied.

Declan and Killean chuckled while Ronan shifted his stance. Kadence's heart leapt into her throat. "No," she croaked.

Once the word was out of her mouth, she knew she'd made a mistake. Until she spoke, everyone had forgotten about her. Now, all eyes turned toward her.

"Kadence, leave!" Nathan spat.

Her eyes flew around the group. Her hand trembled as she lifted it to her treacherous mouth. However, she couldn't run from here. She couldn't lose her brother, and for some strange reason, she didn't want anything bad to happen to Ronan either.

Later, when she was alone, she would kick herself in her stupid ass for finally encountering vampires in the world and turning into a complete idiot because one of them fascinated her. For now, she had to completely ignore her bizarre reaction to Ronan as the other two did absolutely nothing for her.

"The fight is a draw. No more blood has to spill," she said. "We have the one we came for. There will be other nights to continue this."

"And more innocent deaths before then!" Nathan sneered.

"Nathan, please, I can't lose you too!" she cried.

So the hunter, Nathan, was her lover or husband, Ronan realized. He eyed the vein in Nathan's throat and licked his lips as he contemplated ending his competition for her.

"Get out of here, Kadence!" Nathan yelled at her.

A low growl emanated from him over the way Nathan spoke to her. Declan and Killean exchanged startled glances, but neither of them could be as surprised as he was over it.

Nathan tightened his hold on Joseph's throat. He seemed to think Ronan was going to charge him to take Joseph back. However, Ronan had no intention of going anywhere near Nathan, not if it meant leaving Kadence unprotected.

"Nathan—" Kadence started.

"I said *leave!*"

The roared order echoed throughout the alley. Kadence preferred not to see the bloodbath she was certain was about to unfold, but she wouldn't let it happen if she could somehow stop it. Her fingers slid away from one of her stakes as she looked to Ronan, whose head was turned in her direction.

Everything she'd been taught over the years told her he was evil. However, something within her said he wasn't. That belief might get her killed tonight. If it did, then she well deserved to die for her stupidity, but she couldn't bring herself to attack someone who hadn't come after her.

"I'm not leaving," she declared as she looked back to her brother.

Nathan's eyes widened. Declan glanced over his shoulder at her, an approving smile curving his full mouth. Before she could think about what that smile meant, a large hand enclosed on her arm. She spun to face the two men who materialized from the shadows behind her.

The one holding her stared back at her. His pitiless black eyes caused chills to run down her spine. His sandy blond hair framed his handsome face as his upper lip twisted into a sneer of disapproval. She didn't have to see his fangs to know this was another vampire. Dread flared through her as his grip became bruising. The other vamp who had appeared with him moved forward to join Ronan and his group. Kadence's heart sank as she realized the hunters were now outnumbered.

She didn't get any murderous vibes from Ronan, but she had no doubt the vamp holding her would break her neck and step over her dead body with the same amount of consideration he gave to pulling on his socks.

"Hello, boys," the vamp holding her greeted, his voice as glacial as the rest of him.

"About time you showed up, Lucien," Killean said.

"Looks like Saxon and I are just in time, Killean," Lucien replied with a shrug. "Quite the pickle we're all in. Especially Joseph there," he nodded to the vamp Nathan held. "Looks like everyone's after your blood, asshole."

Joseph opened his mouth to respond, but only a choked *ugh* sound came out. Hatred churned in her gut as Kadence gazed at the vamp who had killed her father. She knew his name now, but to her he would always be the vamp who had torn her world apart. The one who had propelled her into breaking free of the boundaries she'd chafed against her whole life.

"Let go of her!" Nathan snapped at Lucien.

"Is she what I think she is?" Lucien inquired, completely ignoring her brother's command as he bent toward her to inspect her more closely.

"She is a born hunter," Killean answered.

Kadence leaned away from him and, before she could think about it, kicked him in the shin. Lucien jumped and surveyed her with more interest. "Feisty little hunter, aren't you?" he murmured.

"Let go of her, Lucien," Ronan said. "She has no part in this."

Kadence gawked at him. Was Ronan, the *vampire*, trying to protect *her*? Even Nathan looked confused by his words.

"From what I can tell, they have Joseph and we have her, so I think she has a big part in this," Lucien replied. "Not to mention, *no* one has seen a born, female hunter. She may be something we can use to our advantage against these do-gooder, idiotic pricks."

Ronan spun toward them. The fury emanating from his body caused her to step back. Lucien squeezed her arm, eliciting an involuntary wince from her. Adrenaline spiked through her as Ronan stalked toward them with menace exuding from every inch of him. She'd been wrong about him; he was going to drain her dry before tossing her lifeless body aside.

Kadence refused to cower from his approach as she defiantly lifted her chin. She'd put up one hell of a fight against him, though she was certain he could crush her skull with only one of his hands. Her fingers twitched toward the stake at her side while she awaited her opportunity to inflict as much damage as possible. Ronan would remember her years after he'd killed her, she'd make sure of it.

"Stay away from her!" Nathan's bellow rent the air.

Shoving Joseph at Jayce, her brother rushed forward. Killen stepped forward to block his attack. Kadence screamed and lurched forward to help her brother as he barreled into Killean. The two of them tumbled to the ground in a frenzied heap.

Lucien jerked her back before she made it two steps toward them. Ronan's hand lashed out to grasp Lucien's forearm.

"I said let her go!" Ronan ordered.

Kadence's jaw dropped.

"What is the matter with you?" Lucien demanded.

"Let her go." His hand squeezed Lucien's arm to the point where Kadence was certain the bone would break.

Lucien released her, and his brows furrowed as he studied Ronan. "I'd rather fight anyway," he muttered before stalking away from the two of them.

It was then that Kadence realized the battle had commenced again. The only one hanging back now was Jayce, but he'd been saddled with Joseph.

"No!" Kadence stepped forward, determined to stop this, or at least try to help as her brother and Killean circled each other like wolves.

"No." Ronan stepped in front of her, his solid body blocking her way.

He became all she could see as his chest alone was three times the size of hers. He was not as tall as the others, but there was no doubt he was the strongest one here. She didn't have to see him in action to know that. Every strand of her DNA was aware of what stood before her: an old vampire with more power than she could begin to comprehend.

Her lips parted on a breath as her eyes fell on his shaded ones. She had no idea what it was about him, but she couldn't find it in herself to care that he was a vampire—not when her skin felt electrified by his nearness and her nerve endings tingled with her need to touch him.

She craved more of him.

Thousands upon thousands of hunters were turning over in their graves right now. Self-hate skittered through her, but she couldn't bring herself to pull out her stake and attack him.

Ronan shifted as the scent of her arousal on the air caused him to harden. She wanted him too. Her forehead furrowed in confusion over her reaction to him. He completely understood her confusion as he felt it too.

He didn't know what drove him, but he *had* to know if her skin was as supple as it looked. Without thinking, he reached out to touch her cheek. Beneath the pads of his fingers, her skin was like fine spun silk. She didn't recoil from him, didn't look repulsed. Instead, to his amazement, she turned her cheek into his hand so that her lips brushed against his palm.

A loud crash from behind him jerked them both apart and brought the world rushing back in around him.

"Shit!" he hissed.

How could he have forgotten about the fight behind him? How could he have left his friends to fend for themselves against the hunters and Joseph?

"Go!" he gruffly commanded her. "Get to safety."

He turned away from her, knowing he would never see her again.

"Wait!" Her pale hand on his arm seared into his flesh, causing his teeth to scrape together when his cock jumped in response. He was not some horny teen, yet this woman had somehow managed to reduce him to that when his men needed him. He glanced at her over his shoulder. "Please, don't do this."

"We don't want this," he replied coldly, pulling his arm away from her before she distracted him further from his duties.

"I... I don't understand," she whispered.

"No, *your* kind never has."

The anger in his voice would have deterred anyone else; it didn't deter her though.

"Please, I can't lose him," she whispered. Anger surged through Ronan; she was lusting over him, but still pleading for her lover's life. He contemplated killing Nathan, simply so the man couldn't continue to have what he so desperately craved for himself. "Not my brother."

"Your brother?"

"Yes."

"Your brother will be safe." If he wasn't already dead. "Now go!"

"Thank you."

His chest constricted at those words. "Go."

Ronan didn't look back at her as he ran toward the others. A good fight and death were what he needed to purge himself of his reaction to her.

CHAPTER SEVEN

KADENCE ROUNDED THE CORNER, but went no further. She couldn't leave. Her brother was fighting for his life, and that man, that *vampire*, was there. The warmth of Ronan's fingers still lingered on her cheek. He hadn't acted like her enemy. She supposed his strange behavior could be some sort of sick, vampire trick, but she doubted it. He'd had the perfect opportunity to kill her. He could have easily struck her down, or had his friend do so. Instead, he'd told her to run.

The monsters she'd always been taught vampires were would have killed her without a second's hesitation. Those monsters wouldn't have told her that her brother would be safe. What had just happened between them was not normal and she needed answers.

She also hadn't come all this way not to watch Joseph die.

Kadence crept back to the corner of the alley and poked her head out to watch the battle. She pulled her crossbow free and loaded it. Her hand squeezed on her weapon while she watched them all fight in a flurry of fists and blood, but the vampires still didn't go in for the killing blow. Now that she was watching more closely, she realized they spent most of their time deflecting the hunters' attacks. The hunters were outnumbered; this fight should be over. It wasn't.

The more she examined the vampires in action, the more she began to question if Ronan and his friends were the murderous, mindless creatures she'd been taught to hate her whole life. They seemed to be something different, something she'd never known existed when it came to vampires. Something she didn't think *any* hunter had ever known existed.

Ronan cut his way through the thick of the fight. Seizing Logan and Nathan by their necks, he lifted them and threw them toward where Jayce and Asher stood with Joseph. Kadence couldn't help but marvel over the amount of strength Ronan possessed. He'd tossed them both aside as if they weighed no more than a feather. The other vampires fell into line behind him as the hunters grouped together. Blood tricked from the injuries the hunters had sustained, but none of them were mortal wounds.

"Give us Joseph," Ronan commanded. "We will take care of him."

"Set him lose to kill more, you mean," Nathan said as he slid his crossbow free of his hip.

"He'll never know freedom again," Ronan replied. "He's ours to destroy. Give him to me."

Nathan's crossbow dipped a bit before leveling on Ronan's broad chest, right at his heart. Kadence's breath stuck in her throat when Ronan stalked forward as if he didn't see the weapon. The resolute expression on Nathan's face was one she recognized well. The bolt fired less than a split second later.

Ronan didn't change his course or even blink when he plucked the bolt out of thin air and tossed it aside as if it had been an annoying fly. Kadence gaped at him. She'd never seen anyone move that fast before, had never thought it possible that someone could.

Before anyone could react, or Ronan could reach Nathan, Joseph shouted a command. "Now! Attack now!" The words were garbled, but his windpipe had healed enough for him to speak again.

Kadence frowned as she tried to figure out who he was yelling at.

The others in the alley exchanged a questioning glance. Ronan leapt forward, his hand encircling Joseph's throat. He looked about to tear Joseph from Jayce's grasp just as another vampire leapt on top of the brick wall. The feral-looking vamp with the blood-red eyes was followed by a dozen more vampires.

Ronan froze with his hand around Joseph's throat as he gazed at the Savages perched on the wall like gargoyles ready to take flight. Their putrid odor barely pierced through the stench of the alley. It hit him that Joseph had lured them into this area of the alley because of the amount of trash and the fact that his cohorts could remain hidden on the other side of the wall until he was ready to draw them forth. If he hadn't crushed Joseph's windpipe, the Savages would have arrived sooner.

"Well, that's a heap of shit right there," Declan said and reached over his back to slide two swords free from under his coat.

Kadence bit back a shout when the vampires launched themselves off the wall. Right now, no one knew she was there; she could be the hidden weapon they may need, but only if she didn't give away her location. One of the vamps crashed into Ronan, knocking his hold on Joseph free. Another hit Nathan, sending him staggering into Jayce and Joseph.

Joseph twisted in Jayce's grasp and yanked Jayce's hand to the side. The young hunter howled as his wrist broke with a snap of bone. Kadence's stomach nosedived into her toes, but she lifted her crossbow and aimed it at Joseph's heart. Joseph clutched Jayce's head as she fired the bolt.

A bead of blood formed on Jayce's ear from where the bolt nicked him before driving into Joseph's chest, centimeters off his heart. Blood-red eyes briefly met hers before Joseph snapped Jayce's neck to the side. The cracking of his spine echoed down the entire alley. The scream of *No!* burned its way up her throat and choked her as a cruel grin curved Joseph's lips.

Sorrow filled her as Jayce's limp body collapsed to the ground.

She'd grown up with Jayce. They'd played tag and eaten ice cream cones on hot summer days. He'd once told her he would have preferred to be an astronaut, to travel into space, but instead he'd trained to be a pilot for the hunters and to kill. And now he was gone. Kadence wanted nothing more than to sit down and sob for the loss of her friend. Instead, she pulled another bolt free from her pocket and reloaded the crossbow. She lifted it to end the vicious monster who had destroyed her father and her friend.

She was about to fire again when Ronan stalked through the fray and captured Joseph by the throat with one hand. With ease, he lifted Joseph high before smashing him into the pavement. The asphalt cracked and splintered beneath Joseph's body. Ronan drew his other hand back to strike Joseph when two more vamps leapt onto the top of the wall before launching themselves off and onto his back.

Kadence's hand quivered on her crossbow when Ronan vanished beneath their bodies. She searched for Nathan and the other hunters, but they were also nowhere to be seen amid the mass of vamps. She fired more bolts at two of the vamps on Joseph's side, successfully taking them both out.

She'd gone through a fair amount of training over the years to learn how to protect herself, but she'd never been allowed to hunt a vampire. Now, her blood hummed with excitement, her body was alive in a way it never had been before, and she couldn't deny that this felt *right*.

Ronan rose from the mass, shedding the vamps clinging to him. Grabbing one of them, he threw the vamp forward with enough force to shatter some of the bricks in the wall. The indent of the vamp's body was left behind as he slumped to the ground. The wall rocked on its foundation, and for a minute, Kadence thought it would topple over.

She searched for her brother, worry tearing at her insides as she spotted Asher and Declan beating back the wave of vampires coming at them. If they found it weird to be working together, they didn't show it. *The enemy of my enemy,* she realized as they stood nearly back to back with each other. Logan was fighting near the one with the scar, Killean. Lucien and Saxon stood back to back as they fought.

Relief filled her when she finally spotted Nathan next to one of the dumpsters. Blood streaked his face from a nasty gash above his right eye, but it didn't slow him as he drove a stake through the heart of a vamp.

Kadence reloaded her weapon as another vamp rose behind Declan. The vamp was about to grab Declan when Kadence fired a shot that went straight through the vamp's heart. Declan glanced at her over his shoulder, his silver eyes glittering with amusement when they met hers. He nodded to her before driving a sword through the stomach of another vamp and running him into the wall.

The already damaged wall swayed back from the impact and gave an ominous creaking sound.

"Look out!" Asher shouted.

Asher staggered away from the wall as it rocked precariously. Pieces of breaking brick clattered over the concrete and thumped off the dumpsters. The wall swayed back again before crumpling with a loud bang and the clatter of bricks crashing into one another. A cloud of gray dust blew all the way out to where she stood.

Kadence stepped forward as her view of the battle was obscured by the debris filling the air. When it finally cleared enough, she saw the vampires who had joined the fight on Joseph's side were fleeing down the street. Asher and Logan followed them, and ahead of them, she spotted Nathan turning a corner.

Joseph was nowhere to be seen. She suspected he'd been the first one to tuck tail and run like the coward he was.

The other vamps remained standing in the alley, surrounded by the carcasses of the vamps who hadn't survived and Jayce. Kadence tore her attention away from her friend's body before she started to sob and didn't stop. She retreated into the shadows as Ronan wiped some of the debris from his hair. Bits of dust and brick rained down around him.

He glanced idly at the arrow protruding from his shoulder. Without so much as a flinch, he ripped it free and tossed it aside. Kadence winced for him.

"If the hunters get a hold of Joseph—" Lucien started.

"They won't," Ronan replied. "And if we go after them, we'll only end up fighting them again."

"And then we'll inevitably kill one of them," Saxon said.

"I don't see a problem with that," Killean replied.

"The hunters are not our enemies," Ronan said.

Why did he keep saying that? Kadence wondered. Why did he *believe* that?

"Maybe not, but they believe we are *theirs*, and because of that they fucked this night all up," Killean said. "Joseph would be dead right now and everyone on this planet would be a lot safer, if it wasn't for their stupidity."

"Enough, Killean," Ronan said. "You and Saxon gather these bodies and take them somewhere the sun can get them in the morning, or where you can set them on fire."

"I'll get the van," Saxon volunteered. He climbed over the bricks and jogged toward the street.

At the end of the alley, she spotted a crowd of humans growing. The humans whispered behind their hands as they pointed down the alley at the vampires standing where the wall once had stood.

"Declan, take care of the crowd," Ronan ordered.

"With pleasure," Declan replied. He climbed over the bricks and sauntered toward the humans. "Hello, darling," he purred to one. The uneasy look left the girl's face. She giggled and blushed prettily when he ran his finger under her chin.

Kadence watched as Declan spoke with the crowd. She couldn't hear what he said, but when he was done, they all walked away. She'd heard about a vampire's ability to change the memories of another, but she'd never witnessed it in action. She had to admit it was impressive, and scary.

As a hunter, she was immune to a vamp's ability of persuasion—something she was extremely grateful for right then.

"What about the hunter's body?" Lucien inquired.

Kadence almost stepped forward to scream at them to leave it be, but Ronan was already speaking, "The hunters will come back for him."

"And if someone discovers it before then?"

"That's the hunters' problem to deal with, not ours. There are no signs of a vampire attack on him, and the police will have a difficult time trying to figure this all out, but again, not our problem. What about the girl Joseph attacked in the club?" he asked Saxon.

"I couldn't save her," Saxon replied. "I obscured the wound on her neck and hid her body. They should find her by morning."

Ronan clenched his teeth as he gazed down the road where the hunters had vanished in pursuit of Joseph. The human race was a food supply to him, but he'd failed in his mission tonight and an innocent had died because of it. Even worse, more of them would die now that Joseph had gotten away again.

They should have killed the hunters and Joseph and called it a night. They all would have had to deal with aftereffects of the hunters' lives on their hands, but they would have saved countless other lives in the long run. If the hunters interfered again, he may have no choice but to take them down.

Kadence remained in the shadows when she was certain the vampires wouldn't be taking Jayce's body with them. Her brother would be back soon, but even if he didn't return, they would find a way to claim Jayce's body.

If the vamps left soon, she would come back and get Jayce herself. She didn't care if he weighed a good seventy pounds more than her; she would figure out a way to bring him home.

A beat-up gray van pulled up at the end of the alley and backed down toward what remained of the wall. The vehicle didn't come to a full stop before Killean pulled the back doors open and they began to toss the bodies of the vampires into it.

They would all be gone soon, and she should retreat from here until they were. She should have already left this place behind. Her brother was gone, and she was in an alley full of vamps.

CHAPTER EIGHT

SHE EDGED DOWN THE ALLEY, her heart growing heavier with every step as she reloaded her crossbow. She'd lost a friend tonight, and now it was time for her to return to the stronghold where she would be locked away once more and married to Logan.

Kadence tilted her head back to stare at the night sky. She'd seen it every night from the stronghold, but this was the first time she'd seen it outside of the stronghold walls. This was her last night of freedom, the *only* night of freedom she'd ever experienced. She didn't realize she was crying until the first drop of chilly water fell onto her hand.

Startled, she wiped the tears from her cheeks. What was the matter with her? She'd always resented her lot in life, always wanted more freedom, but a part of her also accepted what was to be. Now the idea of returning to the stronghold and being married was more than she could stand.

Taking a deep breath, she started walking again. Her lot in life didn't matter; it was far better than *no* life. Fresh tears welled in her eyes as she recalled Jayce's body at the end of the alley. She had to get to him and return home; she had no other choice.

She didn't know much about this human world. However, the little she'd seen of it, and the vast quantity of reading she'd done about it, fascinated her. The humans were a weaker species, but they were brilliant and creative. Over the years, she'd spent countless hours studying the paintings and numerous pieces of art they had in the stronghold. It amazed her that she found some new detail amongst those canvases and sculptures *every* time she looked at them.

She'd read all the thousands of books in the library of the stronghold, some of them so many times she'd memorized them. Her favorites had always been mysteries and detective novels, especially Sherlock Holmes.

She would give anything to visit all the many places she'd read about and seen pictures of, but she would never be able to do any of those things once she returned to the stronghold. However, she couldn't stay out here.

Her brother would be looking for her soon. Nathan was probably just recalling that he'd left her behind to pursue the monster who had killed their father. He would go crazy if she didn't return. And she might go crazy if she did.

But where could she go? What could she do?

Nothing. There was nothing she could do. She had no ID, no birth certificate, no money, nothing she could use to help her navigate the human world. She was schooled in the arts, science, math, history, and other things. She may never use her education, but the hunters believed everyone should be taught. Some of the males were sent out to become pilots, doctors, nurses, plumbers, electricians, and numerous other things that would benefit their society before returning to the stronghold.

She had no real training unless the job included self-defense techniques, cooking, and being a good wife and mother. She was faster and stronger than humans, a good fighter, and a passable cook, but she'd failed on epic levels at being a good wife and mother during her schooling.

She'd spent twenty of her twenty-three years trying to learn how to sew, and she still couldn't do it. Though, she suspected her instructor, Mrs. Cranon, was right and she'd chosen not to learn the technique. No matter how good it felt to stab things sometimes, she *hated* sewing.

In the end, she had no skills that would help her survive in the human world, a world she knew so little about other than what she'd seen on TV and read in her books. Even her glimpses of the humans on TV had been rare as there were few TVs in the stronghold, and the women were often kept away from them.

Even if she could somehow survive out here on her own, it didn't matter; she had to return for Jayce's body, and she couldn't leave Nathan to worry about her.

Resigned anew to her lot in life, Kadence took a deep breath and continued forward. She was almost to the back door of the club when the garbage stench of the alley rose a little and a shadow moved forward, blocking the way. She froze when she recognized Joseph standing before her.

How had he gotten away and back here? She had no answer for that question, but it didn't matter. He was here.

Kadence took a step back as his red eyes ran leeringly over her body. The faint stench of decay emanating from him was enough to make her gag. At one time, he may have been good looking with his golden-brown hair and narrow features. Now she saw nothing but a twisted creature.

"I came back for you, beautiful," he purred.

Her hand gripped the crossbow tighter, but she had a feeling she wouldn't get the chance to hit him with a bolt again, not now that he was prepared for it. She itched to rip his heart out with her bare hands to avenge her father's death, but her instincts screamed at her to run far and fast from here.

He took another step toward her. The dim illumination of the bulb over the club door revealed his blood-covered shirt, the bruises on his face, a jagged cut on his upper right thigh, and the hole from where her bolt had pierced him in his chest.

"So pretty." His insidious voice washed over her, chilling the marrow of her bones.

He moved suddenly and much faster than she'd anticipated with his injuries. She lifted the crossbow, aimed at his heart, and fired. The bolt sliced across his shirt and the front of his chest when he turned to the side to avoid taking a direct hit. His hand wrapped around her braid and he yanked her against him.

Lifting her hands to his chest, she shoved at him as she tried to pull herself free. His grip on her hair tightened until a sharp pain throbbed in her skull and some of the strands tore from her scalp. Giving up on trying to free herself, she squirmed against him and punched him in the stomach. Her blow against the solid wall of muscle in his abs had the same effect on him as a mouse beating on an elephant would have.

Twisting to the side, she tried to get her leg in between them to knee him in the crouch. He knocked her knee to the side and bile rushed up her throat when he rubbed his erection against her stomach. She clamped her teeth against vomiting on him as she put her fingers together and drove them at his eye.

He chuckled when he swatted her hand aside. "I love it when they fight," he murmured in her ear.

Turning, she finally managed to land a solid punch against the underside of his chin. The monster laughed and leaned back to survey her. "Do it again," he taunted, his face only inches from hers.

It hit her then that all her training in weapons and self-defense had been for nothing. Dummies didn't hit back or block her blows; they didn't laugh in her face when she gave them an uppercut, and they didn't have the strength of twenty men. The women had been taught how to defend themselves, but they'd never been prepared to actually do it against a vampire.

Managing to get her hand up again, her fingers hooked into claws that she raked down the side of his face. As the skin tore away, flesh dug beneath her fingernails and blood welled forth.

"Bitch!" he spat at her before slapping her across the face. Blood exploded into her mouth, a ringing sounded in her ears, and she was certain he'd knocked one of her teeth loose.

Clutching her hand, he twisted her arm behind her back. Agony tore through her shoulder and screamed up her back as he turned the joint a way it was never meant to go. "The power," he murmured against her ear. "I can smell it thrumming through your veins." He jabbed his erection against her again.

Her shoulder popped out of place when she twisted to the side. She cried out as he bent his head to run his revolting tongue across her ear. He propelled her back against the wall, his heavy body plastering her to the cold brick. White fangs glinted when he pulled back to reveal his lethal canines seconds before he struck.

Fire burned through her veins, her heart stuttered in her chest, and her breath froze in her lungs as pain ripped through her, rendering her helpless. Blurred stars filled her field of vision. Tears streamed down her cheeks as her life drained unwillingly from her in slurping gulps.

CHAPTER NINE

"DID YOU HEAR THAT?" Ronan asked.

"Hear what?" Declan inquired.

Ronan's hand fell away from the doors of the van after closing them. The alley remained hushed, but he'd heard something. Blocking out the sound of approaching sirens, the hum of the nearby traffic, and the distant beat of the music from the club. He honed all his senses onto the alley, trying to sense another presence there.

Then, he smelled her vanilla scent and her *blood*. He'd assumed Kadence had run when he told her to, and in the ensuing battle with the vamps, he'd lost her scent, but it was all he could smell now.

"Get out of here, Saxon!" he barked.

Declan, Killean, and Lucien stared at him in surprise as the red taillights of the van washed over them and Saxon pulled forward.

Ronan moved so fast down the alley that the walls around him were a blur. His vision became clouded with a haze of red as he turned the corner and spotted her. Spotted *them*.

Moving faster than he'd ever known he could, Ronan closed the distance between him and Joseph in less than a heartbeat. He tore

Joseph off her and threw him thirty feet through the air before he crashed onto the top of a dumpster.

In all his life, Ronan had never been this hell-bent on murder. It was bad enough that Joseph had touched her, but that he had *hurt* her was intolerable. He'd tear Joseph limb from limb for this.

Joseph spun back toward him as he launched off the dumpster. He braced himself to charge forward, but then he turned and fled down the alley. The muscles in Ronan's legs bunched in preparation to follow the Savage vampire, but Kadence's blood permeating the air froze him in place.

"Follow him!" Ronan commanded, and Lucien and Killean took off after Joseph.

His gaze fell on where Kadence had slumped against the wall. Declan knelt at her side, examining her injuries. Two jagged tears marred her flesh from where Joseph's fangs had torn across the right side of her neck. The vivid red of her blood stood out starkly against her pale skin. Tears streaked her cheeks from the pain she'd endured by having her blood unwillingly taken from her body. Her right arm was twisted at an unnatural angle behind her back. He'd had his shoulders dislocated enough times over the years to recognize the damage done to her.

"She's alive," Declan murmured and moved his fingers to prod at the wounds on her neck.

Stalking forward, Ronan pushed Declan's hand aside. "Don't touch her."

Declan gave him a questioning look, but he edged away from her. Kneeling at her side, Ronan stroked her soft skin in the hopes she would wake. She remained unmoving, her heart beating sluggishly in her chest. Fighting back the rage threatening to consume him over what Joseph had done to her, Ronan leaned forward and scooped her into his arms.

Her head lolled to the side, coming to rest against his chest. Her silver-tipped eyelashes curled against her frightfully pale cheek. Blonde eyebrows drew together as a moan whispered past her lips.

With her slender nose, round cheeks, and full lips, she was exquisite. Despite what he knew her to be, he wanted to hold her close and shelter her from the horror of their violent world. Footsteps in the alley drew his attention as Lucien and Killean emerged from the shadows. Killean's eyes latched onto Kadence; his mouth compressed into a flat line.

"Did you get him?" Ronan asked.

Lucien ran his hands through his sandy blond hair. "No, he was gone before we made it to the end of the alley."

A sneer curved Ronan's upper lip, but he couldn't be mad at them. He should have gone after Joseph himself. If it hadn't been for Kadence, he would have, and Joseph wouldn't have evaded him, not again.

"What are you going to do with her?" Killean demanded.

Ronan glanced at Kadence as red, amber, and white lights flashed over the walls around them. The human's emergency vehicles had arrived. He didn't know when he'd come to his conclusion, but he knew exactly what he would be doing with her. "She's coming with us."

"What?"

Ronan strode past Killean without bothering to respond to his question. He carried Kadence toward the other end of the alley, away from the humans. "Killean, call Saxon and make sure he takes care of those bodies. Lucien where's your vehicle?" he inquired.

Killean stared at him before slipping his phone out of his pocket and hitting a button. He walked away as he spoke into it.

"There." Lucien arrived at Ronan's side and pointed to a black SUV in the parking lot beside the club. "You can't take her. The hunters—"

"What would you have me do, leave her on the street?" he demanded.

"Ronan—"

"The human workers are here. She cannot stay, not with these wounds on her."

"Saxon is taking care of it," Killean said when he hung up the phone. His gaze focused on Kadence. "We will obscure her wounds."

"*No* one is touching her again," Ronan growled.

"The hunters will come back for her," Lucien said.

"They may not find her before the humans do, and we don't know where the hunters are. She's coming with us," he said. "And I don't want to hear one more word about it."

Lucien nodded briskly. Killean opened his mouth to reply, before closing it again. Declan remained silent as he walked beside Lucien. Something about the way Declan watched Kadence caused an uneasy feeling to settle in the pit of Ronan's stomach. With every step he took, he couldn't rid himself of the feeling there would be no turning back from this decision.

RONAN LAID Kadence on his bed, careful not to jar her injuries. She hadn't moved since they'd left the alley, but her breathing and heartbeat remained steady. "Get me some bandages, towels, and water," he ordered.

Declan rushed out of the room. Killean and Lucien stood by the doorway, their disapproval evident on their stony faces. "The hunters are going to be really pissed off when they realize we have one of theirs. A woman no less. They'll tear this city apart looking for her," Lucien said.

"Then they shouldn't have left her in the alley," Ronan replied.

Killean snorted. "*None* of us knew she was still there. We all assumed she'd retreated to safety."

"We should leave her somewhere they can find her," Lucien pressed.

"I'm not leaving her somewhere unprotected!" Ronan snarled.

Lucien's raven eyes narrowed, but his head bowed in acquiescence and he stepped back. Declan returned with a set of towels slung over his shoulder, a pot of water, bandages, and medical supplies in hand that Ronan's friend, Marta, most likely kept somewhere for her and her husband, Baldric. Declan set the supplies down on the nightstand.

"Leave us," Ronan ordered gruffly. He didn't look up to make sure his command had been obeyed; he knew it would be.

Lifting one of the towels, he wet it in the pot of warm water. He sat beside Kadence on the bed and carefully cleaned the jagged tears on her neck. Her bleeding had stopped, but the alluring scent of her blood teased his nostrils.

He took a deep breath to calm his thirst for her and wiped away the last of her blood. She stirred only once while he worked on the wounds already showing signs of healing. Tenderly holding her chin, he sprayed some antibiotic on the injury and taped a bandage over it. Her shoulder remained out of place, but that would have to wait until she was stronger.

Leaning back, he studied the healthy pink color creeping into her cheeks. Her breathing grew stronger with every passing minute, and the solid beat of her heart sounded within her chest.

When he ran his knuckles over her cheek, her head turned slightly toward him. He held his breath as he waited for her eyes to open, but she still didn't wake. If she'd been human she never would have survived the amount of blood Joseph had taken from her.

Reluctantly pulling his hand away from her, he rose and walked to the end of the bed. Careful not to move her too much, he untied her boots and pulled them off. He set them beside the bed before gently removing her coat. A smile curved his lips when he spotted the small arsenal tucked within. He removed the weapons and tossed them into the hallway. If someone else didn't take them away, he would throw them away later.

He draped her coat over a chair in the corner before turning back to her. The collar of the turtleneck she wore had been ripped during her attack, but it still hugged her willowy frame and handful-sized breasts. He deliberated taking her clothes off to make her more comfortable, but it would most likely frighten her if she woke and realized he'd stripped her.

Reluctantly, he pulled the blankets over her slumbering form and ran his fingers over the end of her braid. He didn't understand this strange effect she had on him. Not only did he crave her body, but he also wanted to hold her throughout the night and keep her protected. However, he didn't think she would be pleased to wake up next to a vampire after everything she'd been through tonight.

The desire and tenderness she evoked in him were two things he'd believed himself long ago deadened to. He didn't know how to handle their resurgence. His life was neat and orderly; it had to be if he was going to keep himself from succumbing to the bloodlust. This woman made him feel anything but orderly. Just by being here, she'd upset his structured life. He should resent her for it; instead he found himself craving more of her.

Rising, he moved into the bathroom. A cold shower was exactly what he needed. After pulling his clothes off, he turned the shower on, slipped his glasses off, and stepped beneath the chilly spray. The water washed over him as he tried to drown the need for her pounding through his body.

He bent his head, pressing it against the tiled wall as blood pooled around his feet. The sight of it didn't bother him; he was well used to seeing and smelling his own blood. The puncture in his shoulder was still raw and seeping blood, but healing rapidly. He'd survived worse than this, and he would survive the many more injuries he would sustain for the rest of his life.

He turned the water off and stepped out of the shower. Padding over to the rack, he pulled a towel from it and dried himself off before examining his shoulder. The bleeding had stopped, his muscle had already closed within the hole, and before his eyes, his skin was healing over the top of it. He didn't worry about it getting infected. His vampire DNA wouldn't allow an infection or any diseases to survive in his bloodstream.

He checked to make sure Kadence still slept before tossing his towel aside and striding back into the room. He walked over to the armoire, for the first time noticing the ivy leaves etched into its solid wood surface. The hinges creaked when he opened one of the doors to remove a pair of jeans from within.

He pulled the jeans on before walking over to the picture window facing out on the pool beyond. Bars lined the outside of the window. The moon shone down across the wintry landscape as he gazed out at the night before pushing a button beside the window. Heavy metal shutters slid silently down over the glass.

It had been almost seventy years since he'd killed a hunter and felt the effects of their life on his body. However, having spent his life hunting Savages, he'd adapted to their habits and become a creature of the night himself. Usually, he slept through the day and he preferred the sunlight blocked out when he did.

The fact he'd become more and more like the creatures he hunted over the years was not lost on him. He knew what he was becoming.

His gaze returned to Kadence. He didn't feel quite so Savage around her, or maybe he did, he thought as his gaze lingered on her full lips, but he didn't feel the bloodlust as intensely. With her, he knew one thing, keep her safe. He could do that; he could focus on that.

Grabbing the brown leather chair from the corner, he placed it next to the bed and settled in to watch over her.

CHAPTER TEN

Kᴀᴅᴇɴᴄᴇ ʙʟɪɴᴋᴇᴅ against the darkness as confusion swam through her groggy mind. She normally didn't go to sleep until almost dawn, when she was sure the hunters had all returned safely, but she always had a nightlight on in her room, or the sun would be peaking around the edges of her drapes when she woke in the afternoon.

Struggling to sit up, she groaned as pain tore through her neck and shoulder. She tried to raise her right hand to her neck, but it hung limply at her side. Her left hand flew up to the bandage there as memories of the night before flooded her.

She was not in her room, not in her *home*! She bit back a scream. If Joseph was around somewhere, he couldn't know she was awake.

Kadence forced herself to lie back as she fought against bolting out of bed and fleeing into the night. She had to learn her surroundings first. If she launched out of this bed in a panic, she was sure to draw attention to herself and wouldn't get anywhere.

She remained still while her eyes picked up the small bits of light filtering in from under the door across the room. The nightstand beside her gradually took shape, and then the chair next to it.

Adrenaline shot through her. Someone sat in that chair. She could hear their shallow breathing, see the broad expanse of their shoulders. The fingers of her good arm dug into the sheets. Was it Joseph? She had no idea why he would keep her alive, but if he had, it meant worse things than what had happened in that alley were in her future. And if it wasn't Joseph and she wasn't at home, then her future had become a whole lot more uncertain.

She pushed the blanket aside and slid her feet to the floor. A wave of dizziness assailed her, causing her to sway. She bit into her lower lip, drawing blood in an attempt to keep herself grounded in the moment. She had to remain conscious, and she had to move while whoever sat in that chair remained asleep. Her only chance of survival was to make it to the door and out of here.

Staggering to her feet, another wave of dizziness caused her to lurch to the side and bang into the nightstand. Something rattled on it. Kadence's breath froze in her lungs while she waited to see what would happen. The form in the chair remained unmoving, but the hair on her nape rose as she felt eyes on her.

She saw no movement, heard no sound, but suddenly a warm hand clasped her elbow. A shrill cry escaped her as she flung herself backward. Her frantic movements caused her to knock the nightstand over. Glass shattered when whatever had been perched on the nightstand toppled onto it. Dull thuds sounded as whatever else had been on the nightstand fell onto the carpet.

"Easy," a voice soothed. "It's okay; you're safe here."

Kadence took a deep breath while she strained to see the face of the man holding her. His chest brushed against her arm when he leaned toward her. A wave of heat flooded her, and before he flicked the light switch on, she knew who stood before her.

Kadence went completely still when the light in the ceiling blazed to life and illuminated Ronan's face. Her hand flew to her mouth as his eyes met hers, and she finally got to see what his sunglasses had been covering. She'd never seen eyes like his before. They were such a magnificent combination of red and brown that she couldn't figure out if they were the soulful color of a deer's eyes, or the deep red shade of blood.

The blood comparison should have unnerved her; she found it only fascinated her more as the colors swirled more intricately together until they became the deep hue of burgundy while he watched her.

Heat crept through her cheeks when she realized she was staring at him. It didn't get any better when her gaze dropped lower and she saw he wasn't wearing a shirt. To her horror, her mouth actually watered as she drank in the chiseled muscles of his broad shoulders, chest, and abdomen.

She'd seen men's chests before, when the hunters were training, but none of them had ever affected her in this way. There was no hair on his chest, but a deep brown trail of it ran from his belly button to the edge of the jeans slung low on his hips. She barely kept her fingers restrained from following that trail before tracing the lines etching his abdomen with her tongue. As a vampire, she knew he couldn't be in the sun, but his skin was a bronzed hue that made her think of the sun-kissed beaches she'd never been to but had read about.

The numerous paintings and photos she'd seen of men had nothing on the specimen standing before her. Unable to fight the strange pull he had over her, Kadence swayed toward him. How could she so strongly want someone she barely knew, someone who could kill her with a flick of his wrist?

After last night, she thought her teachings about vampires had been wrong, or at least incomplete, and her instincts were telling her that no matter what he was, he would not hurt her. However, she wasn't about to toss aside twenty-three years of upbringing because she found herself wanting to touch, explore, and kiss a man more than she wanted air right now.

Her eyes lifted to his mouth with its stiff upper lip and full bottom one. She almost licked her lips as she contemplated what he would taste like. If he tasted as good as he smelled, he would be delicious.

Kadence gave herself a mental shake before jerking her gaze back up to his eyes. She bit her lip as she struggled to keep her strange attraction to him restrained. Unfortunately, the action caused his eyes to fasten on her lip and hunger sparked within his gaze. Except, this was not a hunger for her blood. Oh no, she saw and felt the desire in him while he watched her. It caused her breath to hitch as her toes curled into the plush carpet. His palm on her elbow burned into her skin; her nipples tightened and she tried to recall how to breathe from one second to the next.

Ronan watched as the blue of Kadence's eyes deepened in hue and her gaze fell to his mouth again. He moved closer until her arm rested against his chest. His fingers slid over her elbow when he bent over her. His eyes never left hers as his lips hovered only inches above her.

His mouth was about to touch hers when common sense returned to her and she stepped back. What was *wrong* with her? Being attacked by a vampire and having pints of blood drained had completely rattled her intellect. She should be trying to stake every vampire she came across after everything Joseph had done to her loved ones, not thinking about kissing one of them!

She was alone with this man —vampire— apparently in his place. If she didn't keep her wits, she'd end up dead or a vampire blood bag.

Ronan reluctantly released her arm and stepped away from her when she stiffened against him. The last thing he wanted was for her to fear him, yet she edged further away from him. "I'm not going to harm you; there's no reason to be afraid."

Her chin rose. "I'm not afraid."

The small smile curving his lips made him even more irresistible. Ugh, she was a mess, she decided. Just then, her heel connected with something on the ground. Looking down, she spotted the lamp she'd knocked off the nightstand and the scattered medical supplies on the floor—the medical supplies that had been used on her, she realized as she recalled the bandage on her neck.

Monsters didn't help heal their victims. Or maybe they did, what did she know? She had no experience with any of this, and she had contemplated licking the vampire, so her brain cells weren't exactly up to snuff right now.

"Where am I?" she inquired.

"You're in our home."

Her eyes went to the closed door behind him before coming back to him. "Who lives here?"

"Lucien, Saxon, Killean, Declan, and I do, along with Marta and Baldric. Though Lucien has been staying somewhere else lately."

"How come?"

"Because it is necessary for him to be elsewhere. Let me put your shoulder back into place."

Ronan braced himself for her rejection when she frowned at him. Then, she glanced at her sagging shoulder as if just recalling it.

"Yes, that must be done," she murmured.

"It will hurt."

A muscle in her cheek twitched as she eyed him. "I can handle pain. Do you know how to do it?"

"I've dislocated and broken more things than I can count. Most of them I've put back into place myself; some I've had help with. I'm sure, as a hunter, you would prefer not to go to the hospital for it."

"Would you let me go to the hospital?"

Ronan rocked back on his heels. He wanted to put her at ease, but he couldn't lie to her. "No. I will make sure you are safe when I let you go, but I will not leave you to the care of the humans. Even though you are more human than I, there are still differences between you and them that they would find very intriguing."

"I can take care of myself."

"I'm sure you can, but I won't risk your life in such a way." More, he wasn't ready to let her go, but he didn't say that. She already looked like a rabbit ready to bolt, but he couldn't tell if she was frightened of him or wary of the whole situation.

"None of this makes any sense," she said.

"I suppose it doesn't, to you. Perhaps it will make sense by the time you leave." Her lips flattened into a thin line. "Your shoulder," he prodded.

"Yes, of course," she murmured.

"Please turn around and grip the wall."

Swallowing heavily, Kadence turned and did as he suggested. She could handle pain, but she was not looking forward to this at all. However, her shoulder had to be back in place if she was going to defend herself. After what had happened with Joseph, she didn't delude herself into thinking she could take a vamp out on her own, and especially not this one.

The power emanating from him made every other vampire she'd seen look like a child. She had a feeling she'd only seen the surface of what Ronan could be capable of, but she would go down fighting if this was all some ruse and she really was dessert.

Ronan clasped her shoulder and her arm. Her head bowed so that her braid fell forward to reveal her nape. His eyes latched onto her bare skin as images of running his lips over her flooded his mind. She'd be sweet against his lips and tongue. The erotic sounds she would make would be something he'd never get enough of hearing, and he knew her blood would be a rush unlike anything he'd ever experienced before.

Shaking his head to clear it of his thoughts, he pulled back on her arm. A loud crack echoed through the room. The muffled cry she released made his blood boil. Releasing her, he glared at his hands for inflicting hurt on her as she rotated her shoulder back.

He almost drove a fist into the wall. He pulled it back at the last second and rested it on the wall as he battled the turmoil rolling through him. Never again would he be the one to make her issue a sound like that.

He felt too large around her suddenly, too cumbersome. She was not a petite or fragile woman, but he could break her so easily. He teetered on the edge of becoming a Savage, what would he do to her if he plummeted over that edge while she was here?

She looked at him over her shoulder, the shadows lining her eyes emphasizing their blue hue. The breath rushed out of him as the emotions battering him eased and a sense of calm stole through him while he gazed at her.

"I'm sorry I hurt you," he murmured.

Kadence was pretty sure her eyebrows were never going to come out of her hairline after those five words. *He* had apologized to *her*.

"It needed to be done." She rotated her shoulder again and winced. "It will be fine by tomorrow. I heal fast."

"Hmm," he murmured as she turned to face him.

"I know you are Ronan, but what is your full name?" Kadence inquired. "Or do vampires not have a last name?"

His crooked smile revealed the tip of one of his canines. His fangs weren't extended, but those teeth were still sharper than her canine teeth. Oddly, she wasn't unnerved by the sight of that smaller fang.

I have got to get away from this man, she realized. *No, vampire,* she reminded herself again. The reminder didn't have the effect of making her hate this guy like she believed it should.

Less than twenty-four hours away from the stronghold and she was already forgetting her entire upbringing. She should be plotting how to escape, not pondering what his fangs would feel like running over her skin.

She moved further away until her legs hit the wooden bed frame behind her.

"We have last names," he said.

"What?" she asked, completely confused by his words.

His smile widened; his eyes actually *twinkled*. She would have thought that impossible for any vampire. Not only that, but he looked young, carefree, and irresistible when he smiled like that. She was certain that smile had melted more than a few women in his lifetime; it certainly melted her.

"My original surname was Caomhánach, a name I assumed years after my birth. No matter how small a thing it is, vampires must blend in with the humans the best we can, and I assumed the name when it was becoming more popular for the humans to have more than one name. Over the years, the name has been anglicized to Kavanagh, and that is what I go by now."

"Oh." She glanced away from him, embarrassed she'd forgotten she'd asked the question and more than a little unsettled by his answer. How old did that make him if his last name had originated and changed in such a way? Old enough to make her skin dance from the power he emanated.

"And I know you are Kadence, but do you have a last name?" he asked.

Her mind spun as she tried to figure out if there was something he could use her last name for, but she couldn't think of anything. "It's Holter."

"Kadence Holter."

Her name sounded more like a caress as it rolled off his tongue. Was that the faintest hint of an Irish accent she'd detected from him? She'd met a few hunters from Ireland when they visited the stronghold. Their accents had fascinated her, as did their tales of their homeland.

"It's a pleasure to meet you, Kadence."

"Are you going to kill me, Ronan?" the question popped out before she could stop herself.

His eyes narrowed as all amusement vanished from him. "Yes, I brought you back here, dressed your wounds, and took care of you, all so I could kill you."

The deep growl of his voice vibrated through the room. No matter how angry he sounded, she realized he still didn't scare her. "I don't know what to think. Your kind—"

"My kind is *not* your enemy," he interrupted. "No matter what you were raised to believe, we never have been your enemy."

Her mouth opened, then closed again. She didn't know what to say. She shouldn't believe him; her upbringing screamed at her he was a lying. But instinctually she *knew* she could trust him and that he would keep her safe.

If Ronan wanted her dead, she would be already. If he intended to rape her, he would be on her now. She didn't sense any kind of mental games going on here, didn't believe he was toying with her, but maybe he was.

He might have decided to leverage her against her brother and the others. That was a good possibility, but it still didn't feel right. Maybe she'd lost more blood than she realized and her deprived mind was having a breakdown. *Best possibility yet*, she decided.

CHAPTER ELEVEN

"I THINK you should rest some more. Your coloring is still off," Ronan said as her eyes went between him, the door, and her coat.

Her fingers encircled his wrist when he reached behind her to pull back the blankets on the bed. He froze as the feel of her warm skin burned into his flesh. One of her fingers hesitatingly caressed his wrist, as if she couldn't stop herself from feeling more of him.

His eyes came back to hers. She had no idea what she did to him, no idea how badly he wanted to pick her up, put her on the bed, and bury himself inside of her. If she knew, she would run screaming from this room, and she would have every right to.

"I don't understand what you're saying. How are you not my enemy?" she asked. "We were born to kill each other."

He almost grabbed her when she swayed on her feet, but he didn't know how she would react if he did, and she should be spending her energy on recovering instead of fighting him.

"I know you don't understand, know you've been taught differently, but now is not the time to get into it," he told her. "You look about ready to pass out."

"Is Joseph dead?"

Ronan stiffened at the reminder that the one who had done this to her still lived. "No. Lucien and Killean chased him after he attacked you, but they lost him."

She closed her eyes and inhaled deeply. Her hand fell away from his wrist as she hugged her middle. When her head bent, he had no idea what she was doing until the salty scent of tears drifted to him and inaudible sobs shook her.

"Hey now, hey, don't do that."

Unsure of what to do, Ronan awkwardly patted her shoulders. In all his many years, he'd never had to deal with a crying woman, and he had no idea how to make it stop. He patted her head next, but when that did nothing to ease her, he wrapped his arms around her and drew her to him. He cradled her head against his chest as he rocked on his heels with her. Her tears dampened his skin, yet she showed no signs of slowing down or being aware of who held her.

Trying to calm her, he ran his hand over her silken braid. His fingers caught in the band at the end. Unable to stop himself, he slipped the elastic away and undid the braid before spreading its silvery length. The thick mass of her hair fell freely to the middle of her back in waves.

She buried her face against his chest, her breath warming his skin as her tears continued to fall. He felt nothing sexual as he held her; all his lust had been drenched beneath the onslaught of her sorrow. All he wanted was to comfort her as he held her closer.

"He'll never hurt you again," Ronan vowed. "Never get close to you again. I will make sure of it."

Feeling completely mortified over her behavior, Kadence stifled her next sob and willed the tears to stop flowing. Her fingers had a mind of their own as they dug into his back. His skin was smooth against her, but his muscles provided a firm pillow for her head.

Inhaling his scent helped to calm her further. He smelled like cinnamon, and the aroma of ozone, a scent she recognized as power, emanated from his pores. She found herself fighting against pressing her lips to him. Her knees knocked together from the force of her overwhelming craving to taste him. On her next breath, she gave into the impulse and turned her head enough that the corner of her lips brushed over his flesh.

He became rigid against her, and she immediately moved her mouth away. She strained to keep the blush from her face in the hopes he would think it had been an accident and not deliberate on her part.

"Do you feel better now?" he inquired.

She wasn't sure what she felt right now. Confused and exhausted, definitely. Irritated at herself for not being able to stop Joseph and being the reason he got away, without a doubt. Completely confused about her attraction to this creature, yep she could add that to the list of conflicting emotions battering her.

"Yes," she said and finally succeeded in getting her traitorous fingers to release their hold on him.

She clasped her hands before her to keep from grabbing him again. When she saw how wet his chest was from her tears, she was unable to stop her mouth from dropping. She went to wipe her tears off him, but he caught her wrist before she could touch him and held it loosely between his thumb and forefinger.

"I'm sorry!" she blurted.

"You had a rough night." Reluctantly, Ronan released her wrist when she tugged at it.

She turned away from him, ashamed at herself. She wasn't a crier, she never had been, but since her father's death, she'd been constantly fighting back tears and the urge to curl into a ball and sob until she couldn't walk anymore. Now, she'd finally broken, and in front of *him*. He probably thought her a weak child now.

What does it matter what he thinks of you, you idiot? She didn't know why it mattered, but it did.

Kadence had never felt more drained or humiliated in her life. Her legs gave out and she sank onto the thick mattress behind her.

She should be demanding answers, looking for a weapon, planning her getaway, but she couldn't fight the incessant pull of her eyelids closing. She lay back on the mattress and sighed when her head hit the pillow.

Settling the blankets back over her, Ronan tucked them around her. His hand brushed over her cheek, wiping away the wetness lingering there. He began to pull his hand away, but she captured it to stop him.

"Are you going to keep me here?" she inquired.

"No," he answered in a rough voice. "As soon as you are well enough, we will find a way to return you to your brother."

"I don't know what to believe, what to think," she whispered.

He swept the hair away from her forehead. "I know, but for now, you should rest and heal. You are safe here. I will keep you protected."

On her next breath, Kadence fell asleep.

Ronan slipped his hand from hers and made his way around to the other side of the bed. She may not appreciate it if she found out he'd slept beside her for the rest of the day, but he would remain above the covers and he wouldn't touch her. He required sleep, and if he was honest with himself, he couldn't resist the chance to lie beside her, if only for a day. He would make sure to get out of bed before she woke up so he didn't upset her.

He stretched out on the bed and listened to her soft inhalations as he allowed her sweet scent to lure him into sleep.

KADENCE STARTED AWAKE AGAIN. Uncertain of the time or where she was, she nearly fell out of the large bed when she bolted upright.

"Easy," a groggy male voice said from beside her.

She squeaked and spun so fast she was certain she'd given herself whiplash.

"Easy," the male coaxed again.

Had she gotten married? Was it Logan beside her? Then the scent of the male hit her and relief caused her shoulders to sag. Why she felt more relieved to find herself in bed with a vampire instead of her future husband was a question she would never delve into during her lifetime.

"What… what are you doing?" she managed to ask.

"I was sleeping." Her pulse skyrocketed at the lazy murmur of his words and the Irish accent that slipped through more now. "I will get up."

"No, I…" *I what? No please stay and drain my blood? No stay, I like you here?* They all made her sound pathetic and were the last things she should be saying. "It's your bed."

"It is," he agreed. He hadn't meant to still be in it, but for the first time in as long as he could remember, his dreams hadn't been plagued with cravings for blood and death. It wasn't until she'd sat up that he'd awoken again. "I'm more than happy to share it with you, but I will also leave it if you ask me to."

Now that her eyes had adjusted to the dark, she could see him clearly as he lay a few feet away from her. *Why does he have to be so irresistible for a vampire?* She wondered as she gazed at him.

"You can stay on your side," she said.

Ronan chuckled as Kadence settled against the pillow and put her feet back on the bed. She'd lain back down, but her body remained tensed to bolt.

She has to go back, he reminded himself when he found himself pleased by her willingness to lie beside him. For the life of him, he didn't give a fuck about that right now. All he cared about was having the opportunity to be near her while he could.

She relaxed a little more and turned her head to gaze at him. "I shouldn't trust you," she whispered.

"I swear to you, Kadence, you are safe with me. The vampire who did this to you last night is as good as dead."

She let out a breath that blew the hair back from her forehead. "For some reason, I find myself believing you, but we are supposed to be enemies—"

"We are not. Hunters have made us their enemies when we don't have to be," he cut in, more abruptly than he'd intended, but he was tired of this mistaken belief of the hunters. It had taken the lives of numerous innocent vampires over the years and cost the hunters many of their own.

"Joseph tried to kill me last night. He did kill my friend, and he has hurt my family."

Turning on his side, he propped his head on his hand as he gazed down at her. "Joseph is a Savage and no longer one of us."

"What do you mean by no longer one of you?"

"Not all vampires kill innocents. In fact, many don't kill at all. But, there are some vamps who are swayed by the power killing can bring them and give into the bloodlust that resides in all vampires. Many vampires fight giving into that bloodlust every day of their existence. Some of them have to fight it more than others. At one time, Joseph worked with us and fought his destructive nature, but he recently gave up that fight and became what we call a Savage."

"Why do some give in?" she asked.

"Vampires go wrong for many different reasons. They're seeking more power, something inside of them snaps, they are inherently evil to begin with, they are tired of constantly having to fight themselves, or they are simply bored."

"They're *bored*!" she spat.

"Not the best reason, but who knows what finally causes them to lose control. When faced with living for an eternity, things inevitably get... monotonous. Perhaps it is curiosity in some, while others are simply trying to feel something new and exciting again. Whatever it is, once a vampire takes the first step toward becoming a Savage, it is much easier to take the following steps that will make it impossible for them to ever again be what they once were."

"Is that why you wanted Joseph, because you try to stop these Savage vampires?"

Ronan placed his hands on the mattress and lifted himself to a seated position against the headboard. He crossed his ankles as he stared at the blank wall across from him. She would leave here soon, and she couldn't leave with too much knowledge of them, but better educating her about vampires might save a life in the future.

"We *do* stop them," he replied.

"Why?"

"Why does your kind hunt them?"

"Because they're evil, and it is what hunters were created and are bred to do."

He knew that was most likely what the hunters had been created to do. The world had a way of balancing itself out, and it had balanced the birth of the more demon-like vampires with the birth of the more human hunters.

"What do you mean by bred?" he inquired.

She shrugged and lifted her head onto her hand as she rolled toward him. Her fingers played with the stitching in the charcoal-colored blanket as she gazed at the wall behind him. "The hunter line must be kept strong," she said. "The best available men and women are paired together to make sure of that."

Ronan's teeth grated together as she revealed this information. She had no ring on, her brother seemed to have been the one in charge of her, but he realized that one day she would be paired off too.

He'd lived through the days when women were married off like they were no better than cattle, and he hadn't liked it then. He liked it less now. Female vampires, especially the purebred ones, always had a mind of their own and spoke it freely. Those were the type of women he'd grown up with and admired.

They hadn't been mated or in love, but his mother had agreed to bear his father a child because with her second-generation purebred status and his father being the only fourth generation to ever exist, their offspring would be the most powerful vampire created. His mother had loved power and attention, and his birth brought her both of those things. After his creation, his parents had found other lovers, but they remained friends until the day they were both killed.

"I see," he said.

"So not all vampires are Savage," Kadence prodded in the hopes of getting him off the depressing topic of marriage.

"No, they are not. I believe you are right and hunters were created to stop Savages, but you weren't given the whole story."

"And that is?"

"That not all vampires are evil. It is only some who go bad, but *all* vampires are hunted indiscriminately by your kind."

"We didn't know that," she whispered.

"I know."

"Why weren't we taught any of this? Why were we never told? Why would we be enemies from the very beginning if what you say is true?" she demanded.

CHAPTER TWELVE

"Do you know how vampires and hunters were created?" he asked.

"At one point in time, a handful of demons escaped to freely roam the earth. Those demons were unable to tolerate the sun, were creatures of the night, immortal, and slaughtered humans to feast on their blood. When humans learned of their existence, they hunted them to the point where the greatly outnumbered demons were once again forced to seal themselves away in what many believe to be Hell," Kadence recited from her studies on the subject.

"While they were here, the demons also mated with some humans," she continued. "The first vampires were born from those humans. Like the demons, they had a thirst for blood, eternal life, and many other demon capabilities such as the power to bend another to their will or cloak their presences. Unlike the demons, they were more human in appearance, had a heartbeat, breathed, and passed as human. Over time, they came to be known as vampires. Vampires discovered that, by sharing their blood with a human, they could create more of their kind."

"And hunters came about how?" Ronan inquired.

"They were created in the same way, only hunters took after the human species even more than vampires. We are the mortal version of a vampire. We have many of your abilities, such as enhanced strength, senses, and extended lifespans, but not your thirst for blood or immortality. Your powers of persuasion and cloaking do not work on those of us who are born hunters, but we do not possess them."

The hunters also didn't have the restrictions vampires faced when they took too many innocent lives, but he didn't tell her that. He also wouldn't reveal to her that many vampires could walk freely through the day. If she went back and told her fellow hunters, which she most likely would, the revelation could make those of his kind who weren't Savage more vulnerable to the ignorance of the hunters.

"The hunters have also figured out a way for the human allies they recruit to not be susceptible to our ability to change their minds," he said.

Her lips compressed into a flat line, and he knew she wouldn't confirm it. It didn't matter; he'd already encountered an entirely human hunter who resisted a vampire's ability to change her memories. A mixture of herbs and hunter blood had been given to the human to keep her mind blocked from a vampire's mind control.

"Why do you and your friends kill the vampires who go wrong?" she asked.

Ronan draped his arm over his forehead as he lifted his gaze to the ceiling. "Humans aren't the only ones who need protection from the vampires who turn Savage. The Savages attack other vampires too, for our blood gives them the most power and we are a far more thrilling kill than any mortal or hunter could ever be."

She inhaled sharply. "That's awful."

He glanced at her out of the corner of his eyes. "That sounded very *un*-hunter like of you."

"I've never been the hunter I'm supposed to be," she murmured. "I've been a thorn in my family's side since I was old enough to speak."

He imagined she had been, considering she was the firstborn

female hunter who had ever been seen by a vampire, as far as he knew anyway. "And why is that?"

She shrugged absently. "Little things here and there I guess. I was always the rebellious one amongst the women within the stronghold, and I was *never* any good at my classes. I can't sew, I'm not much of a cook, and I've dropped a lot of the baby dolls over the years. *Far* more than any of the other girls in my classes. I still can't pin a diaper without stabbing the doll. Though, I'll admit that's more because it's ridiculous to diaper a fake baby, and it feels good to give it a jab."

Ronan lifted an eyebrow at that admission as he tried not to laugh at the look of consternation on her face.

"Unlike the other women in the stronghold, I always dreamed about going out in the world, to see things, and *experience* them. We're not allowed to do that. We're told from the moment we're born that we shouldn't yearn for things we can never have, and that being a good wife, mother, and continuing the hunter line is what we are meant to do. The world is so big and marvelous that I always wanted to see more of it and explore it *all*."

The longing on her face and the melancholy in her voice had him contemplating booking her the first flight to anywhere she asked to go in the world. She should be set free to enjoy her life, not secluded and locked away.

"Women must be protected and sheltered from the world," he grated out.

Resentment simmered in her eyes when they came back to his. "You sound like my brother."

He realized she'd taken his words the wrong way, but he couldn't resist provoking her further as it brought color back to her face and more life to her than he'd seen since her attack. "Your brother sounds like a wise man."

He was certain visions of strangling him were dancing through her head while she glowered at him. Her anger also made her forget her wariness of him as she leaned closer to him.

"I do not wish to be paired off for breeding purposes or want a husband," she said.

Not married then. He ignored the relief her confirmation of that brought with it.

"I am perfectly capable of taking care of myself," she declared.

"Yes, you take great care of yourself. That's why you're here," he replied, hoping to bait her even closer.

She bolted upright, sputtering with indignation. Realizing he'd pushed her too far, he moved to calm her before she reopened her wounds, but she slapped his hand away. Ronan did a double take as he gazed between her and his hand. In over a thousand years, *no* one had dared to rebuke him in such a way.

She swung her legs over the side of the bed. Getting over his shock, he wrapped his arm around her waist and pulled her back before she could rise. She slapped at his arm. Her attempts to get free would have made him laugh, if he hadn't known it would only piss her off more.

"Let go of me!" she cried.

"No." He may not have the same beliefs as her kin, but she would learn he was the one who ruled here. "Relax, before you hurt yourself. I pushed too far, and I am sorry for that."

Her hair whipped into her eyes when her head spun toward him. "That's the second time you've done that."

"Done what?" he asked.

"Said you were sorry. I'm always the one apologizing for doing something wrong, for not obeying when I should or not doing as I'm told. I'm supposed to be sorry for not being overjoyed about my glorious role as soon-to-be bride. Or at least that's what my instructors tell me."

Ronan kept his arm around her waist, his fingers caressing her flat stomach while she spoke. "Then they are idiots."

"Do vampires not have the same rules for women as hunters do?"

"There would be no caging a female vampire, especially not a purebred one."

"What is a purebred?"

"A vampire who is born to two vampires instead of being a human who is turned by one."

Her breath exploded from her. "There's such a thing?"

"Yes. I am a purebred as are the other vampires who live here."

"Oh," she breathed as her eyes ran over him. That revelation, and his age, had to be why she sensed so much power in him. "What about a human and a vampire? What would their offspring be?"

"It depends on which side is stronger. I've seen some be more like hunters, but not as strong, and some be entirely human. The combination of a human and a vampire doesn't happen often, but it has in the past. Most live normal, human lives, some choose to be turned later in life. If they are turned, they can be stronger than an average turned vamp, but not as strong as a purebred."

"Vampires are able to conceive and bear children," she murmured. "We believed they were all turned."

"We are part human too after all, which is why not all of us are killers. We have as much human DNA as demon. I'm not an overly big fan of the human race, they're rather annoying, but I don't like seeing them slaughtered for sport, even if they do it to each other on a daily basis."

Kadence felt as if he'd given her a combo punch that left her lying flat in the middle of the boxing ring. Never in a million years had she expected to learn these things about vampires, never would she have considered they had *any* compassion within them.

"Do vampires have a difficult time conceiving?" she asked.

"No. Do hunters?" Her eyes went to the shuttered windows behind him. "So that is why they lock their women away," he guessed, and knew he was right when her jaw clenched. "The demon

DNA must have reacted differently with the hunters, making it difficult for them to conceive."

She didn't reply.

"Lie down," he coaxed, knowing he would get no more out of her on the subject. He gave a tug on her waist, but she didn't budge. "Joseph didn't take enough blood to permanently damage you, but he took enough to weaken you for a while."

"The permanent damage he's done to me happened before last night," she muttered more to herself than to him.

He frowned as he realized more than a rebellious streak had brought her out last night. "Why were you in that alley, Kadence?"

Her gaze was fixed on the blanket as she responded. "Nathan has been tracking Joseph for a while."

"Why is your brother so interested in him? Why did you disobey everything you've been raised to believe to be there?"

"I never obey when I'm supposed to."

"I get that, but why risk leaving your home now?"

"It took me a while to figure out a way to break free of the stronghold."

"How did you get out?" he asked.

"I can't tell you that."

"Fair enough." He wouldn't ask her to divulge any information he wouldn't divulge himself. "So why were you so determined to escape and see Joseph brought down?"

Fire burned in her eyes when they met his again. "He killed my father."

No wonder she'd been determined to achieve freedom and her brother had been so determined to destroy Joseph himself. Nathan wouldn't back down and would get in the way again, but that was something he would have to deal with later.

"I'm sorry for your loss," he said honestly. He knew how it felt to lose a parent to a Savage.

Kadence gazed at him, trying to decide if he was playing with her or not, but she saw only sincerity on his face and in his eyes. "Thank you. I'm hoping that watching Joseph die will make me feel better. That this... this emptiness in me will ease once he's gone."

He didn't want to take the hope away from her, but he knew nothing completely eased the pain of losing a loved one. It had been nearly a thousand years since he'd lost his parents. He'd had such a short time with them, but their guidance had forged him and the hole of their passing had never been filled.

The young, idealistic man he'd been before their deaths never would have believed himself capable of slipping into the darkness. That man hadn't been plagued with the need to kill, as at twenty-eight, he'd just reached maturity, stopped aging, and started to come more fully into his powers.

Back then, he'd been a young fool who had no idea that soon after becoming fully matured, there would be little left of the vampire race to lead. He hadn't known that centuries of delivering death, even to those who deserved it, would stain and warp his soul. He'd been told by his father that as a mature, purebred vampire he would start to crave something insatiably and that he would have to fight giving into that craving every day of his life, but he'd never fully understood it until his need for blood and death became an ever-constant companion.

He knew the truth of it all now.

"The emptiness of a lost loved one never goes away completely," he told her.

"Never?" she whispered.

"No, but time makes you better capable of dealing with it. Revenge is never the salve you think it will be. It is often necessary and must be carried out, but it will not make everything better."

When he realized he was still holding her and she didn't seem about to jump up and run off, he removed his arm from her waist and leaned back against the headboard. Her haunted eyes met his, her raw anguish evident in her gaze. He'd give anything to take the hurt from her, but that was impossible.

"You should lie down before you make yourself sick," he said.

"I don't get sick," she mumbled as she slid back onto the bed.

"Exhausted then."

She rolled toward him. "It was a tiring night."

Kadence's heart leapt in her chest when he gave her a darling, lopsided smile. She may be exhausted, but she doubted she'd get any sleep with a half-naked Ronan lying in the bed with her.

She bit her lip as she thought about what her brother and the other hunters would say if they could see her now. They'd probably believe she went crazy and lock her away, just as they'd locked away some of the other hunters who had broken their laws or lost their minds over the years.

Nothing she'd revealed to Ronan could be used against her or the hunters, but she was lying in bed with him, and she found herself content to be there. He brought a strange sense of calm to her, one she hadn't experienced in years, if ever. Her kind would consider her a traitor for her actions. She kind of considered herself one by staying beside him, but she wouldn't crawl out of this bed, and she didn't ask him to leave it.

She inched subtly closer until the heat of his body warmed hers. Maybe tomorrow she would get her mind together enough to realize the situation she was in and plot a way out of it, but for now, she didn't have the energy or the will to fight this draw to him.

"I imagine that it was," he said.

"That what was?" she asked as she stifled a yawn.

"A tiring night."

"Oh, yes."

The tips of his fingers briefly caressed her cheek, causing her eyelids to close as she turned into his touch. She smiled when he tucked a strand of hair behind her ear before tracing the outer shell.

"This is all so strange," she murmured and opened her eyes as he ran his finger over her bottom lip.

Her heart rate accelerated when he leaned toward her. Would he kiss her? She wanted that so badly, yet she remained unmoving as she waited to see what he would do next.

Ronan heard the hitch in her breath when his finger stilled on her lip, and he lifted his gaze to hers again. She watched him as one would a predator, afraid to take her eyes away, but he sensed no fear from her. Leaning toward her, he slid his finger away to brush his lips over hers.

Kadence's eyes crossed as she watched him. The butterfly caress made her body melt, but she couldn't tear her gaze away from him as she waited to see what he would do next. Out of everything she'd been anticipating, it was not to have him abruptly pull away from her.

"You must sleep," he said gruffly. "You are not at full strength."

And if he kept touching her, he would be inside her. She may not be aware of where this would lead, but he was, and she was a temptation he wouldn't refuse. He could be a heartless prick on his best days, but not even he was so callous as to take advantage of her now.

Kadence refused to let her disappointment show as she gave a brisk nod. She should feel relieved, not as if she'd missed out on something. *Blood loss, it's screwed up your brain.* She told herself this, but she knew it was wrong.

Kadence closed her eyes and feigned sleep. It was at least an hour before sleep claimed her again; she knew he was still awake when it did.

CHAPTER THIRTEEN

Ronan woke with the hardest erection he'd ever had. Gritting his teeth, he glanced down at the cause of his raging hard-on. Sometime during the remainder of the day, Kadence had rolled over and draped herself across his chest. Her head was tucked beneath his chin, her hand resting against the side of his cheek.

She'd hooked her leg over his waist so that her thigh rubbed against his cock, and her breasts were pressed to his chest. He realized, not only had she sprawled across him, he'd also draped his arms around her and held her against him. *Idiot!*

Stifling a groan, he resisted running his hands over her until she woke as desperate for him as he was for her. If he could convince himself she wasn't an innocent, he would have done just that. But, the hunters kept their women too locked away not to make sure they were virginal when they were ready for breeding.

The seconds of the clock on the wall gave way to minutes before his conscience finally won the war with his dick. Easing his way out from under her, he shifted her over a little to get free. She settled in with a murmur that caused his heart to constrict. Swinging his legs over the side of the bed, he launched to his feet in his rush to be away from her. She whimpered and curled her hand into the pillow his head had been on.

Stepping back, he ran his hand over his face and winced when he realized his fangs had also extended with their need to be inside her. With wooden movements, he turned and strode into the bathroom. A cold shower, some blood, and he would regain control of himself. Having a woman in his bed again, and the unfinished fight with Joseph, had him on edge.

Turning the shower on, he tugged off his jeans and stepped beneath the icy spray. While Kadence remained here, he had a feeling he and cold showers would be getting to know each other a *lot* better. Leaning his forearm against the wall, he rested his head on the tile as he grappled to get himself under control.

The more he tried to shut them out, the more images of Kadence moving over his body, kissing him, and sucking him off flooded his mind. The feel of her breasts against him had been burned into his flesh. He found his hand wrapping around his shaft and giving it a long stroke as he recalled the way her breath had warmed his skin.

It had been years since he'd jerked off, centuries maybe, he couldn't really recall. He still got erections, but he'd felt no compulsion to ease them with a woman or with his own hand. A long time ago, his need for sex had been eclipsed by his never-ending need for death, and he hadn't missed it.

Until now. With images of Kadence in mind, he found himself becoming more aroused than he'd been in years. His hips thrust as he imagined it was the muscles of her sheathe gripping him. Throwing his head back, the cold water hit him in the face as he found his release.

His muscles quaked, his head tilted back down, and he gazed at his still hard dick in his hand. He'd just come, yet he craved more. He wanted *her* holding him now, not himself. His mind whispered at him to go to Kadence, to wake her and claim her. She didn't know what to make of everything, but she wouldn't turn him away.

Through sheer strength of will, he remained in the shower. After another half-an-hour passed, and he jerked off again, he shut the water off and stepped out of the shower. He still felt as tense as a wild, caged animal as he strode over to pull a towel from the rack and dried himself off, but at least he trusted himself not to crawl back into bed with her and take her.

Stepping before the mirror, he wasn't at all surprised to find his eyes more red than brown right now. That demon part of him was still close to the surface, and like him, it wanted *her*. Neither of them could have her though.

She was a hunter, but she'd grown up sheltered from the true brutality of the world her brother lived in. Sheltered from the world *he* lived in. She deserved better than someone who had killed more vampires and a couple of hunters than he cared to recall. He wasn't proud of any of the deaths he'd delivered, but he was proud he'd kept many innocents safer throughout his life.

Turning away from the mirror, he ran a hand over the stubble lining his jaw before grabbing his jeans off the floor. He hastily pulled them on and stepped from the room. His heart clenched when he found Kadence still sleeping. What would it be like to find her like this every day for the rest of his life?

Before he could think about the fact that thought had even entered his mind, never mind how much he found himself wanting to know the answer to it, a faint knock sounded on the door. He hurried to open it before it woke Kadence. Declan stood on the other side, looking far more relaxed than Ronan felt right now. Declan's hair was still damp from a recent shower, one Ronan was certain had been nice and hot.

"What is it?" Ronan demanded as he slipped into the hallway and quietly closed the door behind him.

"Aren't we testy. Did you not get enough beauty rest?"

"I slept fine. Why are you here?"

Declan flashed a grin as his eyes danced with merriment. Out of everyone, Declan could get away with pushing him the farthest. He'd earned that right after their many centuries together, but he was grating on Ronan's nerves.

All amusement vanished from Declan's face as he glanced at the door. "We were curious about what was going to happen with the hunter."

Ronan ran a hand through his disheveled hair. He'd prefer not to leave her, it might scare her to wake up alone, but he had to deal with this. "I'll meet you and the others in the dining room after I speak with Marta about Kadence."

Declan's eyes took on an odd gleam as he appraised Ronan. "Kadence, is it?"

"It is her name," Ronan bit out.

"You like this girl."

"She will be taken care of while here. She's been through a lot."

"We've been together a long time. I've never seen you like this with a woman."

"You don't know what you're talking about."

Declan held up his hands and backed away. "My mistake then. I'll see you in a few minutes."

Ronan noted the amusement in Declan's eyes before he turned and strolled down the hall.

NATHAN PACED the grounds of the stronghold. His tracks taking him from the front gate to Kadence's window. He scowled at the rose trellis beside her window. Surveillance video revealed nothing of her, but he suspected she'd climbed down it last night. Someone most likely would have at least seen her exit the house otherwise.

Somehow, she'd managed to take one of the cars from the garage, punch in the gate code, and leave the stronghold all before he'd left to go hunting for the night. He only knew that because he recalled the white Ford sedan she'd taken already missing from its space when he left, but he'd assumed one of the other hunting teams had taken it.

They'd located the car near the club and brought it back. He'd still been here when Kadence left the stronghold, and he'd never known it. She must have parked somewhere and waited for them to exit before following them.

Over the years, he'd taken her driving around the stronghold and taught her how to use a vehicle. Those drives had been the only times he'd really seen her laugh or smile as they'd traveled through the hundreds of acres of woods and dirt roads crisscrossing the property.

Most of the women weren't taught how to drive, there was no real reason for them to be, but when Kadence had asked him to teach her five years ago, he couldn't resist. There were so many things she was denied; he saw no reason to deny her that too.

Now he was kicking himself in the ass for it. He didn't think she'd asked him to teach her with escape in mind, but now she was in danger, possibly dead, because of his lessons.

What he didn't know was how she had discovered what the gate code was and managed to stay off camera? Those were questions only she could answer, but he was curious about them. If Kadence had managed to do it, then others could get past their defenses too.

No, not true, he realized. No matter what her instructors said about her, Kadence had always been extremely intelligent. She'd always been eager to learn and more inquisitive than most of the more submissive females in the stronghold.

Because of her spirit, he'd believed Logan to be a fine match for her—one he suspected she didn't want—but she had remained silent about the arrangement. Having grown up together and gone through all their training together, Logan was one of his best friends. Logan would be strong enough to keep her safe. He also cared for her and knew her well enough that Nathan didn't worry he would want to break her spirit. Kadence had to be married, but he'd be damned if it was to someone who would try to crush her.

But then, after this, he may throw her in a cage himself. If he ever found her!

The idea of her out there, completely unprepared for the world and all its horrors, was a lead weight around his heart. He'd failed to prepare her for what resided beyond their twenty-foot-high walls and sprawling, secluded property, but then he'd never thought she'd be out there *alone*.

Had she fallen into the hands of the vampires? He couldn't think of a more horrifying and cruel fate for her. She was willful, but she also had one of the biggest hearts he'd ever encountered. The vampires would abuse her until there was nothing left of the Kadence he knew.

And she was alive. They'd always been close; he'd *know* if she were gone.

He kicked himself in the ass again for taking off after Joseph like he had and leaving her behind. He'd just been so determined to destroy the monster himself, that it had been his only thought. When he'd recalled that Kadence had unexpectedly arrived in the club, he'd abandoned his pursuit of Joseph and returned to the alley.

By the time he made it back, the humans were swarming all over it and there had been no sign of Kadence in the alley or club. The humans had also already roped off Jayce's body. It had taken some maneuvering, but they'd been able to steal his body this afternoon. Thankfully, Kadence's body hadn't been in the morgue with him.

He spun on his heel and stalked back the other way. No matter how pissed off and concerned he was about her, he had to admit Kadence was resourceful. She was also more determined than he'd realized to see their father's killer brought down. If she'd been born a man, she would have been a strong asset out in the field.

He glared at the wall as he marched toward it. Why hadn't he known what she'd been planning? He should have known the show of obedience she'd been giving recently was an act. He should have known she was up to something.

They had shared the same womb, they had spent the early part of their childhood playing together, and they were the closest of friends as well as siblings. Then, he'd turned ten and left his boyhood behind to embrace his hunter training.

Kadence, on the other hand, had resisted her training every step of the way. She'd been a constant thorn in her instructors' sides. She'd never wanted to accept her lot as a woman within the stronghold. Their father had believed she'd outgrow it; Nathan hadn't been as convinced, but he'd kept that opinion to himself.

When they were younger, Nathan was amused by her antics of skipping classes, setting her cooking on fire, catching and putting a couple dozen frogs and snakes into the schoolroom, and flat out refusing to do as she was told. He'd believed she wasn't ready to leave her childhood behind. That amusement faded to sadness as it became increasingly obvious his sister was truly unhappy with her designated future.

Then, their father had been killed. Over the years, Kadence had always known things, so he hadn't been surprised to find her waiting for him when he returned with their father's body. Many had tried to keep her from seeing it, but she succeeded in getting past all of them to stand beside their father as he was carried into the mourning chamber.

She hadn't cried or demanded revenge. She'd simply… retreated was the only way he could think to describe it. Her docility had been out of place. He'd believed it was because of the weight of her grief, but he realized now she'd been plotting.

He should have known better. The loss of their father wouldn't have broken Kadence's willful nature. However, he'd been so happy she finally settled into her role, that he hadn't looked past the façade. And he'd lost her because of it.

Nathan slammed his fist into the brick wall running the entire length of the nearly three square miles that made up the stronghold property in this rural area of Massachusetts. Pain lanced through his hand and up to his elbow, but he barely acknowledged the cracking of one of his knuckles. The broken bone would heal soon enough.

That rapid healing ability, along with many of his other enhanced senses, had been what made him the leader upon his father's passing. There were other male hunters here with more experience than him, but his bloodline had led from the beginning and would continue to do so while it survived.

The older hunters accepted this, just as they had accepted he would be bringing his own men with him on the hunts. The men who had fought closely with his father continued to hunt, but they were no longer the seconds-in-command to their leader. He still asked them for their guidance and advice, but the new generation was rising, taking over now.

Besides, his father had been over a hundred years old when he'd been killed, as were many of his friends. They all still had many good years in them, but it was time for the older ones to start stepping aside. Sometimes, Nathan took some of the ones in their fifties and sixties with him on hunts, but last night he hadn't expected to encounter so many vamps, or to have Kadence show up.

He wanted to wring her neck as badly as he wanted to hug her.

"Nathan."

Nathan turned to find Logan crossing the grounds toward him. "Has anything new been learned?" he demanded.

Logan stopped before him. "No, nothing."

"She's not dead."

Logan nodded, but his eyes were distant. There had been so many vamps in that alley. Yes, they'd chased many of them away, but there had also been those *others*. He still couldn't explain them, and he didn't care to. They were vamps and they would die, especially if they had hurt his sister.

"I would *know* if she were dead," he insisted. Where was she though? What had happened to her? If she wasn't being held by vampires, then why hadn't she called? Nathan paced faster. "Get everyone together; we're going out in full force tonight to find her."

"Nathan—"

"She's alive!" he snapped.

"I believe you, but I think we should leave extra enforcements here, just in case."

Nathan closed his eyes; he should have considered that. Kadence would never willingly disclose any information about them, but the strongest man could crack under torture. The gate code had been changed and men stood guard outside, watching for her in case she came back and couldn't get in. However, even with their numerous security measures, there was still a chance the vamps could get in if Kadence was coerced into disclosing their location.

"Double the guard for tonight and increase the electricity on the wall. Day break tomorrow, we'll move the women to the mission to be on the safe side."

"I will have them start preparing for the move," Logan said.

He wasn't concerned that Kadence would reveal the location of the mission; she didn't know where it was. All the history of the hunters was housed within the mission, an underground bunker in the center of the stronghold. There were enough supplies within for the women and children to live there for at least a month, but they would be blindfolded before they were taken to it.

None of their enemies could ever know where the mission was. It had been designed to provide shelter in times of a crises as well as protect the documentation of the hunters' history. Only four people knew its location, himself and three of the eldest hunter men. All of them would kill themselves before ever revealing where it was.

Nathan resumed pacing as Logan turned back toward the numerous cabins laid out in a circular pattern around the large brick house in the middle. The brick house had been home to his family since they'd owned this property. It had also been the original building here. The cabins were all added over the years.

Over three hundred hunters lived on the grounds. At one time there had been nearly four hundred, but some had left to work with other strongholds or marry women there, and others were killed. They were in a drought of sorts when it came to children with only a handful of them being under ten.

There were fifteen more strongholds such as this throughout the world. Some of them had more hunters, others less. All of them were run by hunters who were nominated by the elders within that stronghold and who his father had agreed to appoint. When the next new leader was required in one of those strongholds, Nathan would have to travel there in order to agree or disagree with the nomination. It was not something he looked forward to, but it was his role now.

He stopped pacing when his gaze fell on the archway the women had recently been decorating for Kadence's wedding. The white ribbon covering it stood out starkly against the growing dusk.

No one had asked Kadence if this was what she wanted, he realized. But they'd never asked any of the women or men who were paired together when the time came. It was simply accepted that it would happen, as it had always happened over the years.

He spent enough time in the human world to know it was an archaic tradition. He'd never questioned if things should be different though. When a woman was ready to breed, they were to be married off as soon as possible, with the hopes that within the next seventy years, while she was still capable of doing so, she would conceive a child.

Some did not.

Nathan knew the elder men and women of the stronghold would choose a woman for him soon. Mostly, it was elder women who made the choice as few men lived to a hundred, never mind the two hundred that gave one the lauded status of an elder. If there were no acceptable women here, they would choose one from another location, but he suspected his wife would be Kadence's friend Simone.

He would be happy with Simone. She was beautiful and docile. She excelled in her classes and would make a suitable mother and wife. She was everything he'd ever wanted in a woman.

He told himself this, but he could feel the noose cinching around his neck and he realized what Kadence was going through. When he married, he would at least be able to keep hunting and have freedom beyond these walls. Kadence would simply be locked away here for the rest of her life.

No wonder Kadence had rebelled; he certainly would have. However, none of that mattered right now. The most important thing was getting her back, and he was hell-bent on doing that.

CHAPTER FOURTEEN

EMERGING from the bathroom after her shower, Kadence tied the belt of the robe she'd discovered hanging over the back of the chair around her waist. Not only had someone left the robe for her, but they'd also brought her a change of clothes and a toothbrush.

She didn't know who the clothes belonged to, and she didn't care. Her clothes weren't so ruined she couldn't wear them again, but the idea of climbing back into them after Joseph's attack made her skin crawl.

She glanced at the bedroom door before retreating to the bathroom again. Ronan had been gone when she'd woken. She didn't know when he'd come back, and the last thing she wanted was to be caught naked. Releasing the towel, she slipped on the white bra set out for her. The bra was a little too big on her, but fit well enough. Opening the package of underwear, she removed a white, cotton pair and pulled them on before sliding the yellow sundress over her head.

Wandering over to the sink, she lifted her wet hair to inspect the wound on her neck. It was mostly healed with only the two original puncture marks from Joseph's fangs remaining. Her stomach turned at the reminder of the degradation she'd endured from his attack. She didn't care what they all believed, female hunters should be trained better.

She discovered a hairbrush amongst the sparse toiletries set beside the sink. Her fingers trembled as she ran her fingers over the brush before the shaving cream can and a disposable razor that wouldn't be much of a weapon. These were *Ronan's* personal things. Standing here, touching his things, seemed almost as intimate as sleeping beside him all night had been—something she'd known he'd done, judging by the still warm dent in his pillow she discovered upon waking.

Her fingers settled on the hairbrush. She turned it over in her hand, admiring the fine ivory handle before using it to work out the tangles in her hair. Placing the brush down, she left the bathroom again.

Her stomach grumbled, but she ignored the food on the platter as she inspected the room. From its gray walls to the large armoire and chestnut head and footboard of the bed, there was no sign of any softness in the personality of the man who slept in this room or of anything personal.

She had more signs of her personality on her small nightstand at home—with its ever-present Shasta daisy from the greenhouses and the only photo she had of her entire family together, taken when she was five, before her mother had died from a fall off a horse—than this entire room possessed. Looking around, she would assume the man who slept here was cold and stern, that he was nothing like the man who had talked with her during the day and who stared at her with such heat in his gaze. *Which side is the real him?*

It didn't matter; she wouldn't get to know him well enough to learn the answer to that.

Padding over to the window, she ran her hands over the metal shutters covering them before spotting the button beside them. Pushing it, she stepped back as the shutters rolled up and folded themselves neatly above the picture window. Bars covered the outside of the glass.

Kadence stepped closer to the window to stare down at the large pool below. The puddles on the pool cover were frozen, and the shrubs encircling it were all weighed down with a layer of ice. It had rained sometime last night and frozen over again. Even the black, wrought iron fence surrounding the pool was covered in a sheet of ice.

The fence was high enough that it blocked her view of what lay beyond the pool area. Frustration filled her as she stepped back to survey the room once more. Nothing about the room or the outdoors gave any indication as to where she was, other than she hadn't been transported to a tropical climate while she'd been unconscious.

Inspecting the walls, she frowned as she noted the patches of darker gray paint on them. It took her a minute to realize the patches with their outlines were where photos or paintings had once hung. Now that she was looking for them, she also saw the holes in the walls from the nails that had been removed. There were at least ten places where something had been taken off the walls.

What had happened to it all? She didn't think Ronan was planning to redecorate—she had a feeling he didn't have much time for color schemes—but then why had all the paintings or photos been removed?

In the long run, it really didn't matter what had happened to them all. However, her curiosity was piqued.

When her stomach rumbled again, she walked over to the tray and picked up a piece of bacon. Why vampires had food in their house was another thing she didn't know how to explain, but she happily ate the bacon before grabbing another piece and biting into it.

She doubted any weapons remained in her coat, but she still searched its pockets to confirm it. Dropping her coat back over the chair, she rotated her shoulder, relieved to find she no longer felt any discomfort.

Lifting the navy blue cardigan that was set out with the dress, she slid it around her shoulders and buttoned it. She *really* didn't want to go through Ronan's things, but with nothing else of use in view, she saw no other option.

She pulled open the heavy wood doors on the armoire. The crisp scent of cedar met her as she gazed at the clothes hanging neatly within. Most of them were jeans and button down shirts in an assorted array of colors. There were some black pants of the cargo variety and a black, three-piece suit she bet Ronan looked striking in.

The idea of peeling that suit off him to reveal all the ridges and carved muscles of his chest and abdomen made her mouth water.

Stop it! She was no longer missing at least two pints of blood and could no longer blame her strange attraction to a vampire on that. She had to plan her escape, not stand here wondering what it would be like if Ronan kissed her. She'd broken free of the stronghold; she could figure this place out too.

Although, it had taken a lot of plotting before she'd succeeded in breaking out of the stronghold. In a book she'd once read, the detective used baby powder to uncover fingerprints, so she'd decided to give that a shot. One night, shortly after Nathan and the hunters had gone out, she snuck out to use the baby powder on the keypad by the gate. All the numbers had fingerprints on them, as the code was changed once a month, but she'd used the four most visible fingerprints to figure out the right combination of numbers.

Over the years, she'd spent a lot of time with Roland, the man who ran the security system at the stronghold. She'd never sat with Roland with the intention of escaping. She resented the plans for her life, but she'd never thought she'd do anything other than what had been laid out for her. She'd spent time with Roland because he was one of the few elder men alive, and his stories were fascinating.

However, during all the time she'd spent with him, she'd also watched the cameras as they talked. There were no cameras on the homes or the massive garage with all the vehicles. No one saw any need for that. All the cameras were focused on the outside world.

Eventually, Kadence had realized that the three cameras covering the gate and roadway had a minute, every hour, at the twenty-three mark when none of them were focused on the gate. That minute had been enough time for her to run up and punch two new combinations into the pad every night after the hunters left.

Over her years in the stronghold, she'd learned that three wrong combinations in a twenty-four-hour period set the entire system off. Two wrong tries went by unnoticed though. She had hoped and prayed no other hunters entered the wrong combination on their exits and entrances after her; they would have known something was wrong then.

It had taken her weeks of patience and wrong tries before she finally lucked out on the right combination. She'd closed the gate before it could open more than an inch and fled.

She'd broken free the next night and ended up in the hands of a vampire.

With a sigh, she closed the armoire and turned back to the sparse room. She wanted to know where Ronan was and what was going to happen to her, but she couldn't walk around this place without some kind of weapon.

If I'm not locked in…

Her gaze went to the door as the possibility occurred to her, but she'd leap that obstacle if she came to it. She could only handle one thing at a time right now. Walking away from the armoire, she bent to peer under the bed. There wasn't even a dust bunny under there.

Sitting back, she rested her hands on her knees as she surveyed the room again. Her eyes fell on the metal serving cart and the platter of food before returning to the room. Unless she planned on destroying some furniture, there was nothing she could use in this room to defend herself with against a vampire. The only thing she'd be able to break anyway was the nightstand, and that would defeat the whole purpose of being secretly armed.

Rising, she walked over to the cart and snatched the butter knife laid out neatly next to the fork. The silver knife may not kill a vamp, but she could at least inflict some damage with it. She slipped the knife up the sleeve of her cardigan before snatching the rest of the bacon. She greedily ate it as she walked to the door and grabbed the handle. Taking a deep breath, she braced herself for it to be locked.

The handle turned within her grasp and the door inched open. Stepping forward, Kadence pressed her eye against the crack and peered into the hall beyond. She couldn't see much of what was on the other side, but she heard no movement and detected no one out there. Feeling like a thief in the night, she slid out of the room and closed the door. Thick, dark wood doors lined the long hall before her.

Her bare feet made no sound on the plush, red rug lining the hall as she walked. She was halfway down the hall when her step faltered, and she stopped to take in the bare, white walls. The walls were lit by dim, candle-flame-shaped bulbs housed within the glass sconces lining the walls. Those small bulbs illuminated the numerous places where things had once hung on the walls.

What is up with this place? She wondered as her fingers touched against the handle of the knife. The weapon gave her zero reassurance.

Despite the electricity, she felt as if she'd stepped into the eighteenth century as she continued onward. She saw no bare spots or stains to indicate the rug was anything other than brand new, but something about it, or maybe it was the vibe of this whole place, made it feel ancient.

She crept forward until she came to a large, curving staircase at the end of the hall. The mahogany banister shone in the light spilling from the chandelier above. The hundreds of bulbs within the chandelier created a rainbow of colors amongst the crystals that danced over the white and gray marble foyer below. She had no idea who changed those bulbs when they burnt out, but she didn't envy them their job.

The dome of the ceiling had been painted with an exquisite landscape. Animals were gathered within a beautiful meadow as the sun shone down on a glistening lake. It was an outdoor scene she was certain none of the inhabitants of this place had seen, at least not by day. She hadn't asked, but she assumed since Ronan had been born a vampire that he'd never seen the sun.

Feeling ridiculously saddened for his inability to feel the warmth of the sun, Kadence turned her attention to the stairs. She tiptoed down the steps so as not to make a sound.

Her feet became instantly chilled when she stepped off the wood and onto the marble. Pausing with her hand on the banister, she glanced left and right, uncertain of where to go from here. Her gaze went to the front door across from her, but there would be no walking out of it as a heavy metal gate blocked the way.

Voices drifted from down the hall on her left. Kadence crept toward the voices, her hand slipping into her sleeve to grip the knife handle. Arriving at a set of sliding double doors, she stopped when the voices within became louder and more distinct. The doors had been mostly closed, but a small crack ran down the middle of them to allow the light from within to spill out.

Moving closer, she stepped to the side of one of the doors to peer in at the large men gathered around the ten-foot-long table within. Ronan was on his feet, his arm resting on the mantle of the gray stone fireplace at the far end of the room. His dark hair was disheveled, and an air of angry tension surrounded him.

"She cannot stay here," Killean said, his hands flattened on the table before him. His scar stood out more starkly in the glow of the small chandelier hanging over the table.

Ronan had been focused on the wall, but his head turned toward Killean when he spoke. "I never said she could. However, I am not going to turn her out on the streets and hope the hunters find her or that she can find her own way home. She's been secluded her whole life; she may not survive on her own."

Killean shrugged. "I don't see anything wrong with a dead hunter."

Kadence winced at his callousness, but she knew her brother would have the same attitude if the roles were reversed. *She* had the same attitude about Killean. She may not want to see anything bad happen to Ronan, but Killean could bite it for all she cared.

Ronan's eyes became redder as they narrowed on Killean. "I do," he grated between his teeth.

Killean bowed his head before speaking again. "So we'll arrange a meeting with the hunters and release her somewhere."

"And how do you plan to do that?" Saxon inquired.

"She has to know some way to get in touch with them," Killean replied. "We should arrange something tonight. The sooner she is out of here, the better off we'll all be. The hunters will be out in force and far more of a nuisance to us while searching for her."

Kadence's heart leapt in her chest and disappointment crashed through her. She opened her mouth to shout, *no*, before closing it again. She should be elated they didn't plan to kill her, didn't plan to use her as leverage over her brother and her kind. Instead, she felt... deflated.

She wanted to see her brother and friends again and let Nathan know she was safe. He *had* to be told she was fine. He would go crazy with worry otherwise, and the hunters would be out looking for her. Someone could get killed because of her.

However, she wasn't ready to go back yet. She was free—well, as free as she could be while being held by her enemies...

Not my enemies. She didn't understand how it all worked yet, and it would take her time to get used to the idea, but these vampires were not her enemies.

Ronan wasn't going to just turn her loose. However, she felt freer here than she'd ever felt at the stronghold. There were no expectations for her to be docile here. No looming marriage. No sequestered, endlessly boring days where she sat idly by while her brother and the others went out to make a difference in the world.

And Ronan was here. Her eyes ran over him again. There could never be anything between them, but she couldn't help admiring the way his maroon shirt molded to his broad shoulders and chest. Her gaze lingered on the jeans hugging his powerful thighs and taut ass.

He stepped away from the mantle, drawing her attention back to his face. His gaze was focused on the crack in the doors. She gulped when she realized he knew she stood there.

CHAPTER FIFTEEN

"Come in," he ordered.

She didn't pretend to hide or duck away. She'd been caught. Releasing the knife, she made sure it was tucked securely away before pushing open one of the doors and stepping into the dining room. Like the rest of the walls she'd seen in the house, the white walls within here were also bare.

Her gaze finally settled on Ronan. Her fingers itched to touch him as she recalled the warmth of his body so near hers when he'd lain beside her and how he had nearly kissed her. She almost lifted her fingers to her lips as desire coiled within her belly. She'd thought maybe her weakened state yesterday had caused her to imagine some of her intense attraction to him; she'd been mistake. If anything, it felt stronger.

When Kadence's heightened scent drifted to him, Ronan was unable to stop himself from taking a step toward her. He halted abruptly as he restrained himself from going any closer. If he did, he would take her in his arms and carry her from this room. She wanted him, and all he could think of was easing her need.

No one within the room spoke as their eyes traveled between

Kadence and him. A blush crept through her cheeks as she fiddled with the sleeves of her sweater. Then, Declan cleared his throat and gave a discreet cough.

"How much did you hear?" Ronan inquired, his voice more gravelly than normal.

"Enough to know you plan to release me to my brother," she replied.

Ronan stepped back to rest his arm on the mantle and focused on the wall across from him, but not before she saw a flash of pure red in his eyes.

"You must know where you came from," Saxon said.

She met his hazel eyes head on. "I do, but I can't let you know that."

"I told you we aren't your enemies," Ronan growled.

"I realize that now, but you also said Joseph was once one of you. How can I trust that none of you will become a monster like him? I won't divulge our location to you. There are too many lives at stake."

Kadence braced herself as she waited to see how they would react to her refusal. Declan smiled as he sat forward and rested his hands on the table. Killean and Saxon stared at her as if she were a snake with the head of a spider, but Declan gazed at her as if he understood her, or at the very least maybe kind of liked her. She smiled back at him.

"Is there any guarantee none of you will ever become a Savage?" she asked.

"Fate is a fickle bitch, and sometimes she takes even the best of us down, but sometimes she also intervenes to save us," Declan replied.

Kadence blinked at him, uncertain of what *that* was supposed to mean, but she didn't have time to get into it.

"Enough, Declan," Ronan said as he glowered at his friend.

"He's a little testy right now," Declan said to her before leaning back in his seat and crossing his legs. His expression was innocent when he focused on Ronan.

"Why are you testy?" Kadence blurted.

Ronan refused to answer her question or react to Declan's antics. He had no idea what his friend was trying to get at, and he didn't care. All that mattered was getting Kadence safely back to where she belonged. His nails scraped across the stone of the mantle as he balled his hands.

Declan's silver eyes ran appraisingly over her before he grinned. "Because not only is fate fickle, but sometimes she's downright *devious*."

"Huh?" she asked.

"I said *enough!*" Ronan roared, causing her to jump as her attention swung back to him.

He'd stepped away from the mantle once more. His hands were fisted at his sides, making the muscles in his forearms and biceps bulge beneath his shirt. For a second, she thought the seams of that shirt would burst open as his eyes became almost entirely red.

Fear raced over her skin, not for herself, but for Declan. The vamp became as still as stone while Ronan stared at him. Before she could think about it, she stepped forward, drawing Ronan's gaze to her. She didn't know what she'd expected, but his shoulders relaxed, some of the red bled away from his eyes, and the tension in the room eased.

Saxon cleared his throat. "You must know of another way you can get in contact with your kind then."

"I could call my brother," she said.

"And was your brother one of the annoyances there last night?" Killean inquired.

"That annoyance could kick your ass," she retorted.

Killean lifted an eyebrow, causing his scar to pull upward with the gesture. "Doubtful, but I will give him a go if you'd like."

"Would he be able to trace the call?" Saxon asked, sending Killean a quelling look.

She'd read enough books to know what tracing a call meant, even if she'd never been around as much technology as the male hunters had. There were computers in the stronghold, but only a few of them had the Internet, and she'd never been granted access to those. If she hadn't read those books though, she would have no idea what Saxon was talking about.

For the first time, she felt not only resentful but infuriated by all she'd been denied. There was so much out in the world, so much for her to see and do. She didn't want to just learn other languages; she wanted to travel to the places where they were spoken and immerse herself in the culture and people there. She didn't want to simply stare at pictures of art in books; she wanted to breathe it in as she stood in the Sistine Chapel or the Louvre.

She yearned to stand somewhere and feel small and to learn without any limitations. There were thousands upon thousands of books in the stronghold, ones for recreation and others for learning, but all she would ever know was what was in those pages. Never would she experience it for herself.

And it pissed her off.

She'd once asked one of her instructors why the women could read about and see photos of the outside world, but not use the computers or experience the world firsthand. Her instructor had replied it was because they had no reason to learn about computers, and as women they must be kept safe. However, as women, they also had to be educated so they were intelligent enough to carry on a conversation with their husband and not bore him.

At the time, she hadn't understood why the response had exasperated her so much that she'd walked out of the class, but she understood it now. They'd given her a taste of things she could never have to educate her for her husband, but they'd never taken into account that maybe her husband would bore *her*.

Kadence took a deep breath to steady herself. She could rage against her fate until she became bitter, or she could accept it for what it was. She couldn't stay here; it would only cause more problems between the hunters and vamps. It was more than obvious Killean didn't want her here, and Saxon would prefer her gone.

Her temples throbbed as she tried to figure everything out, but she could feel time slipping away from her.

"Can he trace the call, Kadence?" Declan nudged.

"I'm not sure the depth of their technology," she replied, "but I know they have a lot."

"Then we'll give her a burner phone, take her out of here, and have her call from somewhere else," Killean declared.

Burner phone, something untraceable, a onetime thing, she knew. Nathan had told her they used burner phones when they hunted in case one of their phones fell into the wrong hands. He gave her the number to each new phone he had, and she memorized it before he went out to hunt. He'd had the same phone for two weeks now, unless something had happened to it, and then she would have to call Logan.

"The sun will set in an hour," Saxon said.

"We can take her out to call then," Killean said.

Ronan ran a hand through his hair, tugging at it as his other hand gripped the edge of the mantle. Bits of rock broke off and bit into his palm, but he didn't release his hold on it. If he let it go, he may attack Killean. Ronan knew his friend was right, that she had to be returned, but did Killean have to be in such a rush to see it done?

A jagged piece of rock sliced into his palm, drawing blood as he remained focused on the wall across from him. The best thing would be to get her out of here as soon as possible, but he wasn't ready to see her go.

Though he didn't look at any of them, Kadence saw the pure red color of Ronan's eyes. She held her breath as she waited to hear what he would say.

"We'll leave in an hour," he finally said in a voice so hoarse she barely recognized it.

Kadence felt as if she'd been punched in the gut. Unless she planned something quick, she would be back in the stronghold tonight and married within the month.

Ronan's eyes had become their burgundy hue again when he finally turned to look at her. "Are you hungry?" he asked.

The bacon hadn't been enough to fill her, but whatever hunger she'd been experiencing was effectively swallowed by the pit in her stomach. She shook her head, not trusting her voice to speak. Without another word, she turned, left the room, and fled up the steps. By the time she made it to the top, she was running, but there was nowhere for her to run to.

CHAPTER SIXTEEN

A SHORT TIME LATER, Ronan opened the door to his bedroom. He'd meant to stay completely away from Kadence until it was time for her to leave, but with every passing second he'd become increasingly compelled to return to her. Eventually, he'd given up the battle. He told himself he was going to see her to make sure she was ready to leave, but he knew he lied.

Kadence sat on the bed, her back to him and her head bent forward. Her pale hair cascaded down her back in thick waves that shone in the light. She'd removed the sweater and draped it over the back of the chair; her coat lay beside her on the bed. The sundress Marta had given her exposed the creamy skin of her bare shoulders and clung to her slender curves.

Her head rose when the door click closed, but she didn't turn to look at him. "It's almost time to go," he stated. "I'm sure you'll be happy to see your brother again."

"I will," she replied in a clipped tone.

He frowned as he tried to puzzle out why she didn't seem more excited by the prospect of being reunited with her family. Moving around the bed, he stopped before her. Her face was completely serene and impassive, like a statue. She revealed no emotion as she clasped her hands demurely before her and stared at him.

It took him a moment to realize this was the docile, female hunter she was supposed to be. He didn't like it one bit.

"What is wrong?"

That odd mask of composure never slipped. "I am to be married soon."

Out of everything he'd expected her to say, that hadn't been it. His gaze ran over her slender body and alluring breasts that would fit perfectly in the palm of his hand. His fangs lengthened at the idea of any other man knowing what it was like to feel her body against his while they slept, to be *inside* of her.

He managed to suppress a snarl. "When?"

"Within the month."

He recalled what she'd said earlier, *"I'm supposed to be sorry for not being overjoyed about my glorious role as soon-to-be bride."* At the time, he'd assumed she meant far in the future, not within a month.

"To who?" he demanded.

"Logan. He is an outstanding hunter from a strong family line. Our children will be fine hunters. He is a good man, a good friend, and loyal to Nathan."

"Your brother arranged this?"

"The elders chose Logan for me when I became capable of reproducing."

"You're not a *fucking horse!*"

She blinked, but it was the only reaction she showed to his explosive response.

"Do you want to marry Logan?" he demanded.

"It is a great honor to marry a hunter and bear him children. I must be grateful that I am of an age to do so and that a fine husband has been chosen for me."

She sounded as if she were reciting something drilled into her head over the years. "You accept this?"

Her blank eyes met his as she spoke in a dull monotone. "Of course. It is why I was born. It will be a privilege to carry on the legacy of my heritage."

He didn't understand this complacent person who had taken the place of the spirited woman he believed her to be, but he wanted to shake her to reveal the woman she truly was. The woman he wanted for himself alone.

The irrational urge to possess her was back again, but this time it refused to be buried in the cold recesses of his heart once more. Unthinkingly, he stroked her cheek with the tips of his fingers. She didn't nuzzle him like she had before, but at least she didn't turn away from him.

Crouching before her, he grasped her chin so she had to look him in the eye. "Do you really accept this?"

Something flickered in her eyes, but her mask didn't change. "I have no choice. What else am I to do?"

He had no answer for her, no solutions. There was nothing he could give her, nothing he could say that would help. "You could tell them you are not ready to be married."

She let out a harsh laugh. He winced inwardly, hating the bitterness of the sound. "I can no more fight who I am and what is expected of me than you can. My turn has come. I have known since I was a child it would happen. There's nothing I can do to change it, and Logan is a good man. We've been friends since childhood. I know he won't abuse me, and he will make a fine father for our children."

Not only would another man know her body, but he would also get to share the bond of raising their children with her. Ronan stilled at the realization, even as he wanted to tear the room apart.

He released her chin and rocked back on his heels. "What happens if Logan dies?"

"Then I will become an instructor. I will show the young our heritage, teach them our ways, and I will guard over our ancestry."

"What if he dies before you have a child, or six months from now?"

"If I am still at a good breeding age, and a hunter loses his wife, then I may be considered to fill the role."

No wonder she'd rebelled against her life, there was no hope within it, he realized.

Removing his hand from her cheek, he rose to pace across the floor. He couldn't stand the thought of her being locked away for the rest of her life. Couldn't stand the idea of someone so beautiful and alive being caged so remorselessly and used like cattle.

He turned back to gaze at her as she remained sitting rigidly on the bed. He couldn't begin to imagine what she faced when she returned. Spinning on his heel, he paced back and forth once more. He couldn't help her. If they didn't return her, the hunters would go on a rampage, slaughtering every vampire they came across. Many innocents could become caught in the crossfire of the sudden onslaught. Many of his kind could die.

He couldn't allow that. For his entire life, it had been his duty to protect them.

Being married was her destiny, her fate. Who was he to go against the ways of the hunters, even if he didn't approve of it?

Stalking back, he stopped before her. "I can't help you."

She showed no reaction to his callous words. "I didn't ask you to."

Ronan ignored the fierce pounding of his heart as he pushed aside the clamoring in his head telling him to keep her, that she belonged to him.

"Maybe your brother can stop it—"

"It is my fate. It is who I am, who my people are. No one can stop that," she cut in.

"Shit," Ronan mumbled. He ran his hand through his hair as he started pacing again. A solid rap on the door drew him to an abrupt stop. "What?" he barked.

"It's time, Ronan," Declan replied in a subdued tone.

"We'll be right there."

Kadence rose from the bed with her hands still held demurely before her. Slowly, she met his gaze. "I will tell Nathan to come alone. He may believe it's a trap, but he'll do whatever he believes is necessary to get me back."

"He loves you," Ronan realized.

"Yes."

"And you him?"

"He's my twin and my best friend. Twins are very rare amongst our kind so we were exceptionally close."

"How rare are they?"

"We are the first ones born in nearly seven hundred years and the first girl/boy twins born in over a thousand years."

Ronan folded his arms over his chest. "I see. Would he stop this marriage if you asked him to?"

"He might try, for me, but I would never put him in such a position by asking him to do that."

"Is he the leader of your people?"

"We have many different leaders in different places," she replied vaguely.

He is at least one of those leaders then, Ronan realized and she would sacrifice herself not to cause her brother any trouble. He assumed Nathan had taken over after their father was killed, if the leadership role passed with hunters the same way it used to pass with the vampires.

"Kadence." He moved back to her, and placing his finger under her chin, he lifted it. For the rest of his life, he would recall every detail of her. He brushed her hair back, letting the silken strands run through his fingers.

Stepping closer, he stopped when his chest brushed against hers. Her eyes searched his as he stood over her, but her face remained serene. He found himself unable to resist the lure of her plump, red lips as he bent his head to hers. He only meant to have a little taste, but the minute his lips touched hers, he knew he was gone.

CHAPTER SEVENTEEN

His hand rested on her hip before wrapping around her waist. When she didn't try to resist him, he pulled her lush body firmly against his and lifted her. Not even with his first bedding had he been concerned about coming in his pants, but he was now as she sighed when she rubbed against the rigid length of his erection and pressed her breasts against his chest.

Tangling his fingers in her hair, he pulled her head back and ran his tongue over her lips. Her lips parted to his prodding and he delved into her mouth. She gasped then melted against him as he tasted her. Her tongue hesitantly touched his before becoming bolder as she eagerly met each of his thrusts.

He needed to feel more of her, to know what every inch of her looked and tasted like. Releasing her hair, he ran his hand down the velvet expanse of her shoulders. Gripping the strap of her dress and bra, he pulled them both down until her entire breast fit his hand perfectly. He ran his thumb over her nipple until she moaned and the bud puckered against his flesh, branding him for eternity.

Kadence squirmed in Ronan's hold, wanting to get closer to him yet unable to do so. No one had ever touched her so intimately before or made her feel this alive. For the first time in her life, she didn't know uncertainty and dread. With complete clarity, she knew she didn't give a damn what this man was, she just craved more of him.

Her heart beat against her ribs when he ran his thumb and forefinger over her nipple before pinching it. She didn't know how to react to the overwhelming sensations he ceaselessly stoked to life in her. It was almost too much, but nowhere near enough.

Her fingers curled into his hair when he broke their kiss to leave a trail of heat over her skin with his lips and tongue as they moved over her ear and down her neck. The graze of his fangs against her flesh didn't scare her. Instead, she drew him closer when his head dipped toward her breast. He hesitated for a second before his mouth clamped onto her nipple.

The low groan he issued and his tongue laving her nipple caused her to cry out as a wet heat spread between her legs. When he drew her nipple deeper into his mouth and sucked at her, she nearly screamed as she ground her hips against him with a wildness she hadn't known she possessed until him.

"Ronan!"

Killean's yell from outside the door jolted through the haze of lust consuming Ronan. Still, he couldn't tear himself away from the inviting warmth of her body.

"It's time!" Killean shouted and pounded once on the door.

Ronan's hands clenched on her. He didn't think he would ever be able to let her go now that he'd tasted her, now that he knew how responsive she could be and how ensnaring the scent of her passion was.

With a ragged breath, he succeeded in tearing his mouth away from her. Rising over her, he gazed at her face. She was flushed not from embarrassment but from unquenched desire. He couldn't leave her in this state, not when she would *let* him ease her, but he couldn't take her innocence and ship her back to the hunters. He had no idea what they would do if they discovered she was no longer a virgin.

His head dropped down so his forehead rested against hers as she gazed at him with wide-eyed awe. She was his for the taking, and he was going to hand her over to never see her again.

Suddenly feeling more Savage than he'd ever felt in his life, he was hit with the impulse to sink his fangs into her, drain her to near death, and turn her. To make her his completely. The sharp points of his fangs pressed against his lower lips. The thump of the blood beating within the vein in the pale column of her throat called to him. He would make her the thing she hated most and he didn't care, not if it meant he could be selfish and keep her for himself.

Then, her hand rose to pull her dress and bra back up, covering the breast he'd exposed. The tremor in her hand pierced through the demon to his more human side. He set her on her feet and stepped away from her before he lost control.

"I'm sorry," he managed to get out. "I didn't mean for that to happen."

Kadence rested her fingers against her swollen lips. She longed to have him replace her fingers with his mouth once more, but they couldn't continue this. A lump formed in her throat. If things had been different…

It didn't matter, she decided. Things weren't different and hoping for things that could never be was a fool's game.

"Don't apologize," she said. "I wanted it as much as you did."

To hear her say she wanted him too was more than he could tolerate. There was no point in denying either of them this. He *would* have her. He stepped toward her, not caring about anything anymore except possessing her.

"Ronan!" Killean shouted again.

His friend's incessant yells cleared his mind, but he wouldn't mind ripping Killean's tongue out before they left here. "We'll be right there!" he barked.

Kadence flinched at his words, but she didn't move away from him. Turning on his heel, Ronan strode away from her. He removed his coat from the armoire and slid it on to cover his erection.

"Ronan." He turned at his name. "Thank you."

"For what?"

"For being kind to me, for showing me that not all vampires are evil. I will tell the hunters that. I will tell my brother we have it wrong. They probably won't listen to me, but I will try to make them understand. Thank you for giving me an extra day of freedom." She paused as her fingers touched her lips again. "For showing me what it is like to be kissed. For letting me experience something I probably never will again."

"Your husband will kiss you," he growled, his fingernails digging into his palm and tearing into flesh at the thought.

"Yes, but he won't make me feel like you do."

Ronan let out a hiss as an invisible fist socked him in the stomach. A red haze shaded his vision as the demon part of him screamed at him to take her. When her hand fell from her lips and she edged away from him, he knew that what she saw of him rattled her.

The sight of her distress eased the turmoil of his emotions, and he was left to deal with the disbelief of what had thundered through him. He needed to get this woman out of his house and out of his life before he plummeted over the edge and became the thing they both hated most.

He couldn't stand it if he ever hurt her or if she looked at him with disgust. If he stayed with her, both those things could come to pass.

Turning on his heel, he stormed across the room and threw the door open. Killean and Declan staggered away from him as the door rebounded off the wall. "Let's go!" he spat.

CHAPTER EIGHTEEN

N<small>OW THAT THEY</small>'<small>D</small> removed her blindfold, Kadence watched as the woods whipped by her at an extraordinary speed from the back seat of the SUV. Her skin was still electrified, the hair on her arms stood up from the lingering effects of Ronan's body pressed against hers. Her lips tingled with the reminder of his kiss. She had meant what she said, even if it upset him, no man would ever make her feel the way he did.

That was why she *almost* felt bad about what she planned to do.

Declan sat beside her, his brow furrowed as if in deep thought. Occasionally, he would glance between her and Ronan. Every time those impossibly silver eyes swung to her, she felt as if he stared straight into her soul, and she prayed he hadn't somehow figured out what she intended.

That was impossible. He would have told Ronan if he knew, and he'd definitely try to stop her, but he didn't say a word. He probably suspected that something had transpired between them and was curious about it. She was only being paranoid.

She met his gaze head on as he peered at her again. To her surprise, his mouth quirked into a small smile. Before she could decide what to make of that smile, he turned away from her to stare at Ronan in the seat before him.

"Here," Ronan commanded.

Killean pulled to the side of the back road. Kadence's heartbeat kicked up a notch as, before Killean could put the car in park, Ronan threw his door open and climbed out. She barely saw him through the heavily tinted windows as he stalked past Declan's door and made his way toward the back of the vehicle.

She jumped when the door next to Saxon swung open far sooner than she'd expected. Ronan stood outside of it, his large body filling the entire doorway.

Saxon slid out of the vehicle and shuffled past Ronan, who only moved back an inch or two to give Saxon the room to maneuver. Ronan's eyes were more red than brown when they met hers. He stepped aside and gestured for her to climb out. Kadence clutched her coat to her as she slid across the leather seat and exited the vehicle.

The January wind howled down the lonely road, causing the barren tree branches to click against each other, and the dress to billow around her calves. The frigid air wasn't cold enough to explain the ice creeping through her veins. Her hands trembled when she reached for the phone Ronan handed her. Most likely he would attribute her shaking to the winter night, but she knew it was because she had no idea how he would react to what she was about to do.

Ronan's fingers brushed hers before he jerked away as if she'd burned him. Kadence studied his face, trying to find some hint of the man who had kissed her with such intensity. She was met with a wall of stone.

What she planned to do now would infuriate the most powerful being she'd ever encountered. With one hand, he could break her neck between this heartbeat and the next. He wouldn't though, that much she knew. He might go on a tirade, but he would not harm her.

Kadence's eyes inadvertently darted toward Declan. He leaned against the side of the SUV as he stared at the woods with a look that said he'd rather be anywhere but here. He didn't look at her while he dipped into his pocket and pulled a lollipop free. She gawked at him as he opened it and popped the candy in his mouth before shoving the wrapper into his pocket.

What is a vamp doing eating a lollipop? She'd never seen anything so absurd as he twirled it in his mouth while remaining focused on the woods. Kadence had the feeling he was aware of her stare, but refused to acknowledge it.

Killean walked a little way down the dirt road, his eyes constantly searching the area around them. Saxon strode to the front of the vehicle and crossed his legs as he leaned against the hood. Lucien must have returned to wherever else he was staying, something she was grateful for now.

For the first time, she considered how they would *all* react to what she was about to do. They would be as angry, if not angrier, than Ronan. She looked back to Declan again. He turned toward her and gave a barely perceptible nod.

Kadence nearly dropped the phone. He *did* know! Somehow, he knew or suspected what she planned to do. That knowledge was more than a little unnerving, yet she found her confidence growing as her shoulders relaxed a little. He either believed it would all be okay, or he was trying to get her killed. Whichever it was didn't matter, she was going through with this.

"Call your brother!" Ronan ordered.

Kadence scowled at him, not at all pleased with the command or the tone of his voice. "I'm not yours to order around!" she retorted and held his gaze when a muscle in his cheek twitched and a vein appeared in his forehead.

After a minute of tense silence, Kadence turned away from him and flipped the phone open. Her fingers felt thick as she punched in the last number she'd had for Nathan. It took three tries before she finally got the number right. She stared at the screen as she waited for something to happen, but nothing did. Knowing she must have missed something, she searched the phone for the answer.

Ronan winced when he realized that Kadence wasn't familiar with cell phones. The hunters kept her so sheltered that she only had a rudimentary knowledge of things that most took for granted. Before he could intervene to show her what to do, she hit the send button and lifted the phone to her ear.

Holding her breath, Kadence closed her eyes as she waited for her brother to answer. "Who is this?" Nathan demanded after the fifth ring.

Kadence winced at the raw anger coming across the phone even as love and sorrow swelled within her. She took a deep breath to steady her wire-taut nerves before plunging in. "It's me, Nathan."

"Kadence! Thank God! Are you okay? *Where are you?*"

Guilt burrowed into her at the relief in her brother's voice. She would have given almost anything to ease the anguish she heard, to see him one more time, but she couldn't, she *wouldn't*, give up her freedom again. One thing she'd realized after Ronan's kiss was that life was too short to continue to do as she'd always done. There were so many new experiences out there for her, and she wanted all of them.

She'd rot in the stronghold; she'd die someone far different from the woman she was now if she went back, and she couldn't do it.

"I'm fine, Nathan, really."

"Where are you? What happened?"

Kadence glanced over her shoulder. All the vampires were staring at anything other than her, but she knew they were listening to every word she was saying. "After what happened in the alley, I ran, and I kept running."

"To where?" he demanded. "Where are you? Tell me and I'll come get you."

"No."

The silence on the other end stretched on for a full minute before her brother spoke again. "What do you mean, *no*?"

"I ran as far as I could, and I'm not coming back!" she blurted before she completely lost her nerve. She had no idea what she would do with her life now. That knowledge should terrify her; instead, she felt like a baby bird spreading its wings for the first time, and she nearly laughed aloud from the free-falling experience of plunging out of the nest.

Saxon gawked at her as he turned toward her. Killean's head swiveled on his shoulder, as he leveled her with the stare of a snake ready to strike. A small smile curved Declan's lips and he tossed the lollipop aside. Ronan's breath exploded from him as he whirled toward her.

"What?" Nathan yelled into the phone. "Have you lost your mind? Where are you? I'm coming to get you *right now*! You can't survive out there on your own!"

Kadence grimaced and started moving backward when Ronan came toward her. His eyes became a more vibrant red with every step he took. She couldn't let him get his hands on the phone; he would tell her brother everything if he did. He would make her go back.

"I'm not coming back!" Kadence gushed into the phone. "I'm sorry, Nathan. I can't be what you need me to be, and I want to see, to learn, to *experience*. Please forgive me, and tell Logan this has nothing to do with him. I'll call you as soon as I can. I'll be all right. I love you."

"Kadence!" Nathan's shout resonated through the phone as she pulled it away from her ear and snapped it in half.

"*What are you doing?*"

Kadence jumped at Ronan's bellowed words. He wasn't mad. He was *irate*!

"Give me that phone." The steady calm of Ronan's command unnerved her more than if he'd yelled again.

Kadence shook her head, her hair flying around her face. "No," she managed to choke out.

Shock briefly registered on his face before his wrath blazed back to life. He looked mad enough to strangle her.

"Give me that phone," he growled.

"I... I broke it," she stammered.

"Then you will give me his number and I will call him back."

Kadence jumped back as he grabbed at her. She spun to flee, but his hand snagged her coat and he pulled her against him. The air in her lungs rushed out of her when her back crashed into his solid chest. His grip on her instantly gentled, though she remained firmly trapped against him.

She had no idea if he'd somehow be able to get the number off the broken phone. She released the remains of the phone and stomped them beneath her feet. The satisfying crack of the material sounded seconds before he spun her to face him.

Ronan's face was inches from hers as he gripped her upper arms. His lips skimmed back to reveal the lethal points of his fangs. Despite his furious countenance and the lethalness of him, she still didn't believe he would attack her.

Ronan had no idea how to react to what she'd done. Part of him wanted to shake her for disobeying him when *no one* else did. The other part wanted to hug her close. Had she told her brother that because of him? Did she want to stay with *him*?

He shut the hope down. It wouldn't be possible, no matter what. His life was far too treacherous for her to stay with him. She had to go back, or at least go somewhere away from him.

"What are you doing?" he demanded.

Kadence lifted her chin as she met his stare. She'd made her choice, she wouldn't back down from it now.

"From the second I was born, my entire life has been plotted out for me. I've resented it, I've rebelled against it, but I still followed along with that plan. I succeeded in breaking free of the stronghold, and I was going to return to it. I was going to allow myself to be married off, to be caged again, because I'm afraid of what is out here.

"However, I refuse to be a coward. I'm letting my people and family down by doing this, but I'm free, and I have to see what is out here. Once the monster who killed my father is dead, I will go out and experience all the things I've read and dreamt about my entire life. Maybe one day I'll return to the stronghold, but today is not that day. My brother has no idea I'm with you, he knows I'm alive, and believes I'm free, so the hunters won't blame vampires for my disappearance. I made sure of that."

For the first time in his life, Ronan had *no* idea what to do. Forcing her back to her people would destroy her, but so would keeping her locked up with him. He couldn't just turn her loose on the streets. With her beauty and naiveté, the humans would eat her alive. He loathed all of the options, but she would be safest with the hunters.

He tore his eyes away from her and looked over her shoulder to Killean, who had retrieved the broken pieces of the phone. "Give them to me."

Killean's hand stretched over her shoulder and Ronan released her to take the phone. Kadence couldn't bring herself to look at the device for fear she hadn't destroyed it as badly as she'd hoped. Ronan stared at the pieces in his hand as she held her breath and waited.

"Shit!" he exploded.

Kadence jumped as he spun away from her and heaved the phone into the woods. The remains shattered off a tree with a crack of mechanical bits. Kadence stiffened her spine, refusing to be intimidated by him when he turned back to her.

"I am not going back there. You can't make me, so leave me here," she said coldly.

His hand swallowed her bicep when he clasped her arm and dragged her toward the SUV. Declan stepped toward them, but he didn't try to intervene. Kadence dug her heels into the asphalt to stop Ronan as he pulled her onward.

Her attempt was as futile as a gnat trying to stop a raging rhino. "Stop it! Let me go!"

He didn't stop. Without thinking, she kicked him in the back of his calf. Her mouth dropped open as he spun toward her. She couldn't believe she'd done that, but she couldn't take it back now. He stared at her with his full lips compressed into a flat line and a look that said he might splat her like a fly. Despite her possible impending splatting, Kadence ripped her arm free of his grasp and glowered back at him.

Ronan took a step toward her, but she didn't back away. Meeting him toe to toe, she stuck out her chin. Her insolence maddened him, yet he couldn't help admiring her. She was strong, but nowhere near as strong as the vampires standing here. *None* of them would dare to stand up to him in such a way.

"You are going back to your brother," he stated.

"No. I. Am. Not," she enunciated clearly.

She didn't think he'd ever been denied before if the look on his face was any indication, and she'd done it twice in less than three minutes. She could almost feel the breeze of the flyswatter over her head, but she wouldn't back down from this.

"You are going to do what I tell you to do," he said as if this would resolve the issue.

"The hell I am! You have no say over me or my life. And yes, this is *my* life; I finally get to have one! I don't expect you to understand, but I am not going back there. I won't give up this opportunity. I know it's selfish, I know it's insensitive to my people, but I must do this *for me*. This may be the only chance I ever have to be free, and if I waste it, I will hate myself for the rest of my life.

"The hunters will not come for you; they will come for *me*. There will still be a lot of them looking for Joseph, but once he's dead, things will calm down again. I will not let you take this chance from me!"

CHAPTER NINETEEN

Ronan couldn't deny the sway of her impassioned words. What awaited her at the stronghold wasn't the life he wanted for her. He would prefer to keep her with him, but that would be impossible. If any of his enemies learned of her, they would go after her to take him down.

And then he also had to worry about himself around her. If he turned Savage, Kadence's life may be the first one he took.

No, he hated what awaited her at the stronghold, but she was safest there. She'd be a broodmare, but she'd be alive and protected. Best of all, he wouldn't be able to find her again and she would be safe from *him*.

"You have to go back to your family," he told her, his voice softening at the desperation in her eyes.

"No, I don't."

"What do you plan to do?" he demanded. "You have no money, no ID, and no job prospects. You have nothing."

She pointed a finger at him as she yelled at him. "You are wrong. I will have my freedom!"

Lowering his head into his hand, he rubbed the bridge of his nose as he tried to decide what to do with her. He couldn't leave her here as she'd asked; she'd never survive on her own. But then, maybe she'd smarten up and return to her family if he did drive away. That was if she didn't get herself killed or raped first. At least if she'd returned to her brother he would have known she was safe. He couldn't leave her here without knowing what had become of her.

Lifting his head, he met her steely gaze. "I can't leave you here."

She grabbed his arms, squeezing them as her fingers dug into him. "You owe me *nothing*, Ronan. Let me do this!"

"I will not leave you here! You'll never survive in this world. You are too much of an innocent. Some of the human race is as bad as the worst of my kind. The humans may not be as strong or fast as you, but they can still destroy you."

Kadence contained her rising temper over his condescending words. Shouting at him now wouldn't help her situation at all. Only reason would break through his stubborn façade. He was right, she was over her head in many ways, but she'd made it out of the stronghold, she would figure this out too. She'd have to take it one day at a time, but she needed that first day in order to start living her own life.

"I am very strong, capable, and intelligent. I *can* survive," she replied.

"This world will destroy you."

"No—"

"Enough! You are not staying here and that is final!"

Kadence gaped at him in disbelief. "But—"

He started dragging her forward again, completely ignoring the protests she sputtered. Killean's golden eyes narrowed to slits as she was pulled past him. Declan held the back door open, a nonchalant look plastered on his handsome face. He barely glanced at her as Ronan pushed her into the SUV, climbed in beside her, and slammed the door.

Kadence was about to scramble out the other side when that door opened and Saxon slid in. He looked completely baffled as he stared at her.

"Where to?" Killean inquired gruffly when he settled into the driver's seat.

"Head back to the mansion; we'll figure something out there," Ronan commanded.

"Leave me here," Kadence said. "I'm not your responsibility."

Ronan glowered at her. "Never going to happen."

She fell back against the seat and hunched her shoulders to avoid touching him and Saxon as she silently fumed over his refusal to set her free. After ten minutes of driving, Ronan slid a blindfold over her eyes. She stiffened at his touch and fought the impulse to slap his hand away. A few minutes later, they came to a stop. Ronan pulled the blindfold off her and climbed out of the vehicle. He held the door for her, but didn't look at her.

Kadence glared at him as she stepped out of the SUV. Finally, she tore her attention away to focus on the building looming over her. She'd been blindfolded when she'd been led outside earlier so she hadn't seen it, and she wished she hadn't seen it now.

The place was a monstrosity. No one ever would have guessed the spartan beauty of the inside by the ugliness of the outside. The mansion towered into the night sky, its peaks and turrets looking like something straight out of a gothic novel. The huge gargoyles on the peaks and outside the doorways didn't help that image at all. Bars covered all the arched windows, the front door was painted black, and the entire place had been built using a dreary, gray stone. Long wings fanned out behind the building and to the sides of the main structure.

It was the largest building she'd ever seen, and the ugliest.

"Doesn't meet your fine standards?" Ronan murmured in her ear.

"Really trying to uphold that Dracula image, aren't you?" she retorted.

A spark of humor crossed his face before he buried it. "Get inside."

Kadence snorted, but did as he said, mainly because the place unnerved her. She was almost to the front door when it opened. Her hand flew to her heart as she jumped back into Ronan's massive chest.

Killean's low laugh came from behind her. "You should be scared."

She shot him a dirty look, straightened her shoulders, and strode forward. A tall man stood inside the foyer, his hand resting on the doorknob. Gray speckled his brown hair at his temples, and a pair of round spectacles were perched crookedly on the tip of his large nose. He offered her a small smile before sweeping low in a grand bow.

"Good evening, madam. May I take your coat?"

Kadence almost tripped over her own feet when she came to an abrupt halt. They had a butler? Yes, apparently they did, and he was staring at her expectantly. "Um, yeah." She slid it off and handed it over to him.

"We'll be in the poolroom, Baldric, if you could please bring some food for the human," Ronan instructed.

His icy tone caused a shiver to run down her spine. She'd never heard him sound so distant and reserved. He'd been kind to her before, but she might have pushed him to a breaking point with her actions tonight. Well too bad, because she wasn't exactly jumping for joy right now either.

"Of course, sir," Baldric replied.

Ronan clasped her arm, leading her across the foyer and down the hall. She allowed him to pull her along, mainly because she didn't know what else to do. She was trapped here, with them. Maybe she should have gone home after all.

The second the idea crossed her mind, she buried it. They couldn't keep her here forever, and she couldn't think of any way they could find her brother without risking a fight. Hopefully, they couldn't think of one either.

Ronan paused outside a set of wooden doors and slid them open to reveal the sumptuous room beyond. Red velvet couches were set on either side of a beautiful red and gold oriental rug. She'd never seen anything like these couches with their etched wood backs and arms. The dainty legs barely looked strong enough to support her weight, never mind the weight of any of the vampires spreading out to stand in the room.

Two large pool tables with their smooth green surfaces were set in the middle of the room. One had balls scattered across the top of it. The numerous arching windows in the room were covered with sheer, crimson curtains and each had a red window seat. A bar lined the entire back wall; the large mirror behind it reflected light onto a multitude of liquor bottles. Like all the other rooms, the walls in here were bare. Nothing in this room fit any of these men except for maybe the pool tables and the bar, if vampires drank liquor.

"Sit."

Kadence frowned at Ronan's rude tone, but moved toward one of the couches. She'd read about settees in a few books and imagined this is what the author must have been describing as she carefully perched on the edge of one. Settling her dress, she folded her hands demurely in her lap. She plastered the look of serenity, the one that had managed to get her through so many boring days in the stronghold, on her face.

Ronan strode past her, and moments later she heard the clatter of a glass behind the bar and liquid being poured into it. *Guess that answers my question about vampires and liquor*, she thought.

Killean and Saxon followed Ronan, but Declan walked over to one of the windows and leaned against the wall beside it. Baldric wheeled in a cart loaded with all sorts of food. Kadence's stomach grumbled and saliva filled her mouth. She hadn't realized how famished she was until then. Baldric swept out of the room, closing the doors behind him. Kadence licked her lips, itching to get her hands on some of the food.

"Eat," Ronan said from where he stood by the bar.

Her pride wanted her to refuse to eat anything from him, but her common sense told her she was an idiot if she starved herself to be spiteful.

Climbing to her feet, she made her way to the cart. She loaded a plate with cheeses, crackers, sliced meats, fruits, and vegetables. She munched on the food as she made her way back to her seat.

Kadence was finishing the last bite when Ronan started in. "You can't stay here. It is too risky."

Putting her plate down on the table beside her, she wiped her hands on her napkin while she bided for time to regain her mask of composure. "I never asked to stay here. If you do recall, I was quite satisfied with staying on the side of the road. Plus, I'm sure you have enough security around here to keep anyone from getting in or me from escaping." Though, if she figured out the stronghold, she'd figure out this place too.

Ronan cursed loudly, and liquid sloshed out of his glass when he set it on the bar. Kadence remained stoic as she turned to face him. "That is not what I meant!" he snapped.

"Then what exactly did you mean?"

His jaw locked, but he didn't answer her. A new, disturbing possibility occurred to her. Did he mean *he* was the threat to her?

Before she could question him, Declan stepped forward. "I'm sure she'll be perfectly safe here until we can figure something out."

"You can't be serious!" Killean retorted. "For all we know she could be spying on us, just waiting to give the hunters information about us."

"Oh come on, Killean, even you know that is ridiculous," Saxon drawled.

"She doesn't belong here and we all know it," Killean spat.

"We can't put her out on the street," Declan said.

"No we can't, and until she comes to her senses, she will stay here," Ronan said and shook his head as if he were annoyed with a child.

Kadence's mask of serenity slipped. "I have come to my senses! You have no right or reason to interfere in my life!"

"She's right," Killean said. "Put her out on the street, let her get killed. It's no loss to us. Besides, she'll probably call her brother and beg him to come get her within in an hour of being on her own."

"Fuck you!" Kadence shouted as she leapt to her feet.

She threw a hand over her mouth when she realized what she'd said, but his disdain had infuriated her into reacting before she could stop herself. She'd rarely heard swears from her father and brother. Occasionally, she'd said a few in private, testing out how they would feel on her tongue, but she'd never said one in front of others before. It was not appropriate for the women in the stronghold to curse, and she'd never heard another female utter one.

She had to admit it felt… *good*. Especially considering it was Killean she'd said it to. She wouldn't mind staking the guy.

Killean snorted. "I'd bet that's the first time you've ever said that going by your reaction. I was wrong, you'll be crying and calling your brother in five minutes."

She opened her mouth to tell him where to go with that, but Ronan spoke first. "I won't have her death on my conscience. She'll stay."

Her eyes swung to him, and for the first time in her life, she wanted to claw the eyes out of someone. "I can take care of myself!"

"It will be okay." Declan touched her arm as he offered her some reassurance.

She'd been so focused on the two complete asses in the room that she hadn't realized he'd approached her. She smiled hesitatingly at him, grateful for his reassurance. He was the only one who didn't seem to hate her for what she'd done.

A low growl emanated through the room. Before she could

comprehend where the sound had come from, Ronan stalked toward them. Declan's hand slipped away and he stepped hastily away from her.

Ronan inserted himself between them, his hand encircling her upper arm as he moved her away from his friend. She frowned at him as she tried to figure out where his strange aggression toward Declan had come from. Declan edged further away, his eyes twinkling with an amusement Kadence didn't understand.

"I'll have Marta and Baldric set up one of the rooms for her," Ronan said.

Despite her continued annoyance with Ronan for denying her freedom, a twinge of disappointment went through her. She should be grateful they were going to be in separate rooms while she remained here. Grateful he was giving her at least some distance.

She didn't feel at all grateful though. She'd never admit it to him, but she'd enjoyed sleeping beside him.

She tugged on her arm to get him to release her. She had to put some distance between them if she was going to break free of this odd pull he had over her. He let her go.

"The three of you get ready to go out for the night," he said to the others. "We'll go hunting as soon as our guest is situated."

Kadence scoffed. "Let's not pretend I'm anything other than a prisoner here."

He shot her a dark look, which she returned. "That was the choice you made when you pulled your little stunt earlier."

CHAPTER TWENTY

RONAN LED Kadence to the room Baldric and his wife, Marta, had readied for her. He cursed inwardly when he realized they'd prepared the room next to his. The covers on the bed were already pulled back for her. Marta had managed to find more women's clothes close to her size. They hung neatly in the wardrobe, the doors left open so Kadence would know they were there.

"I'm sure there are fresh towels and shampoo in the bathroom," he said to her.

Kadence walked around the room before stopping to examine the clothes inside the wardrobe. "Whose are these?"

Ronan shrugged. "I don't know. I suppose various women may have left them here."

"You have that many women coming through here that you can't remember their names or what they wore?" she demanded, unprepared for the flare of anger that realization brought with it. He was a vampire, he was old, he'd probably had countless women in his lifetime, but she did *not* want to be wearing their clothes!

Ronan leaned against the doorway as he surveyed her. He thought he'd detected a hint of jealousy in her tone, but her face remained blank. "I have had no women come through here, none of us have yet."

"Then where did the clothes come from?"

"Left behind by the previous owners."

"Why would they leave their clothes behind?"

"Because they left in a rush," he replied.

Kadence gazed at him and then the clothes in confusion. Some of the dresses and shirts were really pretty. It wasn't her style, she'd always worn simpler clothing, usually a plain skirt with a blouse, but sometimes she'd worn pants or a cotton dress. White, gray, or black were their options in the stronghold.

She had to admit, she was looking forward to trying on some of these more colorful clothes. Her fingers itched to pull the orange skirt and bright pink tank top out. It didn't matter they didn't match; they were so colorful!

"Why did they leave in such a hurry? What happened to them?"

Ronan really didn't want to give her any answers, not after what she'd pulled earlier, but he found himself reluctant to leave her here.

He wasn't going to tell her that they traveled so often they had numerous bases of location, none of them as ostentatious or ugly as this one. Most were simple homes, some condos, a few cottages, and a couple of chateaus and wineries that were more investment properties. He'd spent so little time in any of those places that he could barely recall any of them.

The only problem was that Joseph knew about most of those places. It had been many years since they'd had a central base of location, but they spent most of their time on the East Coast as that was where the training facility was located. The training facility had never been the Defender's main home, but they had wanted to be near it to help train the recruits if they had the time, which they rarely did. With Joseph turning and staying near the area, this place had become their first central base of operations in nearly a century.

Right now, Baldric and Marta were working on selling the rest of their numerous properties and purchasing new ones. If the new properties didn't come heavily secured, as this one had, they were having security systems installed in them. Ronan had instructed them to sell all of his personal properties too. Joseph didn't know where they were located, but it was time to make some changes.

The only property they'd considered retaining was the training compound, but that plan had changed. Before Lucien returned to the facility, Ronan had ordered him to get everyone prepared to leave it and asked Baldric to sell the old one and find a suitable new location. If Joseph was organizing the Savages, they couldn't take the risk he would be brave enough or strong enough to attack the training facility. There were a fair number of vampires who could fight there, but not enough to survive an onslaught of Savages.

He couldn't take the chance of losing their fighters now.

He hadn't told the others yet, but he was also contemplating bringing some of the turned vampire recruits into their group. The Defenders had been composed of purebreds ever since the creation of vampires, but these were precarious times and sticking with tradition may get them all killed.

It was a decision he was loathe to make, as he did not want to break with the old ways, but the world had changed vastly since the laws of the Defenders were first laid down.

"What happened to the previous owners of these clothes?" Kadence asked again, drawing Ronan's attention back to her.

"Nothing happened to them. We simply made them an offer on this place they couldn't refuse, not even with all of their money."

She released the orange skirt and stepped away from the closet. "I don't understand."

"We wanted this place, so we offered the previous owners far more than it was worth. Under the conditions that they vacate within two days and leave the furniture behind," he replied.

"*That's* why all the walls are bare and none of the furniture or really anything here goes with any of your personalities. Why did you want this place so badly?"

"It was heavily secured and Joseph doesn't know about it."

"I see," she murmured as she gazed at the bare walls. "Did Baldric and Marta come with the place? And by the way, who is Marta?"

"Marta is Baldric's wife; they've been married for almost thirty years. No, they did not come with the place. Baldric's family has been with mine for over two thousand years. When the family member who works with me passes, a new one takes over."

"So they're your slaves?"

"Hardly," he retorted. "It is their choice to stay and work. They are free to go at any time, as are their children. They know if they ever reveal anything, they will be slaughtered outright, but they also know few would believe them. I trust each one of them to uphold their family's history. When Marta and Baldric pass on or retire, their son Lamont has already chosen to take over for them. He has been out traveling the world, but he will join us when he's ready to learn about the estates and how things work."

"Why do they chose to stay and be your help?" she asked.

"They are far more than my *help*," he grated. "They are extremely well taken care of, as is their whole family, and they are as much my family as Killean, Lucien, Saxon, and Declan."

"I see," she murmured. "Why has his family worked with yours for so long?"

"The very first vampire king, my ancestor, saved Baldric's ancestor from an attack by a Savage. Instead of the king changing the man's memories, when the man asked to serve the king to repay the debt, the king agreed to it. It was only supposed to be that man, but his son stepped forward, and then the next, and so on. Over the years, many men and women have served the vampire kings who have risen and fallen. They have all had the option of moving on, but at least one member of their family has chosen to remain working with my bloodline until now they work for me."

"Amazing," she breathed. "And your bloodline leads the vampires?"

"That is the way it always was."

"So you are the vampire king?"

"No."

"Why not?"

He contemplated his answer as she stared at him curiously. He shouldn't be telling her anything after earlier, but he couldn't deny that it pleased him that she wanted to learn more about him, and none of what he would tell her could be used against them.

"At one time, there was a ruling vampire senate and a king. All turned and purebred vampires who weren't Savage were organized and ruled by that government. My father was the last king to rule. I was supposed to claim the crown when he died. However, the battle that took my parents also took most of the senate and the king's followers. After the conflict, there were few vampires left to rule over."

"How awful," she murmured. "What happened to cause such a thing?"

He preferred not to think about it, but he found himself having a difficult time denying her.

"It was a battle no one saw coming until it was too late. A Savage vamp, one who had been a member of the senate and a purebred vampire before giving in to the bloodlust, organized the other Savages. They prepared an attack against all those who hunted them. When they realized what was happening, the senate and my father gathered as many Defenders and other vampires as they could to counteract the growing threat, but it was already too late. The ensuing battle left the number of vampires decimated, especially the purebred ones."

He didn't reveal to her that those numbers had never recovered in the nearly thousand years since the battle. Few vampires reproduced, unless they were of the royal line and required an heir, and that practice had fallen away after the war with the Savages. Other vampires found their mates over the years and wanted to have children with them, but mates were a sporadic thing and sometimes even mated vamps didn't want offspring.

To this day, he only knew of a little over a hundred purebreds in existence. Their numbers were growing, but not fast enough. If there were other purebreds alive that he didn't know about, they weren't many. Ronan sighed and ran a hand through his hair as he thought back to the stark night that had forever altered his world.

"So much time has passed since then," he murmured, "but I can clearly recall standing on that field and gazing out at the thousands of bodies surrounding me. Blood soaked the ground so much that the dirt no longer absorbed it, and it turned the green field into a lake of red."

Kadence realized he was stuck in the past, haunted by the memories when his unseeing gaze focused on the wall behind her. Sorrow swelled within her as she watched him. She didn't know how long ago it had been, but it was clear that battle had forged him into the man he was now, and it still haunted him.

"I found my parents amongst the carnage. My mother was decapitated, but my father had been torn to shreds, and bits and pieces of him were scattered across the earth. The stench of their blood stuck in my nostrils as I stepped over the bodies of the many vampires who raised me, yelled at me, trained me, and laughed with me."

Kadence's hand flew to her mouth as she stifled a cry over what he had witnessed and how much he had lost. He would not want her sadness, and she knew he would stop speaking if he believed she was giving him any kind of pity. And she didn't pity him; she admired him and understood him far better. He'd survived something horrific, yet he continued to fight every day for his kind. Her heart swelled with emotion. Despite her anger with him for bringing her back here, all she wanted was to hold him against her and try to soothe the lingering grief she sensed in him.

"Everything I'd ever known before then was slaughtered on that field, my life forever altered, my hatred of the Savages secured," Ronan recalled. Yet, he still teetered on becoming one of them no matter how much he despised them.

"Were you hurt?" she asked when he stopped speaking.

He tore his eyes away from the wall to focus on her. "My arm had been nearly severed by a broadsword and hung on by a thread of muscle. I had more cuts and stab wounds than I could ever count, but somehow, I survived. I left Ireland the following week, and I've never stayed longer than a week the few times I've returned to my homeland."

"And the Savages who attacked you, what became of them?"

"They were all slaughtered in the war, but not before the number of vampires on both sides were wiped out to the point of near extinction.

"How many vampires survived?" she asked.

"Myself and fifteen others. Some of the survivors were turned vamps, and some were purebreds, but only one other purebred was a Defender, and I was the only one with royal blood who survived, so most of our old ways were lost after the war."

"What happened to those survivors?" Kadence inquired.

"Some turned Savage and had to be destroyed, others were taken out by hunters, and some were killed by other vampires. Before they died though, those survivors turned humans, or had children of their own to keep the vampire race from going extinct. I am the only one who remains of the original survivors."

Kadence's heart twisted and tears unwittingly sprang into her eyes. Her life in the stronghold had been lonely, but so had Ronan's. She couldn't imagine what it must be like to be the only one who remembered such an awful event, or the time before it occurred, when things had been far different for him.

"Who was the other Defender that survived?" she asked.

"Declan's father, Aengus. He'd been my toughest and most demanding instructor while I was going through Defender training. After, he became one of my closest friends."

"What happened to him?"

"He left Ireland with me and we worked together until he turned Savage about forty years after Declan was born. I killed him so that Declan wouldn't have to."

Kadence bit on her lip to keep from gasping at that revelation. Ronan's gaze was challenging as he stared at her, almost as if he dared her to condemn him for it.

"That must have been very difficult for you to do," she whispered, feeling like she'd uttered a *huge* understatement.

Ronan clamped his teeth and gave a brisk nod as the memory of destroying Aengus played through his mind. He'd never thought it possible that Aengus would ever succumb to his darker nature. Ronan had believed him to be far stronger than that; believed Aengus to be a better man than him. He'd been wrong.

Killing Aengus had been the most difficult thing he'd ever done. Aengus had been his last tie to a life all but forgotten by the other vampires, his closest advisor and friend, but his death had been necessary. The destruction Aengus wrought before his death had caused a panic amongst the humans, and Declan hadn't been physically strong enough to kill his father at the time, even if he had wanted to be the one to do it, which he hadn't.

"It was very difficult," he murmured.

"Declan doesn't hold any anger towards you for it."

"He understands it had to be done and that I didn't enjoy having to be the one who did it. Now, I have a feeling history might be trying to repeat itself and that the Savages are organizing," he said.

Her mouth parted and her eyes widened as realization sank in. "Joseph and those vamps who arrived to help him."

"Yes."

"Can you bring in more vampires to help fight him?"

"I can and I will, but there are many who have remained scattered over the years. Many who don't even know their true heritage, or that there are Defenders amongst them, or that the ones who fall to the bloodlust are called Savages. As long as a vampire doesn't turn Savage, they have no reason to know we work to keep them safe from the worst of our kind."

He hadn't helped with the lack of knowledge most vampires possessed. Because they had become so scattered over the years, he hadn't bothered to regroup them or try to educate them. He simply hadn't seen a reason to inform the turned vampires he knew, and the purebreds who knew all their history and their ways were Defenders.

However, those who did know of his existence looked to him as their leader. He was the eldest of their kind, the most powerful, and not just because of his age, but also his breeding and lineage. No other purebred such as himself had ever existed in the history of vampires.

"They know nothing of what you do, yet you still protect them," she said.

"And I will until the day I die." *Or have to be destroyed,* but he kept that to himself.

"You are one of these Defenders?"

"Yes."

"What does that mean?"

"From the time I was old enough to learn how, I've been trained in fighting and war and how to protect my kind. Defenders are the best trained purebred warriors who uphold the vampire laws, and they track down the Savages in order to keep the innocents safe."

"So, you have sacrificed your freedom and happiness for the vampires, and they don't even know it," she whispered.

"I have sacrificed nothing; I have chosen my course in life. I may not be the king as my father was, but I will keep vampires and humans protected from the Savages. I don't have to be king to fulfill that duty."

"How old were you when the battle against the Savages happened?"

"It was less than a year after I reached maturity, so twenty-eight."

"What do you mean by reached maturity?"

"When a purebred stops aging and starts to really come into their vampire powers. I stopped aging later than most vampires do, but I was more powerful than many of them before then."

"I see," she said. "How old are you now?"

"I was born a vampire one thousand twenty-three years ago."

Kadence gawked at him. "You're exactly a thousand years older than me!"

"I feel every one of those thousand years," he replied.

"Amazing," she murmured. "In all that time, you have never felt the sun on your skin without pain. Have you ever seen it?"

The sadness in her tone tugged at his heart. He opened his mouth to tell her he could walk freely through the day, but stopped himself. She would most likely still be going back to her brother. "I have seen the sun," he replied, unwilling to lie to her.

"Would you like me to tell you about it?" she asked.

His heart leapt in his chest as he gazed at her. Despite the rod of steel going down her spine, she was achingly sweet and innocent. He had never imagined anyone could be like her. He didn't know what he'd done to deserve her throwing his life into a tailspin, but he was suddenly thankful she had.

"Maybe someday, but not tonight."

She crossed her hands before her, but he was not fooled by the demure gesture. There was nothing demure about this little hunter.

"It is only the five of you who fight?" she inquired.

"No, there are others who are not Defenders who also fight the Savages. Some of them train with us to become better at it, and others do it on their own."

"Why has your family always led? Why were you supposed to lead?"

"Like your bloodline amongst the hunters, my line is the strongest and I am also the only vampire still alive who can trace my line back to the original demon offspring. I am the first vampire in existence that is fifth generation purebred. Most are only first generation purebreds, some are two, and a couple are three, but that is all."

"I see," she murmured.

Kadence moved away from the wardrobe and walked over to the king-sized bed as she tried to process everything he told her. She didn't think that would ever be possible. At least now she understood better what drove him and why he could be so demanding and unbending. Now she also knew why he emanated such a vast amount of power.

"Would you let me come with you to hunt Joseph?" she inquired.

"No."

"I have every right to be there."

Ronan's nostrils flared. She could see the outline of his fangs behind his lips as he watched her. "You are a mortal. You have no training—"

"I was taught to defend myself in the stronghold, and I can expertly handle numerous weapons!" she interrupted.

"Let me guess, you can kill a stuffed dummy with ease," he drawled. "You have no training where it counts, in the field. The hunters failed you in that. You will be more of a hindrance out there than an asset, and I refuse to put my men in danger to satisfy your vendetta."

Kadence opened her mouth to protest, but he was right and she knew it. She'd left the stronghold thinking she had the training to fend off any vampire. Joseph had proved her completely wrong.

"And you also don't want me there because I'm a woman," she said bitterly.

Ronan snorted. "I know women are just as capable as men when it comes to inflicting damage and death. This is because you are not prepared."

"Will you… will you teach me? Prepare me?" she asked and held her breath as she waited for his rejection.

Ronan studied her as he tried to decide what to do. "I will until we find a way to return you," he replied. "I'd rather have you actually *able* to protect yourself rather than just thinking you can. That will only get you killed faster."

"Gee thanks," she muttered.

"It's the truth. I think you'll find all you need for tonight. If you do need something else, Marta or Baldric will be happy to help you," he said as he turned toward the door.

"Do you have any books?"

He stopped in the doorway. "Books?"

She smiled at him, an amused gleam in her azure eyes. "Yes, you know, bound paper you read from. My sleeping habits are much like yours and I often stay up all night."

"There is a library downstairs. I will ask Marta to show it to you."

"Thank you."

"I'll send her up."

"Ronan." Her voice stopped him from leaving again. The light cascading over her lit her pale hair and emphasized the curves of her willowy frame. He found himself growing aroused as he gazed at her. "Be careful tonight."

The words rocked him. No one had said those words to him before, and the fact it was her…

She's leaving, he reminded himself. His jaw locked as he stormed out the door. Stalking into his room, he slammed the door closed with so much force it shook the frame, but it did nothing to ease his frustration.

Changing into a pair of black pants and a black shirt, he strapped on some stakes, a crossbow, and slipped two daggers into the holsters at his sides. He never wore so much weaponry while hunting, but after what he'd seen with Joseph and the Savages, he wasn't taking any chances.

He slipped his coat on, effectively covering the weapons before he left his room. Kadence's door was closed when he walked past it to the stairs, but her scent still floated to him.

Killean and Saxon waited for him by the door. "Where's Declan?" he asked of them.

"Still in the poolroom the last I saw him," Saxon replied.

"Wait here."

He turned away from them and strode toward the poolroom. He found Declan leaning against the bar with a snifter of whiskey in hand. Declan rested his elbow on the bar while he gazed out the window. Ronan didn't know all of Declan's secrets, but he did know his friend had a special affinity for knowing or at least sensing things.

"Did you know she didn't intend to return home?" Ronan demanded.

Declan didn't look at him as he responded with his usual self-assurance. "I had my suspicions she was up to something."

Ronan grit his teeth. "Why didn't you try to stop her, or warn me about what you suspected?"

"It's not my place to interfere with someone else's life," Declan replied. "Nor was it my place to clip her wings; everyone deserves a chance to fly."

"Declan—"

"It's too late now, Ronan. She's here. I thought you would be happy about it."

"What are you talking about?" Ronan snarled. "Why would I be happy a *hunter* is still in our house?"

Declan casually swirled the amber liquid in his glass. "If she had told her brother a place to meet her, would you have let her go?"

"Of course."

Declan gazed at him before taking a sip of his whiskey. "You say that because she is here now, but we both know you're lying. You would have kept her."

Ronan was across the room between one heartbeat and the next. Lifting Declan by the throat, Ronan smashed his back against the bar and bent the larger man backward. "I realize that you have your own way of doing things, but this is the first and the *last* time you will go against me in anything, do you understand me?"

Declan lifted his hands in a pacifying gesture. It was the first time Ronan had ever laid a hand on any of his friends in anger, yet Declan didn't seem surprised. "Yes."

Ronan released him. Pacing away, he ran his hands through his hair as he tried to understand what had happened. He'd never believed he'd ever attack one of his friends, unless they turned Savage, but there had been a moment when he'd truly contemplated sinking his fangs into Declan's throat and feasting on him. A good kill would help to calm him.

"It's time to hunt," he said and turned away.

"Ronan." He stopped and looked over his shoulder at Declan. "You may not believe me, but I did not go against you in this. One day I hope you will get the chance to see I did this for you. Killean, Lucien, and Saxon, they haven't been here long enough to know."

"To know what?" Ronan demanded.

"That at one time your eyes were entirely brown. That they've changed over the centuries."

It was true. Ronan didn't just feel the madness creeping over him, he *saw* it every time he looked in the mirror. "What is your point, Declan?" he bit out.

"We all fight our more malevolent side every day. Because of your lineage, you fight it more than the rest of us. I've watched you descend into the darkness more and more over the years, but for one brief second in the alley, when you first held Kadence against you, your eyes were entirely brown again."

"You're losing your mind."

Declan lifted a shoulder and finished off the rest of his whiskey. "I think we all are, but I also think we're coming to a head with something."

"With what?"

Declan set the glass on the bar, lifted his bomber jacket, and slid it on. "That I do not know. Now, let's kill something. It will make us all feel better."

CHAPTER TWENTY-ONE

THE GRANDFATHER CLOCK in the corner chimed 3:00 a.m. Kadence stared at the creeping hands, the book in her lap all but forgotten. She hadn't been able to concentrate on anything since Ronan and the others left. Setting the book on the small stand beside the chair she reclined in, she climbed to her feet. Pacing the large room, she scanned the thousands of volumes lining the floor-to-ceiling shelves of the two-story library.

Marta had explained that Ronan and the others had brought the books with them from wherever they'd been before. The older woman had stayed with her for a good hour, pointing out her favorite books while she gave Kadence a tour. Marta exuded enthusiasm and warmth as she shared her love of the books and the vampires in residence. She hadn't left until Baldric came to retrieve her for help with something.

Normally, being alone in a room such as this would be her idea of heaven. Reading was the way she spent most of her days. It was her only refuge from a life of boredom. Now, she found herself unable to concentrate on the endless spines lining the shelves.

Kadence pulled back the navy blue curtains covering the

windows. She peered into the night, barely able to discern the bars on the outside. Releasing the curtain, she strode to the center of the room. She had traded one prison for another, but at least there were no expectations of perfection for her here, no one for her to marry. She may not be free to go outside or travel at will, but she still had more freedom than she'd had before.

She felt liberated. Yet, there was a constricting grip on her chest that she'd never experienced before.

Turning away from the multitude of shelves, she left the library. Baldric was descending the staircase when she walked into the foyer. He smiled at her as he stepped off the last stair and onto the marble. His brown eyes were warm when they met hers.

"Can I get you anything, miss?"

"No, I'm all set. Thank you."

He bowed his head to her and started walking toward where Marta had told her the kitchen was located. "Let us know if you require anything. There is a buzzer in almost every room." He rested his hand beneath a small golden button on the wall and pointed to it. Kadence recalled seeing one in her room earlier too. "It goes straight to the back hall where we can hear it even if we're sleeping."

"Thank you," she said though she suspected Ronan and his men would never bother them by hitting that button while Marta and Baldric slept, unless it was an absolute emergency, and neither would she.

"Good night, miss."

"Good night, Baldric."

She remained standing in the foyer after he'd vanished into the shadows beyond. She glanced back at the hall leading to the library as she debated returning there, going to her room, or wandering the large mansion and seeing what she could discover now that Marta and Baldric were going to sleep. She might be able to figure out how to get out of this place while no one was around.

She decided it was time to explore seconds before the front door flung open, letting in a rush of wind and fresh snow. Ronan strode into the house, his coat swirling around his calves. Declan, Saxon, and Killean followed him into the foyer. A large, ugly gash seeped blood down the side of Killean's face. Kadence let out a gasp of horror. Forgetting all about her dislike of Killean, she rushed toward him.

"What happened?" Before she could reach him, Ronan grasped her outstretched wrist and pulled her back a step. "I only want to help him!" she protested as she uselessly tried to tug her arm from Ronan's grasp.

"Declan and Saxon will take care of him," Ronan replied.

"But I'm good at tending wounds," Kadence protested.

"Not this one."

"What happened?" she demanded.

"Savages."

"Joseph?" she managed to choke out.

Ronan's body vibrated with barely contained power as he stared at her. "Joseph wasn't there."

"But he sent his friends," Saxon muttered.

Kadence bit her lower lip. "Joseph sent them?"

"I believe so," Ronan answered.

"Was my brother there?"

"No."

She turned to look at Killean's brutalized face. The skin of his unscarred cheek hung down to reveal the fine white bone beneath, and blood continued to ooze from the injury. "Please let me help him."

"No. It will heal on its own and he will be fine. I will not have you around this. You are going upstairs," Ronan replied.

"No, I'm—"

Her protest was cut off when he tugged her toward the steps. Kadence glared at his back as he stalked up the stairs ahead of her, every muscle in his body rigid. "What happened out there?" she inquired as they arrived at the top and he pulled her forward.

"Nothing good," was the crisp reply.

"I *can* help him."

"I won't have you near a vampire who has lost so much blood and is still geared for the kill."

"Oh," she said as realization dawned on her. These were not hunters returning from a battle. These vampires hadn't hurt her, but they were still lethal creatures with a lot of power and a thirst for blood. She shivered at the thought and hurried to walk beside Ronan.

He opened the door to her room and she stepped inside. "I'm sorry for what happened tonight."

He took hold of her chin. "Joseph is organizing the Savages, Kadence. After tonight, I am certain of it. It is not safe for you here."

"Then let me go."

His finger rubbed her chin, melting her bones from the inside out. Heat pooled through her body, causing her toes to curl. Like everyone else in her life, he'd taken her freedom from her, but she found she couldn't be mad at him when he was gazing at her like she was the most precious thing he'd ever seen.

"Where would you go?" he asked.

"Everywhere," she breathed. "I'd go to Machu Picchu and Venice and Rome. I'd stand on the Great Wall and try to puzzle out the mysteries of Stonehenge before kissing the Blarney Stone and drinking ale at a pub. I'd breathe in the air of history, soak in the arts, speak the languages I've learned, and immerse myself in the people and cultures. I'd *laugh*. I've done so little laughing in my life. I want to know what it is like to throw open my arms, laugh to the skies, and inhale freedom."

Ronan was stunned speechless by her impassioned words and the vision she created with them. He could well imagine her laughing and celebrating all those places. This young, vibrant woman had been caged so much she'd rarely laughed in her life, and now he was placing bars around her all over again. Now, he was the one denying her the life she deserved.

Was he keeping her here because she had disobeyed him and he was concerned about her safety, or was it because Declan was right and he really didn't want to let her go?

He'd done some atrocious things in his lengthy life. Holding her captive here until she bent to his will was one of the worst of them. Self-hatred burned into him as he caressed her chin.

"All wonderful things," he murmured. "So you would go Machu Picchu first then?"

"Maybe the Grand Canyon or Niagara Falls, it doesn't matter as long as I see it *all*."

"And what about money?"

"I would figure it out. I'm not stupid or as naïve as you believe me to be. I know it will be difficult, but I *can* do it. I'm not used to the human world, but I'm a hard worker and I am stronger than others. I'm sure I can find something to do while I travel."

He didn't remind her that she had no ID either. There were some times it was best to let things go. "If anyone could do it, I think it would be you, Kadence."

A beautiful smile lit her face. "That's not what you were saying earlier."

"Even with my many years of experience, I am sometimes wrong."

She chuckled and gripped his hand on her chin. "I imagine someone could live for all of time and still get things wrong. We were born to be flawed after all."

"We were. I can't let you go out into this world alone. You have no idea what it is like out there."

Her crestfallen expression tore at his heart. "I realize there is a lot I don't know, but no one has ever given me the chance to learn it either."

"I know they haven't. I wish I could take you to all of those places myself." He would give anything to see her face the first time she saw Ireland or the Colosseum, to hear her laughter as she looked on each new sight with delight. "My duty is to my kind, especially now, and that means that I have to stay here, where the threat is located."

Her delicate fingers tightened around his. "I know."

"Baldric and Marta can take you." The words were out of his mouth before he realized he'd intended to say them. He fought against drawing her against his chest and holding her there as denial raced across his mind. He'd just found her and now he intended to send her away. No, he would set her *free*.

They may only be human, but Marta and Baldric were better trained at fighting vampires than Kadence was. They would keep her safe. They knew places to bring her that would be safe if they ever ran into trouble, and they knew vampires around the world who would help them if it became necessary.

He didn't want her out in the world without him, but that selfishness only made him a bigger monster than Joseph.

"I will give you money and they can go with you wherever you wish to go," he told her. "With the condition and the understanding that you are to stay with them throughout your journey. I know it is not the complete freedom you seek, but they will help keep you safe, and they won't stand in the way of anything you do as long as they believe it's not too dangerous."

He'd make sure they didn't stand in her way if she found a man she loved and decided to settle down with him. His fangs ached in his gums at the thought. She was *his*. But she wasn't.

Kadence's heart hammered as hope bloomed in her chest. He was offering her dreams to her. "Do you mean it?"

He gave a brisk nod as the demon clawed at his chest, seeking to break free to claim her. It took everything he had to keep it securely locked away. "Yes, but if you try to run away from them, they will bring you back. If you get away from them, or do anything to hurt them, I will hunt you to the ends of the earth, Kadence. Do you understand?"

"I would never hurt them or try to escape them, I promise. Will they bring me back when I'm done exploring?"

"That is up to you. It is your life to live now. They will only be there to help guide and protect you through your travels. If they feel you are safe to be on your own, and that is what you ask of them, they will also leave you, but *only* if they feel you will be safe."

"You... you would do that? You would have them leave here with me? You would give me money and let me go?"

No! The denial rang throughout every part of him. "Yes. It will take about a week to get everything organized and to get you a passport and ID that will make it through security everywhere in the world."

"What about Joseph? I left my home to witness his death."

"You stayed away from your home because you wanted your freedom. Now, you must decide what you want more; to possibly witness a death that will never fill the hole inside of you and may leave you feeling more hollow after, or to live out your dreams?"

Kadence rocked back on her heels as she contemplated his words. "I can always go after Joseph is dead."

"No. This is a now or never deal, Kadence." He may decide to keep her if she were here for more than a week. It would be difficult enough to let her go after spending that much time with her, never mind longer. "Things may change in the future and I may be unable to offer this to you. I can't promise you that you will be there when Joseph dies either. Not with your lack of training."

"I see," she whispered.

She churned his words over in her mind. What would her dad want her to do? Easy enough to answer, he would want her back in the stronghold, but since that wasn't an option for her right now, she knew he wouldn't have her living her life for revenge.

She so badly wanted to see Joseph dead, but was witnessing his death worth giving up everything else for? Especially since she might not even get the chance to see it. Ronan would let her go travel, but he would keep her out of the fight until he believed her better prepared to be there.

"I... I will go," she managed to stammer out.

Ronan clasped his hands behind his back, nearly tearing the skin from them as he restrained himself from grabbing her. "I will inform Marta and Baldric and have them set everything in motion."

Before he could change his mind, he turned and walked out of the room. His fangs extended further with every step he took away from her.

CHAPTER TWENTY-TWO

HER SLEEP PLAGUED with dreams of Ronan, Kadence had risen earlier than normal and decided to explore the mansion. Maybe she should still be plotting her getaway. She felt in some way she was betraying her own kind by not doing so, but her kind had been wrong about so many things that she found herself not looking for a way out as she prowled through the rambling structure. It didn't matter anyway. After this week, she wouldn't be here anymore.

She should be overjoyed about that. She should have been kept awake with excitement, and not because she was fighting the urge to cry. She was finally going to be free; she was going to be able to do all the things she'd always dreamed about doing. Instead of being elated, all she wanted was to seek out Ronan and spend as much time with him as possible before leaving.

She kept waiting for someone to tell her she shouldn't be in this area or that one, but no one bothered her as she strolled through the place. She explored the numerous rooms on the first floor. Some of them were empty, but most had furniture to mark what they were. There was an elaborate dining room with a table that easily fit fifty, what she assumed was a parlor with its tables and chairs, another room with sofas and a fireplace that took up the entire back wall, and another with an old desk and floor-to-ceiling shelves behind it.

She only went down one wing before realizing it was mostly empty rooms. She had no idea why anyone needed a place so big, and she felt completely overwhelmed by the vastness of it while she made her way back to the main foyer.

She stopped when she spotted Ronan standing at the bottom of the steps, his elbow resting on the banister as he watched her. "What do you think of the place?" he inquired.

"It's huge."

"And?"

"It's kind of depressing. I don't know if that's because it's so empty or because what they left behind feels like the remnants of ghosts instead of people."

Ronan gazed around the foyer as he tried to see it through her eyes. To him, it didn't matter. This place already had heavy security, was in a part of Massachusetts that was relatively peaceful, but Boston, Providence, Hartford, and New York City were all easily accessible by car.

It had been ideal for their needs. He hadn't cared what it looked like when he purchased it, never would have taken a second look at the interior or had the time to do anything about it, but seeing it through her eyes made him realize the place was bleak.

"You're right," he said and moved away from the stairs. "Come with me."

"Where are we going?"

"You wanted training, you're going to get it, or at least a crash course in it. Marta and Baldric will continue working with you while you're traveling. They're highly skilled fighters."

Kadence couldn't help but smile as she pictured the plump woman, with her kind smile, kicking a vampire's ass.

Their footsteps rang against the marble as she followed him to a door leading to a set of stairs. She'd opened the door earlier, but after looking down the shadowed staircase, she'd decided against exploring it.

Ronan flicked on a switch and descended the stairs before her. "I've asked Marta and Baldric to make sure most of your time outdoors is during the daytime. They will also take you overseas first, anywhere you ask to go, but across the ocean."

"Why?" she inquired.

"The more they kill, the more Savages have a difficult time of crossing bodies of water. The ones following Joseph will mostly be located on this continent, and it seems in this area. For now, I'd prefer to have you away from them. You can explore this continent once they've been destroyed."

What if something happened to *him* while she was gone? The idea caused a tug on her heart and a lump to form in her throat. He was ancient and powerful, but vampires could be killed. What about her brother? What if something happened to Nathan?

She tried to shake the worries off, but once they lodged in her mind, it was difficult for her to get rid of them.

At the end of the stairs, Ronan turned on another switch. Kadence's step faltered when numerous overhead lights flickered on to reveal the broad expanse of the gym. It was easily the size of the entire main floor of the house. The light shone off the weights, the stainless-steel doors at the other end of the room, and the entire back wall of weapons.

"Don't get any ideas about those weapons," he said to her over his shoulder as she gawked at them.

"Wouldn't dream of it," she replied, but her fingers itched to touch some of those knives and throwing stars.

He stepped onto one of the mats and turned to face her. He bounced on the balls of his feet as he backed a few feet away. "So, young hunter, let's see what you've got."

Kadence glanced down at her jeans, baggy blouse, and socks. "I'm not exactly dressed for sparring."

"And you most likely won't be dressed to fight if you're attacked on the street either."

"True," she admitted and stepped onto the mat across from him.

He held his hands up before her as she circled him, stretching her arms as she moved. She was about to stretch her calves when she found herself flat on her back, staring at the sparkly lights above her. Ronan leaned over her, blocking out the lights with his broad shoulders. She didn't know how he'd managed to knock her feet out from under her when she'd never seen him move, but he had.

"An attacker isn't going to give you time to stretch, Kadydid," he told her.

"It's a katydid." It was a ridiculous point to make, but it was better than glaring uselessly at him.

"Not anymore," he replied.

The sexy smile he gave her made her realize she didn't care what he called her when he smiled like that. He stretched his hand out to her. She sat up to clutch it and somehow found herself lying on her back, staring at the lights again. The exasperating man was faster than lightning.

"An attacker won't help you up either," he stated.

His infuriating chuckle had her launching to her feet and glowering at him. She adjusted her blouse and ended up on her ass again. She almost thumped her hands off the mat and yelled at him to stop it. She bit her tongue before she could speak. He may be pissing her off, but he was also exposing how woefully unprepared she was.

She pushed herself back to her feet and danced back before he could knock her down again. He circled around her, his body flowing with grace around the mat. "You're spry," he told her. "You'll never overpower a vampire, but you can outmaneuver one enough to get away."

"I want to kill, not run."

He stopped moving to face her. "You're not strong enough for that. You need to know how to defend yourself enough to escape one, but you're not strong enough to face a vamp one on one and take them down. There's a reason hunters work in packs against us. An experienced hunter may be able to take down a turned vamp on their own, but you're not experienced."

"Okay, so teach me how to outmaneuver one."

He came at her then, a rush of muscle and male that robbed her of her breath far more than her exertion to keep away from him did. He worked her through a series of punches and kicks as he came at her again and again. She found herself staring at the lights more often than she was on her feet, but she was getting actual *experience*.

She had no idea what time it was when the sound of a throat clearing from the doorway drew both their eyes to where Declan lounged against the frame. "What is it?" Ronan inquired.

"Will you be hunting with us tonight?" Declan asked.

Ronan glanced at the clock on the wall. "Shit," he said when he realized it was almost eight. "Yes, I'll be up shortly."

Declan disappeared from the doorway. Ronan shifted his attention to Kadence as she wiped a few strands of hair from her eyes. The blouse, damp with sweat, emphasized her breasts as it cleaved to them. He found his gaze locked onto them and the outline of the simple bra beneath.

"It was a good start," he said gruffly as his cock swelled with his need for her. "We'll continue this tomorrow."

"I look forward to it."

He turned and started for the door before realizing she wasn't behind him. "Are you coming?"

"I'm going to train with some weights and weapons," she said. "I think you've proven I have more work to do."

"Kadence—"

"It's not a bad thing," she broke in with a wave of her hand. "I needed the wake-up call, and I *will* get better. I won't be much longer, but I'm not ready to stop yet either. Go. I won't take any weapons with me. Besides, I'm sure you would know if I did."

"I would," he replied. "Don't overdo it or you'll be useless tomorrow."

"I won't. Be careful out there."

This time, he found himself pleased by her concern instead of angered by it. "I will," he vowed.

OVER THE FOLLOWING DAYS, she continued to find herself still staring at the ceiling more often than she remained on her feet, but she was getting better. Already she had more muscle definition in her arms and legs, and she was faster. She'd even managed to get in a couple of blows against Ronan before staring at the pretty lights again.

Her endurance was also better. Though, every night she still crawled into a hot bath to ease the soreness in her muscles and stayed there until she was more pruned than a raisin. Then, she would go down to the library and read until Ronan and the others returned. Her eyelids were always drooping by then, but she couldn't sleep until she knew he was safe.

Tonight, while waiting for him to come down to work with her, Kadence wandered into the poolroom. She was examining the chess table near one of the windows when he found her. The table had been carved from the trunk of a tree and appeared to be at least a couple hundred years old. Judging by the grain of the wood, each of the chess pieces had also been carved from the same kind of tree and polished until they shone.

"Do you play chess?" he asked.

"I have a basic knowledge of the game," she replied. "Enough so that I would be able to play with my husband, if he enjoyed the game."

He strode into the room, his eyes running over her lithe figure in the black yoga pants and form-fitting, pink tank top. He'd asked Marta to purchase some workout clothes for her, but he'd expected sweatpants and sweatshirts, not this temptation. He'd have kept her in jeans had he known Marta was going to torment him with this outfit.

"And what if you enjoyed the game and your husband didn't?" he asked.

She shrugged and glanced back at the pieces. "Then I probably wouldn't have played again, at least not often."

"Ridiculous," he muttered.

"It's the way of things with us," she replied. "I was educated enough to converse with my husband without boring him."

"And what if he bored you?" The radiant smile that lit her face struck straight to his heart.

"I wondered the same thing recently!" she exclaimed.

Ronan had to take a minute to gather himself as she continued to beam at him. "Well, it is not something you will have to be concerned about anymore."

"No, it's not," she agreed.

"Would you like to play now?" he asked.

She glanced back at the table and then him. He saw the longing on her face before she shook her head. "No, I should train more."

"You've done well. You could use a break."

"Maybe tomorrow night," she replied. "After you left last night, I mastered throwing the shuriken and want to show you."

"Mastered it, did you?" he inquired as they made their way out of the room and to the basement door.

"Okay, maybe not mastered, but I hit the target multiple times."

"Good," he said as he opened the basement door and followed her down to the gym. "They're easily concealed and will allow you to impair your attacker without getting close. It may not kill them, but it will slow them down and might make them rethink coming after you."

"I like that," she said as she walked across the room to the weapons.

Stepping back, Ronan admired her taut ass in those pants. He was going to spend the next couple of hours trying to conceal his erection from her, but it would be completely worth it. She stretched to grab some shurikens from the wall, and he almost groaned aloud when the action exposed a patch of the creamy skin on her lower back.

She came back toward him, her breasts swaying with each step as she took up a position across from the dummy he'd set up for her to work with. Unlike the dummies the hunters had given her to train with, this one was hooked to a rope and could be jerked around by hand or by a machine. She pushed a button and the machine came to life, jerking the dummy one way and then another.

The weapons sliced through the air as she released them with deadly speed and accuracy. She may not be able to take on a vampire by herself, but she was extremely talented, and he couldn't deny that she was faster than the hunters he'd come across, except for maybe her brother. She was also stronger than they were and growing more so every day.

When she was done, she'd hit the target with all six of the shurikens and bounced on her toes as she spun to face him. Drawn toward her, he stalked across the mat and hit the button on the machine, shutting it down.

"Much better," he said, his gaze dipping to her red lips before he tore his eyes away. "Now let's try some live training with the shurikens."

Kadence stopped bouncing and frowned at him. "What do you mean?"

He didn't respond as he crossed over and pulled the shurikens free of the dummy. He carried them back to her and handed them over. "See if you can hit me with them."

"No," she said and tried to shove them back at him.

"Yes." He folded her fingers around them before walking away from her. "Remember, if you hit me, it won't kill me."

"I'm not throwing these at you."

"You have to know how to react against a vampire. Your hunter blood is exceptionally strong, but that doesn't matter if you're not properly trained. You can do this, and if you don't, I'm going to spend the next couple of hours knocking you on your ass until you can't sit for a week."

"I've spent plenty of time on my ass these past days," she retorted.

"I've been taking it easy on you."

Kadence gawked at him as he turned to face her, the cocky look on his face both endearing and maddening.

"Don't be afraid, Kadydid. I won't hurt you."

She scoffed at his words, but before she could formulate a reply, he was coming at her in a blur of speed and muscle.

CHAPTER TWENTY-THREE

KADENCE HAD GOTTEN BETTER at being able to discern where he was as they worked together, and her eyes adjusted to his fluid movements. Reacting on instinct, she released the shurikens in rapid fire, purposely aiming not to hit him, but making a point. When she released the last one, she darted to the side. She didn't move fast enough to avoid him though.

Wrapping his arm around her waist, he lifted her off her feet before taking her down to the mat. Though he'd knocked her on her ass more times than she could recall recently, he'd never gone to the ground with her. Now, she found herself staring into his burgundy eyes when he planted his fists beside her head and his thighs between hers as he knelt over her. They didn't touch, but the heat of him melted her body as if they were flesh to flesh.

"You got a little close on that last one," he said with a glance at the blood beading from the scratch on his corded bicep.

Glancing down his body, she noted the slices in his black shirt and the one in his baggy pants. She could have hit him with each one she'd thrown, something she'd made sure he knew.

"Maybe I didn't get close enough with the others," she replied.

"Is that so?" he inquired and lowered himself so that his chest barely touched her.

Kadence sucked in her breath, but didn't release it as his eyes dropped to her mouth and they heated with desire. All the nerve endings in her body screamed for him to touch her, to ease this need he so easily brought to life in her.

Just when she thought she might pass out from lack of oxygen, he bent his head until their lips brushed against each other. He seemed to be waging a silent battle with himself as he remained unmoving above her. Then, he let out a low groan and took possession of her mouth. Her heart knocked into her ribcage as his tongue slid over her lips before she opened her mouth to his.

The scent and feel of him filled all her senses. Her legs opened further to him, and he settled himself between her thighs. He growled against her lips and thrust his hips forward. The rigid evidence of his arousal rubbing against her made it impossible to think as sensation took her over completely. The delicious sensations his body evoked in hers made it impossible to catch her breath as his tongue drove into her mouth in the same rhythm of his hips moving against her.

Ronan stroked his hand over her face before running it down her shoulder and lower as her hips rose to meet his. He had no idea how any of this had happened, but he lost himself to the wonder of her body as he cupped and kneaded her breast.

For nearly a week, he'd kept himself restrained from touching her in an intimate way. He hadn't planned for anything to change tonight, but he'd been unable to stop himself from bringing her down beneath him, and then there had been no denying him after.

Her back arched to press her breast more firmly into his palm. His hand twisted in her shirt to tear it away from her. He wanted to shred her clothing, bare her to him, and take her with all the savagery of the demon within him.

She's an innocent! The reminder made him realize that, if he took her the way he planned, he would hurt her, badly. He would ruin her, but worst of all, she would hate him for it.

Ronan launched himself off her so fast, Kadence didn't realize he wasn't there until cold air flowed in to chill her overheated skin. She blinked at the empty space above her before turning to find him stalking across the room. His body was so rigid she thought he might break apart with the way he carried himself.

Kadence rolled over as he turned back to face her from fifty feet away.

"I am sorry," he said in a clipped tone she barely recognized.

"For what?" she inquired as she pushed herself to her feet. When she stepped toward him, he took one back like she was a magnet repelling him.

"I did not mean for that to happen. If I hurt you—"

"You didn't."

"Frightened you then."

"You didn't," she said. "I can handle myself, Ronan."

"You think you could stop me from hurting you?"

"I wouldn't have to."

"You have no idea what I'm capable of."

"Yes, I do. It's *you* who doesn't know."

Ronan couldn't stop his mouth from dropping at her words. In all his many years, no one had shocked him as much as she just had. "I am well aware of what I am capable of doing. I have witnessed the blood staining my hands for over a thousand years."

"Yes, you are aware of your capability for violence, but are you also aware that you are capable of kindness and being gentle?"

"You have no idea what I want to do to you right now, and there is nothing gentle about it!"

"You could have done it, but you didn't."

"I would ruin you, do you understand that, Kadence? What I would do to you would ruin you for any other man."

"I don't want any other man. I only want you."

Nope, he'd been wrong, she'd just managed to shock him even more. Before he could respond to her, footsteps sounded behind him. He turned to find Declan standing in the doorway ten feet behind him.

"What is it?" he demanded.

"It is time to hunt," Declan replied. "Marta also asked me to inform you that everything is ready for them to leave tomorrow."

Those final words hit Ronan like a punch between his eyes. "Good," he somehow managed to say. He glanced at Kadence over his shoulder. "Pack what you will take with you. Marta and Baldric will make sure to buy you whatever else you require on your travels. If you have decided where you would like to go first, let Marta know. It will mean less time for you at the airport."

"I have decided, and I will let her know," she murmured.

He followed Declan into the stairwell. "Ronan, be careful."

He smashed his fist into the wall before storming up the stairs behind Declan. Tomorrow, he would have no one to tell him to be careful again. Tomorrow she would be gone. He should be relieved; instead, he knew he would make the death of any Savage they came across tonight exceptionally brutal.

KADENCE STIRRED when she felt arms slipping beneath her. Warmth enveloped her as she was braced against a solid chest and something was removed from her hands. Her eyes blinked open as Ronan set the book she'd been holding on the chair he'd lifted her from.

She hadn't meant to fall asleep while waiting for him, but after he'd left she'd worked out for another two hours in the hopes of burying the sadness that leaving him brought to her. Then she'd packed her things and spent the rest of the night pacing the library before trying to read. Her emotional and physical exhaustion had caught up with her.

"What time is it?"

"Almost three," he replied.

She took in the wet hair falling across his forehead and curling at the corners of his eyes. "You showered."

"Long night," he replied.

He refused to tell her that he'd been covered in blood when he'd returned twenty minutes ago. He'd been unwilling to see her like that, been determined not to see her at all before she left, but when he realized she wasn't in her room, he couldn't resist following the lure of her scent here.

"Is everyone okay?" she asked as she came more awake.

"Yes."

He carried her from the room and down the hall to the stairs. She nestled closer to him, savoring the scent of the spiced soap on his body. Unable to resist, she rested her fingers against his chest and sighed when she felt the powerful flex of his muscles with every step he took. She slid her fingers down his flesh. The yearning to taste him grew until she turned her mouth into his chest and slid her tongue out to lick his salty skin.

Ronan's fangs tingled as they lengthened, and he found himself drawing her closer as her tongue slid over him again. He shifted his hold on her to grip the knob of her door and pushed it open.

She withdrew from him as he set her on her feet. Before, she would have blushed over her actions with him; now she couldn't find it in herself to be embarrassed, not if this was to be their last night together for a while, possibly forever. Resting her hand on his cheek, she stepped into him.

Ronan told himself to back away from her, but his feet were planted to the floor as her breasts brushed against his chest and her eyes searched his. He knew he had to look half wild with his need for her, yet she showed no fear as she rose onto her toes.

Her gaze never left his when she kissed him. Her breath warmed his mouth as they stared at each other and Ronan resisted drawing her closer. If he did, if this continued, there would be no stopping, not this time.

CHAPTER TWENTY-FOUR

THE HEIGHTENED SCENT of her arousal filled his nostrils and permeated his body. He was taken off guard by the intensity of her longing for him as he remained unmoving against her. Her lashes fell to shadow her eyes, and she broke the kiss.

As she moved to pull away, his arm lashed out and drew her to him. Her eyes deepened in color when they met his again. He caressed her cheek before his hand slid back to entwine in her silken hair.

His eyes were drawn to her mouth as he waited for her to tell him no. Waited for her to pull away. She did neither of those things; instead, she leaned into him, her breath coming faster as her fingers dug into his chest.

He knew he shouldn't do this, knew it would only make it more difficult to let her go. She would fly free from here and the brutal life she'd been born into. He would remain and continue to fight until he died or succumbed to the lure of becoming a Savage.

But none of that mattered. All he wanted now was to be inside of her, moving over her, listening to her sensual moans as he claimed her for this brief period of time.

When she kissed him again, he pulled her so firmly against him that no air flowed between their bodies. She belonged with *him* and him alone.

Something niggled at the back of his mind, an intuition that he should acknowledge, but couldn't, as everything in him became focused on her alone.

He pulled her hair back, deepening the kiss and catching her sigh when her mouth parted and her tongue entwined with his. Lifting his mouth from hers, he ran his tongue along the slender column of her throat before he nipped at her supple flesh.

His fangs ached to pierce her skin, to taste the blood pulsing through her vein and calling to him like a siren on the rocks, but he resisted the impulse. It could drive her away if he took from her now.

Her knees buckled when his other hand slid up to cup her breast. He supported her weight as she cried out and her head fell back to allow him better access to her throat. Lifting her, he swung her into his arms, kicked the door shut behind them, and carried her further into the room.

Stopping beside the bed, he set her on her feet and stepped back to drink in the sight of her. She stared up at him, her lips swollen, her eyes heavy lidded and seductive. She was the most beautiful thing he'd ever seen.

A trickle of unease slid through her as Ronan's eyes ran ravenously over her body. His raw need for her was evident on his face and in the heavy bulge behind his pants. No matter what he believed about himself, if she asked him to stop this now, he would walk away from her, but despite her apprehension over what she knew was to come, she didn't want to stop it.

At one time, she'd believed him to be a monster simply because of what he was. Now he was the only man who had ever made her feel like she truly mattered in this world because of who she was, and not because she might be able to have children one day. He was the only man she had ever wanted to share this experience with.

He was setting her free today, and before she left, she would have the memory of this night to hold close while she was gone. Swallowing heavily, she pushed aside her fear as he remained where he was, giving her a chance to change her mind, she knew. The elder women had prepared her for her wedding night, told her what to expect and what would happen. They hadn't prepared her for her overwhelming desire for him too.

His eyes were almost entirely red when she met them. The outline of his fangs pressed against his lips, but the obvious signs of what he was didn't scare her. "I want this. I want *you*."

Ronan released an explosive exhale as he gripped the hem of her shirt. He pulled it slowly up, giving her the time to change her mind as he revealed more of supple flesh and curves. Her eyes never left his as she lifted her arms for him. He pulled the shirt over her head and tossed it aside. The black sports bar she wore kept her handful-sized breasts concealed, but there was something incredibly sexy about this tomboyish look on her.

Hooking his fingers into the band of her sweatpants, he pulled her a step closer until their chests were flush against each other. He tugged her sweats and underwear lower over her rounded hips. He kept waiting for her to tell him to stop, but all he saw in her gaze was yearning as she watched every move he made.

When he'd been in the gym with her earlier, all he could think of was tearing the clothes from her and burying himself inside her before she could stop him. Now, when he knew he would have her, all he wanted was to savor every inch of her. He bent to slide the sweats over her supple thighs and down her shapely calves. She stepped out of them as he rose to stand before her again.

He grasped the edges of her bra and slid it over her head. Her silvery hair cascaded around her shoulders when her arms settled at her sides. Her luscious curves and the small triangle of darker blonde hair shielding her sex from his view caused his mouth to water.

Stepping closer, he gritted his teeth against the throbbing need of his cock while he leisurely slid the backs of his knuckles up her sides. She bit on her lower lip as she raptly watched him, and he memorized her every reaction to his touch. His gaze latched onto her pert breasts with their pink nipples standing out tantalizingly, but he didn't touch them, not yet. Instead, he continued to explore her as he ran his hands over her flat stomach and round hips.

Smelling her desire on the air, he knew she was most likely wet for him already, and he wanted to feel that wetness slipping over his fingers. However, if he slid his fingers between her legs now, he knew he would be lost to her, and he wanted to take this as slow as possible. Her breath hitched in when his hands cupped her firm ass.

"You're exquisite," he murmured.

A spark lit her eyes when her gaze ran hungrily over him. "You're not so bad yourself," she said as her hands gliding over his chest caused his muscles to contract beneath her gentle ministrations.

No one had ever touched him with such reverence before. When he'd still cared enough to have it, sex had always been enjoyable enough for him, but it had always been a scratching of an itch with a willing woman who had understood that was all he wanted from her. It had also been all she wanted from him too.

However, Kadence touched him as if she cared for him.

He stiffened as that realization sank in. She cared for him when none of his other lovers ever had, and he couldn't deny that she'd become special to him too. Dipping his head, he nuzzled her ear with his lips as his hands slid up the slender curve of her spine. "If we do this, Kadence, there will be no turning back."

"I don't want to turn back, ever."

"You could regret—"

"No. Even if for some reason I decide to return home, I will *never* regret this night, or you."

Kadence held her breath as Ronan shifted so his forehead was against hers and his reddened eyes burned into hers. Then his mouth took hers in a kiss that burned all the way to the tips of her toes.

His hands fell to her waist, and he lifted her easily. Taking two steps forward, he placed her on the bed and stepped back to admire her. She lay before him, her skin flushed with passion and her lips swollen from his kiss. Unbuttoning his pants, he hastily pulled them off and tossed them aside.

Kadence's eyes widened as he revealed himself completely to her. A fresh trickle of alarm slid through her as she gazed at the erection jutting proudly out from his body. The elder women had told her what to expect, but they hadn't prepared her for how *big* he would be. It stood a good eight inches away from him and was so thick she knew she wouldn't be able to wrap her hand completely around it.

Swallowing heavily, she pushed aside her trepidation over what was to come. It would hurt, but this was Ronan, and she would deal with the pain if it meant easing this incessant ache for him.

He climbed onto the bed with her and took her into his arms to cradle her against him. The warmth and strength of his body enveloping hers eased her fear. She clasped his back when he reclaimed her mouth and moaned when her breasts rubbed against his chest. The movement sent shivers over her body. He cupped one of her breasts in his palm, running his thumb over her nipple before rolling it between his fingers.

Releasing her breast, he skimmed his hand over her hip and down her thigh. "Open your legs for me," he whispered against her mouth.

Unable to resist, Kadence spread her legs at his command. Small electrical currents coursed through her body as his hand slid between her thighs. His fingers stroking her caused her belly to clench with need.

Ronan rubbed his thumb against her clit, relishing in her increased breaths as her body reacted to his touch. Already wet with her want for him, he spread that wetness over her before dipping his finger into her. Her inner heat enveloped him as her tight muscles gripped his finger and he began to move it within her.

Kadence's mind spun as his finger and thumb stroked her. Her hips instinctively rose and fell in rhythm to his movement within her. His finger was *inside her* and doing such wonderfully decadent things to her body that she could barely think straight. It was all happening so fast that she thought it should be at least a little over-whelming, but all she wanted was to experience more of him.

She ran her hand over the muscles of his chest before dipping down to explore the ridges of his abdomen. She couldn't get enough of him as she traced the trail of hair running from his bellybutton to his erection. Unable to resist, she ran a finger over the taut skin of his shaft before touching the bead of liquid forming on the head of it.

Ronan grasped her hand when she ran her fingers tentatively over his head once more. Holding her hand within his grasp, he turned it and wrapped it around his cock. He worked her hand up and then back down the length of him.

"Like this," he whispered against her mouth.

Kadence almost jerked away when his shaft jumped in her hand as he guided her up and down him. Then, he groaned and his head tipped back until the muscles in his neck stood out. His reaction to her touch fascinated her as did the heat of him against her palm. She forgot all about the delicious sensations he evoked in her as she concentrated on the pleasure she gave him.

Then, he began to move his finger in a completely different way within her and his palm rubbed against her. She ground against his hand as he pushed her closer and closer to the brink of something far beyond anything she'd experienced those times when she'd woken after a dream and felt unfulfilled. During those times, she had touched herself in an attempt to ease what those dreams had awoken in her, but her touch and those dreams were nothing compared to the passion Ronan evoked within her.

"Ronan," she groaned when he slid his hand away from her.

"Easy," he whispered in her ear and eased her hand away from his cock. "I want to be in you the first time a man makes you come."

She wasn't entirely sure what his words meant, but she was impatient to find out. He moved over her, his massive body filling her field of vision and all her senses, as he nudged her legs apart with his thigh.

The corded muscles of his arms stood out as he held himself above her and he no longer tried to keep his lethal fangs concealed. She lifted her hips invitingly to him, needing him to quench the fire he'd created within her.

Leaning down, he took hold of her mouth again and delved his tongue into her. He grasped her hips, holding her as he positioned the head of his dick against her inviting folds and began to inch forward. Gritting his jaw, it took all his restraint not to plunge into her as her wet heat enveloped him more and more. He stopped when he felt the barrier of her virginity. Releasing her hips, he lifted his lips from hers to take in the vision of her beneath him.

"This is going to hurt," he warned.

"I know," she murmured as she ran her fingers over his high cheekbones before slipping them around his neck. "The elder women told me what to expect."

Kadence's breath caught when, for the briefest of seconds, she stared into a pair of eyes the same color as a deer's. She'd seen hints of this rich, deep brown in his eyes before, but never this clearly. She knew she was being gifted a glimpse of Ronan while at peace and not the brutal, unyielding warrior she'd come to know. As fast as it had come, the brown faded away to become burgundy once more.

She had no time to ponder what had caused the change before he thrust forward to penetrate deep into her. Kadence cried out, her nails dug into his nape and her thighs clamped against his sides.

"I'm sorry," he whispered, his hands caressing her face as he kissed her again. "The pain will ease."

She nodded as he ran his lips across her collarbone before dipping lower to run his tongue over her nipple. He remained unmoving within her as he caressed her flesh, slowly evoking her desire for him again. He drew her nipple into his mouth and sucked on it as he ran his tongue around it once more.

The coiling tension built within her once more as he turned his attention to her other breast. The sight of his dark head bent over her, the heat of his mouth, and the scrape of his fangs became an overwhelming sensation she almost couldn't take, but she didn't want it to stop.

Instinctively, she lifted her hips to take him deeper into her as her fingers entwined in his hair and she drew him closer to her breast. He growled against her flesh as she lowered her hips and gasped when a wave of bliss speared through her.

Ronan kept himself still as he waited for her to adjust to the feel of him inside her and to explore him in her own way and own time. It had been years since he'd last had sex, yet he didn't feel out of control with need. A calm had descended over him the second she gave herself to him, a tranquility he'd never expected to experience in his life.

She lifted her hips again, and he groaned as she fell and rose on his cock once more, drawing him deeper into her. He had wanted to take his time, but when she wrapped her legs around his back and arched against him, he knew he was lost. He couldn't stop himself from moving faster, harder, deeper until all he could feel was her pliant body against his and her tight muscles squeezing his cock.

Kadence's hands gripped his hard ass as she held him closer to her. "Please," she panted as the tension coiling higher in her body felt ready to unravel.

She was close to orgasm; he could sense it in her rapid pulse and the demanding movements of her body beneath his. "Please what?" he asked as he nipped at her ear.

"I... I don't know."

He would have laughed at her words, if they hadn't unleashed something primitive within him, something he'd never experienced before. She was *his*, and only his. She may not know what she wanted, but he did, and he would give her the answer. He would be the only one to *ever* ease her in such a way.

Driving deeper into her, he reached between them to rub his finger against her clit until she was writhing and her body was moving wantonly beneath his. Her head fell back as she arched off the bed.

"Ronan!"

The cry erupted from her as waves of pleasure crashed through her, causing her whole body to shake. She could only cling to him as she completely unraveled. She had never felt anything like this, never thought to experience such bliss.

With a shout, he plunged into her a final time and the clenching muscles of her sheath milked his release from him. Tremors shook him as he continued to come inside her in a seemingly endless stream. Finally spent, his head fell to her shoulder and he remained buried within her as he rolled to the side with her trapped in his arms.

He savored the astonishing feelings she evoked in him. Most of them were feelings he was experiencing for the first time. He'd never felt so protective of another before, never wanted to cherish and hold someone as close as he held her.

He inhaled her sweet scent, pleased to realize he could smell himself all over her too. Others would smell him on her skin and within her as well. Her hands released their death grip on his shoulders, and she trailed her fingers leisurely up his back.

He inhaled again, drawing her essence deeper into him. Then, the scent changed. In an instant, all he could smell was her sweet blood pounding through her veins. And he wanted to have *his* blood coursing as strongly within her as her own. He also wanted to feel her flowing through him to form an unbreakable connection to her.

Without warning, the demon part of him rushed to the forefront.

CHAPTER TWENTY-FIVE

HIS FANGS LENGTHENED against her skin as his instincts screamed at him to drain her blood and replace it with his own. To make it so they would be bound for eternity and she would never be able to walk away from here or return to her family. His fangs grazed her neck. The vein pulsing beneath her flesh was right there; he could pierce it before she ever knew what he intended.

He'd have her drained to the point of death within a minute and his own blood filling her in the next minute.

She'll hate you for an eternity if you cage her against her will and in such a way! A small sliver of reason pierced through his bloodlust.

Pulling himself out of her, he flung himself back so fast that he nearly toppled off the bed.

"Ronan, are you okay?"

Her hand rubbed his back. His control unraveled further at her touch. "Don't!" he snarled.

Kadence recoiled as if she'd been slapped. She had no idea what was wrong with him, but she suspected it had something to do with what had just transpired between them. Had she done something wrong?

Well, if she had, then it was *his* fault, she decided. He had a lot more experience in this than she did after all.

What if they had both done something wrong? He may have a lot more experience in this area than her, but she could guarantee he'd never been with a hunter before. Maybe their kinds were never supposed to come together in such a way and now something was happening to him because of it.

She pulled the blanket up against her chest as he launched to his feet and stalked away from her. He didn't look at her as he prowled the room.

"Did we do something wrong?" she asked. "Is this because I'm a hunter and you're a vampire?"

He gave a bitter laugh as realization settled over him and he lifted his head to find her blue eyes locked on him. Something had gone completely off the tracks wrong, but not because of what she was. It was because of *who* she was to him. He was a train wreck waiting to happen because she was not simply a woman he'd come to care for, not a hunter, but his *mate*.

Fuck! He tugged at his hair, trying to keep himself calm as the realization rocked him. How had he not seen it earlier?

Then, Declan's words replayed in his head, *"You say that because she is here now, but we both know you're lying. You would have kept her."*

Wouldn't he have let her go? He'd been determined to do so; he still was. It didn't matter she was his mate, didn't matter he'd accelerated the need to complete the mating bond by taking her, he would not chain her as she'd been chained her whole life, and he would *not* chain her to his world. The danger of her life as a hunter was a day at the circus compared to what came with his life.

The constant fights and death that made up every day of his existence. The treacherous edge he walked. *She* would be the first one he

190 BRENDA K DAVIES

killed if he turned Savage. Or she could calm the demon within him and make it so he never again walked the line between the darkness and the light. It was what mates did for a vampire after all, especially a purebred vampire.

But no other vampire like him had ever existed before. It could be possible he was so completely bound to the demon part of him that she wouldn't calm him, that nothing would change within him, and he would be pushed over the edge by that realization.

Who are you trying to convince of that? He wondered, knowing it was a lie even as he thought it. She'd already calmed him in so many ways. Declan had said that when he first held her, his eyes had been entirely brown again. In that instant, she'd brought forth something in him that hadn't been there in centuries. If she was his, he knew, his constant drive to deliver death would not plague him so badly.

But with the bond not completed between them, she'd also made him far more explosive in other ways. He now understood why his temper had been more unstable lately, why he could barely control himself around her when no other female had ever made him lose control before. A vampire who encountered their mate was more volatile until the bond between the mates was completed.

However, if she were bonded to him, she may never be able to live out her dreams. He could guarantee her nothing but fighting and uncertainty in his foreseeable future, maybe forever.

She deserved better, and he would make sure she had it.

"No, Kadence, this is not because you're a hunter and I'm a vampire. We did nothing wrong."

"Then what is the matter with you?" Her eyes narrowed on him and she pulled the covers more firmly against her chest. "Or is this how you treat all women after you have sex with them?"

He closed his eyes against the misery in her voice. He was a bastard. He should be in that bed now, holding her close. Instead, he was scared if he got too close to her, he might drain her dry, change her, and never let her go.

"No, this is not the way I treat women after sex."

"I guess I'm the lucky one then." Her tone dripped acid as she spoke.

"No… This isn't *you*."

Taking a deep breath, he braced himself to meet her gaze again. She stared back at him, her eyes glittering with fury, but also with a hurt he'd never wanted to inflict on her. Her anguish shoved the demon within him aside. He took a step toward her, and when the thirst for her blood didn't immediately rush back to the surface, he closed the distance between them.

Her hair fell into one of her eyes when she tilted her head back to stare at him. He brushed the strand aside to tuck it behind her ear. Maybe he could control himself enough to crawl back into the bed with her and hold her the way she deserved to be held.

He stroked his hand over her cheek and lower to her neck. His gaze fastened on the vein running just under her skin. He dropped his hand and stepped back as his veins became as scorched as a desert.

"I can't."

He moved further away as he closed his eyes against the hunger tearing at him. Lifting his hands, he scrubbed his palms over his cheeks, pulling at his flesh.

Kadence had never seen anyone look so distraught before. She didn't understand what was going on with him, but the fact it was Ronan tore at her heart. "Maybe I can help."

Oh, she could help, he ruminated bitterly. She was the only one who *could* help. Lowering his hands from his face, he lifted his eyes to hers.

Kadence's mouth parted on a breathless *oh* when Ronan met her gaze again. His eyes were a glittering ruby color that blazed out at her and his fangs had elongated past his lower lip. She'd seen his fangs and red eyes before, but this was somehow different.

Because he's not in control, she realized and her heart leapt into her throat. Before, she'd always been able to see Ronan behind the vampire traits. Now, she saw only the demon.

This was what Joseph had looked like before he'd bit her. There had been no humanity in his gaze, nothing other than evil. Her hand involuntarily went to the place on her neck where Joseph had sank his fangs. The memory of the pain he'd inflicted on her came readily back to life.

"I scare you," he said.

Kadence closed her eyes against her self-disgust over her cowardice. "No," she lied.

"I can smell the fear on you."

"Not of you, not really. The bite, it's painful."

Refusing to be cowed by the memory of Joseph, she opened her eyes. Her heart sank when she realized Ronan was gone.

RONAN STORMED DOWN THE STAIRS, heedless of his nudity. He moved swiftly across the marble foyer, not noticing the coldness of it beneath his bare feet as he made his way to the basement door, flung it open, and swiftly descended.

He stepped off the last stair and strode across the matted floor of the gym. He would head straight for one of the treadmills as soon as he fed. He'd run his body for so long and hard that he would be too tired to move, too tired to do anything but crawl into bed and pass out. He would be too tired to think about anything, especially *her*. Though, he suspected he'd have to be dead before he stopped thinking of Kadence.

"Some of us prefer clothes to work out in, but to each their own."

Ronan ground his teeth together as the words drifted across the room from the stairwell he'd left behind. The last thing, the last *one*, he wanted to deal with right now was Declan. Ronan refused to look back at him as continued through the set of swinging steel doors and into the storage room beyond. A tall, stainless steel refrigerator was set against the far wall. They kept emergency supplies of blood stashed inside, and with the way he felt right now, this definitely classified as an emergency.

Pulling one of the doors open, he snatched a blood bag from within. He ripped the top off it, and heedless of the cold temperature, downed the contents in one gulp. He crumpled the bag, tossed it aside, and grabbed another one. He drank it down before flinging it aside.

He had never required a third bag to sate his thirst before, but fire still raged through his veins. Seizing another bag, he consumed it and was reaching for a fourth when the doors swung open behind him. Declan's footsteps sounded on the tile floor as he entered the room.

"Get out," Ronan commanded.

He still wouldn't look at Declan as he ripped the top off the fourth bag and drank it. The hunger continued to shred his insides with its incessant demand for more. For something *other* than this bagged shit, or rather, *someone* else. No matter how much he drank, he wouldn't be satisfied until it was Kadence's vein his lips were pressed against.

Throwing the bag away, he cursed loudly before slamming his fist into the fridge. Metal screeched as it crumpled from the impact of the blow.

"What did the fridge ever do to you?" Declan quipped.

Ronan whirled on him. "I said *get out!*"

Declan held his hands up as he backed away. Ronan barely glanced at whatever was hanging from Declan's fingers before his friend tossed it at him. "Easy, Ronan, I'm not here to start anything with you."

"Then why are you here?"

Declan's nostrils flared as he scented the air. Ronan stiffened when he realized Declan had caught his scent, which meant he could smell what had transpired between him and Kadence.

"You're in a feeding frenzy," Declan said flatly, wisely choosing not to comment on his relationship with Kadence.

"Your powers of observation are astronomical!" Ronan spat.

"When was the last time you fed?"

"What business is that of yours?"

"You're out of control. That makes it my business. If this were me in here, you would lock me away or destroy me."

"Try it," Ronan dared him.

"I'm not going to try anything. We both know you could kill me, just as we both know why you're like this."

Ronan turned away from him and removed another bag of blood. This time, he didn't bother to tear off the top but sank his fangs into the bottom and drained the contents. He would drink every drop of blood in the fridge, and when he was done, he would return upstairs, take her again and drain her.

He stretched a shaky hand in for the sixth bag. In all his years, he'd never been this out of control.

CHAPTER TWENTY-SIX

"W HEN WAS the last time you fed?" Declan asked again.

"Two days ago." He occasionally went two days at a time, never longer. When he'd been younger, he'd been able to go for almost a week without much of a problem. Now, he tried to feed every day to keep the part of him that craved blood and death at bay.

"You slept with her," Declan stated.

Ronan's head swiveled on his shoulders toward Declan. His friend edged back until his heel connected with one of the swinging doors. "That's none of your fucking business."

"I know, I know," Declan said quickly. "But come on, Ronan, you must realize what she is to you."

"I do," Ronan admitted.

"What happened between you tonight has accelerated things for you. That is why you're so out of control right now."

"A *hunter* for a mate. How is this possible?"

"We don't pick our mates. A lot of us don't find them. But when we do—"

"I am well aware of what happens when we do." A loss of control until the bond between them was completed, and since she was mortal, Kadence would also have to be turned. Which meant she would have to die.

"Then you know what must happen now," Declan said.

Ronan closed his eyes and rubbed at the bridge of his nose. "Even if she would agree to such a thing, I would never allow it. She deserves better than this brutal existence."

"She's a hunter who lost her father to a Savage. She may have led a life of seclusion, but she is no innocent to the brutality of our world, or her own."

"I promised her freedom, and she will have it," he said hoarsely.

Declan exhaled sharply. "You know what will happen if she leaves here, leaves *you*."

"I will not chain her to me! What was it you said to me? *'Everyone deserves a chance to fly.'* You wouldn't clip her wings, yet you expect me to do it. It will not happen."

Declan looked at him as if he'd lost his mind, and perhaps he had.

"It already has happened, Ronan. The more you fight it, the worse it's going to get, until you lose all control and turn Savage, or you end up forcing the change on her. If you take her by force, you may kill her, and you will kill the trust she has in you. You won't be able to live with yourself if you do that to her."

Ronan's skin felt as if it were drawing taut against him, strangling him. He resisted the urge to dig his fingers in and shred the skin from his body so he could breathe again.

"I've promised her the world she dreams of, and she will be leaving in mere hours. I won't be able to hurt her, because she won't be here. I'll make sure Marta and Baldric know not to tell me where they are so I can't go after her. She'll be set free to live, instead of caged here."

Declan gawked at him. "That's not an option for you."

"It *is* an option for me! I know what they say about mates going crazy without each other, I've witnessed it, but that doesn't mean it will happen to me. The bond is not completed between us. We have not shared blood. If anyone can control this, *I* can."

"You may be the strongest and oldest vampire to ever walk this earth, but not even you can control this. You're *already* losing control. No one has ever come back after they've given into their Savage nature. *She* may not even be able to bring you back if you cross that line, and if you did encounter her again as a Savage, there is no telling what you would do to her."

Declan gestured at the bags of blood scattered across the ground at Ronan's feet. "If you become Savage, we won't be able to stop you. Everything you've worked for will be for naught. The Savages will eventually win because, if you don't take your own life, you will take all of *ours*. You will most likely rise up to become their leader and there will be no stopping that, Ronan. Are you ready to deal with that?"

"I have dealt with it for centuries. You felt it necessary to make a point about the color of my eyes before, so it is no secret to you that I've been battling bloodlust for centuries. It will be worse when she goes, but I will control it just as I always have."

"You just drank six bags of blood, yet I can still feel the hunger coming off you. You've never had to deal with finding your mate before."

Ronan eyed Declan as wrath burnt through him. "You knew what she was to me when she pulled that little stunt with her brother." He stalked toward Declan as he spoke. Declan's heel pushed open one of the doors as he backed into the gym. "You could have stopped this. She would have been gone from here before our relationship ever progressed to this point."

He'd regretted going after Declan in the poolroom before; now he would like nothing more than to tear his friend's arms off and beat Declan with them. If that didn't satisfy him, he would tear Declan's head off next.

"After what I saw with you in that alley, I did suspect it," Declan admitted, apparently unaware of how close to death he was. "But this was going to happen no matter what. Even if she had told her brother where to find her, you never would have handed her over to be married to another man. You're unraveling fast, Ronan, faster than I thought possible; most likely because of your age, power, and lineage."

Declan's gaze was sad when he stopped retreating. "You have no control over this. It will claw at you until you go mad."

Ronan turned away from him, no longer able to meet Declan's gaze. "I *promised* her she could see everything she ever dreamed about seeing. *I* can't take her to see those things, I can't give her the life she deserves, not now. The traveling we do consists of: arrive, hunt, kill, return. There's no time for sightseeing and tourist traps. Even if there was time and I did take her with me, I would be dropping her off to go kill before returning to take her on a guided tour. What kind of fucked-up life is that?

"Not to mention, I don't think any of us will be going anywhere anytime soon, not with Joseph here. My life revolves around death. She's too vibrant and beautiful for hers to be the same way. She risked everything to gain freedom, and I won't be the monster who rips it away from her."

"You can figure all that out, and one day, maybe you will be able to take her everywhere she wants to go."

"That's a big maybe. She's also frightened because of what Joseph did to her in that alley."

"You'll get her past that. You need to change her and mark her so that every vampire will know who she belongs to and so you don't completely lose it."

"Mark her for death, you mean," Ronan replied. "Because I will be painting a bullseye on her for all of our enemies if I do that."

"If anyone can keep her safe, you can, and we will all help you do so."

"She won't understand any of this."

"She will, if you explain it to her."

Ronan laughed harshly. "She'll understand that any hope of freedom she ever had is gone?"

"That's not true. Things can change over time."

"There will always be vampires who turn Savage."

"Yes," Declan said. "But maybe one day we won't be the only ones fighting them. She gave herself to you; I would say she cares about you a great deal if she did that. In fact, I think she has already given you her heart. She's a good woman, Ronan."

"Too good for the likes of me," he muttered.

"Tell her what is going on and see what she decides."

"I won't put this burden on her."

"She's strong and she's smart. You deserve some calm in your life; deserve someone who cares for you. Tell her and let her make the choice."

The scent of vanilla drifting to him silenced Ronan's response. He took a step back toward the swinging doors and nudged one open with his heel as the sound of Kadence's footsteps on the stairs reached him.

He'd considered himself somewhat settled, but having her so close caused hunger to surge through him once more. "Get her out of here, Declan."

"Ronan, you know what must be done."

"I need more control over myself before I can see her again. Get her out of here."

"Ronan—"

"Now," he hissed. "I might hurt her otherwise." Declan turned to leave. "Declan." He looked back, his silvery eyes troubled. "I understand why you didn't stop her from doing what she did with her brother, and that you weren't trying to go against me, but she can't stay."

"She can if you give her a chance to decide."

Ronan didn't have the time to get into it with Declan again as

Kadence's scent strengthened on the air. "Keep her away from Saxon and Killean; I don't want them to know about this yet."

"I will. I threw a pair of sweats at you earlier."

As Ronan slipped back into the storage room, he vaguely recalled Declan tossing him something earlier. He spotted the blue sweats on the floor amid the bags of blood as their hushed voices drifted to him through the swinging doors.

Ronan returned to the fridge and took out more blood. He was determined that one of these bags would finally drench the fire within him.

CHAPTER TWENTY-SEVEN

"Is he okay?" Kadence inquired.

Declan heard the concern in her voice, saw it in the way she kept turning her head to look over her shoulder for Ronan. A spurt of jealousy went through him. He wasn't jealous of the condition Ronan was in now, for he wouldn't wish that on his worst enemy, but of the relationship he and Kadence could have together.

They already cared for each other, that much was obvious. It was only a matter of time before it deepened into love.

He shook his head to rid himself of the crazy ideas running through it. No, he was much better off the way he was. The last thing he wanted was to get shot by the bullet that was taking Ronan down. Ronan was going insane, and Declan was calmly walking the cause of his insanity away from the gym.

"Declan?"

He returned his attention to her as he tried to recall her question. "He'll be fine," he assured her.

"Are you sure?"

Declan nodded, but he couldn't be completely sure until everything was settled between the two of them. If everything went well, within the next day or two, Ronan *would* be fine. Hopefully, Ronan still had a day or two left in him before the impending meltdown occurred.

Kadence bit her lip as she twisted her hands in front of her. She was beautiful, yet there was an inner beauty and strength to her that outshone her looks. Enemy or not, he liked this little hunter and hoped she would make the right choice.

"He'll be fine," Declan assured her again.

"I may not know as much as I thought about vampires, but whatever this is doesn't seem like him. Is it because of me?"

She was completely out of her depth in this whole mess and didn't understand the greedy, unpredictable nature of the demon lurking within them. She had given herself to a man she cared for, and in doing so she'd escalated a chain of events she never could have known were already starting to unfold.

To be fair, even if she hadn't given herself to Ronan, it would have only been a matter of time before Ronan recognized she was his mate.

"This isn't like him," he replied, uncertain of how to respond. "But it will all work out soon."

Her mouth pursed as they stepped into the main foyer. He guided her toward the stairs, eager to get her to her room before Killean or Saxon arrived and caught the scent of Ronan all over her. Killean would not react well to such a thing.

Maybe he should tell her what Ronan was going through and how she could help. He shut the idea down as soon as he thought it. Even if he were stable, Ronan might kill him for interfering in such a way. He'd definitely kill him now for it.

This was not his place, and he knew better than to interfere in others' lives.

"What's going on?"

Kadence stopped short when Killean strolled into the foyer from the hall. He held a glass of scotch in his hand and his golden eyes surveyed them with curiosity.

"What are the two of you doing?" Killean inquired.

"I gave her a tour of the place," Declan lied.

Killean took a sip of his drink as he walked closer to rest his elbow on the banister of the stairs. The tension in his body belied the casual gesture. "Why, she won't be staying for much longer?"

"It was something to do," Kadence replied flippantly.

Killean swirled the liquid in his glass as he inhaled deeply and his upper lip twisted into a sneer. Declan braced himself for whatever was about to unfold.

KADENCE'S STOMACH twisted at the look on Killean's face. She knew he didn't like her, but when he looked at her like that, she realized that she also repulsed him.

"Where's Ronan?" Killean demanded.

"In the gym," Declan replied. "I would suggest leaving him be."

"Leaving him be," Killean snorted. "I can smell him all over her. What is he thinking screwing her?"

Color flooded her cheeks, but she managed to stop herself from gaping at Killean's blunt words. She should have known the vamps would be able to tell what had transpired between her and Ronan tonight. She didn't know if she wanted to melt through the floor or kick Killean in the nuts more. Driving his nuts into his throat would feel really, *really* good right now, she decided.

"Watch yourself, Killean," Declan advised.

"It's not you I smell on her, Declan. Why are you being so protective?" Killean demanded.

"It's not her he's protecting. It's *you*." The hair on Kadence's arms rose as Ronan growled the words from the doorway behind her. "Because if you say another goddamn word, I'll rip your throat out."

~

DECLAN CRINGED INWARDLY as Ronan's words filled the foyer. He released Kadence's arm, surreptitiously pushing her a little away from Killean and himself. The last thing they needed was to provoke Ronan any more by having her so close to them.

A scarlet haze clouded Declan's vision as Ronan's wrath reverberated within him. He blinked the cloud away, desperate to get his vision back, but Ronan's emotions were too wild to be shoved away.

He wanted to reach out to someone, to grab them in order to stay grounded. Killean was out of the question unless he wanted to experience more anger. He couldn't touch Kadence, not with Ronan so wound up. He settled for resting his fingers against the wall, if only to keep standing. It did nothing to wash away the red tide shading his eyes.

"Are you okay?"

Kadence's voice filled his ears as her hand latched onto his arm. The red cloud intensified tenfold, causing his ears to hum and his head to throb. Ronan must have seen her grab him. "Let go!" he ordered and tried to shake off her hand.

"You don't look so good." She clung to him as her voice took on a frantic tone.

He didn't feel so good. He was either going to pass out or his head was going to explode. He didn't care which happened first as long as the awful haze stopped. It had been centuries since anyone had broken through his carefully constructed barriers this bad. He'd spent years armoring himself against others, but Ronan was far more out of control than he'd realized, and he was far more powerful than Declan's walls.

"Let go of him!" Ronan snarled.

"But he looks ill," Kadence protested.

"Let go!" Declan finally succeeded in getting her to release him. "Calm down, Ronan," he managed to choke out.

He couldn't see Ronan right now, but Declan knew his friend approached when the haze grew darker. *Breathe, just breathe,* he counseled himself. The deep inhalations helped him to piece his broken walls back together and the pressure inside him eased.

Gradually, the red haze faded until he saw parts of the foyer once more. He took in the shadows, the stairs, and then Ronan. His eyes widened on the vamp coming at them, and he wished he couldn't see again.

CHAPTER TWENTY-EIGHT

KADENCE COULDN'T STOP the tremor that went through her as Ronan stalked across the room. His eyes were a shade of red she would have only thought possible in Hell before she saw him like this. They were so bright they lit the shadows around him as his attention remained focused on Killean.

She'd never seen the normally distant, often asshole vampire look at all ruffled. Now, Killean straightened away from the banister and fear flashed briefly across his face before his expression became void of all emotion. Declan took a hitching breath. His cheeks had regained some color, but he still had a blank look in his eyes that troubled her.

The anger Ronan radiated was impossible to ignore as it pulsated through the room like a living entity. The veins in his arms bulged, and every muscle through his chest and arms stood out. She didn't know where they'd come from, but the pair of blue sweats he wore hung low on his hips. He looked ready to kill, yet his hand was gentle when he clasped her elbow and drew her closer to him.

Ever since he'd walked out of her room, she'd felt a strange sense of loss and an odd stretching of her skin, as if it didn't fit her body right. It made no sense, but the second he touched her again, the sensation eased and she found herself able to breathe easier again.

Ronan pierced Killean with a look that would have made most men cower. Killean's golden eyes filled with disbelief. The only reaction he showed to the hostility Ronan directed at him was a tensing of his fingers around his glass.

"You're not to talk to her like that ever again," Ronan said, the hint of his Irish accent more pronounced. "You're not to do anything but treat her with respect and defend her life with yours. If I see or hear you doing anything disrespectful to her ever again, I'll beat you to within an inch of your life, and when you heal, I'll do it all over again."

Kadence gasped at Ronan's threat. She opened her mouth to deny his words, but Killean was already speaking. "You're the boss."

Ronan took a step toward Killean, who had the good sense to back away. Killean's eyes darted toward her, but instead of his normal antipathy toward her, she sensed only curiosity.

"Don't fuck with me on this, Killean," Ronan stated.

"I have no intention of doing so," Killean replied.

Kadence glanced over her shoulder as Ronan nudged her forward and started leading her up the steps. Killean stared blankly back at her as he took another sip of his drink, while Declan rubbed at his temples.

Turning away from them, she focused on Ronan. With every step they took, his eyes shifted back to that amazing burgundy color, but now that she knew the true depth of the brown in his eyes, she wanted to see more of it.

He pushed open the door to her room and stepped aside to let her enter first. She was instantly assailed with the lingering scent of their sex. Her heart kicked up a notch, and to her horror, she felt herself growing aroused again. After what had happened earlier, she'd been certain she'd never have sex with him again. She wanted answers about what had happened to him, but she would not be fooled twice. Unfortunately, her body seemed to have other ideas.

She couldn't meet his gaze as he stepped into the room beside her. His fingers stroked briefly over her skin before he released her arm. He strode over to her bed and pulled the blanket back. Kadence's jaw clenched as the sight of her blood staining the white sheets brought back the horrible events of him fleeing her room earlier. His hand stilled and his shoulders hunched up as if he were preparing himself for a blow when he looked at her over his shoulder.

"Did you not know I was a virgin?" she asked coldly when the stunned look didn't leave his eyes.

"No, I knew you were," he said. Turning away, he spoke so softly she barely heard his following words. "It wasn't supposed to be like this."

Yanking the sheets from the bed, Ronan wadded them into a ball. He hadn't thought it possible, but seeing her blood made him hate himself even more for the way he'd treated her tonight. Seeing her blood on the sheets slammed home the reality of what an asshole he was.

"I'll get you some new sheets," he said.

He couldn't meet her eyes as he walked past her and into the hallway. He opened a few doors before he found the closet with the sheets Marta kept stacked within. Staring at them, he struggled to maintain the thin thread of control he'd managed to reclaim after glutting himself on ten bags of blood.

Finally feeling capable of being near her again, he removed a set of sheets from within and returned to the room. Kadence remained where he'd left her, her eyes guarded as she watched him remake the bed.

"You should probably try to get some sleep," he said when he was done.

"I'm not tired."

"You've had a rough night; you should rest."

She glared at him as she crossed her arms over her chest. He'd hurt her, he knew. When she should have had comfort and security, he'd abandoned her. He wasn't surprised she was mad at him; he was surprised by how much he didn't like it.

"It wouldn't be a rough night if you would tell me what is wrong with you. Besides, I don't recall having to take orders from you," she said.

Ronan gritted his teeth as he met her gaze. Her face was suffused with color; her hair cascaded around her face in waves that emphasized her striking features. She was exquisite and *his*. There was no denying it. Even after she left here, she would always be his.

"There is something we must discuss," he said.

"Noooo," she retorted sarcastically.

He lifted an eyebrow at her, but he deserved her anger. She hadn't cried and carried on about her circumstances and what he'd done to her tonight, but what would she say when he told her he wanted to bind her to him for eternity? That he wanted to turn her into something else entirely and deny her the freedom she so rightly deserved to have?

If they completed the mating bond, it would be for him; there would be nothing for her. Just as there had been nothing for her amongst her own kind. He'd thought the hunters archaic for marrying her off like they intended to, so what was he now? Because his demon DNA recognized her as his mate, he believed he had more of a right to her than her own family and her own kind?

He'd fought against losing his humanity for years; he could fight it longer, for her.

"I'm sorry for what transpired here earlier."

Her eyes became a vivid shade of blue as fury emanated from her. "I see."

He didn't understand why that had pissed her off more. He was trying to apologize. He knew it would never be enough, but it was a beginning at least. "I must explain—"

"Don't bother," she cut in. "It was a mistake, a passing fling."

"It was not a mistake!" he snapped, unable to control the flare of temper her words provoked in him. Taking a deep breath, he took a second to steady himself before continuing. "I am not sorry for what happened between us; I am sorry for my behavior afterward."

"Oh." Her arms fell to her sides as some of her ire faded. "Okay."

He couldn't help but smile at her even as his insides twisted into knots at the words he knew he would be issuing soon. "Okay."

"Why did you act like that then?"

Tell her. The words screamed across his mind, the selfish part of him roaring to life. She cared enough for him to have given herself to him; she might agree to stay with him if she knew his sanity could depend on it. However, he couldn't bring himself to place that responsibility on her, not when she was so close to being free.

"It had been a while since I fed." Not a lie, not a truth.

Her brow furrowed then cleared when his eyes were involuntarily drawn to the vein in her neck. "Oh," she said. "And you've fed now?"

That was not the word for what he'd done. "I have."

"So you're better now?"

No. "Yes," he lied.

"What about what happened with Killean and Declan just now? I've never seen you so angry at Killean, and I think something was wrong with Declan."

"No one is going to talk to you in such a way. Killean knows that now. And Declan is... well, he's different from others. Before you ask, I don't know exactly how he's different. I just know he is. I've never asked him to reveal all of his secrets to me, but his difference can be useful to him, or stressful."

"I see."

"You should rest before you leave."

Kadence blinked at him, thrown off by the abrupt change in conversation. "Excuse me?"

"Rest. It is going to be a tiring day for you, and you will be leaving shortly."

"Oh... ah... yeah," she muttered. She had no idea what was wrong with her. She should be jumping for joy. Soon she'd be leaving this place and *him* behind to do everything she'd always dreamed about doing. The knowledge brought her no joy. Instead, it made that awful tightening of her skin start all over again.

Her fingers bit into her arms as she held back the tears burning her eyes. She would not cry in front of him. She *refused* to do so again, especially since she had no idea why she wanted to cry. Okay, well, she had a little bit of one. She had come to care for this man who she would have gladly staked two weeks ago, and she wasn't ready to leave him.

Do I want to go? she asked herself. *Of course you do, you idiot. You abandoned your whole family for a shot at freedom, and Ronan is offering you more than you ever could have hoped for.*

Then why did her heart feel like it was being squeezed in a vise?

"Do you want to leave, Kadydid?" he asked.

Her heart squeezed further at the nickname he'd given her; one she'd come to cherish over the past week. Was that a measure of hope she heard in his voice, or was she only trying to hear it there?

"I want... I want to see the world and learn things," she whispered.

He glanced to the windows, his hands fisting as on the horizon the night sky began to lighten toward dawn. "And I will give that to you," he murmured. "I must speak with Marta and Baldric now."

He kept his head averted from her as he strode toward the door. "Ronan." He flinched away from her hand when she rested it on his arm. "I should speak with my brother."

His head swiveled toward her. She couldn't stop herself from taking a step back from the burning red of his eyes. "Why?" he asked.

Kadence swallowed. "To let him know we were wrong, that you are not all bad, that we all fight a common enemy. Maybe... maybe you could work together. Think of the good that could be done and the lives that could be saved if hunters and vampires united."

"And do you think he would listen to you?"

She contemplated his question before sighing. "Probably not, but don't you think it's worth a chance?"

His hand briefly rested over hers, his fingers squeezing her before releasing her. "I think it's best if you get away from here. If you leave behind the violence and death of both our worlds and live the life you are meant to live."

"And what life is that?" she inquired.

"One of happiness."

"Ronan—"

Pulling her close, he kissed her forehead before releasing her. "Let this go."

The lump in her throat choked her as he strode toward the doorway. "Ronan!" she blurted when he stepped out the door. He hesitated in the threshold, his shoulders drawn up to his ears and his back hunched. "Thank you, for everything. No matter what, I will never regret anything that transpired between us."

"Neither will I."

"When I come back—"

He looked at her over his shoulder. "If you come back, I will be here, waiting for you."

"You'll have found someone else by then," she said with what felt like the worst smile.

"No, Kadydid, there will never be anyone else for me, only you. Do not return here unless you're ready for an eternity with me."

Before she could reply, he was gone from the doorway and she was left gawking after him.

CHAPTER TWENTY-NINE

KADENCE STOOD IN THE FOYER, her small bag in hand as Marta bustled around her. For the thousandth time, Kadence's eyes went to the hallway where the poolroom was located. Somehow, she knew Ronan was down there. She kept waiting for him to come to say goodbye, but she hadn't seen him again since he'd left her room.

"Are you ready, miss?"

Kadence glanced at Marta before focusing on the hall again. That awful feeling of not belonging in her own skin hadn't eased, but now she found it nearly impossible to breathe as she kept waiting.

"Miss?" This time it was Baldric who stepped before her.

Go, or stay for an eternity? And what did he mean by an eternity with him? He couldn't have *really* meant what she'd thought when he said that? She wasn't a vampire. There was no eternity for her.

Kadence looked over at where Marta stood by the door with a small duffel bag in hand. Her mostly gray hair had been pulled into a ponytail. Her round face only showed lines around her eyes and mouth when she smiled. Plump with kind hazel eyes, Marta had become someone Kadence really liked.

"Yes," she croaked. "Yes. I am ready."

Baldric stepped back and opened the door for her. Kadence glanced over her shoulder, but there was still no sign of Ronan. She took a step toward the poolroom before retreating. If she went to say goodbye to him now, she might never leave.

She forced herself to walk out the door. She'd turned against her brother and all her kind for this opportunity at freedom. She'd forsaken everything she knew; she could not change her mind now, even if she was contemplating staying for a man she'd only known for a short while.

A man she had willingly given herself to. By doing so, she'd chosen a course she could never take back and didn't want to. If she tried to return to the hunters now, and they somehow learned who she had given herself to, they may label her a traitor and kill her. Even Nathan wouldn't be able to stop that from happening if they decided that's what she was.

Not like she would ever willingly tell them she had given herself to a vampire, but like Declan, there were those of her kind who had gifts. She certainly did. She had the same strength, speed, and enhanced senses her father and Nathan possessed and her strange knowing of things.

Stepping into the day, Kadence tipped her head back and let the warmth of the sun wash over her. Baldric opened the back door of a black car with heavily tinted windows for her. Every step she took caused her shoulders to sag more, but she tossed her bag into the back seat and climbed in behind it.

She winced at the clicking sound of the door closing behind her. Huddling into herself, she watched as Baldric and Marta climbed in and Baldric started the vehicle. She couldn't look back as they drove down the tree-lined, cobblestone drive to the thirty-foot-high gate at the end.

"Put your blindfold on now, miss," Marta said.

"Please call me Kadence. It's going to be an extremely long time together if you keep calling me miss."

"Kadence then," Marta said with a smile. "Do you need help with the blindfold?"

"No," she whispered and slid the thick material over her eyes.

"WHAT HAVE YOU DONE, RONAN?"

"If you want to survive to hunt tonight, I would suggest leaving," Ronan didn't look back at his friend as he replied to Declan's question.

"You have to stop them. You can't let her go."

"I can and I did."

He kept his gaze focused on the bar as he swirled the whiskey in his glass. He was going on his third bottle of Jameson, and he still didn't feel any effects from the alcohol, which was probably a good thing. In his current mood, he might tear this entire house down if he were drunk.

The people who had lived here before them had shitty taste in décor, but they had fantastic taste in alcohol, he decided as he took another sip of the Jameson Vintage Reserve he'd discovered beneath the bar. At one time, he'd lived on Irish whiskey and women.

He couldn't remember the last time he'd taken a sip of alcohol, but he could clearly recall the last time he'd taken a woman. Every second of that encounter had been emblazoned on his mind, along with the fiasco of an ending. And now she was gone, set free by none other than himself.

Had he hoped she'd stay? Right up until she walked out the door. He would have denied it, but he realized now, he'd been holding out hope she would decide to stay for him.

Now he was trying to remember the last time whiskey had burned its way down his throat instead of thinking about who had walked out the door.

The light Declan let in when he'd slid open the doors flashed, but not because he was closing them again; it was because Declan was coming closer. Ronan had closed the shutters over all the windows, unable to handle that small amount of sun right now as the demon churned within him. He definitely couldn't deal with Declan's worry for him.

"Ronan—"

The tumbler shattered in his hand, and liquid splashed over him as shards drove deep into his flesh. He didn't bother to pull the glass from his palm before he lifted the bottle he'd set next to his chair. Declan remained mute as he padded by him to the bar where he removed a couple of bottles before walking over to him. Grabbing the back of one of the ugly chairs, Declan set it beside him, placed one of the bottles between them, and opened the other.

"Not one more word about her, Declan."

"Understood."

The light shifted again and Killean's resin scent drifted to him. Ronan's fangs lengthened in anticipation of one of Killean's remarks, but the vampire only walked by him to the bar before moving a chair to sit on Ronan's other side. Saxon joined minutes later, and when Ronan heard the click of the front door shutting, he knew Lucien had also arrived.

He'd forgotten Lucien was supposed to be coming today to discuss the moving of the training facility. *Ah well, the more the merrier,* he thought as he lifted the bottle to his lips and drank half of it down.

Ronan closed his eyes and took another pull on the bottle. The bloodlust slithered through his veins like an insidious snake waiting to strike. Every beat of his heart caused his temples to pulse with it. Yet there was still so much to deal with, so many still counting on him.

If he gave in and gorged himself on the blood, he wouldn't have to deal with it ever again. He'd only have to deal with himself, and Kadence's hatred of him should she return.

Mate or not, she was gone and he had to accept that she may never return. He had to continue with what he'd been born to do. Rising to his feet, he drank the rest of the bottle as he made his way toward the bar.

He waited until Lucien walked in and settled into another chair before speaking. "We have to take out Joseph before he continues to organize."

Declan passed his bottle to Lucien and opened the one he'd set on the floor. "We've had no new leads on him, even Brian is coming up blank," Lucien said.

"How is that possible?" Declan inquired.

Lucien shrugged. "Brian said he's not a GPS. Sometimes whatever he does just doesn't work. He also said Joseph is most likely staying in a large crowd or city if he can't pinpoint him."

"A large crowd of Savages?" Saxon asked.

"Perhaps," Lucien replied.

"Not good," Declan muttered.

"The trainees, do they know what is going on? Why the facility is being closed and moved?" Saxon asked.

"I saw no reason to keep it from them," Lucien replied and teepeed his hands before his face. "If they decide to bail instead of fight, then good riddance. I hope they get butchered by a Savage."

"Nice," Declan muttered and took another drink.

Lucien scowled at him. "You'd wish them well?"

"I wouldn't wish them death."

"We have to discuss if we will bring the turned vamps in to work with us," Ronan said. Some of the glass still embedded in his hand clattered against the bar when it succeeded in working its way out of his flesh. He glanced at the blood splattered piece before focusing on the others.

"It goes against tradition," Saxon said.

"It does," Ronan agreed. "And the turned vamps aren't as strong as we are, but they can take on a Savage. I lived through an attack from the Savages before. If Joseph comes at us with numbers like what they had back then, it will be a war the likes of which none of you have ever experienced."

They stared stonily back at him. He understood their reluctance to add turned vampires to their ranks and their pride. There were so few purebred vamps left, even fewer who had made it through the extreme training that elevated them to the status of Defender. The turned vamps went through a lot of training, but they didn't go through the same kind of training they had all endured and survived.

"They still don't have to be one of us," Lucien said. "We can call them something else if we want to use them for this battle."

"I vote we call them pissants," Killean said.

"I like it," Lucien agreed. "They many not even be willing to fight."

"I'm sure you've inspired no loyalty," Declan replied.

Lucien gave him the finger. "I'm not there to inspire them. I'm there to make sure they don't get killed by a Savage, and as soon as we find a replacement for me, I'm done with training them. Joseph boned me the most when he went Savage on us, and I got stuck with all the idiot newbies."

Thankfully, Joseph had given into the demon part of him outside of the training facility. Most likely because there had been enough recruits there to possibly take him down when they realized he'd become a Savage. Joseph had known that. Despite their endless thirst for blood, Savages were far from stupid. Before Joseph, they'd had no one to organize them, to lead them, but Joseph was a purebred, something different and stronger than they were, and the Savages were falling into line with him.

"Bring the turned vamps in training, who agree to fight with us, here," Ronan said to Lucien. "There will be enough room for them to stay here between the carriage house and the guest house, but make sure they have no idea where this place is located." His teeth ground together at the idea of having to be so close to the recruits, but there was little else that could be done about it. As long as they stayed out of his way, they'd survive. "Cut the ones who aren't willing to fight loose."

"What about Aiden, the purebred in training?" Lucien inquired. "His sisters and Brian are still at the training facility too."

Aiden had already been in training when his sister, Vicky, was captured by vampires looking to sell off her blood to the highest bidder. She'd been chained and held with other purebreds. It had taken them a while, but Ronan and the others had hunted down and destroyed most of that remaining threat against purebreds.

What remained of those vampires were a far smaller threat than what the vampire race faced with Joseph. But then, Joseph and the Savages were a danger to everyone who crossed their paths. For the first time, he was glad Kadence would be far from here.

"Bring Aiden and his family here too, if they agree to it," Ronan replied.

Lucien took another swig of his bottle.

"There are other turned vamps who have already gone through the training and are out there hunting Savages," Saxon said. "Do we bring them in?"

Having as much help as they could get would be the smart thing to do, but having vampires crawling over this place and the nearby cities and towns in search of food would be a sure-fire way to draw Joseph's attention, along with that of the humans.

However, if Joseph was accruing Savages, it was only a matter of time before he caught the attention of someone he shouldn't.

"Let's get the recruits here first, and then we'll discuss bringing more turned vamps in," Ronan replied as the last of the glass in his hand worked its way out of his flesh and clattered onto the bar.

"When should I bring them?" Lucien inquired.

"Now. I want this over with," Ronan replied.

CHAPTER THIRTY

"I'D LIKE to make a phone call, if I can," Kadence said.

"Of course, miss... ah, Kadence," Baldric replied with a smile. "You're not a prisoner. We're only here to make sure you're safe."

She smiled at him as he held one of the cell phones out to her and she took it. "Thank you."

"If you're going to call your brother, I'd keep it short. That may be a throwaway phone, but we don't want to take the chance they could find you."

"I will. It's... ah... it's okay if I call him?"

"Ronan said you could do whatever you wanted once you were free, as long as it didn't put you at risk, and I am to use my judgment on that. Since you can't do anything to hurt yourself, or Ronan, I see no reason why you can't call him. I don't believe you would do anything to put Marta or I at risk either."

"Of course not," she whispered.

"Don't forget our flight leaves in ten minutes."

Kadence resisted tugging on the collar of her shirt at the reminder. "I know."

She tried to tune out the crowd of people around her as she walked away from Baldric. It was quieter in this area of the airport than it had been when they were going through security, but she was ready to leave Logan Airport far behind her. Though she knew all the airports would have the hectic hustle and bustle of travelers trying to reach their destinations, she found the activity she'd assumed she'd love difficult to handle when a growing weight was bearing down on her chest.

She started dialing as Marta walked by with a stack of magazines and books in hand. The crawling in her skin had increased since she'd left Ronan, but she didn't know if that was from being away from him or from her unfamiliar surroundings. Not to mention, there were so many people; they were *everywhere*.

Her head pounded from all the noise. The scents of cooking food, coffee, body odor, and one woman who had enough perfume on to drown an elephant filled her nose. Kadence couldn't stop her nose from wrinkling as she passed the woman. She returned the dirty look the woman shot her and got as far from the woman as she could, but the heavy floral scent followed her.

She hadn't expected to be this overwhelmed by the human world, but her senses were being bombarded, and her body ached. Someone bumped against her, and she nearly jumped out of her skin before she hastily sidestepped them.

Taking a deep breath, she tried to steady the riotous beat of her heart as she punched in Nathan's number and held her breath in the hopes her brother still had the same phone. She knew he would have done everything he could to keep it, knowing it was her only connection to him, but sometimes things went horribly wrong.

"Kadence?"

"Yes, it's me," she whispered and wiped away the tear that slid down her cheek at the much-loved voice coming through the line.

"Oh, thank God," Nathan breathed. "I've been so worried about you."

Guilt filled her at the relief in his voice. "I'm sorry, I really am. I hope you know that."

"It doesn't matter. Just tell me where you are and I'll come get you. We can forget all about this when you get home."

Even if she did go home, she could never forget about any of this. "No, Nathan, I'm still not coming back. I... I'm doing this for me. Please understand, and don't ask me to come back again, not now."

"Kadence—"

"Listen to me, I didn't call you to hear a lecture or to come home. I'm not coming back. I'm not going to marry someone I don't love—"

"Then we will find you someone else!" he exploded.

She couldn't tell him that there was no one else for her, not after Ronan. She rubbed at one of her temples as she tried to ease the headache pounding there before shaking her head to clear it of the absurd notion. Of course there could be someone else for her, eventually, maybe.

She told herself this, but her skin felt stretched so tight that she had the urge to tear it away from her, and her heart yearned to go back to him. Did she love Ronan? No, that couldn't be possible. She'd only known him for a little over a week; it was impossible to fall in love with someone so fast. She kept telling herself this, but now that the possibility had taken hold it wouldn't let go.

He was a vampire, but he was a good man. Strong and caring, he made her feel things no other man had ever made her feel. She knew vampires weren't the enemies she'd always believed them to be, but to fall in love with one, to...

What? Settle down and marry him? She didn't exactly see Ronan as the marrying kind, and just because he'd tossed out that eternity comment to her, it didn't mean he wanted anything more with her. She was standing here after all when he could have made her stay.

No, he would have never done that, she knew. But he could have *asked* her to stay, and he hadn't.

Kadence kept that in mind as she inhaled a shuddery breath and focused on speaking with Nathan.

"I didn't call to be talked into coming home or because of marriage. I called because…" She had no idea how to say to him what she wanted to say to him. She'd been trying to figure it out since she'd left Ronan behind, but it always sounded the same to her, ridiculous. "We have it wrong, Nathan," she blurted.

Not exactly the smooth words she'd hoped to be able to come up with, but the truth.

"We have what wrong?" he demanded.

"The vampires, we have it wrong."

"What are you talking about?"

She glanced over at Baldric when he stepped into her line of view and tapped his watch. This was never going to be elegant, it would never be received well, but she couldn't leave here without at least trying to make a difference, and she was running out of time.

"Not all vampires are evil," she said. "Some of them are good. Some of them are trying to do exactly what we are. They protect innocents from those vampires who kill—"

"Kadence—"

"Listen to me! It could save so many lives if you do! They could have killed you in that alley. They didn't. They could have killed me. They didn't!"

"You're with the vampires who were in the alley?" he barked.

"No, not anymore. They set me free. I'm leaving, Nathan."

"Did they twist your mind in some way? Where are you? Tell me, and we will get you help."

"You know I'm not susceptible to their persuasion. No one twisted my mind. They opened it."

Silence met her statement. Baldric tapped his watch faster.

"I have to go."

"Did they hurt you?" Nathan asked.

"No. They knew who and what I was too, Nathan, and they let me go. Ronan would never hurt me."

"*Who the fuck is Ronan?*"

She had to move the phone away from her ear as Nathan's words reverberated through it.

"He's… he's… the one who set me free to live my dreams, and gave me the means to do so," she finished lamely, knowing he was so much more than that to her.

"If he set you free, then he's trying to kill you, Kadence. This world—"

"I know. It's big, it's cruel, and I have no idea about it." Being in this airport had hammered that fact home. "But I'll learn, just as I learned to walk and talk. Just as I've learned everything else. And I'm not alone; I have friends to help me through and money."

"What friends do you have with you? How do you have money? Where can you go? You have no ID; you have nothing."

"That's not important. What is important is that you listen to me. Not all vampires are brutal killers; not all of them are our enemies." A line was forming outside the gateway for her plane. Baldric had stopped tapping his watch and was coming toward her as the first person in line handed over their ticket. "Vampires and hunters can do good, together," she said as she watched more people moving through the ticket line.

Her gaze went to the silver airplane outside the floor-to-ceiling windows. The setting sun lit the plane in a multitude of different colors and caused the windows of the plane to reflect the growing pink of the sky. That plane would take her from here and deliver her to the first stop on her journey.

Baldric stopped before her and pointed toward the shortening line. "I have to go, Nathan. I'll be in touch again soon. Take care of yourself, and remember what I said. I love you."

She flipped the phone closed before he could respond. Baldric took it from her and tossed it in a trashcan. "We have to go," he said. Lifting her bag from the floor, she walked with him toward the line.

RONAN LEANED against the wall of the club to watch the humans grinding against each other. Saliva filled his mouth at the possibility of sinking his fangs into every one of their necks. Draining them all dry and leaving them nothing more than shriveled husks was the only thing he could think about doing right now.

Declan stepped in front of him, drawing his attention away from the crowd. "Perhaps you shouldn't be here."

Ronan straightened away from the wall. "And where should I be?"

"There are a lot of humans here."

"There are, and they're all prime targets for Joseph."

And me. It was what Declan was thinking too, but he was wise enough not to say it.

A shifting behind Declan's shoulder drew Ronan's attention to the dance floor as Killean and Lucien cut across it toward them. Saxon followed behind, moving slower due to a woman with blue hair and another redheaded woman grinding against his sides. Saxon bestowed his charming smile on them, causing them to nearly swoon.

Ronan's teeth ground together so forcefully, he thought he might shatter his fangs. Now was not the time for Saxon's playboy shit.

Saxon finally succeeded in extricating himself from the women. Ronan's attention was drawn away from them, and his desire to feast on their blood, when the distinct odor of garbage filled the air. Saxon's head swiveled on his shoulders seconds before a Savage crashed into his side.

Ronan leapt forward, shoving his way through the crowd as the Savage propelled Saxon across ten feet of dance floor and into the exit door. The impact of their weight caused the door to burst open. They both tumbled outside and vanished from view. Ronan heedlessly shoved humans out of his way as he ran forward.

Never had he seen such a brazen attack from a Savage in public before. Some of the humans were still staring at the closing metal door when he pushed them out of his way. A few were creeping closer, trying to see what was going on outside. They scrambled away when he snarled at them before plunging out the door.

He didn't get a chance to look around before he was assailed with the stench of garbage and something hit him in the side of his head. Staggering to the side, the scent of his blood filled his nostrils as the glasses he'd been wearing fell to the ground. He spun, lashing out at whoever had hit him and catching them under the jaw with an uppercut that shattered bone with a crack.

He heard the scuffle of another fight, but before he could look for the source, a whistling sound came from behind him. Throwing his arm up, he caught the blade of the sword that would have sliced his head from his body. The blade bit into his palm, slicing deep as he yanked the sword from the grasp of the Savage wielding it.

His blood coating the weapon made it slippery as he spun around and stabbed it through the Savage's throat. Lunging forward, he drove it into the wall, shattering bricks and breaking the tip of the blade off. The Savage clawed at the weapon as Ronan twisted it deeper and yanked it to the side, severing the vamp's head from his shoulders.

Ronan spun to face three Savages racing at him, their shoulders hunched up and their fangs fully extended. He braced his legs apart and grinned as the first one ran into him. He'd been itching for a fight, and these assholes had delivered it to him.

Capturing the Savage by the shoulders, Ronan lifted him up and slammed him facedown onto the pavement as the second one launched onto him. The thin thread of control he'd been retaining over himself shattered. Red shaded his vision, and his fangs ached to be buried in someone's throat. Death was the only thing that would fill the hole Kadence's leaving had torn into him.

He didn't recognize the sound that came out of him as he stomped his foot onto the back of the one he'd driven into the ground. He wrapped his hand around the throat of the one clawing at his back and tore the vampire's head off with his other hand.

The next Savage spun two daggers through his fingers while he eyed Ronan, looking for a weakness. Blood dripped from Ronan's hand as he stepped onto the one still lying on the pavement, unable to move due to his broken back. He stalked forward, ignoring the spinning blades the Savage swung back and forth at him. The daggers whistled as they sliced through the air in front of his face, but he didn't ease in his pursuit.

The Savage backed steadily away, his eagerness for a fight lessening when Ronan grinned at him. The Savage swung at him. Ronan leaned away from the blade as it sliced so close to his nose he felt the nick of the blade across his skin. When the Savage swung at him again, Ronan clutched his arm and brought it down over his knee, snapping it in half.

The Savage howled and stumbled back as Ronan pounced on him, sinking his fangs into his throat. Putrid blood filled his mouth and he spit it out. The Savage drove the next dagger at his eye, but Ronan clasped hold of the wrist, halting it before it could blind him.

He bared down on the Savage's wrist, shattering bone and causing the knife to clatter onto the pavement. The Savage gagged when Ronan punched him in the face, knocking his fangs down his throat. Before the Savage could react, Ronan seized his throat and ripped backward, tearing it out.

He spun the vamp's head around and tore it from his shoulders before tossing it aside. He whirled to find the others entangled with a handful of Savages. Ronan raced toward the one climbing over

Saxon's back and wrenched the Savage away. The vampire's startled red eyes met his before Ronan drove his fist through the vamp's chest and ripped out his heart. He crushed the still beating organ in his hand as the vamp fell before him.

The scent of the blood and the thrill of the kill had his pulse racing and his temples pulsing with the adrenaline coursing through him. *More.* He needed more death, more blood, more of this mindlessness. It was the only thing that made any sense to him anymore.

He pulled another Savage off Killean and twisted its head completely around. Killean ran a hand through his hair, pushing it away from his face and streaking more blood over him.

"Ronan—"

Footsteps silenced Killean and drew Ronan's attention to the end of the alley. A crossbow bolt fired out of the darkness. He sprinted to the side to avoid taking the hit as more were fired at them. Saxon cursed as one of the bolts hit him in the upper shoulder.

Ronan bounded down the alley toward the half a dozen hunters emerging from the shadows. The hunter's blood wouldn't be putrid. No, it would be delicious, powerful. It would finally satisfy the unending thirst he'd been dealing with his entire life.

A small part of him still recognized that once he gave into the bloodlust, it would never be eased, that it would haunt him until he was destroyed. The far larger part didn't care as he slammed into the first hunter. Ronan struck the hunter in the nose, shattering it.

The enticing aroma of the hunter's blood filled his nostrils and caused his veins to burn with hunger. The hunter's startled blue eyes met his. Ronan hesitated when he recognized it was Kadence's brother, but then he heard the release mechanism of a crossbow and a bolt slammed into his shoulder. Ronan grinned as he dragged the man beneath him.

CHAPTER THIRTY-ONE

"WHAT HAPPENED TO YOU GUYS?"

Ronan didn't bother to respond as Lucien strolled across the grounds toward them. His body language remained casual, but his gaze raked Ronan's blood-soaked frame from head to toe and back again before his black eyes darted nervously to the others.

"Savages and hunters," Saxon replied.

"Looks like a bloodbath."

"It was," Ronan grated.

"It was ugly," Declan said.

"I can tell," Lucien remarked.

"How are things here?" Ronan demanded.

"I just returned with everyone," Lucien replied. "The recruits are settling into the carriage house and the guest house. All of them decided to come."

"Good." Ronan turned away from him. His body still thrummed with his need to kill; he hadn't had enough of it tonight, but that would have to wait until their next hunt. He could feel the eyes of the others boring into his back as he stalked toward the hideous house that had nothing on the hideousness creeping into his veins.

He threw open the door and walked into the foyer, pausing when the aroma of vanilla drifted to him. Kadence's lingering scent caused a stabbing pain to shoot through him as he strode toward the stairs.

Something shifted in the shadows and Baldric emerged from the area of the kitchen. Ronan's hand fell onto the banister at the same time his foot hit the first stair. Baldric's eyes widened on him and he stumbled back. Ronan could only stare at him as he tried to figure out why the man was back here.

Had she returned to her brother? Had she been trying to spy on them and betrayed him, or had she run away from Marta and Baldric?

"Where. Is. She?" Ronan bit out even as he realized that none of his questions were right.

He turned away before Baldric could respond and followed the enticing lure of her scent toward the library. Every step had him feeling more keyed up than the one before it. "Ronan—"

He didn't look back at Declan, but he heard his footsteps as Declan hurried after him.

"Ronan, you're covered in blood. Some of it is her brother's."

Ronan ignored him as he stepped into the doorway of the library to find Kadence lying on one of the couches with her head resting on her hand and her eyes closed as she slept. Her silvery hair cascaded around her shoulders in waves. The sight of her calmed him even as his body roused to her nearness and his fangs lengthened in anticipation of tasting her.

"Ronan—"

"Leave us be," Ronan commanded. Spinning, he grabbed the doors. Declan's troubled eyes held his as he slid the doors closed, shutting Declan out.

"Ronan?"

He turned toward the beautiful sound of her voice to find her eyebrows in her hairline as she surveyed him. The rays of the moon spilling through the windows were the only illumination in the room as she rose. The increased beat of her heart sounded in his ears; her hand went to her mouth.

"What happened? Are you injured?" Kadence took a step toward him and froze when he remained unmoving and staring at her as if he didn't know what to make of her. "Ronan?"

"What are you doing here?" he grated out.

Kadence didn't know how to respond, what to say to this man standing across from her. No, not a man. Right now, he was every inch the demon that had created the vampire line. Blood streaked him from head to toe. It coated his hair, making it stand up from where he'd been running his hand through it.

His torn shirt exposed a swath of his chest that hadn't been spared any blood either. The hole in his upper chest near his shoulder oozed blood, but most of the blood covering him was not his own. He didn't have enough injuries for that to be possible.

She'd never been afraid of Ronan before, but he looked Savage, and damn if he didn't smell like one of those murderous things too. Her nose wrinkled at the stench wafting off him. She felt every beat of her heart against her ribs.

What had happened to him while she'd been gone? What had she returned to?

"What are you doing here?" he asked again.

The tone of his voice, the way the shadows caressed his body, and the fiery glow of his red eyes caused her to gulp and wipe her palms on her pants.

"I... I came back."

"Why?" he demanded as he prowled forward.

She couldn't stop herself from stepping back as he glided across the room with lethal grace. He didn't come at her; instead, he circled her like a shark circling its prey. She was nothing more than the guppy.

"Ronan, what happened tonight?" she asked, unable to keep the tremor from her voice.

"Why are you here, Kadence?"

The hair on her nape rose when he uttered the words from behind her. Why did he smell like those Savages who had attacked in the alley? Was it because it was Savage blood on him, or was it something more? Had he given in? Before, she never would have believed it possible; now she shared the room with a lethal predator, and she wasn't sure she knew this man.

"I'm here because I called my brother from the airport."

"Did you now?" The words were murmured in her ear, but when she spun to face him, he was ten feet away from her again, circling once more. Despite her excellent night vision, she briefly lost him in the shadows near the back of the room. "And what did you say to him?"

"I… I told him the truth," she whispered and stepped away from where she'd last seen him. "I told him not all vampires are killers. That the hunters have it wrong."

"I see. And why would you do that?"

"Because we're trying to accomplish the same thing and working against each other is just going to help Joseph and the Savages rise in power. You need help, the hunters need help, coming together to fight a common enemy will benefit both sides and prevent unnecessary deaths."

"And that's why you're here now?"

"Ye-yes," she stammered when she felt his breath against her neck once more, and he inhaled her scent. She didn't bother to try to face him; she knew he would be gone before she could turn around. "Maybe I can help bring both sides together."

His bitter laugh caused her to wince. "I don't think your brother cared much for what you had to say."

"What happened tonight?" she whispered.

"Savages and hunters. Your brother was there."

Kadence's stomach turned, and a cold sweat coated her body. "Is… is… did you kill my brother?" Silence stretched on so long she nearly screamed in frustration as her fingernails bit into her palms. "Ronan?"

"He is alive," he replied, and Kadence heaved a sigh of relief. "Though I didn't want to leave him that way, not after he shot me with his crossbow."

Kadence took an involuntary step toward where she'd last seen him, but movement to her right alerted her that he'd already moved on. "Are you okay?"

"What do you think?"

"No," she admitted. "Something is wrong, and I don't know what it is."

"You sacrificed yourself, Kadence. Sacrificed your freedom because you believe you can help forge an alliance between the hunters and vampires."

"No, not a sacrifice. I never thought of it like that, but right now you're making me feel like one!" she blurted, unnerved by the creature in this room with her.

She felt a brush against her nape before his hand clasped it and he held her loosely within his grasp. He had her flight-or-fight response kicked into hyperdrive, yet she couldn't help but reach out to him in some way. She tried to touch his hand, but he was gone so fast that she took a stumbling step back from where he'd been.

"But you have sacrificed yourself. I told you, don't come back here unless you're ready for an eternity with me. Yet here you are."

She wiped her palms on her pants again. "Ronan—"

"Did you think I was playing with you, Kadence? Did you think my words were an idle promise? Did you think you could come back here, try to play peacekeeper, and then take off again?"

"I… I don't know," she admitted. "I didn't know what to expect."

She'd simply known she couldn't get on that plane and abandon her family and Ronan. No, she'd never known freedom before. Yes, there was so much in this world she dreamed of seeing and doing, but she would enjoy none of it if she left them behind. Not if there was something she could do to bring both sides together and possibly save some lives.

"I couldn't go, not while knowing you and Nathan would be here fighting. I've always been caged, but I was born into this life. How could I abandon everyone I know and love because *I* want to see the world? How could I live with myself if something were to happen to him or to you? Your deaths would be on my hands, and I couldn't allow that. I would have been back earlier, but the humans weren't exactly pleased that we weren't going to board our flight even though we didn't check any baggage."

"You have no idea what you've unleashed by coming back here."

The words were uttered from her left, but when she turned to face him, she didn't see him there. Then, on her right, he emerged from the dark, stalking toward her like the predator he was. He stopped before her, his ruby eyes burning into hers.

"I had to come back," she said.

He reached for her before recalling the wound the sword had sliced across his palm and the blood splattering him. "There are more things you don't know about vampires, Kadence. You have no idea what you are to me, but *I* do."

"And what am I to you?"

"My mate. We will be bonded. I can't and won't let you go again. It nearly drove me over the edge to do so this time; it won't happen again. I'll turn you because I must claim you as mine. If I don't, I will have to be destroyed. I gave you the chance to be free; you should have taken it and never come back here."

Her mouth parted on a gasp when he spun away from her and stalked toward the doors. "I'll give you time to absorb that knowlededge, but know you will either become a vampire or I will be destroyed. I can't turn Savage; it would spell doom for everyone, including you."

He threw the doors open and strode away before she could form a response to his proclamation. What had she done by coming back here? He'd told her not to come back unless she was prepared for an eternity, but she hadn't really believed him when he'd said that, or had she and it was what she wanted too?

Being in his presence again had caused her skin to stop crawling, and her chest no longer felt like someone was trying to rip it open. He'd unnerved her with his strange behavior, and his declaration was frightening, but she finally felt almost normal again.

When she was with Ronan, she felt like she'd finally found her home.

But become a vampire? She hadn't been expecting that.

What else would eternity mean, you idiot?

She was staring at the doorway and trying to puzzle that out when Declan appeared. "Are you okay?" he inquired.

"Yes." Declan started to turn away from her, but she stopped him before he could leave. "Declan?"

"Yeah?" he asked over his shoulder.

"Would he really have to be destroyed if I left here again?"

"If he allowed himself to be taken down by one of us, yes, he would have to be killed. Ronan is the strongest creature in existence on this planet. If he turns Savage, we're all doomed. I told him it was a horrible mistake for him to let you go without telling you all this to begin with. I like you, Kadence, really I do, but make the right choice here, and make it fast, or I may turn you myself. Ronan will kill me for it, but if you're already a vampire, he can complete the bond with you after. I will do what must be done to save his life just as he's saved mine countless times over the years."

Kadence gawked after him when he vanished from the doorway. She'd stepped into a steaming pile of crap, but no matter what happened now, what she became, she'd made the right choice by coming back here. She could save lives, and she would. Even if she lost hers in the process.

CHAPTER THIRTY-TWO

NATHAN HELD the icepack to his nose as he paced back and forth within the living room of the brick house. His head pounded from the beating he'd taken and every breath he took whistled in and out of his nose, but he was alive.

And for the life of him, he didn't know why. That vampire had had him dead to rights. He should be taking a dirt nap right now. Instead, he was drinking scotch in the hope of numbing the soreness of his body and trying to figure out why that vamp hadn't torn his throat out.

No, not *that* vampire, Ronan. That was what one of the other vamps had called him when he'd thrown Nathan away from him and taken off with them. *Ronan.* The same Ronan that Kadence had mentioned?

It had to be, as it was definitely the same vampire who had been in the alley the night Jayce was killed. None of it made any sense, and trying to figure it out only made his head pound more. The guy had beaten the snot out of him, and Nathan had shot him with his crossbow, yet his throat remained intact.

"I don't get it," he muttered.

Logan and Asher didn't say a word from where they sat on the couch, nursing their own wounds. There was nothing for them to say. None of them understood what had happened tonight or in that alley the first time they'd encountered Ronan and those other vampires. Maybe the first time he could have written it off as the vamps had decided to retreat, but he couldn't tonight. Yes, the vamps had left, but they could have easily killed them before they departed.

He'd felt the power emanating from Ronan, and it had rocked him even before the punch to his nose had. Never had he encountered anything like that. There was no denying they should all be dead, yet they remained standing, or mostly standing anyway.

"Maybe it's a game they're playing or something," Asher muttered.

Nathan hadn't told them about Kadence calling him again. It was a sensitive topic for Logan that she'd fled in the first place. Plus, his sister hadn't exactly sounded like someone they could trust when he'd spoken with her, and no matter what she'd done, he didn't want anyone thinking badly of her when she finally did come back.

Now, he knew he had to tell them about the call. He couldn't figure this out on his own, and he could trust them not to go to the elders with it. If they did, Kadence may never be welcomed back here again.

Nathan finished off his scotch before turning to face them. "There's something I have to tell you. It's not going to make any sense, but you have to know. Kadence called me earlier."

Logan winced and rubbed at his chest, but he raptly listened as Nathan repeated the conversation he'd had with his sister.

Ronan slid the doors to the library open and glanced around the dimly lit room. Someone had closed the shutters over the windows. He had a feeling it was Kadence, who still believed the sunlight would burn him. She was curled up on the sofa, her hand tucked beneath her head and her chest rising and falling with her soft inhalations as she slept soundly.

It had been hours since he'd last seen her, since he'd felt in control of himself enough to come anywhere near her again. His eyes were still red; he believed it might be a permanent condition until the bond between them was complete.

She came back! He'd been too geared up last night, too covered in death to really grasp that concept. Standing there gazing at her, the realization hit him fully now. She may not have been prepared for what she'd walked into, but she'd come back to him.

He couldn't tear his gaze away from her as he walked across the room to kneel at her side. She looked like an angel as she slept, her face serene. He stroked her cheek, relishing the satiny feel of her skin beneath his as she calmed him further.

Her sweeping lashes fluttered open, her azure eyes were dazed as she stared at him. Then, a smile curved her lush mouth. "Hello," she murmured.

He couldn't help but smile back at her. "Hello."

He slid his arms beneath her and lifted her from the sofa. She draped her arms around his neck and nestled closer against him. Her head fell into the hollow of his shoulder as he carried her from the room and up the stairs.

"Why didn't you go up to your room?" he asked her.

"I wasn't sure I still had one here."

"You'll always have a place with me, Kadydid. *Always.*"

She rested her lips against his neck. "You're much calmer now."

"Do not be fooled. I'm barely in control, but I had to see you."

"At least you're not covered in blood anymore."

He bent his head so that his lips rested against her cheek as he spoke. "You never should have seen me like that."

Tilting her head back, her eyes searched his as she heard the self-loathing in his voice. "I know what you are, Ronan. You've never denied it. I know you're lethal, brutal, a killer."

"Hmm."

"It was the smell that had me worried."

He froze in the middle of the hall. "The smell?"

"Yes, you smelled like them."

"Like who?"

"Like the Savages."

"And what do they smell like?" He knew what they smelled like to him, but to learn they may also smell to a hunter wasn't something he'd expected.

"Like garbage," she murmured. "Like death. It's not a strong aroma, but it's there. I smelled it that first night in the alley, then with Joseph, and again on you last night. It must have been because you had their blood on you."

Ronan was too shocked by the revelation to continue forward for a minute. The hunters could smell the difference too, not even a turned vampire had the ability to smell the Savages, only purebreds did, and now hunters. It didn't sound as if she smelled the aroma as strongly as he did, but perhaps there was more demon in the hunters than he'd realized.

"I see. Do other hunters smell it?"

"We assumed it was what all vampires smelled like, something else we were wrong about," she said as she rested her head against his chest and placed her hand over his heart. She loved the solid pulse of it beneath her palm. "You smell like cinnamon and the ozone scent of power. I like it."

"I'm glad you like it," he said and kissed her ear. "To smell the difference between us is an unusual ability to have. All purebred vampires can smell the foulness of the Savages, but the turned ones can't."

"You smell it?"

He smiled at her as he continued walking again. "I do. For every human life a vampire takes, the scent increases. When I was forced to kill hunters before, I acquired the smell for a while. It has faded over the years."

"So hunters can tell the difference between Savages and those who aren't, and we don't know it?"

"It seems that way."

"I will talk to Nathan again and tell him."

"After last night, I'm not sure your brother wants to hear anything you have to say about vampires."

"Did you hurt him?"

"I did, but he will live, and he deserved it."

She didn't flinch away from his blunt words. Her fingers rested against the fading red mark from where a bolt had pierced him. Her brother and her lover could have killed each other last night over a complete misunderstanding. This insanity had to stop.

"Nathan injured you too."

"Barely felt it."

She sniffed. "Tough guy, huh?"

He didn't tell her that he could take a bolt to the chest and barely feel it, yet the idea of losing her again could knock him to his knees. He nudged the door to her room open with his foot.

"I can talk to Nathan. I *can* make him listen, make him see reason," she insisted.

"Not today, Kadence. One battle at a time."

"I couldn't stand it if something happened to either one of you when I might be able to stop it."

Whether she realized it or not, she'd just admitted to caring for him. He didn't know what the strange sensation filling his chest was, didn't know how to react to it as it robbed him of his breath.

"Is there anything else about vampires we have wrong?" she asked.

"There are other things," he replied.

"Such as?"

"Not now."

"You still don't trust me?"

He set her on the bed and stepped away. "There are many things I have to tell you, but there is something else we need to get straight between us first."

"This mate thing?"

"This mate thing," he confirmed.

Taking a deep breath, she gripped the edges of the mattress. "Tell me about it."

"I can't let you go again. I need you to stay here, with me."

She didn't understand the raw need she saw in his eyes, but it touched something primal inside her. Rising, she rested her hands against his cheeks and met the red of his eyes as she pulled him down to her.

The minute his lips touched hers, she knew what the awful tightening of her skin had been—her need for *him*. Her heart swelled, and her body rejoiced as heat pooled through her limbs and she relaxed into his kiss.

It didn't matter what the future held; she never wanted to leave him again either.

His arms wrapped around her. Kadence's fingers slid through his hair to draw him closer. His hands swept over her back, bunching her shirt in his grasp and lifting it up her sides.

He pulled back suddenly, breaking the kiss. Kadence couldn't catch her breath as she gazed at him while he clasped her cheeks in his palms. He stared wordlessly down at her, his face harsh with his barely leashed restraint.

"We cannot do this, not right now." His voice was hoarse and his accent more noticeable again. "I could hurt you if this continues."

"No, you couldn't."

He exhaled loudly. "I *can* hurt you, and it's a chance I'm not willing to take."

"Then I think it's time you fully explain this mate thing to me."

He reluctantly released her and moved as far away from her as he could. Leaning against the wall, he stared at the shuddered window as he spoke. "Sometimes a vampire discovers what is known as their mate. We don't know why it happens, why some of us find them while others don't, but it is most likely tied in with the demon part of us.

"When a vampire encounters their mate, they experience an instantaneous connection to whoever their mate is. The vampire may not realize it is the mate bond at first, I didn't, but I was drawn to you from the second I saw you. When the bond between mates is completed, it can only be severed by death. And if it is severed by death, the remaining mate will either die or go mad. When vampires find their mates, the consequences can be volatile until the bond is completed, especially if one of them is mortal."

She folded her hands in front of her when he started pacing before the window. "And what happens if one of them is mortal?"

"They must be turned into a vampire. There is no other option. It is the only way to calm the vampire again, and it is necessary to seal the bond between them."

"And how is the bond sealed?"

"One of the steps is through sex, which is what escalated the mating bond within me and brought it to the forefront."

"Oh," she murmured, unable to keep the blush from her cheeks. "That's why you reacted like you did afterward."

"Yes. Not only did I want to feed from you, but I also wanted to change you, right then."

Kadence gulped at his words and clenched her hands tighter as she realized how close he'd been to hurting her as Joseph had.

"If both mates are vampires, then they will exchange blood during sex. That will finish creating the bond and opening the pathways between their minds, which will allow them to communicate with each other," Ronan continued. "It will also unify them for as long as they live."

"What if the mortal doesn't want to be turned?"

His eyes swung toward her and she found herself staring at the vampire who had been in the library with her last night. The muscles in his arms and chest stood starkly out as his lips skimmed back. In amazement, Kadence watched his fangs descend. She'd seen them before, but she'd never seen the lengthening of his canines in such a way.

"Then the vampire will go mad, turn Savage, and have to be killed."

"And what happens to the vampire when the bond is completed and the mortal becomes immortal?"

"They regain control of themselves, for the most part, but if their mate is ever threatened, there is no control."

Kadence imagined he'd be Hell on earth in such a scenario.

"The mating bond also makes both the vampires stronger," he continued. "Most likely because, not only does at least one of them continue to feed on humans, but also because they are both feeding from another vampire on a consistent basis. Plus, many mates are deeply in love with each other, and I've been told there isn't anything one won't do for love whether they are vampire or human."

Love, she thought as she watched him pacing a hole into the rug. She cared for him, deeply, but love? *Just get through one thing at a time,* she told herself. *You can figure that out later.*

"What do you mean by at least one of them continues to feed on humans?" she asked.

He stopped pacing and turned to face her. "At least one vampire needs to still have fresh blood from an outside food source, but the other can survive solely off the blood of their mate, if that is what they chose to do."

"I see. And you truly believe me to be your mate?"

"From the moment I saw you, I wanted you, and believe me, that is not something I've experienced in years, and I've *never* experienced it as strongly as I do with you."

"What?" she blurted. "I'm sure you've seen and desired thousands of women over the centuries."

He had the nerve to chuckle.

"I have," he confirmed. "And when I was younger, I found a diversion in those women. As I got older and the years wore on me more, my need for death and blood started to outweigh my desire for women. Eventually, all I cared about was killing and sating the demon within me."

"I'm not really sure what you're telling me. All you want to do is kill?"

"The demon DNA that lurks within all vampires is stronger in purebreds. We are more closely tied to the demon than a turned vampire is, and we have more of the demon's traits. When a male purebred becomes fully mature, the demon becomes this insatiable, clawing thing that is only caged through strength of will, or the finding of a mate. Some set it free and let it do as it will and become Savage; others fight it every day of their lives. The females can experience it too, but not on the same level or with the same intensity as the males. I am assuming this was the way of the demons too.

"In each male purebred, the insatiable demon shows itself in different ways. Some seek out pain, others copious amounts of blood, others want death, some can't have enough sex, some lock themselves away from humans, and others give in and become Savage to make it stop. Turned vampires can experience it too, but not as strongly as purebreds do.

"In all purebred males, maturity means they stop aging, their power increases and continues to do so as they age, and they hunger for things to the point of madness," he continued. "Many experience a combination of heightened urges, but there is usually one that is more dominant than the others.

"For me, that dominant thing is death and blood. I am a bloodthirsty killer, and I enjoy it. I've focused my impulses on hunting Savages, and it has kept the madness at bay for a millennia, but every year it has become increasingly difficult to keep myself in check. Every year, I feel the madness seeping in more and more. And with every year, I stopped wanting women and craved the blood more, until *you*. I want you a thousand times more than I want to kill, which is something I *never* believed I'd be able to say."

Kadence bit on her lip as she tried to understand the battle he'd been waging against himself. She couldn't imagine what it must be like to live only for death, or how hopeless some days must feel for him. Yet, she brought him some hope.

"You could never be like one of those Savages," she murmured.

"I could and I will, without you. I've been more out of control since we had sex, and that is because the bond isn't complete, Kadence. The rest of it must be finished, and you will become a vampire when it is done."

Her hand instinctively flew to her neck when his eyes latched onto it. "No," she said as memories of the suffering Joseph had inflicted on her burst through her mind.

CHAPTER THIRTY-THREE

Ronan didn't like what he would have to do to her, didn't want to bring her any pain, but that is all he would bring to her when she went through the change. There would be no stopping that. He would give anything not to have her become a part of his world, but he couldn't change what had been set into motion, not now that she'd returned here.

"I am sorry, Kadence," he said. "I would change this if I could."

The fear in her eyes was nearly his undoing. "It will hurt."

Never in his life had he felt this helpless and inadequate. "The taking of blood isn't painful, if you're willing. It will be nothing like what you experienced with Joseph if you don't fight me. It's extremely pleasurable to those who are willing."

"Have you ever allowed another to do it to you?" she demanded, not at all liking the idea that another had known him in such a way.

"I've never allowed another to feed from me, but I do know that those I've fed from have never been harmed by it. Some enjoyed it nearly as much as sex, some more so. You will be the first and only vampire who will ever take my blood."

She recoiled from him. "*Me*? Drink blood?"

"That is what vampires do."

"I know that's what you've meant this entire time, but I never really *thought* about what being a vampire completely entailed." She had no idea how to react to anything he was telling her. A vampire, her? Tied to him for an eternity? What if he annoyed her or treated her badly?

He was abrasive, demanding, and used to getting his way. She was certain he would annoy her numerous times over an eternity, but he would never treat her badly. That she knew with absolute certainty. But to drink blood? The idea made her stomach turn. However, when she looked at him again, she had to admit that it didn't seem as repulsive if it was *his* blood. She found herself curious to know what it would actually taste like.

She found herself licking her lips before she shook her head to clear it of the absurd notion. "This is all so much," she muttered.

"I should have told you this before you left here. You might have stayed away if you had known the consequences of your returning, but I didn't want you to have this knowledge hanging over your head. I wanted you to truly know freedom."

He would have sacrificed himself for her; he had, in a way. Her heart swelled with emotion as she gazed at him. Love, she loved this man. She didn't know when it had happened, but it had, and it didn't matter if she hadn't known him for long or not. She loved him, but was she ready to give up everything she'd ever known for him?

She contemplated Declan's promise to change her if she didn't allow Ronan to do it. He knew Ronan would kill him if he did it, but Declan cared enough for Ronan to die for him; everyone in this place did. That said more about him than anything else, she knew.

"If there wasn't some kind of mate connection between us, would you even like me?" she asked.

She didn't know why she required the answer to that, but she did. She respected and admired him, and she wanted the same from him.

His mouth pursed, the lines etching the corners of his lips revealing his strain. "What do you mean?"

"I mean, if I had been a normal woman who you met, would you like my personality? Would you like who I am and want to get to know me better, or would you find me annoying?"

For the briefest of seconds, brown swirled within his eyes again as he strode across the room and cupped her cheek. She turned into his hand, nuzzling his palm and the slice in his flesh from another wound he'd sustained last night.

"Yes, Kadence, even without the mate bond I'd want to get to know you better. You're unlike anyone I've ever met before. You have more courage than most of the men and women I've come across in my lifetime. Though there have been times when you've annoyed me."

His lips quirked at these last words and she smiled back at him. "The feeling is mutual."

"I'm sure it is. You must know, I will protect you and our children with everything I am."

She couldn't breathe as she lifted her hand to clasp his against her cheek. "It is difficult for a hunter to conceive. Whether it's on the male's part, the female's part, or perhaps both, we can often go a lifetime without children."

"Then I will protect *you* with all that I am for every day of our lives together. I am the only purebred who has five generations of purebreds as ancestors before me. None of them were mated, they simply bred to create a stronger line. At one point, such a thing was expected of me, but that was centuries ago. Over the years, it has become an expectation that I never planned to fulfill."

"What changed?" she asked. "Why have you not fathered children?"

"After the Savage attack that killed my parents, I was more focused on revenge, on trying to protect the vampires who remained and slowly rebuilding the Defenders, than on trying to have children.

I never took the king title, so I didn't see it as necessary to have an heir. Then, as time went on, I had no interest in women or having a child, until now."

"But—"

"It doesn't matter if we don't have children, Kadence. All I want is you; a child would only be a bonus."

"I'm scared of this."

"I know, and you have every right to be. My bite will not hurt if you don't fight it. The transition will though. It's excruciating for a mortal to become immortal, but you will never have to experience it again once it's over. It may also be different for you, given what you are. You already have some demon DNA in you, the transition could be worse."

"Or it could be easier."

"It could."

"What would become of me if we are mated and you turn Savage?" she asked.

"I will not turn Savage, not while I have you. The bond between us will keep me grounded; it will be the thing I want most in this world. Not blood, not death, *you*."

She sucked in a breath and bit her lip at this revelation. Then, she recalled Declan's words from before. *"Fate is a fickle bitch, and sometimes she takes even the best of us down, but sometimes she also intervenes to save us."* It suddenly made sense to her now, as did his reason for not intervening when she decided she wouldn't return to the stronghold.

Declan was hoping to save Ronan from becoming a Savage, and he believed she was the key to keeping him sane.

Her fingers fiddled with the edges of her sleeves as she tried to process everything. She'd never feel the sun's warmth again, she'd have to feed on blood for the rest of her life, and the hunters may all turn against her forever. No matter what Ronan said, she thought he might let her walk away again if she asked him to let her go.

And then what? She couldn't return to the stronghold, she wouldn't have Marta and Baldric to help her go somewhere else this time, and she would destroy Ronan if she left. She cared too much for him to inflict that on him. But was she ready to die and be reborn as the one thing she'd been raised to hate? Was she ready to give up the sun and drink blood?

Her gaze went to the shuttered window. No matter what she decided, she had to feel the rays of the sun on her one more time.

"I can give you time to process this," he said.

She tore her eyes away from the window and back to him. "I would really like that."

He hesitated for a minute before caressing her cheek with his thumb. She caught his hand when he went to pull it away.

"If we had been a normal man and woman, I would have chosen you," she told him.

His hand enclosed on hers. "Take the time you need," he murmured, and before she could reply, he was gone.

KADENCE MOVED SWIFTLY down the hall. She glanced behind her at Ronan's closed door, but she knew he wasn't in there. He hadn't entered his room when he left hers. She didn't know where he'd gone. She descended the stairs and hurried to the front door. The gate wasn't blocking it this time.

She glanced up at the cameras on either side of the door, but no one emerged to stop her when she continued toward it. Grasping the knob, she turned it and pulled it open. Sunlight spilled across her as she walked outside and lifted her face to absorb its warmth.

A few birds sang in the barren trees lining the drive. Their melodious songs floated across the vast expanse of snow-covered lawn. The lawn rolled forth as far as she could see. Trees were spaced throughout, and though they had no leaves, she'd spent enough time wandering the stronghold and studying nature books to know that they were maples, pears, cherries, apples, and oaks. The leaves and flowers on them would be breathtaking in the spring.

If she didn't look at the house, it was actually beautiful here.

A large garden was set around a giant fountain in the center of the yard. The plants within were all bare or buried beneath the snow, and the fountain was off, but she was drawn toward it. She stopped at the edge of the fountain and slid her hands into the sleeves of her coat as a breeze blew over the land, lifting snow and swirling it around her. She smiled as she studied the marble cupid in the middle of the fountain. She'd bet anything Ronan *hated* it.

She looked at the sky again, her head falling back as she threw her arms wide and closed her eyes. Over the years, the sun had never failed to make her feel better if she was sad or lost, and this may be her very last day experiencing its rays.

Tears brimmed in her eyes and slid down her cheeks.

"WHAT IS SHE DOING?" Declan asked as he unwrapped a lollipop and stuck it in his mouth. Ronan had no idea why he'd started sucking on the candy a couple months ago, but it had become his new thing.

Declan plopped his feet on the desk and leaned back in the desk chair. "I'm not sure," Ronan replied as he focused on Kadence making her way toward that hideous fountain.

"Perhaps the mortal simply needed fresh air," Saxon suggested.

"Or perhaps she's going to make a run for it," Lucien drawled.

"Probably straight into the enemy's arms," Killean said.

"She's not going to make a run for it," Declan replied and bit down. "Ugh." Grabbing the trashcan, he pulled it forward and spit the remains of the lollipop into it.

"What is it with you and those human things?" Lucien demanded.

Declan set the can down and leaned back in his chair again. "I'm trying to figure out how many licks it takes to get to the center, but I keep biting into it before I get there."

"Why on earth are you doing that?" Saxon asked.

"Might as well solve the mysteries I can in this world," Declan said.

Ronan sensed more behind the man's words and his newfound obsession with human snacks than Declan was saying, but he let it go.

Tears streaked Kadence's face as the sun glistened upon her.

"Why is she crying?" Lucien asked.

"Shit," Ronan hissed as realization sank in.

"What is it?" Declan inquired.

"She doesn't know," he murmured. "I didn't tell her."

"Tell her what?" Saxon asked.

"That we are able to go out in the sun."

Declan's feet hit the floor as he spun to face Ronan. "How could you *not* tell her that?"

Ronan scowled at him. "I wasn't going to reveal everything to her, and then I just… forgot."

"You should go tell her before she decides she likes the sun more than you. Which, she might," Lucien said.

Turning on his heel, Ronan stalked out of the security office where he'd been meeting with the others about their next step in trying to locate Joseph. He cursed himself with every step he took to the front door. The sun's rays hit him as soon as he opened the door, and the cool air brushed over his skin as he strode forward.

Kadence no longer stood by the fountain, but he followed her scent down a trail leading through the privet hedges lining the seashell walkway. At the end of the privet was a far larger garden. It covered at least three acres of land, though there was little to see now except for some heather, lavender, and fountain grasses.

He stopped short when he found her at the end of the walkway, gazing at the remains of the gardens. Seeming to sense him, she turned and her face lit with a smile. Her hand was stretching toward him when it fell back to her side and her mouth dropped open. Her gaze ran over him as if she expected him to burst into flames at any second, and she most likely did.

"Ronan?" she squeaked.

He strode toward her, took her hand, and bent to kiss her. Her eyes remained on his as their lips touched and her breath rushed out of her.

"How is this possible?" she inquired when he rose away from her.

"Only the Savages can't go out in the sun," he told her as her eyes ran over him again and then again. "With each kill, they become stronger, yet they also become weaker."

"But… but… you can be out in the sun?"

"I can," he replied. "There was a time, after I killed those hunters, that it was more difficult for me, but that time has passed. I no longer experience any ill effect from the sun's rays."

"We were so wrong," she murmured, her skin paler than normal and her lower lip trembling. "I don't have to give up the sun if I become a vampire?"

"You don't," he assured her.

"You *have* to let me tell Nathan about this, let me talk to him. The two of you should meet. I will arrange it."

"I doubt your brother would want to see me again, Kadydid. We didn't exactly part on good terms."

"I can help to fix that; let me do this."

He pondered her words as he ran his fingers over her cheek, savoring every detail of her. "Why don't we do one thing at a time and figure us out first?" he suggested.

"I've figured that out," she said and stepped closer to him. Her arms slid around his waist as she rested her head on his chest. "Whatever this is between us scares me, but I won't lose you. You have to agree to let me speak with my brother though when this is done."

"Kadence," he breathed, kissing her neck as he held her to him. "I will not deny you that."

"You also have to promise you won't lock me away. I realize we can't go traveling all over the world right now, but I won't be confined again. I want to help hunt Joseph and stop this growing threat."

"You are not ready for a fight like that."

"You will keep training me," she insisted. "And as a vampire, I will probably be faster and stronger. You also said, as a mated vampire, I would be stronger than other vamps. Don't cage me, Ronan. It will ruin us if you try to lock me away. I am a hunter, and I will hunt."

"The last thing I want to do is ruin us or make you unhappy," he admitted as he ran his lips down the slender column of her throat. "But you will agree to listen to me when it comes to Joseph and the Savages."

"I will," she promised.

He lifted her against him, and she snuggled closer to his chest as he carried her across the property toward the house. His heart hammered with every step, his cock swelling with its need to be inside her made walking difficult, but he didn't slow.

He shoved the front door open and stalked across the foyer to the stairs. He took them three at a time to the top and sped down the hall to his room.

CHAPTER THIRTY-FOUR

KADENCE LIFTED her head from his shoulder to study the angles of his face. She sensed the demon simmering just beneath his surface.

She should be afraid. She wasn't. She'd made her choice; Ronan was her destiny. She wouldn't go back, and she wouldn't dread what was to come. He would protect her, and she would love him.

He set her on her feet before kicking the door shut behind him. Clasping her cheeks, he bent to kiss her. A wave of emotion built within her, warming her to her core as love burst through her. Entwining her fingers in his hair, Kadence kissed him hungrily back. Her body clamored for his as she realized that she never would have been able to leave him again. Her fate had been tied to his since she'd laid eyes on him. Perhaps it had been sealed from the moment of her birth.

Breaking their kiss, he pulled off his shirt before clasping the edges of hers and sliding it up to reveal her body to his voracious gaze. The demon within him clamored to possess her as he pulled off her boots and socks before kicking off his own.

Concerned he would hurt her, he kept his darker impulses leashed, but he was unable to stop himself from tearing her pants off her body. She gasped at the rending sound of the fabric, but she didn't pull away from him when he reclaimed possession of her mouth.

Her hands slid across his shoulders before trailing over his chest and down to his waist. Her touch seared through him and burned its mark upon every inch of his flesh. He'd been in a rush to possess her, but he realized then that she already possessed him in every way.

He shook with his need to be within her while slaking his thirst on her blood. Her fingers gripped the button of his jeans, and she slipped it free before pulling the zipper down. Ronan groaned as she pushed his jeans lower and freed his dick from the confines of his jeans. His body jerked when she gripped his shaft and stroked him the way he had taught her to. His teeth grated together as she squeezed him, causing him to nearly come in her hand.

Kadence watched in awe as his head fell back against the door. The corded muscles of his neck stood out as he thrust his hips in rhythm to the motion of her hand. She couldn't help but marvel at the power she had over this man—a man who was far stronger than her, or anyone she'd ever known, yet he was *hers*. The possessive urge the thought brought forth set something free within her, something she'd never known existed before, something savage. He was hers, and she would kill anyone who tried to take him from her.

Bending her head, she ran her tongue over his chest, tasting the saltiness of his flesh as his cinnamon and ozone scent engulfed her senses. She was wet and aching to be filled by him when she nipped at his flesh.

Ronan jerked against her when she bit him lightly before swirling her tongue over the bite. He growled as she bit him again. This time, hard enough to draw blood.

She licked it away before she bit again, drawing more blood forth. His fingers threaded through her hair as she mewled and her hands dug into his shoulders. She released his dick and bit him again.

"Harder, Kadence," he said, fisting her hair tighter as he held her closer.

Unable to resist his command, she bit down more forcefully and swallowed his blood.

He felt the unraveling within her, the growing desperation as her fingernails scored him. He didn't know what had unleashed this need within her, but he was helpless to deny her what she wanted as she bit him again.

One second, he was leaning against the door, the next his hands were on her hips and he was lifting her. He kicked his jeans from around his ankles seconds before he lowered her onto the swollen length of him.

Kadence cried out as he stretched and filled her, completing her. She froze, her eyes locking on his while he stared raptly at her. He was the most magnificent thing she'd ever seen or experienced as he remained buried deep within her while the potent taste of his blood lingered on her lips.

She had no idea what was wrong with her; she should be repulsed to be yearning his blood in such a way, but she wanted more of it, and him. She'd never tasted anything as delicious as it was, hadn't believed it possible blood could be so sweet.

Her hands cupped his face as she bent to kiss him. A thrill went through her when she ran her tongue over his fangs, feeling the sharp edges of them. He nipped at her lip before drawing it into his mouth to soothe the sting.

Then, his fang pierced his lip, drawing his blood forth. She sucked on it as she laved the puncture. Being buried within her and his ability to feed her calmed the demon within him. Ronan's hands tightened on her hips and he braced his legs apart as her body moved fluidly against his, yet he sensed something more within her, a hunger he'd never expected as he fed her more of his blood.

Pulling away, she studied his face. Her lips, swollen from his kisses, were also tinged red with his blood. Her tongue slid out to lick it away, and she shuddered against him.

She kept her eyes on his as she rose over him again before sliding slowly back down. She was magnificent, and she was his. Completely and utterly *his*. He bent his head to one of her nipples, and rolled his tongue over it as he sucked on her. Her body bowed and her head fell back as she thrust harder against him.

Kadence clung to him as if nothing outside the two of them existed anymore. The building tension in her belly and between her thighs splintered apart when his fangs grazed her breast before his lips tugged at her nipple. She cried out, her fingers digging into his shoulders as she came apart.

Panting for breath, her head fell into the hollow of his shoulder. The enticing scent of her orgasm filled the air, but Ronan held back his release. He intended for this to last longer.

He nipped at her breast again as he strode across the room. Each of his steps drove him in and out of her. She moaned against his shoulder when he laid her on the bed. He remained deep inside her as he climbed on top of her.

"We're not done yet, love," he assured her.

He braced his arms and withdrew from her before burying himself deep again. Her mouth parted, and her legs wrapped around his waist as she lifted her hips and eagerly took his next hard thrust. He knew he was unraveling, that he should be gentler with her, but he couldn't stop himself from driving harder and faster into her. She propelled him heedlessly onward as her body rose and fell to match his pace. The demon burst free of its cage as he took her with a ferocity he couldn't stop.

Kadence held onto him as she felt the unraveling within him and she knew she was the only one who could ease him. He plunged into her again and tossed his head back as his arms went rigid beside her head and a guttural shout escaped him. The pulsations of his release filling her brought forth an answering orgasm from her and she cried out.

Falling back on the bed, she marveled over the beauty of his chiseled body, dampened with sweat, as he remained rigid above her. Slowly, his head came back down and his red eyes met hers. His hair was tussled as it fell almost boyishly across his forehead. There was nothing boyish in the vampire above her as the demon within him was on full display.

What had transpired between them had done nothing to ease his need for her. Instead, it had only whet the demon's appetite for more.

Kadence braced herself for what was to come. However, he didn't strike as he stared unwaveringly down at her and kept her body caged beneath his. He didn't so much as breathe. She knew it was taking all he had not to pounce on her and take the rest of what he needed from her.

She loved him even more for it.

"It's okay," she murmured. "Don't fight it anymore. I want this too."

"The transition is difficult, Kadence, prepare yourself for that, and I have no idea what it will be like for a hunter."

"I know," she whispered and brushed back a strand of his hair.

"Kadence—"

"I have made my decision, Ronan. There is no going back now. This can't be changed for either of us. Whatever happens, we will deal with it together."

He gazed wordlessly at her as some new emotion came to life within him. He wasn't sure what this feeling was, but she was the only one who had ever brought it out in him.

Kadence smiled at him as the red bled away from his eyes and she found herself staring into a pair of beautiful, deep brown eyes once more. "There's the Ronan I love," she whispered.

CHAPTER THIRTY-FIVE

H<small>IS</small> <small>MOUTH PARTED</small> on an explosive breath. He stared at her as if she'd punched him in the gut. "Love?" he choked out.

Kadence took a deep breath, bracing herself against the sorrow that would follow if he rejected her. "Yes, I think… no, I *know* I love you."

His body softened around hers as one of his hands clasped the silken strands of her hair. "I will spend forever trying to be someone who deserves your love."

"You already deserve my love."

He lowered his forehead so it rested against hers and inhaled her enticing scent. She humbled him in ways he'd never expected to be humbled in his life. He was determined she would never again feel trapped and lost. Never again be unhappy.

"I may not be able to give you everything you dreamed of right now, but one day you will have everything you've always wanted. One day, when things settle some, I will take you anywhere you ask to go. I will make you the happiest woman in the world, Kadence."

Her hands ran over his sweat-slicked back as tears burned in her eyes. "I am happy," she whispered.

"Good."

She shivered with delight when his arms tightened around her and she felt him harden within her once more. Her body quickened in response to his arousal. Wrapping her hand around the back of his head, she turned her head as she guided him to her neck and lifted her hips to him.

He slid out of her before burying himself within her again. He ran his tongue over the pulse pounding in the side of her neck as the rush of her blood filled his ears. Thirst burned him when he rested his fangs against her vein.

Taking deep breaths, Kadence tried to stay relaxed even as her body braced for what was to come.

"Don't fight it," he whispered in her ear before he sank his fangs into her neck.

The piercing sting caused her body to jerk beneath his, and she winced as she waited for the excruciating agony she'd experienced with Joseph, but when Ronan gave his first pull, all she felt was joy as he took her blood while his body moved within hers.

Strength flooded through Ronan as her blood filled his cells, branding him forever as hers. He'd never tasted anything as intoxicating as her, or experienced so much power from another's blood. He'd only rarely fed from other vampires, and they'd all been turned ones. It had been centuries since he last fed from another of his kind, but her blood felt far stronger than theirs ever had.

For the first time in centuries, he was free from the burning in his veins and his unquenchable need to kill. Joy swelled within him as a peace he'd never thought to find settled over him. Her fingers curled into his back and her pleasure slid through the connection opening between them.

Turning her face into his neck, she sank her teeth into his shoulder and cried out when she broke through his skin and licked away his blood. Too far gone in the freedom she gave him and the ecstasy of her body, Ronan didn't think about her reaction and craving for his blood.

She arched beneath him and bit into him as she came again. With one final thrust, he found his release within her welcoming body. He pulled out of her as her blood continued to fill him and she bit him again.

Gathering her closer to him, he bit deeper into her vein. Her grip on his back loosened, her fingers eased their hold on him. The slowing beat of her heart sounded in his ears as the life drained from her, and he knew she was almost to the point of no return. Retracting his fangs from her, he licked the drops of blood from her neck when her head lulled to the side.

Panic gripped him as her shallow breaths rattled in and out of her chest. He had to get more of his blood into her soon. He bit into his wrist. Blood welled forth, its new scent causing his nostrils to flare. Kadence was etched into his cells now as her blood flowed through his veins, making him stronger than he'd been before.

He brought his wrist to her mouth and rested it against her parted lips. His blood trickled inside, but whereas she had eagerly consumed it before, she remained limp beneath him now. "Drink, Kadence," he commanded gruffly.

Her dazed eyes met his before fluttering closed again. Gathering her closer to him, he cradled her in his arms. The weakness in her body caused his heart to race as he kissed her forehead, and his fingers entangled in her hair. He could feel his blood seeping into her, but he couldn't feel it making any changes within her or strengthening her.

Terror clawed at his insides. Maybe a hunter couldn't become a vampire; maybe it was impossible to turn them. It had never occurred to him that might be a possibility, but maybe the fact they were already part demon would make them immune to the change.

If that were true, then they were both doomed as he could feel the life slipping from her. Madness crept steadily into the edges of his mind at the realization that he may have destroyed her.

She was his, but more than that, somewhere along the way, he'd fallen in love with her too. He should have told her that before doing this, should have told her what she meant to him, and now he might never get the chance.

Then she shifted and her fingers twitched against his chest. Unexpectedly, love cascaded around him, robbing him of his breath. It took him a second to realize it wasn't his own emotions he felt, but *hers* as her love surrounded him within its comforting embrace.

Excitement hammered him when Kadence seized his arm and she drew more blood from him. Ronan's head lowered to hers while his blood strengthened her and replaced the blood he'd taken from her.

The satisfaction Ronan experienced from her drinking from him brushed against the edges of her mind, as did his concern for her and his love. That love spread in her a warmth stronger than the sun. An unfamiliar, but not unpleasant, tingling sensation started in her gums. Easing her bite on him, she ran her tongue over her teeth. Her canines lengthened when she prodded at them.

"Kadence?" Ronan murmured as he brushed the hair back from her face. Her eyes remained closed, her skin paler than normal, but she'd released her bite on him.

Then, her fangs sank into his wrist. He jerked against her, disbelief filling him as she pulled on his blood. He'd never changed another, but he knew that wasn't normal. All humans had to go through the change before they could be reborn as a vampire. It took hours, sometimes as much as a day for fangs to emerge, not minutes.

He held her tighter when she squirmed against him and bit deeper. He had no idea what he'd unleashed by changing a hunter, but he would never let her go.

RONAN ROLLED over and climbed from the bed. He glanced back at where Kadence remained sleeping peacefully. He'd watched religiously over her for the past few hours, searching for any hint of suffering, but she hadn't so much as twitched as she lay on her side with her hair fanned out around her.

Even in the easiest of transitions, there was still excruciating pain, but there had been none with her. Her body had accepted his blood as if it were her own.

The transition wasn't complete. He could still feel the changes taking place in her through the bond connecting them, the shifting of her cells and molecules as she became immortal. He suspected her transition had been easier because she was already part demon, but he didn't know what that would mean when she woke again.

Whatever she became, she was his now, and they would deal with the consequences of that, if there were any.

Moving away from her, he walked into the bathroom. He turned the sink on and splashed his face with water. He pulled a towel from the rack and dried himself before lifting his head to meet his haggard reflection in the mirror. His face hadn't seen a razor since Kadence left. Thick stubble lined his cheeks and jaw. He'd rubbed her skin raw earlier because of it, something he would not do again, but he couldn't spend the time away from her that it would take him to shave now.

He walked into the bedroom as a knock sounded on the door. Grabbing his pants, he tugged them on and hurried to answer it before it woke Kadence. He cracked the door open, his eyes narrowing on Declan.

"What is it?" He slipped out and closed the door to within an inch.

"How is everything going?"

Ronan glanced at the partially closed door as he sought out his bond to Kadence. "Better than I'd expected."

"Good. We're getting ready to go hunting."

ETERNALLY BOUND   265

"If you come across Joseph, bring him to me if it's possible. We should try to learn what he's been up to."

"We will, but I have a feeling he's going to be lying low for a while."

"So do I."

"Ronan..."

Declan's strangled voice broke off as his eyes darkened until the silver color became almost entirely black. Ronan took a step back as the color drained from Declan's face. Uncertain of what was happening to his friend, Ronan took his arm to steady him when Declan swayed.

Declan fell forward to brace his hand against the wall as tremors wracked his large frame. A blood curdling scream rent the air, piercing deep into the hushed night. Spinning, Ronan flung the door open, shattering plaster when it banged off the wall.

Horror turned the blood in his veins to ice when his eyes landed on Kadence. Her entire body was lifted off the bed, her head and heels the only things touching the mattress. The scream broke off as she flopped onto the bed and began to thrash as if she were in the middle of a seizure.

Ronan raced across the room and gripped her shoulders in an attempt to stop the spasms wracking her. The delicacy of her bones was not lost on him as she jerked against him and he feared she would break something. Sweat rolled down her, plastering the sheets to her slender frame. She fell back, panting heavily as her fingers dug into the bed.

She jerked beneath him, nearly breaking free of his hold when another round of spasms shook her. He glanced at Declan when he slumped heavily against the doorframe. Declan's eyes were closed as he labored to breathe.

"Declan—"

"What's going on?" Lucien burst into the room. Killean and

Saxon were close on his heels as Lucien skidded to a halt inside the doorway.

Kadence whimpered again and her eyes fluttered open. No longer their bright blue color, they'd become a bruised blue as they stared unseeingly up at him.

"The pathways are opening," she whispered.

He stared at her in stunned silence when she slumped listlessly back to the bed, unconsciousness claiming her once more. His heart hammered as he caught the much too faint thump of her pulse. He'd witnessed transitions before, he knew they were never pleasant, but he'd never seen anything like this. Never seen one go so smoothly before going so horribly wrong.

Through the bond connecting them, he felt nothing from her. He turned toward Declan. "What is going on?"

Declan opened his eyes to reveal their still black color. "Pain." His voice came out gravelly. "She was in pain."

"What do you mean *was*?"

"I don't know. It's… it's quiet now."

"Too quiet," Ronan murmured as he gazed down at her parted lips. He ran his fingers over her forehead, brushing back the hair sticking to her pale skin.

"Have any of you heard or seen anything like this before?" he demanded of the others.

Killean and Saxon shook their heads. "No," Lucien answered.

"Get the records," he ordered.

"I'll go." Declan spun and fled from the room as if the hounds of Hell were on his heels.

SAXON SAT in the chair beside the bed, flipping through one of the numerous books that contained much of the vampire's vast history. Declan had disappeared after returning with the records. Uncomfortable with being near Kadence in her current condition, Lucien and Killean had retreated to the hall where they were flipping through more annals, but Saxon was studying her reactions and trying to find something in the records to match.

The records were the only things Ronan had maintained full custody of after the war with the Savages. One of the selling points of this place had been the vault built into a wall in the gym. If one didn't know the vault was there, they would never see it.

Some of the records were so old they were written on parchment and had to be handled with the utmost care. They'd focused on those older documents first, the ones written before Ronan was born.

"Anything?" Ronan demanded when Kadence remained unmoving before him, her hand cold as he held it within both of his. He'd ordered the others from the room earlier and slipped a nightgown on her, but she was still far too exposed for his liking.

"Not yet," Saxon murmured.

Lucien's head emerged at the bottom of the doorway, where he sat with his back against the wall. "No," he said and ducked back again.

Declan walked into the room with a book clasped to his chest.

"Declan?" Ronan asked.

"I discovered nothing in the books I went through," Declan said, his eyes once again a silvery gray color as they met Ronan's. "In all your many years, a hunter has never been turned, and it doesn't seem to have occurred before you were born either. I think if it *had* occurred, it wouldn't have been a secret, but full-blown knowledge. We'll find nothing in these journals, Ronan."

"I didn't think we would," he murmured as he turned his attention back to Kadence.

Rosy color tinged her cheeks once more. Her heart continued to beat within her chest, and her breath warmed her lips when she exhaled, but she hadn't moved in the three hours since she'd collapsed onto the bed again. The transition should be over by now, but it still held her within its unrelenting grasp.

"She will survive this," Saxon said.

And become what? Had he destroyed her? Turned her into something different? What pathways were opening and where would they lead her? His hands tightened around hers at the possibility of something terrible awakening within her. Closing his eyes, he bowed his head. He had no idea what she was going through as the bond remained oddly closed off on her end.

"Get the crossbow and weapons ready, in case she doesn't survive," he ordered.

"Ronan—"

"If you don't put me down immediately, I will kill you all," he interrupted Lucien.

"I'll get them," Killean said and Ronan listened as he rose to his feet.

"Wait," Declan ordered. "She's awake."

Ronan's eyes flew open and his head turned toward Kadence. Her hand remained limp in his grasp, but her eyes were on his. Except, she didn't seem to see him, and the color of her eyes robbed him of his breath. He'd never seen anything like the white blue shade of her eyes as they glowed with an eerie light.

Declan stepped closer when her eyes shifted toward him. "The paths," she croaked. "The paths, they're all broken. They go nowhere. They go everywhere."

Her eyes closed as fierce spasms shook her. Ronan clasped her to his chest until the spasms stopped and she fell silent once more. Her body eased against his as her shallow breaths warmed his neck.

He had done this to her; he had caused this to happen. The uncertainty surrounding her and this hideous pain was his fault. Self-hatred boiled through him, rocking him to the very core of his being.

"What paths, Kadence?" he whispered, but she didn't respond, and he hadn't expected her to. "You will not die."

He didn't know if she heard the order or not, but he willed her to survive as he sought her out through their bond. This time, he found a small opening, but he discovered only a slumber so deep that he could barely connect with her.

"She is strong," Declan said. "Stronger than any of us realize."

"I hope so," Saxon muttered.

"That strength is what is making this more difficult and different from any other transition. The parts of her that have been dormant since birth, possibly since the creation of the hunters, are changing and evolving," Declan said. "We will soon know what she will become."

CHAPTER THIRTY-SIX

KADENCE STIRRED, causing Ronan to nuzzle her forehead with his lips as he held her in his arms. Declan stepped out of the shadows by the back wall when she whimpered.

Her eyelashes fluttered against his skin as she blinked. Hope clutched at Ronan's chest when he leaned away to peer down at her. Shadows circled her eyes, but the brilliant azure color of them had returned.

"Ronan," she whispered.

He exhaled sharply as relief filled every part of him. He kissed her as his hands ran over her face. Warmth radiated from her flesh instead of the unnatural cold she'd been emitting. Her heart beat more solidly within her chest and her breathing was stronger.

"Are you okay? How do you feel?" he inquired.

A small smile curved her lips. "I'm fine now. That wasn't normal, was it?"

"No." He brushed the lank strands of her hair away from her face. "It shouldn't have happened."

"We both knew it may be different for me, but there was no choice. It had to happen. How long have I been out of it for?"

"Almost two days."

"Not too bad." She stifled a yawn and struggled to sit up. Ronan steadied her as she pulled herself up to sit against the headboard. "It's over now. There's only the future to look to."

Her voice took on an odd tone as she said those last words and her eyes became distant.

"Kadence—"

"I'm fine, Ronan," she interrupted and her eyes came back to him. "Truly."

He turned to Declan. "Leave us."

"I'm glad you are well, Kadence," Declan said before he slipped out the door and closed it behind him.

Ronan gathered Kadence's hands in his. "I was worried about you," he admitted.

A tug pulled at Kadence's heart as she inched closer to him. "I know."

Kadence held him as she tried to bury the memory of the murky realm of uncertainty she'd been trapped in. It felt like weeks had passed instead of days. "I could hear you and feel you, but no matter how hard I tried, I couldn't come back to you. There were so many different things."

She knew she didn't make any sense, but she couldn't quite process what had happened to her yet. She rubbed her hand over his back, taking comfort in the familiar strength of his etched muscles. He was something solid when nothing had been solid for the past two days.

"What happened, Kadence? You mentioned something about pathways."

"There were only brief periods of pain," she murmured. "But they were *so* painful." She trembled as she recalled those moments when it had felt like every bone in her body was breaking and snapping back into place. "And then there would be quiet…"

"And pathways?" he prodded when her voice trailed off and her eyes took on that distant look again.

"Yes, or at least they looked like pathways in my mind. They were full of vibrant blues and purples as they unrolled around me to lead me onward. They took me deeper and deeper."

"Toward what?"

"Deeper inside me, I think," she murmured. "It was all so confusing, yet it felt right. The pathways led me to where I was supposed to be." She rested her hand against his cheek. "Here, with you, and... whole?"

"What do you mean by whole?"

Her hand fell into her lap. "When I left here, when I walked away from you, it didn't feel right. *I* didn't feel right. I told myself it was nothing and that I couldn't run away from my family to live my dreams only to give them up for someone I barely knew, even if I did care for you. I tried to convince myself it was the crowd at the airport making me so uncomfortable. I told myself all those things, yet my skin felt too tight, my body ached, and all I wanted was to come back to you."

Ronan scrubbed a hand over his face at this revelation. "That's why you came back."

"That was part of it. I was walking to the plane, getting ready to board and thinking about kissing the Blarney Stone when I realized that I was probably the only person who had a chance of bringing our sides together and that I couldn't go."

"You were going to Ireland?"

She smiled at him as she brushed the hair away from his face, taking note of the shadows under his eyes and the exhaustion radiating from him. "I kind of have a thing for this Irish guy I know. I wanted to see where he came from."

Ronan clasped her hand and kissed the back of it. "You will one day," he promised. "Why did you come back here instead of going to your brother?"

"I knew you would listen to me more than he would, and the minute I decided to return to you, some of the pressure in me eased. Not completely, but it was better, and I almost felt normal again. When I finally saw you, I could breathe easier again."

"It sounds to me like the demon DNA in you also recognized me as your mate."

"I think so too. I sense the bond between us more strongly now that I'm a vampire, but it was there before too; I just didn't know what it was. You're *mine*, Ronan. Nothing will ever change that."

"No, nothing will," he vowed. "Do hunters have mates or something similar?"

"Not that I know of. We are paired off, and some of those pairs come to love each other if they're lucky enough, others don't. Sometimes hunters find someone they would like to marry before they can be paired off, and sometimes they're granted permission to marry, but I've never heard anyone describe anything like what I felt when away from you. However, few love matches occur before marriage, and I've never met one, so I don't know what those couples experience with each other."

"I see," he murmured.

"My family is the strongest line." She stifled a yawn and nestled closer to the warmth of him. "Maybe that has something to do with it. Maybe we are more in tune with the demon part of us."

"Maybe," he agreed.

Kadence lifted her head to gaze around the room and her brow furrowed. "Ronan—"

"It will take some time to get used to your heightened senses. I'm told the sights and sounds can be especially overwhelming in the beginning."

"No," she said. "It all looks and sounds the same to me."

He sat back as he studied her. "It seems our species have a lot more in common than we'd ever realized. You were also seeking out my blood before the change."

"I was," she murmured as her eyebrows drew together over her nose. "And I enjoyed it. I have to speak with Nathan."

"Soon," he promised. "First you should feed and rest."

His words drew her attention to the blood pumping through his veins. She felt the answering pulse of his heart in every molecule of her body. For the first time, his new scent enveloped her, as did her own. The two of them had become intricately woven together.

A new inner strength pulsed within her, and with the next beat of his heart, her fangs lengthened. She recalled sinking those fangs into Ronan earlier, but feeling them now startled her.

She would never change what had passed between them, but she felt thrown off now. She hadn't experienced as many changes in her body as a human would have, but there was no denying she was no longer the woman she'd been before.

She was also extremely aware of another change in her. She felt Ronan at the edges of her mind, and she could feel the edges of his. "We will both have to get used to the mental bond," he said as he ran his hands over her. "It can be shut off again, if you would prefer."

"No," she said. "I will get used to it."

He smiled and kissed the tip of her nose. "We will get through this together, and I will do what I can when it comes to your brother."

Her breath caught in her chest as his pure brown eyes gazed back at her. "Ronan, your eyes, they're completely brown."

"When I was younger, they used to be brown all the time, but as time went on and the urge to kill became more incessant, the color of my eyes changed."

"Why are they different now?"

"Because you calm me more than all the blood and death in the world ever could. They may not remain brown all the time, but I didn't know they could ever be purely brown again until Declan told me they were when I first held you in the alley."

She drew her lip into her mouth to bite on it and winced when she pierced it with one of her fangs. "Easy," he murmured and bent his head to lick the blood away. "It will take time."

"I know," she said and sniffed at the air again. Now that she was adapting to his strong scent within her, and hers within him, she was beginning to smell herself more. "I could really use a shower."

He chuckled and rose to his feet with her locked securely in his arms. "Of course."

"I smell really bad."

He dropped his head down and inhaled deeply. "I think you smell like me, and I smell fantastic."

She couldn't help but laugh as he grinned at her. She'd never seen this side of him; he was almost jovial as his brown eyes twinkled. "Ronan, are you teasing me?"

"I think I might be," he replied, sounding more surprised by it than she was.

"I like it." She rested her head against his chest as he carried her into the bathroom.

"Then I will try to do it more often."

"Good."

CHAPTER THIRTY-SEVEN

HE DIDN'T BOTHER with the light in the bathroom as he strode toward the large, gray tiled shower. Kadence savored the feel of his skin beneath her and the power of the muscles enveloping her. The solid beat of his heart sounded in her ears as her fangs throbbed.

"You need to feed soon to complete the change," he told her when he sensed her hunger.

"You mean it's not complete?"

"Not normally no, but you're not exactly normal."

"No, I'm not."

Bending, he kissed her forehead. "You're hungry."

"I guess I am," she murmured.

"You'll only ever have to feed from me," he assured her as he adjusted his hold on her to pull back the glass encasing the shower. He fiddled with the water until steam rose to swirl around her. Setting her carefully on her feet, he gripped her nightgown and pulled it over her head.

Kadence's nose wrinkled when the sweaty scent of the clothing hit her. Her gaze fell on the toilet when he threw it onto the closed seat cover.

"Will I still have to go to the bathroom?" she asked.

"You will. Even us purebreds have at least some human in us, though you will probably have to go far less than you did before."

"Hmm," she murmured. "So, am I now considered a turned vamp?"

He unbuttoned the pants he wore and tugged them off. Stepping closer to her, he ran his hands over her sides, enjoying the feel of her silken skin. "Technically, yes," he replied. "However, you are so much more than that. I could always sense power within you, but now it is far stronger."

"Maybe that's your blood in me that you're sensing."

"I definitely sense that too, but this is more."

She stepped into him, sighing when her breasts came into contact with his chest. Even with the knots in her muscles, desire for him bloomed within her. She rested her fingers on his chest as his hand cupped her cheek.

His other arm wrapped around her waist and he lifted her against him. Kadence draped her arms around his neck. She nibbled at his bottom lip, drawing it into her mouth as he stepped into the shower with her. A blissful groan escaped her when the hot water beat against her skin and eased some of the soreness from her.

Ronan lowered her to the ground and reached behind her to grab the bottle of shampoo. "Close your eyes," he said gruffly.

Despite her displeasure over the loss of contact between them, Kadence closed her eyes as he guided her around. He worked the shampoo into her hair with a tenderness she never would have suspected from him as he massaged her scalp.

"Marta said women like conditioner," he said after he'd washed the shampoo from her hair and lifted another bottle.

She turned her head to look at him over her shoulder. The water running down his face and broad chest created rivulets she longed to lick away from him. "You asked Marta about women's things?"

His mouth curved into a smile. "I am not well versed in what women require."

She laughed as she brushed the wet hair out of her eyes. "I could argue differently about that, but yes, conditioner does help with the tangles in long hair. I doubt you have to worry about that."

"Not in years, and there was no conditioner the last time I had long hair."

"You had long hair?"

"At one time. I cut it off the first time it got in my way during a fight and never let it grow long again."

"I see," she murmured as he worked the conditioner into her hair.

She closed her eyes as his hands kneaded her cramped muscles afterward. He stepped closer to her, his erection rubbing against the hollow of her back while he worked over her body until all the knots were out of her muscles and her entire body felt electrified with its need for him. He washed the conditioner from her hair before positioning her so that her back was flush to his chest.

Stretching above her head and behind her, she ran her hand over the stubble lining his cheek. His lips pressed into her palm as one of his hands skimmed down her belly while the other rubbed the underside of her breasts.

"We should get you back to bed," he whispered against her palm.

"You read my mind," she replied. She lowered her other hand to grip his rigid shaft. "I want you, Ronan, now."

He should deny himself, she needed rest, but for the life of him he couldn't get the words past his constricted throat. She turned into him, and her gaze latched onto his mouth. The scent of her arousal grew stronger on the air, ensnaring him within its intoxicating depths.

Her fingers threaded through his hair as she rose onto her toes. He gripped her ass as her wet breasts slid over his skin, and she rubbed enticingly against his cock.

"You've been through a lot. You should rest," he said.

"There is no rest for the wicked," she murmured as she ran her tongue over his lower lip before nipping on it. "And I have more than one hunger right now."

Releasing her, he reached behind her to turn the water off. He opened the shower door, lifted her up, and carried her out. He removed a towel from the rack near the shower and enclosed her within the soft, terrycloth material. Her damp hair fell about her shoulders as she wiggled against him and bit at his lip again.

Her fingers glided over his chest, her gaze following everywhere she touched. The muscles of his stomach rippled as she traced them and delighted in the feel of him. He was everything she could have ever wanted and more.

Kadence pushed the towel away from her before gripping his shoulders and lifting herself so she could circle her legs around his waist. His eyes swirled a burgundy color as she rubbed her sex teasingly against the head of his cock. When he went to lower her onto him, she lifted herself away and shook her head as she gave him a playful smile.

Ronan lifted an eyebrow at her when she rubbed teasingly against him again, but didn't take him into her. Stalking forward, he set her on the marble counter near one of the sinks and pulled away from her. She went to grab him, but he caught her wrists and pinned them over her head to the mirror behind her. Her breasts heaved with her inhalations as she gazed at him from passion-darkened eyes.

"Do you enjoy teasing me, Kadence?" he inquired.

A smile curved her mouth as she slid her hips toward him. Her legs parted in invitation to him, but he held back from entering her.

"Now it's my turn to tease," he murmured.

Bending his head, he licked his way down her breast toward her nipple. Kadence's back bowed as he drew the puckered bud into his mouth and ran his tongue around it before turning his attention to her other breast.

Her breath came in shallow pants, the ache in her spread from between her thighs and into her belly as he suckled on her other breast. Then, he sank his fangs into her breast just above her nipple. She cried out, her body bucking on the counter, her wrists jerking in his grasp as overwhelming pleasure speared her.

He kept her wrists firmly within his hold as his tongue laved her nipple while he drew on her blood. Shifting his hold on her wrists into one hand, he kept them pinned as his fingers skimmed over her flesh in a touch so faint that she barely felt it, but it left her skin electrified.

Ronan slid his hand between her thighs, spreading them wider. Her wetness slipped over his fingers as he stroked her, causing her to cry out. He kept his mouth on her breast while he dipped a finger into her.

She writhed against him, her head moving back and forth as he parted her further and slid another finger into her. Her muscles clenched around him when he rubbed his palm over her clit, stoking the fire within her higher.

"Ronan!" she gasped. "I can't!"

He released his bite on her breast and lifted his head to meet her gaze. Leaning closer to her, his mouth brushed over hers as he spoke. "Can't what?"

"I can't take anymore."

He slid his fingers away from her and grinned when she moaned and pressed her hips forward on the counter. "I thought you enjoyed teasing," he said and pulled her wrists down so that he held them against her belly.

Before she could respond, he trailed his fingers up the inside of her thigh in a wispy touch that she barely felt, but her body begged for more of it. She tried to pull her hands from his grasp again, but he kept them firmly in place as he pushed her thighs further apart and knelt before her.

Her eyes widened when he bent his head between her legs.

"Ronan!" Any protest she'd been about to utter died on her lips when his tongue stroked over her aching center.

Her head fell back as he worked his tongue into her in penetrating thrusts. Finally, he released her hands. Kadence grasped his head, not to push him away but to pull him closer.

Ronan growled as her hands curled into his hair and her hips surged toward him. Grabbing her ass, he dragged her closer to his mouth as he tasted the heated wetness of her core. Her hips moved faster as she fucked his tongue with a wild abandon that had him growing impossibly harder.

He sensed her impending release in the tightening of her muscles. Pushing her closer and closer to the brink, he pulled away before she could plummet over the edge. Her hands tugged at his hair as she groaned her disappointment. He rose before her and seized her wrists again with one hand. Drawing them over her head, he pinned them to the glass once more as he met her dazed gaze.

"I love to tease too," he murmured before taking hold of his dick and guiding it to her entrance. He held her gaze as he buried himself within her.

"I love the way you do," she murmured as her eyes drifted closed.

Ronan pulled back to drive into her again. He lost himself to the frenzy of his need as he thrust into her again and again. He was on the brink of spilling, but he gritted his teeth and held back his release.

Kadence's eyes opened, and his breath caught as he found himself gazing into their startling white-blue depths once more. She most certainly was something more than a normal turned vampire, and she was starving.

Releasing her wrists, he wrapped his hand around her head and pulled her face into the hollow of his throat. "Feed," he commanded.

Her fangs slid over his skin before sinking into his vein. His body jerked as she pulled hungrily on his blood and her body kept rhythm with the demands of his. The muscles of her sheath clenched around him and she cried out against his throat. This time, he didn't hold back his own release, but followed her over the edge.

CHAPTER THIRTY-EIGHT

"My brother would never hurt me," Kadence said for what felt like the thousandth time that night.

Ronan barely glanced at her as his eyes remained focused on the trees around them. He tuned out the clacking of the branches in the breeze swirling through the park as he listened for any other sounds. The hunters would come, he had no doubt, but he didn't know what would happen when they did.

Kadence searched the woods for her brother, her hands twisting anxiously before her. She'd spent the past week adapting to her new vampire status and training with Ronan. She'd always been fast before, but now she moved with a speed that still startled her, and her reflexes had amped up.

She'd managed to avoid having Ronan take her down once, but it had been a big improvement. He'd reluctantly admitted to her that she was doing better than he'd expected and, with more training and her added vampire strength, she would be able to take down a Savage on her own. He'd even admitted that, if she kept working as hard as she had been and completed the training, she would make a good Defender one day.

Finally, he had agreed that it was time to contact Nathan, and she'd called him earlier today. She was surrounded by over eight hundred pounds of solid vampire flesh as Ronan and the others stood close by her, yet a shiver of unease raced up her spine. The swings across the way swayed back and forth, their creaking chains adding a creepy air to the already tense night.

Her brother would never hurt her, but the eerie playground, coupled with the fact she knew Nathan wasn't going to react well to what she had to tell him, made her feel like screaming. She'd told Nathan he could bring some of the other hunters with him, but no more than ten. She really hoped he'd listened to her. Otherwise, this night could end badly, and she desperately wanted everything to go right.

The two men she loved the most could die if this blew up in her face.

Killean kept muttering about killing hunters, and Lucien looked like someone had taken away his favorite toy as he studied the woods with a sullen expression. Declan idly twirled a lollipop in his mouth as Saxon tapped a foot while his hand rested on one of the knives strapped to his side. Ronan stepped closer to her.

"My brother won't hurt me," she insisted again.

His hand settled into the small of her back. "You are not one of them anymore, Kadence. There is no way to know how they will react to that revelation."

"I may be a vampire now, but I will always be one of them."

"They're here," Ronan said.

"Where?" Kadence asked as she searched the woods. A fresh, subtle scent wafted from her right, and she turned in that direction as Nathan emerged from the woods with Asher and Logan flanking him.

"There are others still in the woods," Lucien said.

"Yes," Ronan replied.

"We didn't expect them to be brave enough to reveal all their numbers," Killean said.

Kadence glared at him before focusing on her brother. Her heart leapt as joy and love swept through her. She took a step toward Nathan, but Ronan blocked her from going any further with his arm. She turned her angry gaze on him.

"I told you before we came here that you were to stay by me," Ronan said.

"He's my brother."

"And if he wishes to come to us, he can, but you will *not* go to him."

She opened her mouth to protest, but when his eyes shifted to a more volatile red color, she held it back. Everyone was on edge enough without her pushing it to a breaking point. Nathan stopped ten feet away from them; his gaze ran over the vampires before settling on her.

"Are you okay?" he demanded.

"Yes," she assured him. He studied her, as if trying to figure out if she were telling the truth or not. "Really, Nathan, I'm fine."

Logan glanced at her before focusing on Ronan. His lips flattened when he saw the protective way Ronan stood against her. Kadence's heart twisted, and unexpected tears burned her eyes. She'd never loved Logan the way she loved Ronan, but she cared deeply for him. She'd never wanted to hurt him or her brother, but she knew she had, and she would have to live with that for the rest of her life. She could only hope that one day they would forgive her, but she didn't expect it from them.

"I'm sorry," she said, keeping her gaze focused on Logan as she spoke. "Know that the last thing I ever wanted was to hurt anyone. I just…" She trailed off as she tried to think of how to explain what had happened without making it worse. "I broke out only to see Joseph die, but once I was free, I decided to try to see more of the world."

Logan's eyes finally slid to her. "You didn't get very far."

Kadence winced at the accusation in his voice. "I was going to go to Ireland. I was there, in the airport, getting ready to board the plane, but I couldn't do it."

"Why not?" Nathan demanded.

"Because we have it wrong," she told him again. "And if there is a chance I can save one hunter's life, or one innocent vampire, I knew I had to try to make it happen."

"Innocent vampire? Sounds like an oxymoron to me," Logan spat.

"I'd say you're the moron," Killean grumbled, his face stone cold as Logan glowered at him.

Kadence swallowed heavily. She'd cut Logan far deeper than she'd realized. Ronan clasped her nape, drawing her closer. Nathan stiffened at the possessive gesture, and Logan looked as if murder was the only thing he wanted.

"Shit," Asher hissed.

"What have you done, Kadence?" Logan demanded. "You can't be stupid enough to trust them!"

"Watch how you talk to her."

The low, lethal tone of Ronan's voice caused the hair on her neck to rise. She'd known this wouldn't be easy, but it was rapidly deteriorating into an explosive situation. "Listen to me!" she cried and stepped forward.

Ronan moved with her. He bared his fangs at the hunters as he held every one of their gazes. "Know that if you try to harm her, I'll kill you," he promised.

Nathan's eyes darted between them.

"Animals," Logan scoffed.

Nathan held his hand up. "Enough," he said before focusing on Kadence. "Tell me what is going on. What do we have wrong?"

Kadence met her brother's troubled blue eyes, so similar in hue to hers. "Not all vampires are evil. Not all of them kill for fun. Not all of them are like Joseph."

"I see," Nathan murmured. "And we're supposed to believe they're not all evil because…?"

"Because you can smell it," she said in reply to her brother's trailing question. "I didn't realize it until recently, but the stench we believed all vampires to have *doesn't* affect them all. Ronan told me all purebred vampires can smell the difference between a vampire who has turned Savage and one who doesn't kill, but a vampire who has been turned from a human cannot smell the difference."

"What is a purebred vampire?" Nathan inquired.

"A vampire who is born a vampire, and not a human who has been turned into one," Ronan replied.

Nathan's eyebrows shot into his hairline, Asher's mouth dropped, and Logan made a scoffing sound. "Vampires can be born?" Nathan inquired.

"Yes," Kadence replied.

"Holy shit," Asher muttered.

"It's a far bigger world than all you little hunters believed," Killean drawled, earning scowls from everyone.

Choosing not to rise to Killean's baiting, Kadence focused on brother again. "Hunters can smell the difference between the vampires who kill and those that don't too, not as strongly as a purebred, but we can detect it. I know the vampires here don't smell like Joseph did."

Nathan gazed at the men around her before giving a brief nod. "They don't," he agreed. "But just because there's no foul odor, I'm supposed to believe they're not killers?"

"We're killers," Ronan said, and she almost elbowed him in the gut for it. "But we only kill those of our kind who turn Savage and start slaughtering other vampires and humans."

"We've also taken out a hunter or two when they've gotten in our way," Lucien added with a smirk.

"Enough," Ronan said, and Lucien became silent.

"So you've killed an innocent hunter before?" Logan demanded.

"You're not innocent if you're threatening our lives," Ronan replied. "Your kind may have been ignorant to the truth about vampires since the very beginning, but ignorance is not an excuse when our lives are on the line. You better remember that."

"Ronan," Kadence whispered.

Ronan's thumb rubbed her nape reassuringly as he spoke. "They must know the whole truth if there is to be any kind of trust." Ronan kept his attention focused on Nathan. The bruises he'd inflicted a week ago on the hunter had vanished. His broken nose was no longer swollen and crooked. "I could have killed you," Ronan said to him. "I didn't."

A muscle ticked in Nathan's cheek at the reminder. Ronan waited for him to be foolish enough to deny it, but the young hunter nodded. "True," he agreed.

"They saved me from Joseph. He attacked me in the alley," Kadence said. "I'd be dead now if it wasn't for Ronan. He also set me free. I was *free*, Nathan." Anguish flickered in her brother's eyes. "I could have gone anywhere I wanted to, I had money and *humans* who were going to help keep me safe, yet I'm standing here now."

"I know being kept in the stronghold was difficult on you. I didn't realize until recently how difficult it was and how confining. We can work on making it better for you there," Nathan said.

Ronan stiffened beside her. She rested her hand on his chest, but it did nothing to ease the tension he emitted. "Nathan, I'm not returning to the stronghold."

"Then what do you intend to do, Kadence, live with the vampires?" Nathan asked.

"Yes."

Logan threw his arms into the air. "They've corrupted you and you can't even see it!"

"No, they haven't," she replied. "I know it's hard to believe that they aren't our enemies, at least not all of them. I struggled with it too in the beginning, but I know the truth now."

Before coming here, she'd promised Ronan she wouldn't reveal to her brother that they could go out in the day, not until he deemed Nathan trustworthy enough. Now, she had little to work with in order to make them see reason, but she understood Ronan's reasons for guarding some of their secrets.

"Nathan, take her and let's get out of here," Logan said.

"No one will *ever* take her from me," Ronan promised.

"Enough, Logan," Nathan said before focusing on her again. "It seems you have traded one cage for another."

CHAPTER THIRTY-NINE

KADENCE OPENED her mouth to reply, but Ronan spoke before she could. "I would never keep her caged as you did. She had no choices with you, not even on whom she would marry."

His eyes fixed on Logan, the man Kadence had told him she was to marry. Ronan suspected Logan's obvious love for Kadence would turn to loathing when he realized what she was now. The hunter may become an issue that would have to be dealt with later, but for now, he would continue to play nice, for Kadence.

"Every step she has taken with me has been one of her choosing, not someone else's. I tried to make her return to you. She refused. I set her free. She came back. No one will take her choices from her again, not even me."

Nathan rocked back on his heels. "And just what is it between you two?"

He saw the question in Kadence's eyes when she lifted her gaze to him. "Reveal what you will about that," he told her.

She turned back to her brother. Part of her screamed not to say the words out loud. She was afraid he would walk away from her and she would never see him again if she did. The other part knew she couldn't lie, not to Nathan, and it would come out eventually. It was better to know if he would turn against her now, than tomorrow or a month from now.

"I… I love him, Nathan."

"Bullshit!" Logan exploded. He jerked a crossbow up from his hip, and before Kadence could blink, he fired the bolt.

"No!" Nathan shouted as Kadence leapt forward.

Ronan pulled her back with one hand while he snatched the bolt out of the air with the other. Lifting his head, Ronan held Logan's gaze as he broke the bolt in half. The hunter took a startled step back when the vampires closed in around Ronan and started toward Logan.

"Back off," Ronan commanded his men.

They moved back, but all their eyes had taken on a fiery red hue as they stared at Logan. If he allowed it, the hunter would be dead before he could take his next breath. Ronan released Kadence and strode forward. She snagged his hand and tugged on it until he stopped.

"No, this is not… This will *not* happen!" she yelled.

Releasing Ronan's hand, she moved forward with lethal speed to yank the crossbow from Logan's grasp. She threw the weapon onto the ground and stomped it, shattering it into pieces. Her fangs lengthened as she resisted tearing Logan's throat out for trying to kill Ronan. Feeling somewhat more in control of herself, she lifted her head to meet Logan's startled gaze.

Ronan drew her against his chest when her eyes burned that feral, white-blue color. Her brother and the other hunters gasped when they saw her eyes.

"Don't you ever do that again!" she yelled at Logan. "I'm sorry I hurt you, I really am, and I will regret it for the rest of my life. But *I* have chosen Ronan, and no matter what anyone else says or believes, it is a choice I would make over and over for the rest of my life. If you try to attack him again, I'll kill you myself, and don't think I'm not capable of it."

She turned to face her brother who gawked at her as if he didn't know her. She supposed he didn't know her, not really. "I love you, Nathan. I always will no matter what happens. Maybe, one day, if you'll listen to me and accept my choices, you can get to really know *me*. However, none of that matters, not when innocent lives are on the line.

"There are vampires who have been killed that didn't deserve it, and there are hunters who have died that didn't have to. Joseph is bringing together a large group of Savage vampires that we can beat if we all work together, but if the vampires and hunters remain divided and killing each other, then Joseph will only grow stronger until he becomes unstoppable."

Her brother succeeded in closing his mouth, but it fell open again. "Your eyes," he murmured.

Kadence's heart sank. "Are my eyes really what you're most concerned about after everything I just said?"

Nathan closed his mouth and threw back his shoulders. "No, they're not. What is a Savage vampire?"

"Those of our kind who kill for pleasure and take the lives of innocents. There is no humanity left within them," Ronan replied. "They are the ones we hunt."

Nathan's gaze ran over them before focusing on Ronan again. "How big of a threat is this with Joseph and these Savages?"

"It's growing stronger every day," Ronan said.

"You can't seriously be considering this insanity!" Logan hissed.

"Not another word, Logan," Nathan commanded. "Asher, what do you think?"

"I think your sister has hopped on the crazy train express, but I believe there is something to what she says," Asher replied.

"Thanks," Kadence muttered.

"You gotta admit it's a little crazy, kid. I mean, we're all a little crazy in one way or another, but you're rounding out the top of the looney tier right now. I suppose the vampires could have found a way to warp her mind and turn her to their side, but I don't see why he would have set her free if that were the case."

"What do you think of that, Logan?" Nathan inquired.

"He set her free as part of his manipulation to gain her trust," Logan replied.

Kadence almost stomped her foot in frustration, but she managed to stop herself from doing so. Acting like a child would get her nowhere right now.

"True," Nathan said as he rubbed at his jaw. "And judging by the color of my sister's eyes and the speed with which she moved over here, I'm going to say she's not the same as when she left the stronghold. We know a vampire can control a human's mind, perhaps—"

"You know hunters are immune to a vampire's powers of persuasion," she interrupted brusquely.

"True," he said. "But he's no normal vampire, we can all sense that, and you are not a normal hunter anymore."

Ronan didn't speak as he waited for Nathan to figure things out for himself. It wouldn't do any good to rush him or argue with him. Nathan was young, but the fact he was taking time with his decision and listening to the views of the others revealed a maturity beyond his years.

"But then, we've never been normal hunters. Our family line has always been stronger," Nathan continued.

Nathan's gaze traveled to the other vampires. "What makes a vampire turn into a Savage?"

"Death and blood is a temptation many vampires live with every day, and some give into it," Ronan replied. "Those who kill become stronger, especially if they kill our kind or a hunter, though they enjoy slaughtering humans too. A vampire doesn't become completely Savage until the innocent deaths of the humans warp their souls."

"So at any time one of you could also become Savage?"

"Yes." There was no reason to deny it or to lie. If they were to work together, they would have to be honest with each other. If Nathan discovered the truth later, it would sever any relationship they may have built between them.

"Many of us fight it," Declan said. "And that's just it, we *fight* it."

"That's fine. I'm more concerned about thinking we can trust you and having one of you turn on us," Nathan said.

"We could say the same to you," Ronan said and glanced pointedly at Logan. "We're not asking for your secrets."

"I know more about them than they know about us," Kadence said as she silently pleaded with Nathan to believe her.

Nathan stared at her before looking to Ronan. "What will happen to my sister if you turn Savage?"

Ronan slid his arm around her waist. "Because of your sister, I will not become a Savage, not unless something happens to her."

"I don't understand."

"That's something I'd like to keep between us for now at least," Ronan replied before focusing on Logan. "But know I will defend her life above my own and I will kill anyone who threatens her, no matter who they are."

Logan's nostrils flared and hatred burned from his eyes, but he kept his mouth shut.

"I see," Nathan said. "And what of them?" he asked with a wave at the other Defenders.

"I've known all of them for centuries. They battle their demons, but they're as determined to destroy Joseph and the Savages as I am."

Nathan folded his arms over his chest as he speared Kadence with his stare. "Are you a vampire?"

Kadence had hoped not to have to deal with this yet, but she'd given herself away with her eyes. "Yes," she replied.

Logan sucked in a breath. Before anyone could respond, he spun on his heel and stalked away. Kadence took a step after him, but Ronan held her back as Nathan put out a hand to halt her.

"Let him go," Nathan said. "This is something he may never come to terms with, and you have to accept that."

A lump lodged in her throat as Logan vanished into the woods. "I never meant to hurt him."

"I know, but you did, and we're the ones who put you in that position. You shouldn't have taken off the way you did, you could have gotten killed, but we... *I* was wrong for expecting you to accept a life I wouldn't have accepted for myself. I know that now, but that doesn't change what has happened."

"Nathan—" She stepped toward him and froze when he kept his hand up between them.

"I'm not ready either. I love you, but this is a lot to take in."

Tears burned her eyes as she bent her head. Ronan embraced her as he leveled her brother with an unblinking stare.

"We'll work through it in time," she said.

"I have to discuss this with the elders," Nathan said. "They're not going to take it well."

"No, they're not," Kadence agreed.

"Call me tomorrow," he said to Kadence before turning and walking away.

"Crazy or not, I hope you found happiness, Kadence," Asher said before following her brother.

Kadence nestled against Ronan's chest when he lifted her and held her against him. His body remained tensed as he studied the trees. Over his shoulder, her eyes landed on Killean. The pitiless vampire stared back at her for a minute before briefly bowing his head to her.

She may have just lost everyone she had known for her whole life, but she knew then that she'd somehow managed to earn Killean's respect.

CHAPTER FORTY

KADENCE PUT THE BOOK DOWN, rose, and paced over to one of the bookshelves before stopping and turning back to the chair she'd vacated. Her gaze went to the window and the sun spilling inside. She strode over to pull back the curtain and reveal the covered swimming pool.

She should call Nathan, but she dreaded picking up the phone. She knew the elders would never agree to the hunters working with the vampires. They hated and resisted any kind of change, and the hunters had been set in their ways for centuries. She stalked back toward the chair, her dread growing with every step.

There had been a niggling at the back of her mind ever since she'd woken this afternoon. It was the same feeling she got when she somehow knew things. Then, there was always this nagging tug on her mind. Before the tugging had been small, but now it felt like something was digging its way into her brain, and it would not go away.

Before, there had been some sort of revelation, but there were no revelations coming to her now. She sensed nothing more than what she already knew. However, the incessant digging sensation grew with every passing hour, and she could feel it expanding within her brain and taking over.

She shook her head to clear it of the sensation, but it clung like a burr. She rubbed at her temples as they pounded with every beat of her heart.

"Kadence?"

Lifting her head, she found Ronan standing in the doorway. The sweats he wore hung low on his hips, a sheen of sweat emphasized the chiseled ridges of his abs, and his damp hair had been brushed back from the rugged angles of his face. He'd been working out with the others, and the new recruits who had been moved here. Now it was time for the two of them to train together.

"What is wrong?" he asked as he strode toward her.

"I... I don't know," she muttered. "I have this feeling that something is coming, but I don't know what, and I can't shake it."

"You've been through a lot." He rested his hands on her shoulders as he stopped before her. "It's understandable that you're unsettled."

"No, it's more than that. Over the years, I've always just *known* things. This is kind of like what I experienced then, but it's more."

"More how?" he inquired.

She blinked when he blurred before her until he became two and then three. She leaned toward him, inhaling his scent as she tried to stay focused on him, but as she watched, the floor vanished beneath her feet.

Ronan caught her when her legs gave out. Terror burst through him when he felt her distress and uncertainty battering against the bond connecting them. He tried to get deeper into her mind to see if he could soothe her, but something kept him blocked from experiencing more of what she felt.

"Declan!" he bellowed.

He'd left the others in the gym, but seconds later the pounding of footsteps rang across the marble. Kadence hunched forward and her head snapped up. He found himself gazing into her white-blue eyes. Though she stared at him, he didn't think she saw him as she remained focused on something far beyond him.

"What the fuck?" Lucien said from the doorway.

Ronan glanced over to find him standing with Declan and Killean. Lucien and Killean took a step back, but Declan winced as he lifted a hand to his head. "Shit," Declan said.

"What is it?" Ronan demanded.

Kadence wheezed, drawing his attention back to her. He held her cheeks in his hands when she started speaking, "The pathways." Ice slid down his spine as she uttered the same words she'd spoken during her transformation, but this time she spoke in a much more alien tone of voice. "Plymouth, rock, warehouse, bricks, Joseph."

Color flooded back into her eyes and she met his gaze. She trembled in his arms, but determination etched her features. "I know where Joseph is, or at least where he was."

RONAN HAD ORIGINALLY REFUSED to bring her with them, which had resulted in their first big fight. She'd eventually worn him down when she'd reminded him that he'd promised not to cage her, that she was stronger than most turned vamps, and that she had found a way out of the stronghold, she would find a way out of the mansion too.

She also hadn't spilled enough details for them to easily locate Joseph in Plymouth, but she would be able to locate him on her own, once she escaped. The pathway to Joseph's location had unraveled in flashing swirls of brilliant blues and purples in her mind. Each new flash had revealed a landmark she would recognize when she saw it again.

"Joseph killed my father, and you promised me that you would not dictate my life," she said again when Ronan's disapproval vibrated through their bond.

"You may not have seen a lot of vampires in your vision, but there will be a lot there if Joseph's managed to stay hidden from Brian this whole time," Ronan replied, not for the first time.

"I'm not so sure it was a vision, more like a guide or map," she said, refusing to rehash their argument again. "I saw road signs, landmarks, then the warehouse, and finally Joseph."

"You said when you were a hunter you knew things," Ronan said as he turned onto another road leading deeper into the thick woods she'd directed them into. "Becoming a vampire most likely unlocked something that has been within you. It will grow stronger with time and practice."

Wonderful, she thought. Being knocked to her knees by the burst of images flooding her mind earlier had been anything but fun. However, if those images helped them to locate and exterminate Joseph, she'd happily receive them again.

She glanced at the cell phone in her hand. She'd called Nathan earlier and explained what had happened, where they were going, and who they were hunting. She had a feeling that, if she hadn't told him it was Joseph, he wouldn't be meeting them. Her brother had been distant on the phone, and he'd sounded exhausted. She had no idea what had happened since she'd last seen him, but the elders wouldn't have made what he revealed to them easy on him.

The screen on the phone lit up as a large boulder with a tree growing through the center of it appeared ahead. "Turn there," she said and pointed at the rock. She clearly recalled the strange rock from the seventh image she'd received.

Ronan made the turn and continued down a winding road. It was so dark the headlights barely pierced the night surrounding them. She typed a message to Nathan and closed the phone. "We're almost there," she murmured.

"You're going to stay in the SUV," Ronan replied.

"No, I'm not."

"Kadence—"

"No. We're here because of me. I will not allow you to order me about and keep me locked away like the hunters did. Either accept that I will see this through to the end, or get out of my way because you won't be keeping me in this vehicle."

The others inhaled sharply in the back seat, but didn't say a word. Ronan's head turned toward her, and his red eyes lit the night better than the headlights as he gazed at her. Kadence held his gaze, refusing to back down.

"I may not have realized it before, but I was submissive for most of my life; I won't be again," she said.

"You've never been submissive around me," he muttered.

"What can I say? You bring out the best in me," she replied with a smile that didn't ease the tension from him as she'd hoped.

He glanced at her again as the knuckles in his hands turned white from his grip on the wheel. Kadence rested her hand over one of his. "You've been training me. I'm strong and fast, and I promise I won't do anything foolish. I will do what you ask of me as long as you don't ask me to stay behind."

"We've barely gotten any real training in you," he muttered.

"And that is why I'm agreeing to stay out of the way."

Before he could formulate a response, she sat forward in the seat and slapped her hand on the dashboard. "Take the next left. The warehouse is through the woods about a hundred feet beyond that."

She texted the last stage of the directions to her brother before tossing the phone into the glovebox. Her hand rested on the handle and her foot tapped against the floorboard as she prepared to leap from the vehicle.

Pulling to the side of the road, Ronan seized Kadence's arm before she could bolt. She stiffened in his grasp, her gaze swinging back to him. "Know that I will drag you away from here if you don't listen to me. Promises or not, your safety comes first and I won't have you doing anything to risk your life or anyone else's. I'm willing to let Joseph get away again before I allow that to happen."

Kadence glanced at the vampires crowding the back seats before releasing the handle. They were all watching her and Ronan with expressions that clearly said they'd rather be toasting marshmallows in Hell than sitting where they were.

"What do we do?" she asked Ronan.

"You stay close to me. Text your brother and tell him to park off the road behind us and continue to the warehouse on foot."

She retrieved the phone from the glovebox and typed the message before focusing on Ronan again. The red had faded from his eyes, but not completely. He released her arm and slid out of the vehicle. He stood there for a minute before sticking his head back in.

"Landfills smell better," he said.

"Now we know why he's out in the boonies," Lucien said and opened his door.

Ronan focused on Kadence as she shifted in her seat. The last thing he wanted was to have her here, but he'd promised not to cage her again. He was close to breaking that promise and screw the consequences. She could be mad forever as long as she was alive. He glanced at Declan in the back seat, who stared blankly back at him. Declan could stay with her; he'd be able to keep her restrained if it became necessary.

"Don't," she whispered. "I promise, Ronan, I'll do what you say, but don't make me stay here. I won't forgive you if you do."

"You'll be alive."

"Life isn't worth living if you take my freedom away from me again."

He strove to maintain restraint as he inhaled a deep breath and then another. "We'll just check things out for now," he finally said and closed the door.

Walking to her side, he opened her door and took hold of her arm to help her out. Her nose wrinkled as soon as she exited the vehicle, and she stepped back. Her hand flew up to block her nostrils. "It's horrible," she muttered.

"It is," he agreed. "Come."

CHAPTER FORTY-ONE

THEY MOVED DOWN the dirt road with rapid speed before he led her into the forest and around to the side of a dilapidated, three-story, brick building. Judging by its numerous boarded windows and sagging roof, it had been years since anyone had done any upkeep on the warehouse.

"Smart," Declan said as he crouched on the ground beside Kadence. "We'd never think to look for him out here, and there are no humans around to interrupt them."

"He was one of us," Saxon said. "He knows how we work, what we look for, but Brian should have been able to locate him out here."

"Not if he's been moving around a lot," Lucien said. "This most likely isn't where he's staying. Judging by the smell, there are too many Savages in there for his liking."

"Can he smell the Savages still?" Kadence asked.

"No," Ronan replied. "Years ago, Declan and I caught a purebred who turned and questioned him. Once they give in, they no longer smell the rot of another. Probably because they are rotten too."

Kadence shuddered as her eyes drifted back to the building.

Beside her, Ronan's body was coiled so tight, she thought he might snap. "We have to see how many Savages are in there," he murmured. "This way."

He kept her hand in his as he led her around the crumpling structure to a sliding barn door in the front. From inside, laughter and music flowed out, as did the pungent stench of blood and decay. Turning to Kadence, he clasped her shoulders.

"I need you to stay here."

"But—"

"You promised you would do as I say, and I need you to *stay here*. I can get closer by myself, and I don't want you to see what is going on inside."

Kadence glanced at the building as she tried to keep breathing through her mouth. Even still, she could *taste* the horrific stench of this place. She didn't think it was any worse than what she would have experienced before becoming a vampire; there were just far more Savages here than she'd ever encountered before.

"You can't go alone," she whispered.

"I'm only going to look, not attack."

"Okay," she relented. "You have to be careful."

"I will be."

He drew her close, his hand sliding through her hair to cup the back of her head as he held her close and claimed her mouth. Reluctantly, he stepped back and released her before turning to look at the shadows dancing through the trees behind her.

"I'd lower those weapons if you want to live," he said coldly.

Kadence followed Ronan's gaze, as the others turned toward the woods and edged back until they were flanking her and Ronan. The shadows shifted when her brother came forward, lowering his crossbow as he walked. Behind him, Asher and Logan also emerged with half a dozen other hunters.

"Don't ever point a weapon at me again unless you're prepared to fight," Ronan said to Nathan. "And if any of you think to aim one of those at her, you'll all be dead before you know you're missing your throats."

Nathan's gaze flicked to her. "Fair enough," he replied. "I smell garbage, like you said the Savages of your kind smelled, but it's worse than what I've experienced before."

Ronan edged Kadence behind his back as he spoke. He didn't trust Logan anywhere near her. "There are a lot of them inside that building."

Nathan's gaze went to the warehouse. "Joseph is in there?" he asked as he slipped the crossbow onto his back.

"I think so, or at least I saw him in there, sort of," Kadence said.

"What do you mean by that?"

Kadence sighed. "It's tough to explain, but you know how I always kind of *knew* things?"

"Yeah."

"I kind of knew this too, but in a way I've never experienced before. Joseph was in there when I saw how to get here."

"Interesting," Nathan said. "So what do we do now?"

"Now, I'm going to get closer and see what we're up against," Ronan replied.

"I'm coming with you," Nathan stated.

Ronan opened his mouth to tell the hunter no, before deciding against it. They were here to try to work together on this. However, he didn't want to leave Kadence here with the rest of the hunters. Seeming to sense this, Declan moved closer to her while Lucien and Killean stepped into position in front of and behind her. Saxon hedged her in on the other side. Kadence scowled at them, but she didn't protest the box they'd closed her into.

"My men won't harm my sister," Nathan said.

"That's not a chance I'm willing to take, not with her," Ronan replied.

306 BRENDA K DAVIES

Nathan turned to face the remaining hunters. "I'll be back shortly. Make sure Kadence stays safe."

"Oh, for crying out loud, I'm probably stronger than you now," Kadence muttered, earning her a dark look from her brother that she returned.

The two of them didn't look much alike, but in that moment, Ronan saw the striking similarities in the twins' obstinate personalities.

"Let's go," Ronan said and slipped from the woods.

Nathan stayed close by his side, moving noiselessly over the ground toward the back of the building. Stopping beside the warehouse, Ronan edged toward one of the broken windows. The board covering it had slipped to expose the bottom of the window. He knelt beside it, and Nathan crouched down across from him. Nathan's eyes were wary, but Ronan didn't detect a spike in the hunter's heartbeat over being alone together.

Rising slowly, Ronan peered into the window. His teeth clamped together when he saw the vast number of Savages within. There had to be at least a hundred of them, and probably more on the upper floors. Beside him, Nathan's breath hissed in when he rose to look inside too.

Mixed in with the Savages were humans. Most of the humans were dead, their bodies littering the floor, but there were still some who were being feasted on by numerous Savages at once. His gaze ran over the naked bodies covered in blood and writhing over each other as many of them feasted on each other while they screwed in the middle of the floor.

Ronan's forehead furrowed as his eyes were drawn to the back wall and the line of vampires there. All of them had their hands pulled over their heads and were chained to the wall. Their red eyes gleamed in the candlelight and their fangs extended as they jerked against their bonds. Their emaciated frames made it impossible for them to break free of their binds.

Despite the stench of the place, Ronan didn't get an overwhelming sense of power coming from the Savages crowded within. He would bet most of them were no more than a month old.

Sliding away from the window, he rested his fingers on the ground as he tried to puzzle out what was going on within. Anger etched Nathan's face when he knelt in front of him again. Ronan jerked his head to the side and glided back toward the woods. An uneasy feeling grew in the pit of his stomach with every step he took. Something was wrong here; he just didn't know what it was yet.

"Why is my sister here?" Nathan asked, breaking into his thoughts.

Ronan stopped walking to face him. Nathan had a good four inches on him, but he still stepped away from him. "Because she is."

"She doesn't belong here."

"If I forced her to stay behind, I'd have done to her what you did to her, and look at how well that worked out for you. She may love me, but she'll grow to hate me and it will destroy her if I try to lock her away, even if it's what I'd like to do to keep her safe."

Saying the words out loud made him realize how true they were. He'd agreed to allow her to come to make sure she didn't try to find Joseph on her own, but he realized he'd also agreed to it because he knew he could never crush her spirit. He loved her too much for that.

"She belongs here as much as you do. Besides, she's right, she is stronger than you are now. She's stronger than any other turned vampire who has come before her, and I've been training her, *really* training her. She's lethal."

A muscle twitched in Nathan's cheek, but he didn't argue with him. Ronan turned away from him and continued through the woods as his mind churned over what they'd seen in the warehouse. He pulled Nathan back when the missing piece slid into place.

"This is where Joseph is storing his recruits. His *new* recruits," he said.

"Recruits?"

"Yes."

Turning away, he poured on the speed until he came back to the place where he'd left Kadence and the others. She pushed past Killean to come to him. Logan sneered and hatred burned in his eyes as he watched her. Stepping forward, Ronan gathered her in his arms and held her firmly against his chest. He pinned Logan with a remorseless stare that caused him to pull at his collar as he looked away.

"How bad is it?" Kadence asked.

"Bad," he replied, unwilling to release her. "There are at least a hundred Savages inside."

"Is Joseph in there?"

"I don't think so. He's definitely been here, as this is where he's creating and keeping his recruits."

"What do you mean *creating*?" Declan asked.

"I mean, he's turning humans and putting them in there. He's probably feeding them after they turn so they can complete the transformation, but then he's chaining them to the walls until they're so famished they ravish the first human they come into contact with. If they kill often enough, they won't fight their bloodlust anymore. The Savages who aren't chained are in the middle of a feeding and sexual frenzy. They've completely given themselves over to the bloodlust."

"He's also probably recruiting shitty humans who would be more than happy to live forever while continuing to be shitty vampires and killing for sport," Saxon said.

"Probably," Ronan agreed. "The few humans still alive in there won't be for much longer."

"If he plans on turning humans into Savages, he'll build an endless army," Lucien muttered and ran a hand through his hair.

"Yes," Ronan agreed. "And he may have other buildings like this out there."

"How do we stop them from being set loose?" Nathan inquired.

"First things first. At sunrise, we're burning this place down and taking out as many Savages as we can."

"You mean *we* are," Nathan replied and waved at the other hunters.

"You'll learn, young hunter, that I always mean what I say," Ronan replied.

CHAPTER FORTY-TWO

NATHAN RESTED his hand on her arm and drew her away from the others. Ronan lifted his head to watch them. Through the bond connecting them, she sensed his dislike of their distance, but he didn't come after her.

"I don't understand," Nathan said as the rays of the sun lit the earth and fell over them. His gaze ran over her before going to the sun and then beyond her to Ronan. "How is it possible you're all out in the sun? Are they really vampires? Are *you*?"

Kadence glanced at the others as they worked to fill glass bottles with the gasoline they would be using to set the warehouse on fire. Ronan had sent Declan to retrieve the supplies a couple of hours ago; Nathan had sent Asher with him. Kadence recognized it as the first olive branch between the two factions, but it had been a very thin branch. No one had spoken while Asher and Declan were gone, and she doubted the vamp and hunter had done any bonding while on their mission.

"I wouldn't lie to you about that, Nathan," she said. "I am a vampire and so are they. I know you can feel their power."

"I can, and I can feel... a difference in you. Something more than just a vampire."

"I am different than they are. Not much, but my transformation was different. My eyes don't turn red when I'm upset, and I *saw* this place. It was the strangest thing ever, but I saw flashes of different things, which helped to guide my way here. It's like something inside of me was set free when I turned. Most likely some dormant part of our demon DNA."

"How is it possible all of you can be in the sun?"

"I told you, Nathan, we've been wrong all these years. Not completely wrong, but enough that we can all work together to make a difference. Vampires who don't kill innocents can go out in the day. The more vampires kill, the more they are unable to tolerate the sun."

"Holy shit." He ran a hand through his disordered hair before tugging at the ends of it. "Working together is easier said than done, Kadence. The elders—"

"Won't understand this, I know, but *you* have to. You're the leader, Nathan. If we don't work together, if we don't stop fighting vampires who aren't our enemies, we'll all be destroyed. I think this warehouse proves there is something horrible in the works right now."

Nathan's eyes were haunted when they met hers. "It's more than just the elders. Yes, we were wrong about some things, but there are other strongholds around the world. There are others with us who will not understand this or agree to it. Everyone in our stronghold wants to change our location, and I have agreed to it."

She ignored the twinge of sadness his words caused her. She should have known they would decide to do that once they'd learned of her fate. "I would never reveal where it is," she murmured.

"I know, but it doesn't matter. They don't feel safe, and I can't have that. They're in the process of moving as we speak."

"I see."

"How did you escape, Kadence?"

She smiled at him. "Planning," she replied and gave him the shortened rundown on her method.

"Smart," he murmured.

"Determined," she replied. "Nothing is ever easy, Nathan, not in our worlds, but the hunters have followed our family for years, and for more reasons than we were the strongest line. We are born leaders who can do anything we set our minds to. The hunters believe things are one way, and we've always accepted it, but you will make them see that things must change if we are all to survive."

He opened his mouth before closing it again. His head tilted to the side as he studied her. "We've been together our whole lives, but I'm not sure I ever knew you. A part of you would have died if you stayed in the stronghold."

"This was the path I was meant to take in life, and I truly believe that. It's more than seeing things more clearly now, like this place, but I also see them *differently*."

"I can understand that," he said.

Ronan strode over to them and slid his arm around her waist as he handed Nathan a bottle of gasoline with a rag hanging out of the top. "Let's get this over with."

Nathan took the bottle and glanced between the two of them. "We have much to discuss when this is over."

"We do," Ronan agreed. He removed his arm from her waist and turned to face her. She'd come armed with stakes and a crossbow, but he pulled out another crossbow and a lethal-looking switchblade knife. He handed them both to her. "I know you won't return to the vehicle, and I'd prefer to have you where I can see you, but don't you let anything that comes out of that building anywhere near you. The fire and the sun will take care of most of them before they can get close to you, and *I* will take care of anything else."

She nodded and he clasped the lapel of her coat. Pulling her closer, he kissed the end of her nose before his forehead fell briefly against hers and he inhaled her fragrant scent. Every instinct he had said to take her from here before this started.

He couldn't, he knew, but allowing Kadence to embrace who she was becoming may be his undoing. She wrapped her hands around his wrists as she lifted her lips to his. *I love you.* The words were a soothing caress that came from her mind and whispered into his. *I love you too*, he told her.

Lifting his head, he kissed her again before releasing her. "I don't want you in the shadows," he said as he led her toward the edge of the small clearing surrounding the crumpling building. The woods had crept in to reclaim most of their land, but there were still some open patches. "As soon as that building is on fire, get in the sunlight."

"I will," she promised and stroked the thick muscles in his forearm when his body vibrated with tension.

"Don't get out of the sunlight."

"I won't."

His gaze remained latched on her, his eyes turning redder with every passing second. She knew that color wasn't entirely because of his concern for her, but also because of the impending battle. She could feel his growing excitement over what was about to unfold. Their bond would keep him from turning Savage, but she'd never be able to completely ease the compulsion to kill from him, and she didn't want to. She loved him for who he was, a powerful warrior.

Nathan stepped beside them and rested his hand on her shoulder. Kadence grasped his hand and tears burned her eyes at the connection. He squeezed her fingers before releasing her.

He moved swiftly forward with Ronan and the others. Kadence remained in the tree line with Declan and Saxon, watching as half of the hunters and three vampires approached the warehouse. A clammy sweat coated her skin and her heart raced as Ronan and Nathan crept up to the backside of the building.

The strengthening rays warmed Ronan's skin as Lucien and

Killean broke off to head around the building. Nathan stayed by his side as he reached the warehouse. Turning, bricks bit into his back when he pressed it against the wall and lit the rag sticking out of the bottle he held. Nathan did the same with his bottle.

Rising to his feet, Ronan used his fist to smash the board out of the window and tossed the bottle inside before Nathan threw his in. The crack of more boards breaking sounded around the warehouse before the first startled cry pierced the air.

Retreating from the building, Ronan fell back as the screams within rose. Declan led Kadence out of the shade of the trees to stand twenty feet behind him. Saxon moved forward to join the circle near the front of the building. From his spot, Ronan couldn't see the hunters guarding the front.

Flames shot out of a lower window as the first tendril of smoke spiraled from the roof. The back doors burst open and a rush of Savages poured out to take their chances with the sun instead of the flames. Some of them didn't make it ten feet before they shrieked and fell to the ground. They wailed as the sun blistered their skin and smoke poured from them. Others made it to the circle where they were taken out by a hunter or vampire.

Ronan seized the first one coming at him and threw him to the ground before grabbing the next two. He tossed one of them onto the ground before tearing the head from the first. Placing his foot into the back of the one he'd thrown down, he ripped the heart out of the next Savage before finishing off the one pinned beneath him.

From behind him, a bolt whistled past his ear and embedded into the heart of a Savage racing toward him with smoke billowing off his body. The impact of the bolt through his heart threw the Savage back and he fell to the ground, dead. Ronan glanced over his shoulder as Kadence lowered her crossbow and grinned at him.

She reloaded her weapon and spun to take out another Savage barreling toward her brother. Nathan gave her a startled look before returning to the fight.

The next Savage Ronan captured had flames shooting from his eyes when he tore its head off and tossed it aside. One of the hunters on the side of the building fell beneath the weight of three Savages who were barreling toward the woods. Saxon clasped the hunter's hand and yanked him to his feet as flames and smoke trailed behind the escapees.

The hunter turned to follow them, but Ronan's bellow froze him in place. "Do *not* break formation!"

The hunter glanced after the Savages. If they made it to cover and put out the flames, they were still less of a threat than the mass fleeing the warehouse. Ronan had just grabbed another Savage when the clatter of shattering glass and wood sounded. Driving the Savage into the ground, he lifted his head to look up as vampires leapt out of the burning building from the windows above.

His head spun toward where Kadence stood behind him as the first wave of vampires leapt over him. "Kadence!" he roared as the Savages jumped to their feet and fled toward the woods.

Declan yanked her back and caught the first two coming at her. Kadence fired the bolt in her crossbow before releasing the weapon to let it fall against her side. She pulled her stakes free as she prepared for the next wave of Savages.

Adrenaline raced through Kadence as her fangs lengthened. She bounced on the balls of her feet and spun to drive a stake through the heart of a female Savage who had been coming at her with her fangs fully extended. Yanking the stake free, Kadence dashed to the side and drove both her stakes into the hearts of two more Savages as Declan took down another. The Savages parted enough to reveal Ronan carving his way ruthlessly through them toward her.

She ducked to avoid the clawing grasp of another Savage when something hit her in the back. A foot kicked out, knocking the stake from her hand. Her other stake was yanked from her as a heavy weight fell on her, nearly driving her to her knees.

Before she could hit the ground, she was pulled back up by a hand gripping the collar of her jacket. "What do we have here?" a voice murmured in her ear, and she realized the bastard had jumped onto her from above.

For a minute, she thought it was Joseph who held her when an arm cinched around her neck and her head was pulled roughly back. The voice didn't match Joseph's though. She smelled death on the man holding her, but it wasn't as overwhelming as Joseph's stench had been.

Declan took a step toward her and stopped when the arm around her neck jerked, causing her to choke as she was dragged back three feet.

"Tsk, tsk, Declan," the man holding her murmured.

Declan's forehead creased as he gazed at the man. The Savage chuckled and pulled her back another step. "You have no idea who I am."

"Not a clue," Declan said.

"And it doesn't fucking matter," Ronan replied as he stalked toward them.

The fury emanating from him in waves caused her skin to prickle. The hold on her neck tightened until there was no room between her body and the solid wall of flesh behind her.

CHAPTER FORTY-THREE

"Stop!" Ronan snarled when her toes were pulled off the ground. His long fangs glinted in the sun's rays and his eyes became so intense a red that Kadence swore she felt the heat of them against her skin.

Kadence tried to turn to see who held her, but her head was jerked back again, making it impossible for her to move it. Gritting her teeth, she forced herself to go limp. The Savage behind her grunted and then wrapped his other arm around her waist to support her weight.

Ronan's eyes focused on her as the Savage dragged her further back. "Joseph will like my little prize," the Savage muttered and turned his nose into her hair before inhaling deeply. "You and Ronan are entwined with each other. You reek of him, cupcake."

Kadence stiffened when he ran his tongue over her cheek and Ronan's rage blistered across their bond. Her vision blurred when Ronan's emotions swamped her mind. Then, he retreated from her mind and a wall slammed down between them.

Shaking off the lingering effects of Ronan's rage, she lifted her head and gasped when her gaze landed on him once more. The staccato beat of the Savage's heart sounded in her ears and sweat now coated his forearm as he held her closer, something she hadn't considered possible until his body practically molded around hers.

She didn't blame him for being terrified. She was more than a little unnerved herself as a reddish-black hue began to seep insidiously over Ronan's skin. The only time she'd ever seen anything like that color was in pictures of demons. The color seeped over the backs of his hands and crept up from the collar of his shirt to spread across his face. The way the color moved through him reminded her of the flames spreading out to destroy the warehouse behind him. The stare he leveled on the Savage promised death, and not a merciful one.

When something poked her in the chest, she tore her gaze away from Ronan's startling visage to the stake aimed directly at her heart. Yet, she felt no fear of the weapon. Not when she had a very pissed off purebred standing across from her, and the vamp holding her had begun to quake.

The flames of the building rose higher behind Ronan, and she became aware that the screaming had stopped and that all the hunters and Defenders were creeping toward them now. The ground was littered with bodies and drenched in blood. Some of the bodies still had flames consuming them, but most were little more than smoldering ash in the growing daylight.

The Savage holding her hissed and stepped further into the shadows of the forest as his skin blistered and smoke curled into her face. He didn't have the same intense reaction to the sun that most of the others had, leading her to believe that he hadn't killed as much as they had.

Ronan's face became completely encompassed by that insidious color. Though the rest of him was covered by his clothing, she *knew* his entire body was now that reddish black hue. The rest of his men fanned out behind him, but most of the hunters had started to hang back, afraid to move any closer to Ronan. Nathan edged forward, coming toward her from the side.

"Back off, Ronan, or I'll kill her," the Savage said.

"No," Ronan said in a guttural voice she barely recognized. "You won't."

"You're all over her," the Savage spat. "You think I can't recognize your claim on her? A newly turned vampire could realize it, and I am no newly turned vamp!"

The last of his words took on a hysterical tone. Ronan's unblinking stare mixed with the demon-color was the most frightening thing Kadence had ever seen.

"No," Ronan finally said. "You're a purebred, and you're a dead one."

"You won't do anything to me while I have her, and you'll do anything we say once I give her to Joseph."

Ronan's skin swirled and pulsed with those colors as his eyes burned like hot coals. "You won't make it one more step, let alone reach Joseph."

Kadence's fingers inched toward her side as the knees of the Savage literally knocked together. Slipping the knife Ronan had given her from her pocket, her fingers slid over it as she worked to free the blade.

The Savage gave a harsh bark of laughter. "You think you're so strong, Ronan, so powerful, but you don't know what's coming. Not even *you* will be able to stop it, and *I* will be standing there laughing when you're finally taken down."

Kadence finally succeeded in opening the knife and turned it in her grasp. "I can't wait to see you destroyed," the Savage growled.

Gripping the handle, Kadence kept her arm close to her side as she swung the blade back and drove it into the Savage's thigh. She threw her weight to the side to keep from taking a stake to her heart as she twisted the blade in his flesh and jerked it to the side. The putrid scent of his blood hit her as he grunted and fumbled to keep his hold on her. His hand twisted around her braid and he yanked her back.

Kadence never saw Ronan move until he was on top of the Savage, driving him into the ground like a jungle cat taking down its prey. She bit back a cry as her head jerked forward and she was brought to the ground with them. Before she could try to free herself, Ronan tore the hand holding her from the Savage with a brutal twist of bones and sinew. Bile surged up Kadence's throat when the fingers of the severed hand remained entangled in her hair as she scrambled back.

Fumbling awkwardly, she managed to tear the hand free and throw it aside. The Savage wailed in horror as blood sprayed from the stump of his wrist and Ronan remained perched on his chest. With methodical ruthlessness, Ronan tore the other hand away from him.

Kadence crab-crawled backward across the ground, looking to get away as the sour stench of urine filled the air, and she realized the Savage had pissed himself. She didn't blame him.

Hands seized her arms, and her head fell back to take in Nathan standing above her. His mouth fell open when Ronan's head swiveled toward them. Ronan's nostrils flared, and the red of his skin took on a scarlet hue.

"Let her go!" Declan snapped and yanked Nathan's hands away from her.

Nathan released her and took two steps back, but Ronan continued to watch him. Kadence realized the Savage had pushed him too far and he was on the verge of completely snapping.

"I'm okay," Kadence choked out. He'd said that because of their bond he wouldn't turn Savage, but if the man before her wasn't Savage, then she didn't know what was. "Nathan was just trying to help me!"

Nathan lifted his hands in the air as if to prove her point. Ronan watched him for a second more before his attention shifted back to the Savage.

"Don't touch her again, not when he's like this. He won't hurt her, but he'll shred every one of us," Declan warned, and Nathan nodded.

"Where is Joseph?" Ronan snarled.

"I... I don't know!" the Savage wailed. "Not here. He left me here yesterday and went somewhere else!"

Ronan leaned so close to the savage that their noses almost touched. Amusement slithered through him as the man's misery battered him. This vampire had no idea what suffering was yet, but he would by the time Ronan was done with him. The vamp's eyes rolled in his head as his stumpy arms beat against Ronan's sides. Ronan slid his fingers around the vamp's throat, drawing blood as he dug into the Savage's flesh.

"What is coming?" he demanded.

Spittle flew from his mouth when the Savage violently shook his head back and forth. Ronan dug his fingers deeper in until he could feel the Savage's spine. He scraped his fingers across the bone and the Savage blurted out a reply. "A war! Your death!"

"Not my death, but yours. I'll make it quick if you tell me where Joseph is," he promised.

"I really don't know!" the Savage cried.

"Ronan, he doesn't know," Kadence whispered.

His attention was drawn to her, sitting on the ground ten feet away from him. Her neck was still red from where the vamp had choked her. This *thing* had dared to touch her. Yet, he couldn't tear this creature leisurely apart like he longed to do, not in front of her. She understood his darker side, but he wouldn't expose her to such cruelty, not when he knew she was right; this thing didn't know where Joseph was right now.

With a growl, he jerked his hands apart, tearing the savage's throat in half and rending its head from its shoulders. The head rolled away before the rays of the sun lit upon it and flames licked over its skull.

He inhaled a shuddery breath as he struggled to regain control of himself. He'd seen what could happen to a purebred when infuriated or when their mate was in jeopardy, but he'd never experienced it before. He gazed down at the red and black coloring of his skin as he wiped his blood-drenched hands on the ground.

Despite the fact the Savage was dead and Kadence was safe, the color wouldn't retreat from his body. Turning, he looked to Kadence again as she gazed at him in wordless wonder. She'd witnessed him at his most brutal and out of control, yet he saw no revulsion in her eyes.

Scrambling across the ground, she flung herself into his arms. Ronan remained motionless for a second, unwilling to touch her with the putrid blood still on him, but he couldn't resist holding her. His arms closed around her and he drew her against him.

"Did he hurt you badly?" he demanded.

"No, I barely felt anything," she whispered. "Are you all right?"

"There isn't a mark on me."

She ran her hand over the front of him. "What is this?"

"It will fade."

"What…?" Her voice trailed off, and she bit her lip as she glanced at the others who were edging closer to them.

"Purebreds are capable of almost anything when their mate is in trouble," he told her and looked pointedly at the hunters nearby, making it clear that if they tried anything with her, he would joyfully tear them all apart too.

Keeping his arms around her, he lifted her from the ground when he rose to face the others. The roof of the warehouse gave way with a loud crack; smoke and flames burst high into the air as bricks crumpled and fell.

"We have to get out of here before the humans arrive," he said and focused on Nathan. "We have much to discuss."

"We do," Nathan replied, though he was paler than he had been as he stared at Ronan.

"I know a place if you'll follow us."

"We will," Nathan said.

Kadence buried her face in Ronan's neck and inhaled his scent. She slid her fingers into his hair when he started walking across the ground with her. Reluctantly, she leaned away to look at him. His eyes still glistened like rubies, but that reddish-black hue was retreating from his face.

"Why did your skin change like that?" she asked as she ran her fingers over his face. Some of the color remained in his cheeks, but his skin felt no different to her.

Her words drew his attention to the color seeping out of his hands. "Because the demon part of me was close to the surface," he replied. "Closer than it's ever been before. I've witnessed it happening to a purebred before, but I've never experienced it. When that part of a purebred is unleashed, there is little they can't do. They can even enter a house uninvited and break the rules that normally govern our kind."

"Does it only happen with purebreds?"

"Yes... well, at least it only used to be purebreds. You are a new entity, so who knows what you might be capable of doing."

Her lips flattened as her fingers played with the hair at his nape. "I would do anything to destroy someone who attacked you," she replied.

He couldn't help but smile over the possessive tone of her voice. "I believe you."

CHAPTER FORTY-FOUR

RONAN TURNED on the lights within the closed hotel as he moved through it. Baldric purchased the property in Falmouth for him last month, not for the hotel part of it, but for the fifteen acres of land that came with it, a rarity on Cape Cod and an investment for Ronan. The hotel had closed for the winter months before he'd purchased it.

Ronan expected to add the property to his collection and forget about it, but they'd been close enough to it today for it to make a good meeting place for now.

The briny scent of the ocean filled the air as the waves crashed on the shore outside of the boarded-over windows. He kept his arm around Kadence as he walked, not to protect her, but because he needed her calming presence right now. He'd regained most of his control, but it wouldn't take much to push him over the edge again.

Arriving at the restaurant area, he flicked on the lights and strode over to pull a chair from the top of one of the tables. Dust floated up as he set the chair on the ground and settled Kadence onto it.

"Will you be sitting?" he asked Nathan.

"Not unless you are," he replied.

Ronan smiled at him as he pulled down two more chairs and

placed them on the ground. The others spread out around the room, but didn't bother to remove the chairs from any of the remaining tables. Ronan hadn't expected them to.

"Your injuries from last week have healed well," Nathan said. "I would have thought the bolt hole from a crossbow would take longer to close."

The hunter was brave for digging at him in such a way, or stupid, but he'd come to realize Kadence and her brother were far from stupid. Nathan was trying to learn more about him.

"I heal faster than most," Ronan replied. "As it seems, you do too. Broken noses don't often heal within a week."

"Lucky punch," Nathan replied.

Ronan chuckled. "Lucky shot from you. The fact you're her brother made me hesitate in taking you down."

Kadence rolled her eyes as the two of them stared at each other. She could practically taste the amped up testosterone on the air. "Yeah, yeah, you both heal fast and are manly men. Could you please move on so we can discuss more important things sometime today?"

Settling next to Kadence, Ronan rested his hands on the table as he waited for Nathan to sit across from him. Finally, Nathan tore his attention away from Kadence and focused on Ronan again as he settled into the chair across from him.

"What happened back there, I've never seen a vampire do what you did," Nathan said to him. "What was with the weird skin change?"

"You'll probably never see it again," Ronan replied. "It's a trait of purebreds only."

"And that is what you are?"

"I am fifth generation purebred, the only one of my kind to ever exist with such breeding and the only who can trace their lineage back to the first demon offspring."

"So, you are the leader?" Nathan asked.

"When I was younger, I was raised to one day be king; I never took that role."

"Why not?"

"Many reasons."

"Are the other non-Savage vamps unwilling to follow you?"

"We would follow him to Hell and back," Declan said. "You know naught of our history."

Nathan clasped his hands before him as he leaned back in his chair. "We apparently don't know much about you at all. I didn't know there were such things as turned and purebred vampires, Savages, and well... you."

"He looked like a Savage to me earlier," Logan muttered.

Ronan didn't bother to acknowledge him as he remained intent on Nathan. "Almost a thousand years ago, I chose not to become king. It is a decision I will be changing, somewhat. Because they have been so scattered over the years, most vampires don't know our history either, how we were originally created, or the full extent of what some of us can do. It is time that is rectified. I will not be king, that title died with my father as far as I'm concerned, but from now on, I will work to gather the vampires and lead them."

Declan grinned while Saxon, Lucien, and Killean exchanged surprised looks before nodding enthusiastically.

"Why?" Nathan inquired.

"With or without the help of the hunters, Joseph must be taken down and what he is doing must be stopped."

Ronan didn't tell him about the Savage attack he'd survived when he'd been younger. They may end up working together against Joseph, but he couldn't have the hunters knowing about their small purebred numbers.

"The Savage that attacked Kadence, he knew you."

"He did," Ronan confirmed. On the half hour drive it had taken to get here, Declan recalled who the Savage was. "He was a purebred who tried to make it through Defender training under Joseph."

"What is a Defender?" Nathan inquired.

"The purebreds who work to keep humans and innocent vampires safe have always been known as Defenders. While he was with us, Joseph worked to train purebred vampires. He also worked with turned vampires and taught them how to differentiate a Savage from another vampire."

"How can they tell the difference if the turned ones can't smell them?"

"It's easy enough to look for the signs of a Savage hunting in the area. An increase of missing people reports, unexplained deaths, animal attacks, and such. Then they focus on a Savage's favorite places to hunt, like bars and clubs. They prefer anywhere a human is more vulnerable and their defenses are lowered. Once the vampire is located, it's simply a matter of confirming that they are a Savage."

"By witnessing the death of a human?" Nathan asked.

"No," Ronan replied. "When we feed from humans, we do not enjoy making them suffer. It is usually the opposite, and we seek to give them pleasure, or we shut down their emotions so that they feel nothing." That was the way he'd fed from others, with no emotional involvement, until Kadence. "Afterward, we change their memories of what occurred. However, a Savage prefers to experience the pain of their victim. They thrive on the fear and agony. It gives them a bigger rush, as does hunting and killing other vampires in such a way. If you come across a vampire whose victim is suffering during the blood taking, then you have come across a Savage."

Nathan looked dumbfounded by this revelation. Ronan glanced at the other hunters who were hiding their shock with far less success than Nathan as they gawked at him and exchanged looks.

"Plus, you now know you can smell the difference too. Remember that before you stake your next vamp," Ronan continued.

"I will," Nathan replied though some of the hunters scowled behind him. "So the vamp who attacked Kadence was one of you?"

"No, he didn't successfully make it through the training, and it seems Joseph decided to recruit him to his cause. That Savage was a new edition to Joseph's collection. He hadn't killed many, yet. Otherwise, he couldn't tolerate the sun as well as he did. By next week, he probably would have burst into flames like the others. I'd be willing to bet there are others who have also failed their training and that Joseph is looking to recruit them too."

"Others who have been trained to fight by one of your men?" Nathan asked.

"One of our *ex* men," Ronan replied.

"But Joseph is highly trained, they're highly trained, and there's a chance they could have a grudge against all of you."

"They *could* have a grudge against us, but *every* one of them hates hunters," Ronan said pointedly.

"It's hard not to, you stake happy bastards." Lucien smirked.

Ronan shot Lucien a silencing glance before continuing. "They know they can't take us down, not without a lot of help, and they have no idea where to find us. You, on the other hand, unless you plan on calling off all your hunts until this danger is eradicated, they'll be able to take you out with far more ease than us."

Anger flashed through Nathan's eyes before he smothered it. "We are stronger and more capable than you think."

"Believe me, I know that." Ronan clasped one of Kadence's hands within both of his. "But that will get you nowhere if you're outnumbered by Savages. The more they kill, the more limitations they have on them such as not being able to handle sunlight or cross large bodies of water, but they also grow physically stronger."

"Do you really think that Joseph organizing an army is the bigger threat the Savage was talking about, or do you think there is something more out there?"

"I don't know," Ronan admitted. "I can't think of what else it could be, but Savages are extremely cunning, and they do not want to die. They'll do everything in their power to eradicate any threat to their lives."

"It won't be easy to convince the elders we should work together, or the other strongholds around the world," Nathan replied.

"After last night and this morning, it will be easier," Asher chimed in. "I know I would prefer not to kill a vampire who isn't looking to kill me or a human. That whole blood drinking thing is still disgusting, but we all do what we must to survive, and if they're not hurting someone—"

"They're draining the blood of another and changing their memories; there is something wrong with that," Logan sneered.

"There is a difference between that and killing, Logan, and you know it," Asher said.

"There is," Nathan agreed.

"We can continue to work in opposition and possibly all be slaughtered because of that, or we can all work together and destroy the bastard who killed Dad," Kadence said.

Nathan quirked an eyebrow at her. Kadence lifted her chin as she waited to be admonished for her language. If they'd been sitting in the stronghold, she would have been, but Nathan didn't comment on her word choice. She wasn't his to take care of anymore, and she realized her brother was coming to grips with that.

Her hand tightened around Ronan's as she spoke. "Nathan, we can do this together."

Nathan leaned back in his seat and rubbed at the black stubble lining his jaw. Dropping his hand down, he leaned forward again. "You will be taking control of the vampires, rising to the position of leader, the one you claim was supposed to be yours," he said to Ronan.

"Like you, I was specifically bred and groomed to one day take control of my kind. Unprecedented events detoured my course for a while, but unprecedented events have steered me back onto it." Lifting Kadence's hand, he placed a kiss against her knuckles to ensure her brother understood his point.

"And how will you go about taking control?" Nathan inquired.

330 BRENDA K DAVIES

"I will organize them. Most vampires live in peace, but what Joseph is doing is threatening to all our kind and the entire world. For many millennia, only purebreds have been Defenders against the Savages. I was reluctant to bring turned vampires in to become a Defender, reluctant to change our customs, but I realize it has to be done and that living in the past may be the downfall of us all. You will do what you must to protect your kind, and I will do what I must to ensure the same thing, but we are both working toward the same common goal."

"And these vampires you aim to bring in and organize, they won't want to destroy us too?" Nathan asked.

Killean shifted behind him, his face remained stony, but the gleam in his golden eyes told Ronan he'd happily destroy every hunter in this room and consequences be damned.

"I'm sure some of them will," Ronan replied honestly. "Just as some of the hunters you bring in will still prefer to see every vampire dead. Continuing to fight and kill each other is pointless. No matter the resentment and history that is sure to boil forth on both sides, we must find a way to either work together or stay out of each other's way."

"I agree about that," Nathan said. "But what are we going to do? Go on patrols with each other?"

"We can start there," Ronan replied. "And over time work toward more. Perhaps one day, we can train together. It would create some very lethal fighters."

"It is a start," Nathan agreed.

"And what if one of you turns Savage, what then?" Logan demanded.

Ronan pierced him with a remorseless stare. "They will be hunted as ruthlessly as any other Savage. Despite our bonds to one another, we all know that is the consequence of turning. Joseph will be located, he will be brought down, and I will be there to do it."

"*I* will be the one to do it." Nathan's quietly spoken words were more forceful than if he'd bellowed them to the room.

Ronan had destroyed the prick who killed his parents; he would not deny another the opportunity for revenge, even if he knew it would bring no relief. "If it works out that way and you are there, then you will be the one to do it, but Joseph will be taken down the first opportunity we have to do so. It is necessary he is destroyed no matter who does it."

Nathan's hands fisted on the table. "Agreed."

"I will also be there to see it, if it works that way," Kadence said.

Nathan sat back in his seat as he gazed at Ronan in challenge. With that action, Ronan realized Nathan had acknowledged Kadence was now under his protection, but it was clear he didn't approve of her being anywhere near the fight.

"Will you inform the other strongholds about the alliance we will be trying to forge here?" Ronan asked Nathan.

"Not right away. We will see how things play out before bringing them in. They haven't reported an increase in Savage attacks or missing people from their locations. For now, it seems as if this growing threat is located here in the Northeast."

"For now," Ronan agreed. "I'm sure Joseph will be trying to establish more warehouses throughout the area in an attempt to expand. We will locate the other turned and purebred vamps he's trained over the years and either bring them in or learn if they've also turned Savage."

"How do you intend to find them?"

"We know where some of them are. For the others, we have a friend who may be able to help locate them."

"Will this friend be joining in the fight?" Nathan inquired.

Five months ago, Brian would have happily jumped in to help kill as many Savages as possible, but it was unlikely he would now that he was mated. "He will aid us when he can."

"I see. Can he locate Joseph?"

"Not recently, but he has a couple of times in the past, and so has Kadence and she may be able to do so again." Nathan's jaw clenched when he realized Ronan was telling him that he would not keep Kadence out of this. "On our way here, I called Brian and asked him to join us. He should be arriving shortly."

CHAPTER FORTY-FIVE

AN HOUR LATER, Brian strolled into the room with their newest pure-bred recruit, Aiden, at his side. "Someone call some hookers so we can really make this a party," Aiden drawled as he gazed at the brooding occupants of the room.

"That would make it a regular old fuck fest," Lucien replied.

Aiden grinned at him as he hooked his fingers into his belt buckle. "Nice one."

"I thought so."

"Enough," Ronan said. "Did you bring the things I asked for?" he inquired of Brian.

"Yes," Brian replied.

He turned and walked back to the door. Ronan heard whispered voices before the door closed, shutting Brian's mate on the other side. Brian walked over with a stack of folders and placed them before Ronan. The files had been moved from the training facility to the mansion with the rest of the recruits. Everyone moved closer as Ronan spread the folders across the table so that Brian could see the photos attached to the outside of each one.

He'd told Brian to leave behind the numerous files marked deceased and any over fifty years old. Joseph hadn't taken over the running of the training facility before then. They may have to go through the older files eventually, but right now they had to concentrate on the vampires they knew Joseph had direct contact with.

"Which ones do we know where they are now?" he inquired and looked at each of his men.

Hands reached around him to pull out the files of those they would be able to locate without Brian's help. He wasn't entirely sure how Brian's ability worked, but he suspected Brian needed to meet someone in person to locate them again. He didn't think Brian would have met many of the unknowns remaining, but even one of them was one less that they would have to waste time trying to find.

"Which ones do you think you can locate, Brian?"

Brian studied the pictures before pulling out nearly a dozen files, more than Ronan had expected. "These."

"Good," Ronan said and pushed the remaining folders aside before focusing on Nathan. "We will find a more central location to meet next time and go out to hunt together from there. Neither of us will reveal where we live, or be expected to. If anyone is caught trying to find the location of the other, it is a breach of trust and the offender will be dealt with swiftly by the other side. We will send out groups of hunters and vampires together every night. If someone is wrongly injured by someone on the other side or knowingly attacked, the attacker will be dealt with by both sides."

These were details they had already hashed out while waiting for Brian to arrive, but he wanted to make sure they were clear to everyone.

"Agreed," Nathan said.

"It's a solid start," Kadence said.

"It is," Nathan replied.

Ronan rose with Nathan and extended his hand across the table to him. "A good beginning to what could become a strong alliance," he said as he took hold of Nathan's hand.

"Yes, it is," Nathan agreed and shook his hand.

There was only one more thing he had to discuss with Nathan before leaving here.

"I think it is time for us to go. We will be in contact tonight." Nathan said.

Nathan went to step away, but Ronan kept his hand, holding him back as the others started to file out of the room. "I'd like to speak with you and Kadence alone," he said.

Nathan hesitated before waving the rest of his men out the door as Ronan's followed behind them. Ronan released Nathan's hand and drew Kadence against his side.

"You're to make sure your man, Logan, stays away from Kadence," he said to Nathan when the door closed behind the others.

"I never had romantic feeling for Logan, if that's what you're worried about," Kadence said.

"No, you didn't, but he had feelings for you, and now those feelings have turned to anger." His eyes burned into Nathan's as he spoke.

"Logan would never hurt her," Nathan said.

"Maybe not before, but he's bitter and angry now. That's a deadly combination. If he does anything that I deem threatening toward her, I'll kill him, alliance between us or not."

"Ronan!" Kadence gasped.

"No." The look he sent her caused her to hold back any further protest. "On this, I will not budge. He won't be anywhere near you. There will be *no* arguing about that. I have only one weakness, Kadence, and it is you. Everyone who was in this room knows that. They won't exploit it, but Logan might. Not to mention, you both think you can trust him, so your guard will be lowered around him."

"I'll keep him away from her," Nathan promised.

"Good."

"One more thing," Kadence said. "The women in the stronghold need to be better trained. I'm not saying prepare them for going out in the streets, but you have to do more, Nathan. I believed I was prepared when I left the stronghold, but I wasn't. It nearly got me killed."

"Ah hmm," Nathan cleared his throat and gave her a pointed look.

"I know leaving in the first place put me in danger," she agreed, and her brother nodded. "But I was *really* unprepared. The women think they can defend themselves. They can't. I know you think you can keep them all sheltered, but there may come a time when you can't. If that time comes, they'll be lambs to the slaughter, and you would have allowed it to happen by not teaching them more."

Nathan stared at the wall behind her before focusing on her again. "We will train them better."

"Good," Kadence said. "And speaking of women, how is Simone?"

"She is fine," Nathan answered.

"Will you tell her I say hi and that I miss her?"

"I will," he promised.

NATHAN'S MIND spun as he tried to sort through everything that had happened in such a short time. He had no idea how he would get the elders and some of the other male hunters in the stronghold on board with this, but he had to. After what he'd seen with those Savages in the warehouse, he knew it was only a matter of time before they were all completely outnumbered.

There would be no stopping the spread of the Savages once that happened. Sighing, he ran a hand through his hair as he walked out of the room beside Ronan and Kadence. His gaze slid to his head-strong sister. He also had no idea what to make of her newfound vampire status or her relationship to this man—a man who would tear the world and everyone in his way apart to protect her.

He never would have thought he'd be okay with his sister in a relationship with a vampire, and especially not okay with her *being* one, but he had to admit, Ronan may be the only one who could keep her safe. But more than that, Ronan made her happy in a way he'd never seen Kadence happy before.

He wanted to hate Ronan, his entire life had been built on hatred for what he was, but he found he couldn't. Not when Kadence was smiling like that and practically glowing with self-confidence, happiness, and love. More than that, he couldn't deny that the vampire loved her too. He wouldn't have believed a vampire capable of feeling love, but he was beginning to realize he'd been wrong about many things throughout his life.

He never would have chosen this life for his sister, but he was glad she'd stumbled into it. She would have gradually died within the stronghold. He had a feeling she would be blossoming more with every passing day now.

Stepping through the doorway, his gaze traveled over the hunters and vamps standing within the hallway. They stood on opposite sides of the hall while they stared distrustfully at each other, but at least they weren't trying to kill one another.

Baby steps, he reminded himself. Baby steps that had the possibility of leading to a better and safer life for all of them.

His gaze drifted to the two vamps who had brought the files for Ronan. Brian stood next to two pretty blonde women. Brian's shoulders went back and he pulled the one standing closest to him back a step when Nathan's eyes fell on her. Nathan turned away from them to focus on the other woman who was the identical version of the woman with Brian. Her head canted to the side as her green eyes studied him. Nathan found his steps slowing as he gazed inquisitively back at her.

Then, she scowled at him. Despite her apparent dislike of him, Nathan smiled at her before walking out of the hotel. He gave Kadence a hug and climbed into the battered truck he favored for hunting.

CHAPTER FORTY-SIX

"IT'S GOING to work between the hunters and the vampires," Kadence murmured as she trailed her fingers up Ronan's bare chest to his chin and back down again. "It's going to take time, there will be problems, most likely *many* problems in the beginning, but it's going to work out for the better."

"Yes," Ronan agreed as he took her hand and pinned it to his chest.

"I'm going to be there to help with that, and I'm going to be there when Joseph dies. If I get the chance, I'll kill him myself."

She wiggled her way up his body and sprawled across his chest. Against her thigh, she felt him hardening again, but his face remained serious as he gazed at her.

"Joseph is an old, powerful, purebred vampire," he said.

"And I'm a turned hunter, the first of my kind, who knows what I can do. I might be as fierce as a purebred when I'm in a rage. Perhaps my skin will turn color too."

"Hmm," he grunted.

Her smile slid away at the grave look on his face. "Don't lock me away, Ronan."

His hand tightened around hers as he took a deep breath. "I promised you I wouldn't do that, and I won't, but there are some things we should discuss."

"Such as?" she asked warily.

"Such as, you will continue training with me every day, and if you go into the field, it will be with me. If I don't think you're ready, or if I feel you're not working as hard as you have been, I will continue to keep you from the fight."

"I agree," she said. "But you have to be fair and unbiased in your assessment of me."

"I will," he replied.

"Anything else?"

"Not right now, but we'll discuss this again when Joseph is dead."

She smiled as she leaned forward to kiss him. "Are you really going to lead the vampires?"

"It is another thing that will take time, but I will work to gather the vampires again, to lead them, and to better educate them on our history, our ways, and what they are."

"You will make an outstanding ruler," she assured him.

"And you will make an impressive, stubborn ruler at my side," he replied and nipped at her bottom lip.

Kadence giggled as her fingers curled into his chest. "I love you."

"You'd better because you're bound to me for an eternity, and I'm head over fucking heels for you."

"I'm okay with that."

She squealed when he flipped her over to pin her to the mattress beneath him. His beautiful brown eyes met hers before he bent his head to kiss her. Kadence forgot all about the problems waiting for them outside of this room as she lost herself to the rhythm of his body and the strength of his love enveloping her.

The End.

Bound by Vengeance (**The Alliance, Book 2**) is now available and focuses on Nathan and Vicky:
brendakdavies.com/BBVppbk

If you enjoyed *Eternally Bound* you may enjoy the **Vampire Awakening Series** too and get a chance to meet some of the other characters in this book more.

Check out Book 1 of the Vampire Awakening Series, *Awakened*, free everywhere ebooks are sold.
brendakdavies.com/Awwb

Sign up for the mailing list to stay up to date on future releases in this series and others from the author:
Brenda K. Davies/Erica Stevens Mailing List: http://bit.ly/ESBKDNews

Read on for an exclusive excerpt of *Into Hell* (The Road to Hell Series, Book 4).
This is the final book in The Road to Hell Series.

Kobal

My eyes narrowed on the shadows from where the voice had come, but whoever stood there remained concealed by the darkness. Scenting the air, I detected a new aroma within the cavern. Whoever it was had not been there long. I recognized the odor as the same aroma Lucifer and the other angels emitted. It brought to mind water, but whereas River made me think of fresh rain, this was more like a pond.

I focused my gaze on a shifting in the shadows as my lips skimmed back to bare my fangs.

"I have not come here to fight, Kobal," the voice murmured. "I would not have revealed my presence in this cave if I intended to battle you. I would have simply struck while the two of you were focused on whatever it was the oracle revealed to her."

"Then why not show yourself?" I demanded.

The darkness moved and flowed before a raven swept out of it to land fifty feet away. Larger than the ravens on Earth, it stood nearly three feet tall and weighed at least a hundred pounds. It moved with the grace of its mortal counterparts as it settled its feathers against its side with a fluid ripple of motion.

"I've shown myself," the raven murmured and River gasped behind me. "As you can see, I could have remained hidden from you for a lot longer. Even if you scented me, you would not have been looking for me."

"What the fuck is with the talking bird?" Hawk blurted.

"It's not a bird," Bale said and drew her sword from her back.

Into Hell is now available:
brendakdavies.com/IHppbk

The first book in this series, _Good Intentions_,
is free everywhere ebooks are sold:
brendakdavies.com/GIwb

Stay in touch on updates and other new releases from the author
by joining the mailing list.
Mailing list for Brenda K. Davies and Erica Stevens Updates:
brendakdavies.com/ESBKDNews

FIND THE AUTHOR

Erica Stevens/Brenda K. Davies Mailing List:
brendakdavies.com/ESBKDNews

Facebook page: brendakdavies.com/BKDfb
Facebook friend: ericastevensauthor.com/EASfb

Erica Stevens/Brenda K. Davies Book Club:
brendakdavies.com/ESBKDBookClub

Instagram: brendakdavies.com/BKDInsta
Twitter: brendakdavies.com/BKDTweet
Website: www.brendakdavies.com
Blog: ericastevensauthor.com/ESblog

ABOUT THE AUTHOR

Brenda K. Davies is the USA Today Bestselling author of the Vampire Awakening Series, Alliance Series, Road to Hell Series, Hell on Earth Series, and historical romantic fiction. She also writes under the pen name, Erica Stevens. When not out with friends and family, she can be found at home with her husband, son, dog, cat, and horse.

Made in the USA
Monee, IL
28 September 2019